# A PARTICULAR MAN

LESLEY GLAISTER

BLOODHOUND
BOOKS

Copyright © 2024 Lesley Glaister

The right of Lesley Glaister to be identified as the Author of the Work has been asserted by her in accordance with the Copyright, Designs and Patents Act 1988.

First published in 2024 by Bloodhound Books.

Apart from any use permitted under UK copyright law, this publication may only be reproduced, stored, or transmitted, in any form, or by any means, with prior permission in writing of the publisher or, in the case of reprographic production, in accordance with the terms of licences issued by the Copyright Licensing Agency.
All characters in this publication are fictitious and any resemblance to real persons, living or dead, is purely coincidental.

www.bloodhoundbooks.com

Print ISBN: 978-1-916978-94-2

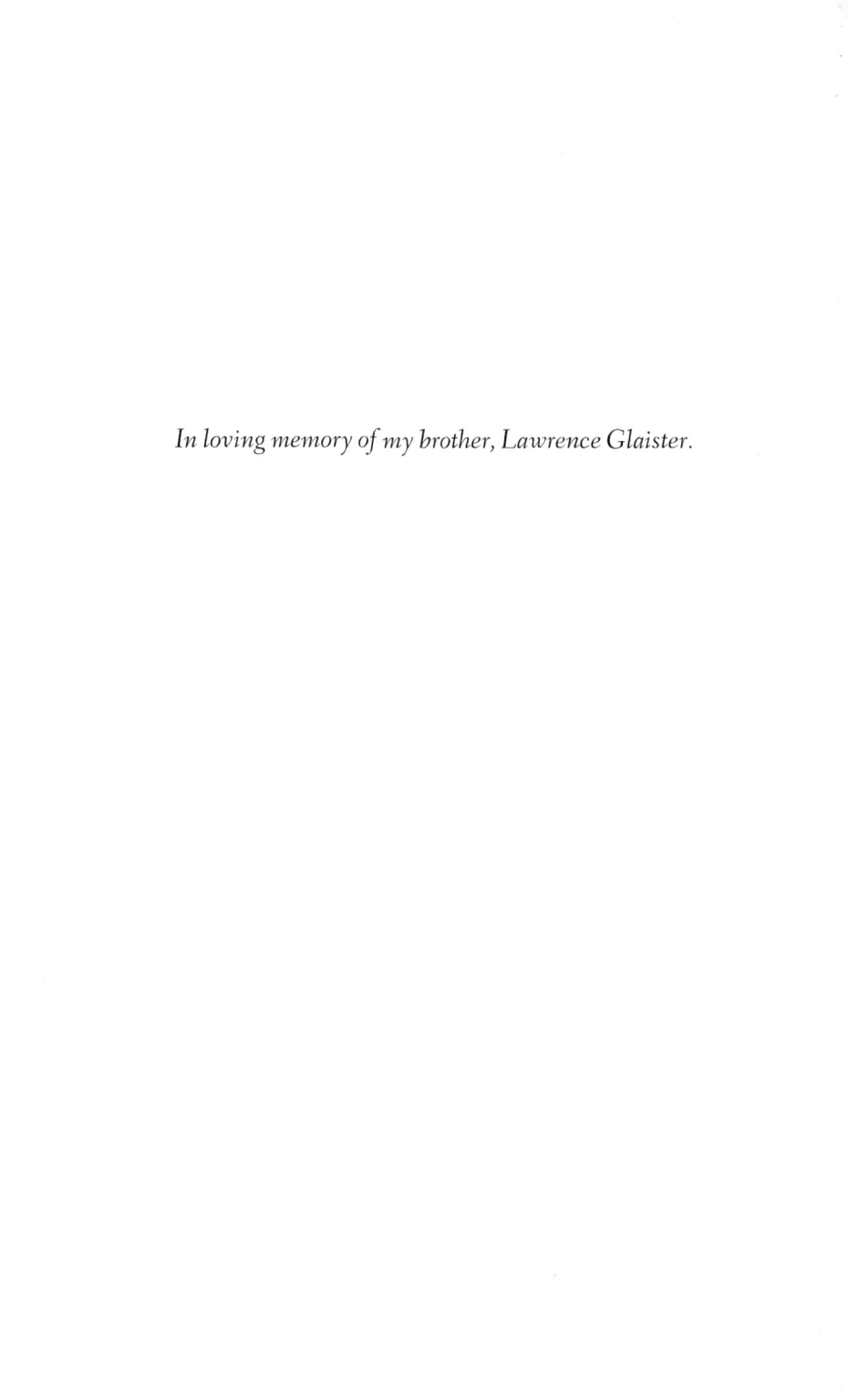

*In loving memory of my brother, Lawrence Glaister.*

# PROLOGUE

October 1945

On the morning of the letter, Clem stood at her easel in the garden. Her aim: to capture the Turkish-carpet colours of the chrysanthemums reflected in the fish pond. Of course (always, always) she will have been thinking of Edgar. The war in the Far East had been over for a month, and every waking moment they awaited news of him, or, please God, *from* him. So dreadfully unfair that other mothers had their boys safely back (those that were coming back), boys from France, Africa, everywhere but the wretched Far East where the war had dragged its filthy feet. But now it was over. And where was he?

Though, in truth, Edgar may not have been prominent in her mind at the precise moment of the letter's arrival. Rather, she may have been absorbed in capturing the light on the pond, rendering it rich, enamelled. Painting is an excellent way to escape your mind. And what a luxury and a *rest* that is, a short liberty from anxiety, a welcome loss of self.

So, it was approaching noon on an exquisite autumn Wednesday. Bees bumbled in the roses; Michaelmas daisies ached in mauve clumps. Dipping in and out of focus she was aware of these things, but there were things of which she was unaware. For instance, she was unaware of the postman coming to the front door; unaware that Linda, having received the official letter and known "in her bones" as she later said, that it was bad news, ran, panic-stricken down to Dennis's surgery. She was unaware of Dennis barking at Linda for the interruption, sending her out, making her wait till he'd finished with his patient before accepting the letter.

Only afterwards did she piece these things together.

What she will always remember is Dennis's heavy trudge into the garden and her fleeting irritation at the interruption. They'd been amid some squabble, and she assumed he'd come to deliver another barb. Until she noticed the way he stood, hands by his sides, letter dangling, a laxness in his face, a face gone suddenly old.

Light sheened his spectacles so that she could not see his eyes. His hair was thick still, badgerishly streaked with white. He remained a handsome figure, though stout. A button was coming loose on his waistcoat. These were the sort of thoughts that her brain released like a flock of frantic birds trying to beat away the truth.

She remembered nothing more until she was seated in the drawing room with a cup of overly sweetened tea, the letter crumpled on her lap. *It is my sad duty to inform you... On or around the 6 July... of jungle fever... Popular and resourceful chap... Much missed... Condolences.*

He had been dead for three months.

The present unpeeled like a wet label, leaving the glass clear for her to peer through to the past. Back then, when he was so tiny and vulnerable, he'd seemed to be the wrong baby, a stranger, not someone who could possibly have emerged from her own body. But the wrong baby had become the right child. *Her* boy, charming, uncomplicated, happy, so *loving*, had grown up to be a brave, funny, handsome, kind young man.

And now, a few words in a letter, a chalk-faced husband, an awful falling and flailing in her mind.

---

Dennis had returned to finish his surgery; what else could he do with patients waiting? And then there was lunch. That they sat down at the table as if everything was normal, struck her as incredible. Outrageous. And he'd been dead for *three months*. They sat in their usual places and picked at some sort of ersatz cutlets brought in by a pink-eyed Linda, who stammered her condolences. Linda had known Edgar since he was a baby. Her own son Alan served in North Africa and was home now, not undamaged, but making the best of it. *Alive*.

Clem stared numbly at the unidentified meat, the grey puddle of gravy. Dennis was eating, though not with his usual vigour. The revulsion she felt at the sounds of his mastication almost overwhelmed her grief. But the grief had not properly yet arrived; this was still shock. But shock? Really? After all, it was *war*. This outcome had never been unlikely. When, four years ago, the telegram had arrived telling them that he'd been taken prisoner in Singapore, Clem had actually been relieved. He wouldn't be fighting now, at least. He'd be safe in a prison camp. Such had been her naivety.

Revulsion she felt – over the cutlets, her husband's chewing, embarrassment at the paucity of their marriage. The news had come, and they'd sat down to lunch! They didn't speak, except for "pass this" or "pass that". Several times Dennis cleared his throat. Once he'd finished his bottled strawberries (picked from the garden in the innocence of the summer, when Edgar might still have been alive) he pushed back his chair and stood, dabbed his lips with a napkin, and came to stand behind her. The weight of his hand arrived on her shoulder. 'I say...' he began, but in fact said nothing more. Paused for a moment, cleared his throat again, left the room. Clem pushed away her untouched dish. The fruit was too red, too sore.

*Three months.*

# PART 1

## GUARD YOUR TONGUE

'You are free now. Anything you say in public or to the press is liable to be published throughout the whole world. You have direct or indirect knowledge of the fate of many of your comrades who died in enemy hands as a result of brutality or neglect. Your story, if published in the more sensational press, would cause much unnecessary unhappiness to relatives and friends. It is felt certain that now you know the reason for this order you will take pains to spare the feelings of others.' (Extracted from typed order from RAPWI: Recovery of Allied Prisoners of War and Internees.)

# 1

## STARLING

### NOVEMBER 1945

The door knocker's a knocking fist, or it's meant to be, but it makes him think of a punch in the gob. Should he knock? Instead, he turns the handle. The door opens straight into the living room, and there's a clench in his vitals at the soupy, doggy smell of home.

Mum grabs him, her hug violent. 'Lennie, Lennie, Lennie.' Scapulas frail under his hands. He scans the room; has it always been so cramped? Stuffed with furniture, armchairs draped in crochet, round table with its layers of tablecloth, chairs crammed under. On the mantel, herds and packs and flocks of tiny glass beasts.

It's been years.

Air comes out of Mum like a puncture. 'Let me look at you, my duck.' She clings to his coat sleeve.

The passage door opens and there's the old man. The dogs burst in, buffeting his ankles. Salt and Pepper, two Jack Russells, black and white. He kneels to embrace their licky welcome. Both have grown fat and grizzled. He staggers as he rises.

The old man looms with folded arms. 'Glad to see you in

one piece, son,' he says, which is rich considering the last thing he said was, "*Never darken my door.*"

'Hello Dad,' says Starling. That's who he is now, not Lennie, but *Starling*. He'll not think of himself as Lennie, that miserable toerag.

'Not quite all in one piece.' He shrugs off his coat, to show his cuff, safety-pinned to conceal the stump.

Mum's hands fly to her mouth; her eyes in their shadowed craters suck in the light.

'Par for the course, I'm afraid.' Christ, he sounds just like Edgar.

'Oh my poor, poor lad. Why didn't you say when you wrote? Oh, I shall have to sit down.' She lowers herself into an armchair, both hands pressed to her mouth.

'You could have warned us, son,' the old man says.

Starling shrugs, shuffles his feet.

'Only trying to be thoughtful, I expect.' Mum stiffens herself protectively, same as ever. Not back two minutes and the old pattern is back in place. 'But you're thin as a rail, my poor duck. Oh, and your specs are cracked; we shall have to get you a new pair.'

'Could be worse,' he says.

'Oh Lennie, how we've dreamt of this day!' Mum carries on. 'Seeing you here, large as life, but oh, your poor hand… When I think of you as a newborn, those tiny fingers.'

'Now, now, Mum, don't go taking on. I'll take bag up,' the old man says. He hoists the khaki holdall over his shoulder, and plods effortfully up the stairs, breath a rasping wheeze.

'He's worse,' observes Starling.

Mum sighs. 'Well, he's no better, and that's a fact. Off work for months, he's been.' She hauls herself up from her chair. 'Cup of tea? Kettle's hot. Or a freshen-up? Water's hot. Or a lie down?

Bed's made up. Dad'll fetch in a jug of beer from pub. I expect you'd like a drink with your tea?'

'Good to be home, Mum.' Lennie holds her thin body, breathes in hairspray. She's made an effort, and he's touched by her stiff hair, the smears of red on her cheekbones.

'Look, Lennie,' she says, 'I don't know what it was went off between you and your dad before you left, and I don't want to know, but do try not to go upsetting him.' She tails off, bright pleading in her eyes. 'A fresh start, Lennie? Eh?'

He snorts. 'Honestly, Mum!'

'I just mean let's keep things nice. He's making such an effort.'

'And so will I.' Wearily, he sets off up the stairs. His bedroom makes him groan. It's like looking down a telescope the wrong way, the narrow space with its iron bedstead and makeshift bookshelves. This is a duty visit, a checking in. He might stay a week or two, just till he gets himself on his feet – or he might only stay the night. *You can make an effort for one night, Starling.*

He flicks the light switch, struggles with his shoelaces. Such a bugger when every simple task reminds you what you've lost. He'll get used to it, he's told, work out ways to do things. People have come off much worse than him. Elastic for shoelaces, for a start. Mum can sort that out – and sew up the rest of his cuffs. He tips back on the bed. There's a squealing creak of springs, as if he's falling back through time. His eyes climb the ivy trellises on the wallpaper that they climbed through all the misery of being Lennie: bookworm, sissy, cry-baby, hopeless at footie, hopeless – to the old man's disgust – at everything except books. And here are his books, his tiny desk where he spent his evenings hunched over Latin, maths, medical encyclopaedias.

As soon as they reached Colombo, then Liverpool, the three and a half years of hell became unreal. Coming home he thought would mean returning to the real, but this, here, doesn't seem it. For most of the time in the jungle, he didn't dare believe he'd be back here one day, stretched out like this on his old bed. *Safe*. He lifts his left arm. No hand but he can still feel it, an itch on the palm, they say that means money on the way. Phantom money for a phantom hand. The itch maddens because there's nowt to scratch. The hand, if it still exists, will be bones now: phalanges and metacarpals and... He tests his memory for the carpals: *capitate, hamate, pisiform, trapezoid, trapezium and what? Two missing.* But then, all the bones of his left hand are missing, in the jungle, gnawed at by animals or greened over.

He gets up and pads to the bathroom – still new to him, fitted just before the war, Mum's pride and joy. He splashes his face, peers into the old mirror that has always reflected his face as mucky, even when it was scrubbed clean. He's taken aback by his hollow cheeks and eye sockets. *Sphenoid...*

*Oh, shut up and shave.*

---

Roast meat and spuds, cabbage and carrots, gravy. A glass of ale. An atmosphere somewhere between Christmas and a wake.

'Shall I cut it up for you?' Mum says, seeing him struggling with his fork. He lets her take his plate, since it will give her satisfaction. The old man chunters in his throat, and looks away.

'I would have got lamb,' she says, 'but not in this day and age. The butcher calls this "steak".'

'Horse, I reckon,' says the old man, with some relish. 'Or whale.'

'Not bad though if you don't think about it,' she says, returning his plate of chopped food. 'There.'

They sit in silence for a moment, and then, 'Cheers,' she says, lifting her glass.

'Welcome back, son.' The old man lifts his.

'That shall be my new motto,' says Starling, smiling at Mum. 'Not bad if you don't think about it! Cheers.'

They chink glasses and begin, wordlessly, to munch until Mum clears her throat – and the way she looks at the old man, it's plain he's put her up to asking. 'Me and your dad have been wondering what you're going to do with yourself now, Lennie?'

He crunches a morsel of roastie. In the jungle they talked about food all the time. Roast spuds, the salty crunch of the outsides, the softness when you bit through. Edgar would go on about custard tart, trifle, eclairs... a sweet-toothed man, sweet all through.

'Well, you're hardly going to be a doctor now, are you?' The old man sounds pleased. He always took it as criticism that Lennie wanted to better himself.

'What with one hand,' he helpfully explains.

'I don't see why not,' objects Mum.

'I daresay Ramsay will find you something at the works, if I have a word. Not manual, obviously, something in office line.'

'Then you could live at home, Lennie. Wouldn't that be grand?' says Mum. 'That'll save you a bob or two till you get yourself back on your feet. But of course, if you still want to go to medical school...?'

A shred of meat between his teeth, his tongue fossicks for it as he breathes. Patience, just keep hold, it's only one meal, one ordeal. Of course, he can't stay.

'Eh, son? Your mum asked you a question.'

Starling sips his beer. It's hard sitting on a chair; he wants to squat like they did in the jungle. Under all the protective layers of tablecloth (plastic, lace, oil-cloth, blanket) his legs twitch. This tabletop is protected like nothing else on earth.

'Give him time,' says Mum, 'all he's been through.'

'What's been going on here, then?' Starling says, to change

the subject.

And while she rattles out the local gossip: him dead, her married, etc, the hard bones of his pelvis press on the chair, the dreamed-of food balls in his gut. On the deliberately slow acclimatisation voyage back, they'd been fed carefully, not too much; too much food all of a sudden in a starved system can kill. Again, the wrong-end-of-the-telescope feeling. Clearly, he no longer belongs... and though he doesn't want to, still it makes him sad; it makes him sad for Mum.

The old man gets up to stoke the fire, rattling coke from the shovel. The flap of flame and smoke coming into the room catches him wrong, brings to mind something he must not remember.

'Scuse me.' He lurches from the table and hurries out back to the old privy, forgetting there's the indoor bathroom now. The dogs follow him excitedly, yipping, and it's the dogs that save him. Once in the cold air, he squats, and the muscles in his hips stretch with relief. The dogs lick his face; there's salty tears and the taste of gravy, and they lick him clean.

Imagine something bright: Edgar's donkey laugh; he could always laugh, till very near the end. The limericks were filthy, funny, sometimes cruel. Edgar was the champ. Starling and darling rhyme, but he could never tell whether the darling was meant.

*A man returned home from a camp*
*And his family gave him the cramp*
*So he left them to see*
*What his new life could be*
*But to see it he needs a headlamp.*

He stands. The beer has filled him with gas and he belches as he opens the back gate, steps out into the road where street lamps make balls of fuzz in the drizzle and the cobbles glisten. Hard to believe that this street is on the same planet as the jungle, where it's probably daylight now and sun will be battering down. That place has burrowed itself into his brain. Without an operation how will he get it out? He watches Pepper lift his leg against a lamp-post, and then Salt sniffs and pees on same spot. He goes back through the yard and into the house where his parents are still sitting at the table.

'Think I'll turn in,' he says. 'Night-night.'

'But I've made you a pudding,' Mum says. 'Apple pie. Your favourite.'

'I can't, Mum, sorry.'

'Your Mum's been saving sugar ration for this moment,' Dad says.

'It's all right, Dad,' she says. 'I'll warm it through for you tomorrow, Lennie. Night-night. Make sure the bugs don't bite.' Her hand flies to her mouth, and she looks appalled at herself. 'Sorry, duckie, I expect there were bugs?'

'Just a few,' he says and finds himself grinning as he trudges up the stairs.

All night he twists and turns, sinking into the lumpy mattress, smothered by the weight of sheet, blanket, eiderdown and bedspread. Metal mesh squeaks underneath him. Straw palliasses might have been hard and lousy, but your bones got used to them. This softness seems dangerous. Can't sleep, scared to sleep any rate, lest he cry out. Bugs: the way they flowed from every crack and crevice when the lights went out. The ooze when you crushed them, then the marzipan smell.

He can hear Mum's feet padding about on the landing; a floorboard creaks as she listens at his door. What if he called her in and told her things, things that would make her hair curl? He snorts. It's just what she'd say, "*He told me things that'd make your hair curl,*" but he won't. "Guard your tongue" is the order, and he will. He'll protect her. It's all he can do for her now. And one day, he'll make her proud.

2

## STARLING

When he gets down in the morning, Dad's already taken the dogs out. Mum insists on boiling him an egg. Probably her egg. All he wants is tea, pints of it, as he sits at the table flicking through *The Mirror*. Stalin wants an H-bomb; the dockers' strike has ended; it's rumoured that Hitler isn't really dead.

'Sorry about last night,' he says. 'Your pie.'

'I know it was miserable out there, love,' she says. In the morning light she looks withered, her dark skin (Egyptian blood) sallow. He wishes he could reach through to her, but there's something in the way now, something that will always be between him and anyone who wasn't there. He longs for Lammy – Corporal Horace Lamb – his mate, who'll be home now with his wife and the kiddie who was born when he was away.

He stares at the bread and marg she's spread for him, wishing for her sake that there was another child, someone who could *really* be here. Before he was born, there was a stillbirth, a girl, barely mentioned. If only she'd lived. She might be married now with kiddies, living round the corner, popping in with a baby on her hip.

The egg sits in its egg cup, but he can't tackle it; you need two hands for a boiled egg.

'You could have that later, in a sandwich,' she says. 'If you don't fancy it now?'

'Mum, I'm off to London.'

'But...'

He can't look at her face. 'Got to see a man about a dog.' He gets up and goes over to the dresser. On the top shelf are the same old books as ever – *Common Ailments*, *The Count of Monte Cristo*, *Successful Dahlias* – and yes, still here, a map of London from a trip taken donkey's years ago. He unfolds it on the table, and finds Catford where Lammy lives. Perhaps he'll have a night there before he finds himself a hostel. He also looks up Lewisham, where Edgar's sister lives. Not far apart, as it happens. Mum starts washing up, humming to herself as she does when she's putting on a brave face.

'I like that old song,' he says. 'Why don't you sing it?'

'You daft ha'peth!'

'Go on, Mum.'

Gone pink, she clears her throat. 'All right then, if you insist.' She dries her soapy hands and composes herself before singing a bit of *"By the Light of the Silvery Moon"* in a thin, childish voice. As she finishes, she splays out her housecoat, and curtseys. He goes to clap before he realises that he can't, that he'll never clap again.

'You used to sing that at bedtime,' he says. 'You were a good mum, you know. Still are. The best.'

'Stop your nonsense!' She turns and busies herself drying a plate. 'I'll pack up some pie for you to take, shall I? And I'll cut you a sandwich. You'll come back soon though? You will, won't you, Lennie?'

The old man comes in with the dogs, does a double take when he sees his son at the table.

'Forget I was here?' Starling says.

Mum pours his tea. 'Lennie's off to London.'

The old man says nothing, eyeing the egg.

'You can have it,' Lennie says.

'He's going to *London*,' Mum repeats. 'Got to see a man about a dog. And I'm putting that in a sandwich for him.' Bravely, she snatches the egg out of the old man's reach. 'Oh, did you hear about poor Frankie Cresswell?' she says, and he nods, forcing tea down his throat. Yes, he knows about Frankie. Of course, the old man never told her what he'd caught them doing, him and Frankie. It was nothing much. Just a kiss, the beginnings of a kiss, might never have been more, but he happened to open the door on them.

'They say he was missing for weeks before the final news,' says Mum. 'Poor Mrs Cresswell. I sent her a letter, Lennie. I said what a nice boy he was, what a good pal he was to you.'

Dad blows and slurps his tea.

'Thanks, Mum.'

'So pleased *you're* back safe, my duck.' Mum's voice is choked. 'You can't imagine what we went through ever since we heard you'd been taken prisoner. The horrors people were coming out with. I hope it wasn't all true, Lennie?'

'It'll have made a man of you, any case,' Dad says. He lifts his cup. 'Mum?'

She drains the teapot into his cup.

The words hang there. *A man of you*. To be beaten, tortured, and starved, to see your friends die in front of your eyes, to see their bodies burn. Is that what makes a man a man?

No, what he means by *man* is clear, and in that sense the war has failed.

The train shunts through woodland. Sunshine lances between bare branches, and he shuts his eyes. Getting away was easy, the old man glad to be shot of him, Mum pressing him with damp packages of apple pie, egg sandwich, a bottle of cold tea. The flickering on his eyelids stops and he opens his eyes, stares out at a flat field, two horses nose-to-nose in the distance. Five other men are in the carriage: two in uniform, three in demob. He's glad he chose the grey chalk-stripe suit, single-breasted, classier than the usual navy or brown. He gets out his fags. Seeing him fumble, a bloke flicks him a light, and they chat a bit but when he says he was in the Far East the conversation flags. This other, who fought in France, seems embarrassed for him. It's true that there was no heroes' welcome for his lot.

Victory was June: September an anticlimax. His lot aren't heroes, but the dirty tail-end of it all, something you want to look away from. The conversation falters before the chap gets off at Derby, lifting a hand, wishing him luck. Starling watches him limp along the platform. Going to meet his girl, he said, but there's no lass in sight. Starling comforts himself that it was a lie.

Fag pinched between his lips he blows smoke from the corner of his mouth. The plan – stop with Lammy tonight, then get himself a hostel. It'll be a relief to see his mate. They travelled back together from that world to this. And when at Liverpool they parted, Lammy said to call if he ever needed a bed. And now he does need a bed – and more than that, a mate.

The train changes rhythm as it edges through the suburbs. He enjoys the backs of houses. There's a pegged-out line of giant underpants, a kiddie's swing, a man bent over a spade. Raindrops wriggle across the glass. He grinds his fag end on the floor, and his hand goes to the tobacco tin – Edgar's – which he must deliver to Edgar's family. How best though? Take it to the sister, who's easiest, nearest – or go to Suffolk and meet Edgar's parents? "Folks," he always called them, "my folks." He's got both addresses. The tin, packed with Edgar's tiny sketches, is his responsibility; to return it, his duty. Since the day he got hold of it, he's kept it close, safe, never even looked inside. It weighs on him now, that responsibility.

The train has stopped. Shouldering his heavy pack, he pushes through King's Cross station. Bomb damage still stinks up the air; it's a dank drizzly afternoon, pale sun or moon, he can't tell which, slumped above splintered roofs.

He walks with his chin up. A man with a purpose. He walks till he finds a phone box, grips the receiver under his chin, fumbles pennies into the slot and dials the number. It's not Lammy but his landlady who answers, and snappishly agrees to go downstairs and see if he's in. His jaw ticks as he waits, intermittently feeding halfpennies into the slot. In the end a woman speaks. It's Lammy's wife – Celia – who tells him her hubby's out. There's a silence when Starling asks if they can put him up tonight. He hears her sighing before she says, 'Sorry, but it's not convenient tonight, what with him being out.' He can hear a child shouting in the background as she tells him they're going away tomorrow. 'Perhaps in a few days? Thursday, say? I'll tell him you rang.'

He stops and sits on a wall, takes the weight off, swigs tea, munches his sandwich. She sounded nice, like she was telling the truth, not just stringing him along. Better this way any rate. Gives him a chance to find a hostel, get himself settled.

He stands and stretches; damp in his joints makes him stiff. He throws a crust to a three-legged dog, sense of fellow feeling there. The skinny mutt trails after him before he mimes a kick, though he'd never really kick a dog. Sends it packing for its own good, can't take on any creature now. Poor pets homeless, families gone, left to scavenge. The dogs of war, ha! He misses his own dogs, but they're all right with the old man, who's softer with them than he ever was with him.

Walk to the sister's first, then find a hostel. The route to Buttress Street turns out to be a grim one, detours round piles of rubble and craters, builders at work everywhere, Polish refugees, Kraut prisoners of war repairing impossible amounts of damage. Sometimes there are untouched streets. In some houses, lights show already against the gloom.

How can it be so dark? Above the cloud it's the same sky here as in Siam. It's the same planet, depending on the same sun. Palm trees come into his mind, tangled vines, air so dense you have to tunnel through it.

It's further than he thought to Buttress Street. His feet ache, and the stump feels tight and hot. Without a hand to run through, the blood must find its way back up his arm. The circulation is ingenious. He should keep fresh his anatomy. He goes through system as he walks, imagining blood moving through those tubes in his own legs: *femoral artery, femoral vein, popliteal artery, popliteal vein, anterior tibial artery, posterior tibial artery,* the red and blue diagrams so neat and organised – unlike the mush of the real.

It's gone five, and properly dark before he locates the sister's flat, between a bookies and a sweetshop. With a surge of confidence, he rings the bell, but there's no reply. Not back from work yet, maybe. He'll wait a bit. He'd forgotten what an English November feels like, the damp of it, the smell of smoke and cinders, dirty drips from the gutter, sooty windowsills. He trudges up and down the road to keep his circulation moving. Time drags on, and he starts to doubt his plan. His confidence trickles in the gutter, gurgles down the drain. She might be away, out with friends, visiting her family in Seckbridge. Or she might have moved away. And then his heart jolts as he sees a girl approaching – it's her. He knows her from a photo of Edgar's.

But with the actuality of her, his nerve fails. *Step forward, hold out your hand, you do still bloody well have a right hand, shake hers and say...* She stoops to pet a cat.

Hatless, straggly hair, scarf trailing, a funny way of walking. A bit knock-kneed. She's pale as milk. When she notices him watching her, he takes a step forward, but her scowl is sudden and ferocious. She swerves away. He starts to follow. She peers over her shoulder, and he drops back. His nerves are shot, and she looks scared. He doesn't want to spook her. He opens his mouth, but she's further off now, leading him away from her door. Isn't there some sort of bird that does that? Drags its wing, leads you away from its nest? He drops back to shelter in a doorway, lights a fag. In a few moments she returns, and he sees her scan the street before she lets herself in, all nervous and jittery. After a minute a light comes on upstairs, and there's a twitch of curtain, a pale face looking out.

He bends to stroke the cat she stroked; it's hunched on a windowsill and rises under his hand, purrs, a buzz of warmth against his palm. He could ring the doorbell now he knows she's in there, but his head aches and it's too late; his nerve has gone. He doesn't want to see her now. Or anyone.

He lopes off to find a bed.

3
---
AIDA

'I'll miss you, little Miss You,' says the American. Around them cutlery clinks, and glass chinks; smoke swims in the filmy light.

Aida crosses her legs under the table, enjoying the nylon slide. 'And I'll miss you, Mister You.' Though it feels rather twittish to trot this out, the tragic thing is that it's true. She likes his voice and the way he is in bed. She likes his wide, easy smile, the texture of his skin, the thick fair hair on his arms, almost like fur, the wholesome, soapy smell of him. And she likes his height. He's taller by far than any British man she's been with; it's excessive and unnecessary – gorgeous. Invisibly, she sighs. Of course, she always knew he was only temporary: that's the deal with GI's.

He waves his arm and orders coffee. "Corfee". This is to be their last night together, a blowout meal at Simpson's in the Strand, though they'll write to each other. They *say* they'll write. But the USA is so far away it might as well be the moon. It's not actual *love*; she has prevented that happening by secretly mocking his name *Duke,* with its pathetic allusion to aristocracy (and anyway, surely, more suitable for a dog?), by thinking of him only as "the American", by searching for and magnifying irritating habits. When he wipes his nose, for instance, he pushes the handkerchief deep into the nostrils with both index fingers. *Awful.* She concentrates on that. You can't love someone who does that. (Though he does have a good nose: straight and triangular.)

He gets up to go to the "john" and she forces her eyes from the lanky way he walks, those long, long legs, looks right away, and sees something that makes her choke on her wine and shrink down in her chair. It's *Daddy*, about to leave the restaurant, and with a *woman*. How did she not see him before? Has he seen her? The woman is a miniature person, a stranger, in a tight blue costume, a silly velvet hat with a little veil. As Aida watches, Daddy helps her on with a mink, then turns her round by the shoulders, laughs at something she says, and dabs the end of her nose affectionately with one finger. It's what he does to Aida when she amuses him. And then they are gone, the two of them, into the night.

She blinks, swallows, feels sick, guilty somehow, for having seen: *complicit*. The American returns, gestures a waiter and asks for the "check". 'Hey, what's up? Looks like you've seen a ghost,' he says. She says nothing at all. 'Let's go,' he says. 'Can I take you home, little Miss You?'

Another thing that could grate, is the way he calls her that. It occurs to her that perhaps he dislikes *her* name, as much as she dislikes his. Taking her home will of course mean coming in, and coming in will of course mean bed, glorious bed, which is all made up ready with clean sheets (mended side-to-middle but still, her best). But having seen Daddy like that does rather put one off. In a month it will be Christmas, and though she'd rather ignore it this year, the first since Edgar's death, she has promised to go home. How will she face Daddy? Should she confront him? If he saw her and knows she saw him, he might think that by keeping silent, she's colluding. But she's pretty sure he didn't see her. Surely, he'd never have dabbed the woman's nose like that if he knew she was a witness?

The American clicks his fingers in front of her face. 'Anyone home?'

She shakes her head, fights a smile, irritated now by how much she likes him, too dangerously much, just when he is leaving. She can do without that sort of turmoil in her life.

'Actually, I think I need an early night.'

'Seriously?'

She nods, stands and walks towards the cloakroom. They await their coats in silence though she lets him help her wriggle into her tatty musquash when it comes. Outside, they stand in the light that's shed from the restaurant (still some thrill in that after years of blackout). 'What did I say?' He looms over her, wide shoulders already glistening with drizzle.

She pulls her hat over her ears, takes a breath. 'Look *Duke*,' pronouncing the frightful name with English emphasis rather than "Dook" as he does, 'You're leaving tomorrow, and then we shall never see each other again.'

'Never say never,' he says.

'Don't see any point in prolonging things.'

There are taxis crawling everywhere, and she hails one.

'Thank you for dinner,' she says, opening the door. 'Thanks for everything. Good luck.'

'Seriously!' His voice sounds angry for the first time since she's known him, which is only a few weeks. She met him soon after the news about Edgar and, though he isn't aware of it, he's partly what's been holding her together. She lifts a hand, gazes back at his angry, puzzled face, at his frame – wide-shouldered, tall, spare – and then, as the taxi rounds a corner, he's gone.

Almost immediately she regrets it. The driver tries to engage her in conversation about the weather, rationing,

Nuremberg, a tirade of grumbles. He seems quite content with her lack of response. She disappointed him, of course, her lovely, lanky, sexy, generous American. And after he'd just bought her such an expensive dinner – lobster mayonnaise, chocolate meringue. He's only done the thing that GI's do, love you and leave you, that was the joke, there was never any talk of marriage. What if he'd asked? *Might* she have considered it? Her twin cousins both married Americans and live now in Philadelphia. The taxi nearly hits a cyclist, the driver slams on the brakes, swears, turns, 'All right back there?' and then resumes his grumbling.

No. She couldn't go to America. It's too soon; she's too sore about Edgar, the idea of leaving her country, her folks, scares her. And there will be other men; she will keep herself busy and find another, easy as pie, easy as that; pathetically, she tries to snap her gloved fingers. And then Daddy comes into her head again. Such a shock to see him with another woman, she hardly knows how to manage it. *Daddy!* The most boring moralistic stuffed shirt in the world. Of course, it could be perfectly innocent. The woman could be... what? A patient, or a... No, Aida, it clearly is not innocent. The way he dabbed her on the nose, the way he put the coat around her, the simpering glance she threw over her shoulder as they left.

'Have to drop you here, treacle,' the driver says. And of course, the end of the road is up, like half the roads in London with gas mains and water mains and whatnot.

'Cheer up, it may never happen,' he says.

'Already has.' She withdraws the extra sixpence for the tip.

It's darker here; the street lamps aren't all back yet, and some people still have their blackouts up. Some of the houses are empty, there's a gap in a terrace, a direct hit, a space like a missing tooth, a smell of ruin. As she walks, she's unnerved by the feeling that someone's following, and she turns sharply, but it's too dark to see. She walks faster, heels clacking on the pavement. She strains her ears for sounds of footsteps behind her; there's a breeze and litter skitters, tarpaulins flap. The other day when she returned from work she felt the same thing, as if there were someone following her. With relief she turns into her own street, where the street lamps work, and the betting shop casts a cheery oblong of light onto the road. When she reaches her doorstep she turns, stands with her back to the door, scanning. There is a chap, young, maybe a youth, but he walks straight past, never so much as a glance at her, and there's no one else about.

The ginger cat that always begs to come in winds round her ankles, and though she usually sends it packing, this time she lets it in and up the stairs. She locks the door and trudges up to the cold messy room, which has the single advantage of being hers, and hers alone. Before she left this morning, she had a cursory tidy, draped her pink chiffon scarf over the lamp to soften the light and set the fire ready to be lit.

She removes her hat then slaps herself hard on the cheek. *Ouch. Why do that? Why deny yourself that pleasure, you utter fool? What will the glorious chap be doing now? Finding another girl to say goodbye to Blighty with?* She kneels and lights the fire before she sheds her coat. With the kettle on the stove, she opens a tin of pilchards, forks a scrap onto a saucer for the cat. She'll have the rest tomorrow. For now, it's a cup of tea and Agatha Christie like a miserable spinster.

If the American really cares, he might follow; he knows the way. He might be in a taxi right this minute. She warms at the thought. One more night *would* be lovely. Headstrong is what the parents call her. Not so much strong as wrong this time. Idiotic. *Cut off your nose to spite your face.* Jittering, she makes herself wait for the kettle to boil and pours water over this morning's tea leaves before she goes to the window, yanks back the curtain to peer down onto the street. She sees Gladys, the mad old woman with her pramful of lost toys, turning the corner, then there's no one. No lanky American striding along, of course, though just as the curtain falls, she catches a glimpse of movement, and lifts it again to see, in the doorway of the derelict shop opposite, the glow of a cigarette. She strains her eyes to focus, and out of the darkness resolves a slight shape. She drops the curtain and stands frowning and flexing her fists. Could it be the same youth she saw before? What's he doing there? She tunes the wireless to some band music, pours tea, can't resist looking out again. This time the doorway is empty, and all is dark. She wraps a shawl round her shoulders and, with the cat warming her lap, settles by the fire for her winterish, spinsterish evening.

4
―――

## STARLING

*The Beeches*, the house is called, and beech trees stand guard, leaves dripping rust, and a beech hedge stretches between the two gateways. Two polished Austin Siddeleys wait by the door; there's room for a fleet of the buggers.

He waits, half-hidden behind a tree trunk, fag pinched in the corner of his mouth, peering from under the brim of his hat. Must look a dodgy bastard to anyone who spots him. In the end, a woman emerges from the front door. Big and posh is the glimpse he gets through a porch into a hall, stained glass and lamplight. Edgar's mum? "Mummy", he called her. Normally you'd take the piss out of a bloke who said *Mummy* – not Edgar, though. He kept a creased-up photo in his paybook. Dark dad and fair mum seated, fair girl and dark boy posed behind. All stiff as pokers.

And this is the woman (though older and thinner). She comes down the steps, tying on a headscarf. It'd be the easiest thing in the world to step forward now, hand over the tin, but before he can summon himself, she's got into one of the cars. The door slams, the engine starts, and she's gone. His heart punches like a fist. Failed again.

A bird of some sort sings from above, not a song so much as a complaint. He dares to walk right to the entrance – entrances. Up the steps is the wide front door, brass numbers, 107, polished letter flap, by the side an iron hedgehog boot scraper. He pokes an experimental toe between its bristles. And down a meaner set of steps is the surgery door. "Dr D.B.J. Everett MD" says the plaque on the pillar beside. *"We live above the shop,"* Edgar used to say. His name would have gone on there when he'd qualified; there's space for it. The joke is Edgar never wanted to be a doctor, while Starling had to fight for his place at medical school, securing the one annual scholarship available at his grammar school.

The surgery door opens, and up the steps climbs a vastly pregnant woman. He goes back to the shelter of the tree. Now the car's gone he can see a line of prams parked outside.

No point going to the door now, not with the doctor at work, the mother out, the sister in London. Every bloody time he's been near the sister, he's lost his nerve. Nerves all shot to smithereens. Hung about in that filthy doorway like a spare part, pathetic, then slunk back to the hostel. What's up with him? Lost the trick of it. The trick of what? *Life.* How to do it. If he'd stepped up and given the sister the tin right away, he'd have saved himself the trouble and the cost of the two trains it took to get here.

Though he did want to see where Edgar used to live. In the dark of the jungle, Edgar used to walk him through the place – the streets, the River Deben – till he thought he could picture it, but he'd got it all wrong in his head. *You must visit; the folks will love you.* What he'd pictured was something from a calendar, summery, hollyhocks, thatch and all that bollocks... not wet roads, gravel, and mulching leaves.

Why not shove the tin through the letter flap and be done with it? The bloody taste of rust hangs in the air. He lights a fag from the stub of the last, pinches it between his lips and walks away, hunched inside his coat. He does want to meet Edgar's family – wants them to know him. Edgar would want that too. It's starting to pelt down with rain; he'll find shelter and come back later on.

He lopes uphill into town, finds a café to shelter in, water dripping from his brim, glasses steaming up as he orders tea and a bun. A nice enough girl gives him the eye, and he plays up to her. 'You're not from round here, are you?' she says in the local accent Edgar sometimes used to do. At Christmas in camp they got up a sad effort of a pantomime every year. Once, Edgar was an ugly sister, who put on an accent just like that. His teeth grit together through the dull and heavy bun.

Condensation weeps down the tea-shop windows, an old bloke frowns over a crossword, a mother feeds scraps of cake to a baby. It's warm and homey till the door opens with such a sharp ping it shocks him and at once the place is too hot and small and he has to get out, and he knocks his chair over in his rush and someone says, 'I say, old man!' and he is out of there and panting in the dusk. Can't go back to The Beeches in this state. *Breathe, breathe, pull yourself together.* He finds his way back to the station, though there's two hours yet till his train. He crosses the bridge to the river. How Edgar went on about it, and the boat he spent all his time messing about in as a boy. *Speedwell*, was it? *"One day, Starling, my old chapster, I shall take you out in her."*

In the late light at low tide there's miles of mud, the colour of gunmetal. He didn't picture it like this, but green and lush with ducks and willows. He can't imagine Edgar here. Miles across the water, trees are like scratches on tin. The rain begins again, the scratches vanish, and suddenly it's dark. The river smells thick and soupy, a tang of malt in it, a brewery nearby. Didn't Edgar mention that? At the station there's a pub. A drink before he tries again, there's time, he won't impose, just meet them, pass over the tin, condole. Can you say that? Condole?

He stands at the counter, gulping down pint after brown pint, but he's not used to it and his shrunken stomach aches. Landlord asks no questions; something soothing about him, his kind Suffolk voice, the way he minds his business, refills the glass *gratis*.

But somehow time goes by, until it's too late to go back to Edgar's. His train is in and there's nothing for it but to climb aboard, bloated in the gut, ragged in the head, unfinished business, duty undone. Rain lashes black windows as the train chugs into nothing. Go back to the sister's then. Just ring her doorbell, get it over and done with, or shove it through the bloody letter flap. With the rhythm of the train, he shuts his eyes.

# 5
## AIDA

Blankly, she stares at the slab of papers on her desk. Reports of food production for logging and filing, forms filled with incomprehensible codes and acts and paragraphs and references to other indecipherable codes and acts and references. To think how thrilled she was when she took this post to have to sign the Official Secrets Act. It seemed so deliciously cloak and dagger, and she'd thought she might become privy to important national secrets, or at least something *interesting*. But it's all piffle, baffling as hell and twice as boring. Basically, she's helping build a – terribly well indexed – bureaucratic midden. Whoever, in the future, will want to dig through and study the minutiae of, for instance, she peers at the top sheet of paper, animal slaughter in Midlothian in 1942?

She took the job gratefully. After ambulance work it promised to be regular, and safe, and clean. And it has, admittedly, kept those promises. But now she misses the excitement, the unpredictability... even, peculiarly, the *fear*. Who'd have thought she'd miss the war! Since VE-day the country's gone dull and grey. The lightbulb buzzes like a fly. No window in this tiny basement office (or cupboard, really). Across the desk, Dora hums *"Daisy, Daisy"*. At least there's tea upstairs in the kitchenette, actual fresh tea leaves that haven't been used before. A governmental perk. Her eyes creep to the clock – ten to three.

'Nearly time,' she says. 'I'll do the hons.'

Dora looks up, pencil poised. 'Isn't it my turn?' She pats her mouth in a neat yawn. She's a mousey girl, straight beige hair parted to one side, clipped with a hairgrip, wire-rimmed specs. You'd call her plain, but for her ridiculously sweet retroussé nose. Entirely wasted.

'Let me go,' pleads Aida, 'I'm going crackers. Need to see the light of day. We may as well be moles down here.'

Dora gives another yawn, and stretches her head from side to side so that the vertebrae pop. 'Anyway, how did last night turn out?'

'Nothing doing.' Aida stands. At last! All day she's been waiting for Dora to ask but she's maddening like that. She makes you wait.

Dora frowns. 'But I saw him pick you up. Tall, isn't he? Over six foot, I reckon.'

'We had a meal and then a squabble. Six foot three.'

'Phew, do you get a crick in the neck? But you didn't...?'

Aida shakes her head.

Nodding approvingly, Dora adjusts her specs, which will keep slipping down that dinky nose. She's smugly engaged, primly moral – mostly.

Aida glances at the framed photos Dora's taken the trouble to tack to the wall: the fiancé; a King Charles spaniel; the fiancé holding the King Charles spaniel. There's nothing on Aida's side except a calendar, turned to the wrong month. 'You see,' she explains, 'it was going to be our love you and leave you moment, and I–'

'Came to your senses? Good for you.' Dora sticks her pencil

into a sharpener and turns the handle. They both watch the petals of shaved wood drop into its chamber. Dora withdraws the pencil and tests the sharp point with a fingertip. 'Why are Yanks so tall?'

Aida laughs. 'For goodness' sake! Yours wasn't! What was he called again? Midge?'

'Nat. He was a gnome. And he *wasn't* mine; it was only when...' She sniffs, and reaches up her sleeve for her hanky.

'All right, all right,' Aida says quickly. Dora's Chris went missing in Algiers for some time and, apparently in her distraction, she'd allowed herself to be comforted by a miniature GI. Just *how* comforted, she's never let on.

'Better nutrition,' Aida says, getting up from her desk. 'Lots of beef. They reach their optimum potential, don't they?'

Dora tucks her handkerchief back up her sleeve, smiling bravely. 'Are you sad?'

'No,' Aida lies.

The door flies open. 'Ladies?' Mr Frampton appears, frowning. The usual smell of onions emanates from his greasy suit, and Aida takes a step back. 'Sounds like a lot of chitter-chatter going on.'

'Just fetching the tea,' she says.

He peers dubiously at the clock but can hardly object to five minutes. 'Run along then, and remember we need *all* these dealt with before close of play, and there's plenty more where they came from.' He indicates the haphazardly paper-stacked trolley: it seems as if all the paperwork from the entire war is flooding down to their basement office, boxes of it every day. He gives an approving nod at the stacked work on Dora's desk. '*You* don't seem to have done much,' he points out to Aida. 'You spend all your time chattering. I can hear you, you know, yap, yap, yap. It's usually you.'

'Getting to it,' she says, and runs up the stairs to the kitchen to stack the trolley with green government-issue cups and saucers and the giant brown enamel teapot.

---

Onions barely raises his head when she delivers his tea, only grunts at her to get a move on. She saves Mr Neville Guthrie till last, and when she backs the trolley into his office, it's flooded with tangerine light. How she envies him his window with its panorama of West London: sunsets, trees, planes, and steeples. In the windowless basement there's no difference between night and day, and despite a clanking radiator, it's perpetually chilly.

Neville lifts his head, wavy red hair tousled, tie loose and top shirt button unfastened. He pushes his chair back from his desk to stretch out his legs and smiles his pleasingly crooked smile. A warm look passes between them for a little too long, and she snatches her eyes away. Like herself, Neville's been here a few months, but he's more senior, with the luxury of an office to himself. Before the war he was a draughtsman but now, for some unfathomable reason, seems to have settled for the Ministry. He's older – a proper grown-up, with whom she's been out now and then, to the flicks or for a drink. He's *nice*, far too nice for her, though she likes his faint Scottish accent, his air of apartness. Being a Quaker, he took no part in active service, spent the war shifting between outdoorsy kinds of work: farms and forestry. Onions holds that against him, but Aida has no issue with his principles. It's certainly not cowardice; it takes a hell of a lot more guts to stand against everyone than to fall in with them. After all, even Daddy didn't fight in the Great War, having been a doctor. There's no shame. And *someone* needs to do that work. Not everyone can be off fighting and getting themselves killed.

She swallows hard, distracts herself by studying Neville's

hands, strong from all that manual toil. When he first arrived they were rough and calloused but, she notices as he reaches for his tea, they've grown smoother. He carves wooden spoons in his spare time though, and there are always nicks on his fingers. He has reassuringly broad palms and stubby fingers but weirdly shaped thumbnails, almost wider than they're long, which she finds oddly disturbing.

'Busy on Friday?' he asks. 'They're showing *Grapes of Wrath* at the Regal. Thought I'd take it in – marvellous novel. Read it?'

'No.' She pours his tea.

'Fancy coming along?'

'I'll have to check my diary.' She grins over her shoulder as she trundles off. 'Now back to the grind, mister.'

Neville's a pleasant sort of standby when there's nothing more exciting on the go. A safe, attractive, reliable chap. He's respectful, never having tried to get her into bed which, if she was a better type of person, she might appreciate. As she pushes the trolley back towards the kitchen, she allows herself, with little jumps in her heart and belly, to picture the more exciting ones as a sort of frieze running along the corridor wall: the American; the married lawyer; the fairly famous actor and the less famous actor; three other GI's (though none a patch on *Dook*), an almost elderly librarian (must have been at least forty). These men all had one thing in common. They saw her as a temporary distraction or entertainment, or however men think about these things. Not since the awful Brian Burk has anyone taken her seriously. She shudders at the memory of Brian, then, as she parks her trolley beside the stained and dripping ministry kitchen sink, giggles. That was preposterous! Incredible that for a short time, she actually contemplated marrying *Brian*, a pal of Edgar's at Westminster. She went out with him for a few months before the war. He wasn't *bad*-looking exactly, but had a portentous way of speaking, eyes retreating into his head as he cleared his throat, as if preparing to pronounce. She shudders at the memory of their single kiss. He'd lunged at her in the hall after a party, thoroughly jamming his tongue into her mouth. She scrubs at it now, wincing. Amazing that it didn't put her off kissing for evermore.

She carries down a tray with tea for herself and Dora, and hoists a new slab of papers onto her desk: *Ministry of Food, Livestock Policy*. In her handkerchief there's a twist of tea leaves for tonight – if they won't give you perks it's fair enough to take them. She yawns, sits back, sips the tea: stewed, and not quite hot enough. 'Might go out with Guthrie on Friday,' she says.

Dora looks up, pencil poised, peering at Aida over her slipped-down specs. 'What on earth *is* it about you?' she says.

Aida chooses not to take offence. It's true that men seem to like her, seek her out; she's rarely short of a date. 'Not my nose, that's for definite!' she says.

'It is rather a stately nose.'

Aida flicks a paperclip at her. 'Must be a throwback thing,' she muses. 'My parents have both got nice little hooters. And my brother, too.' She swallows at a sudden lump. God, she's barely thought about Edgar today. Is this how it happens, how you start to forget?

Dora lifts a finger to her lips. 'Onions!'

The two of them duck their heads and begin industriously sorting, numbering, logging, shifting papers from one pile into another.

'Poor old Guthrie,' Dora says after a while. She's stopped to sip her tea. She prefers it lukewarm. Better for the digestion, apparently.

'Why *poor old*? I really do like him, you know.'

Dora's expression begs to differ. Her Chris eventually came back in one piece, bearing a ring with a tiny diamond, which sparkles modestly under the dull pear of the office lightbulb. They will marry in spring next year, and Dora will leave the Ministry behind and continue her tidy, well-planned life. She will produce two boys and a girl, and breed King Charles spaniels. If all goes to plan, the tiny Yank will turn out to have been her one and only fling. Aida hopes she did at least allow herself to be *thoroughly* comforted.

Once Onions is safely back in his office, she nips back into Neville's. 'I do happen to be free on Friday,' she says, with mock surprise.

He grins, pushes back a flop of hair from his brow. 'We'll take in the early showing, shall we, then have some dinner?' It's properly dark outside the window now, and she sees herself reflected deflatingly in the glass, pale and crumpled, her hair flat and limp.

'*À bientôt.*' She gives him a mock salute and wanders into the Ladies' to gaze at her tired face, her shining stately nose; she tries to pinch a bit of colour into her cheeks. No one would ever call her pretty, so what *is* it? She likes men, she likes sex. Maybe it's just that they can tell? She's too pale, straight-haired, thin – and lavishly behootered – to be considered *pretty*. Edgar's friends always liked her though. He couldn't see it himself, he mused once, being her brother, but she must have IT – whatever IT is. IT is something you can't get; you either have IT or you don't. *Oh Edgar, Edgar, Edgar*. She notices her lashes are wet. It's disconcerting. He was missing for nearly a year before they knew he was a prisoner, and then he was a prisoner for almost the rest of the war. In all that time she was buoyed by a stubborn bubble of hope that would not pop. But now it's popped, and tears will come, sometimes actually roll down her face, without warning, as if some sort of valve or gauge has broken. He's been dead four months, now, and for the first three they didn't even *know*. You'd think you'd know.

She scrubs her eyes and groans. *Pull yourself together, Aida.* You're twenty-four. Stop moping. Get married. Neville Guthrie isn't a bad prospect. Intelligent, principled, kind, good-looking in a reassuring, tweedy way. Why not take him more seriously? After all, once Dora has gone, you don't want to be stuck in the bloody Ministry dodging old Onions on your own.

---

On Friday she dresses up, "making the most of herself", as Mummy, irritatingly, would say. She wears her nicest outfit: a navy cashmere two-piece with a pleated skirt and pearly buttons on the snugly fitted jacket, a sort of magic garment that gives her figure the illusion of curves. It was a twenty-first birthday present, the cloth procured by Daddy (black market), and tailored by Mummy's favourite dressmaker. Under the jacket she wears a cream shirt (seven coupons) and on the lapel, a sparkly paste brooch, given by a beau, that at a cursory glance might pass for diamonds. Under the skirt are her last new nylons, a gift from the American, who will be on his ship by now, somewhere mid-Atlantic. *Don't think about him. Best that he's out of reach.*

When she rushes, late, into their broom cupboard, Dora widens her eyes. 'Ooh, bringing out the big guns I see.'

Aida shrugs. 'Might as well give him a run for his money.'

'Poor mug.'

'He's not a mug; I like him.'

Nothing but a slight raise of an eyebrow from Dora at this.

'I *do*.'

'Be gentle with him. He's a lamb.'

Aida works hard and fast and, for the first time ever, the day's trolley is empty by five o'clock, when the Ministry shuts for the weekend. On her way out, she goes to the Ladies' to complete her preparations. Last night she set her hair, and it still rises satisfactorily from her brow in a pale wave. She pencils over her fair brows, adds a spot of rouge to each cheek, coral lipstick (anything darker and she looks half dead), and a dab of *Evening in Paris*. Dora, popping in to spend a penny before catching her bus, pulls a face, but refrains, ostentatiously, from comment.

Neville seems not to notice any difference, but looks pleased when she takes his tweedy arm. The picture starts at six o'clock so they have time for a drink, a gin sling each, which though watery makes Aida's head pleasantly swimmy. It's a relief when he joins her in a drink; last time he stuck to lemonade, and she got tiddly on her own, which she finds faintly embarrassing, and much less fun. When they're settled into a snug corner of the pub, Neville says, 'Now, tell me, what would you rather be doing with your life?' He taps his cigarette on the rim of the ashtray.

'That's a queer sort of question! What do you mean?'

'You seem always to want to be elsewhere. As if you're about to spring away.'

'Do I?' She leans forward eagerly, fascinated to be so closely observed, then sits back to consider. 'Nothing in particular,' she admits. 'It's nice to be right here, right now, with *you*.' She touches his knee, smiling brightly, flirting and mock flirting all at once. He dips his head, pleased and bashful, possibly not picking up on the mocking part.

'What about work?' he asks. 'If you could do anything?'

'Well,' she considers. 'I liked ambulance driving. It was awful, of course, but exciting. Weirdly, sort of fun. Time went so *fast*. You never knew what was coming next. Well, you sort of knew, but you never knew *quite* what...'

He nods, sips, puffs, content for her to rattle on, recounting the night her ambulance broke down just in time to stop herself, her crew and the wounded family in the back being crushed by a collapsing building.

Quickly, she shakes away the memory; it's all right to tell stories but you don't want to have to feel the feelings again. 'But I don't want to do anything medical, not with Daddy being a doctor, and anyway I can't be bothered to train.' She gulps her drink. 'And certainly not the Ministry,' she says. 'It's so deadly dull, isn't it? Paper, paper, everywhere, and not a drop to drink! And they're all papers that are over and done with. Basically rubbish. What's the point of archiving them all? A great big bonfire would be more fun.'

'Might be useful, in future.'

'Useful for what? Loo paper?'

He has rather a darling way of shaking his head as he laughs, gazing at her with a warm light in his chestnut eyes.

'Useful info if there's another war, say, or an economic collapse,' he says seriously. 'And for historians of the future.' He never laughs for long, she notices. His default temperament is earnest, and she's afraid he'll go off on one of his political rambles. But it seems he's content tonight to keep his interest on her, which is endearing. *You see, Aida: a good prospect.*

'What do you like to do outside work? At weekends, say?'

Embarrassingly, she's stumped. If only she could say something like play the cello, or write, or ballet dance (or even like watching ballet) or grow roses or breed dogs or play tennis.

'Read, walk, think,' she says, hoping he can't hear the sound of a barrel being scraped. 'I don't have an actual *hobby*.' How dull he must be thinking her, how ordinary. She wags a finger. 'Warning: I contain no hidden depths,' she says, 'so don't go splashing about, trying to find any!'

He pulls on his ciggie, smiling and shaking his head.

'What about *you*?' she says. 'Surely you'd rather go back to being a draughtsman.'

'Indeed, if the right opportunity comes along. In the meantime–'

'And you've got your spoon carving,' she interrupts. 'And your... your Quakerism.'

He nods, mouth curving. He has not one but two dimples in each cheek, reddish bristles, firm lips, straight teeth.

'I wouldn't call the Quakers a *hobby*,' he says. 'Do you go to church?'

'Christmas and Easter and weddings, the usual thing.' *And funerals,* she doesn't add, beating from her mind Sunday, when she ought to be going home. When she ought to be going, with her parents, to a memorial service for the local Far East POWs who will never be coming home.

'Must be lovely to have a passion for something,' she says. It's rather despicable, she thinks, that the only thing on her mind these days is men. Except for Edgar, except for grief. But then almost everyone is grieving. Grief is not a distinction. Last time they went out, Neville told her about friends lost in the war. One in particular, a fellow conchie killed in a tractor accident, seemed to hurt the most. Seeing the raw hurt, the outrage on his face, had been too much. It had brought her own loss blasting back. Once you've had a big brother it feels impossible to go through the rest of your life without one.

'Let's get going,' she says.

---

During the film (long, miserable) he takes her hand, and squeezes rhythmically, rather as if he's milking a cow. She's distracted by wondering if he has ever, in fact, milked a cow. Afterwards they go to dinner in a place of his choice: a dark, stuffy little café with a snuffling waitress who serves them the dish of the day: cottage pie and bottled peas. As they eat, a black cat winds between the tables, and there is a slight catty odour underlying that of smoke and stewing meat. The café doesn't serve alcohol, though by now she could have done with a top-up. He confesses that the gin has given him a headache; he barely drinks, preferring to stay in his right mind.

A dull heavy feeling descends. The film was depressing, the food depressing, the evening depressing. She'd like to get drunk and dance the soles off her shoes, walk home barefoot at dawn.

'In your right mind,' she ponders. 'Not sure I can claim to *have* a right mind.'

He blows smoke and smiles, apparently oblivious to her dip in mood.

'No, I mean it,' she says. 'I don't think my mind has ever been what you'd call *right*.'

'What's wrong with it?' he asks.

The oilcloth tablecloth is scrubbed almost bare of pattern, you can just make out the faintest memory of flowers.

'Eh?'

'Oh, I don't know.' She takes out a ciggie, and he clicks his lighter for her. 'It just doesn't want to do anything much. It reads – nothing clever. It likes whodunnits best. It thinks about clothes and food and what, next. And...' *My brother,* she thinks, inhaling a steadying bite of smoke.

'Well, I think your mind is perfectly all right,' he says. 'And it's a mind to which I'm becoming partial. You're refreshingly straightforward, Miss Everett. You don't put up any pretence.'

She gives a surprised snort. 'Oh yes I do! You *really* don't know me at all!'

'I'd like to get to know more.'

'But there's nothing to me. I'm empty. Like a shell.'

'I doubt that.' He takes her hand.

She writhes under the sincerity of his gaze. 'Dancing!' she

says suddenly. 'I do love dancing, that's something. Body and mind both. We could go now. Shall we? There's a dance at the–'

He raises a quelling hand. 'Really, darling, I'd sooner not.'

'Come on anyway.' She jumps up, impatient to leave the dismal atmosphere. 'Let's walk.'

'I'll walk you home,' he says, getting to his feet.

'Too far,' she says. 'I'd sooner get the bus.'

---

As the trolley-bus trundles her towards Lewisham, she feels like weeping. He's much too grown-up for her, and too, too depressingly nice. There's nothing to hold against him, nothing to actually dislike. He's earnest, but what's wrong with that? He's fascinated by her, which is a novelty. She sighs. It's her own fault the evening went wrong. One day, maybe, she could be the person for him; she could transform into someone well-meaning and well-intentioned and sincere. Hell, maybe she could even become a Quaker! Or a Quaker's wife anyway. One day, but not *yet*. Have a bit more fun first before things become too real. Do more dancing, live more *life*.

6

## CLEMENTINE

Flames waver above thick white candles and the air shivers with wax, fur, perfume, camphor. Holly and ivy wreathe the columns; berries like frozen drips of blood. It's the first Sunday of Advent. Morning service, followed by the POW memorial, is over. The queue down the aisle rustles and murmurs as it makes its way towards the door, impeded by the new vicar who takes his time shaking hands with everyone in turn. Clem shivers and steadies herself on the end of a pew. St Mary's is chilly and dim, rather like this new vicar himself, with his tone-deaf, impersonal homily. Last time they attended St Mary's, which must have been Easter, the elderly relict was still in place. At least he *knew* Edgar. To this gauche replacement, Edgar Leonard Dennis Everett was nothing but a name in a list of names, an abstract sorrow.

Incongruously, after the sermon, the prayers, and the roll-call of the lost, this new vicar said, 'In the spirit of advent and of the Holy Spirit within each of us, which endures in this joyous season, let us conclude with a carol.' Startled glances travelled between the congregation, and uncertain voices struggled against an ugly mush of organ music. *"Oh Come, All Ye Faithful"* still jangles her ears.

The only sign of Dennis's grief is his tight and ticking jaw. He's immaculate in his black cashmere overcoat, hair newly cut and flattened with Brilliantine, Homburg tucked under his arm. He stands as erect as the soldier he never was. During the service, expressionless, he sat, stood, knelt promptly as requested, closed his eyes as if he were praying, conducted himself like a dignified automaton. As, she supposes, did she. Oh, if *only* Aida had come. No doubt she'd have found something to poke fun at, laugh at even; she'd have made Dennis react like a human being. And now they'd all be going back for lunch together rather than just the two of them. The thought of sitting at that table, barely speaking... Aida's irreverent presence would have jollied things up. But, of course, she made an excuse to stay away. Since the news of Edgar, they've seen neither hide nor hair.

After the vicar's limp handshake, the polite and solemn sentiments, and the dim of the church, it's wetly bright outside, the moss on the gravestones violently green. Blinking, she clutches Dennis's arm. The churchyard is filling, a gabble rising. *So sorry for your loss, sorry for your loss, loss, loss, loss* washing between the gravestones. Everyone has lost or is sorry for loss. Hats and veils and sober coats: wool, tweed, musquash, mink and squirrel. Wet handkerchiefs clutched in hands, powdered cheeks, grief-reddened noses.

Corin and Eleanor are here, she sees with a tiny, surprised lift of her heart. Corin's a devout atheist, but in honour of Edgar, here he is today!

Since the day of the letter, two months ago now, more information has emerged. It seems that the camp Edgar and his regiment were in – somewhere on the Burma/Siam border – was, like many smaller ones, unknown to the authorities. So he never got the Red Cross parcels, never got the Marmite or the Spam or the tins of lard, never got the chocolate or the Ovaltine, or the socks or the cards or the letters they all spent hours writing. In late 1942, after he'd been missing for months, there was a pre-printed postcard bearing the words: *I am a prisoner of the Japanese. I am well.* with Edgar's childishly scrawled signature. But then he was moved from Changi to somewhere deep in the jungle, maybe from camp to camp, they'll never know. And that's where he died. They will never have a body to bury.

She scans the carved stones, angels, wreaths, anchors, lilies, thinks of the bones beneath. Her boy's bones, bones which grew inside her, must be somewhere in the tangle of jungle. Her idea of jungle is Rousseau-like, ferns and creepers, spiky alien blooms and beady animal eyes.

Dennis accepts and offers condolences from friends, patients, strangers... and after his, her hand is shaken too, her glove squeezed and squeezed, and sympathetic and curious eyes search hers, which thanks to a pill administered by Dennis, remain hard and dry. The pill has put a sheet of glass between herself and her own feelings, between herself and others.

She needs to sit; there's the drag in her stomach and the leak between her legs. Since the day of the letter, the impulsive visit to Corin... Through the sober crowd, the tilting stones, she looks for him again, and there he is with Eleanor, talking to some stranger. Preposterously tidy he looks, though hatless, his too-long hair brushed back, face shaved. Eleanor has done her utmost, but still there's something disreputable about him. Tiny Eleanor in her black coat and neat netted hat is dinkily perfect, like a woman carved on a mechanical clock, nodding, lifting her hand in jerky greeting. Her eyes might slice jealously through any gaze between Clem and Corin, but they can't sever the meaning of those gazes.

'I'm going to sit down,' she tells Dennis.

'Only a few more minutes, old girl,' he says, 'then home for lunch.'

'No Aida?' says some impertinent person. 'I'd have thought she'd have been here.'

'She couldn't get down from town,' Clem says. 'I'll be over there.' She indicates a bench, pulls her arm from Dennis, picks across the ground, uneven with roots under the wet grass, roots and bones. *Sadly Missed*, the stones say. *Fondly Remembered, Devoted Husband, Devoted Wife, Devoted Mother. Devoted, Devoted, Devoted*. She wobbles a detour to her favourite stone, an angel, stone wings raised, a noseless, kindly, greenish face. *Beloved by all who knew him*.

Corin's watching; she can feel his eyes. On the day of the letter, when she and Dennis sat down as usual, ate lunch as usual, she thought she'd go insane. She'd not planned on running to Corin, but after the first numbness, she had been seized with a wild, febrile energy and left the house with no plan and no goodbye, driven to the river, left the car and, for the first time in years, *ran*, with no destination in mind, lumpy, hectic and sweating, ignoring the curious looks she garnered as she pounded along. It was as if, if she could run fast enough, she could escape the truth. It was her feet that had decided on her destination, thumping her past the boatyards and the Maltings, all the way to the wooden boatshed, above which was Corin's studio.

For over twenty years she'd been coming here at two o'clock on Fridays for her painting lesson with Sir Corin Murray-Hill, and in all that time she'd never visited on any other day of the week, though years ago, Corin gave her a key "just in case". In case of what, he'd never specified.

*Safe in the arms of Jesus*. She reaches the bench – damp, bird-splattered, shadowed by a twisty black yew. But needs must. She wipes a bit of seat with her handkerchief and sits, the relief from abdominal dragging immediate. Probably nothing to worry about. Another ghastly manifestation of the change of life. Soon it will go off, the hot flushes are already tailing away. Checking first that no one's looking, she sneaks out her flask and takes a sip of brandy. The yew drips onto her shoulders, and onto her stupid velvet hat, her only black one, with its trivial diamanté butterfly. From here the people seem a dismal flock grazing on grief from which, thanks to the lovely pill, she is protected.

Eleanor has her back half turned to greet someone, and Corin takes the opportunity to nod across, to smile and blink, signalling sympathy and love. His hand goes to his heart. Eleanor, turning back, catches Clem's returning smile and sends her a daggery look. She takes Corin by the arm, and drags him through the lych-gate, out of sight.

Clem sips brandy, enjoys the soothing burn of it in her gullet. She closes her eyes, allowing herself to remember the day of the letter, when she had climbed the rickety stairs to the studio. With what relief she'd inhaled the miasma of linseed, turps, cat and smoke, as she collapsed on the filthy old sofa. Through the skylight, sun slanted onto easels, paint tubes, books, jars of brushes, cups, socks, screwed-up paper, crusted palettes, cat food – and Pablo the cat.

'Edgar's dead,' she said aloud, and waited. 'Three months,' she said. '*Three months.*' But nothing. Yet. Something was still holding her together as it had held Dennis over lunch, oh, the dreadful control of that lunch. After all, so many men and boys – and women and girls, too – were killed. Edgar was only another, and one must not indulge. The ultimate sacrifice they call it, the vicar trotted that out, of course. But for it to be a sacrifice, shouldn't one have had a say?

A blade of light slashed her knees, her feet in their neat

wifely brogues among the detritus of the studio floor. She got up to pour whisky into a cup. It was a teacup, a saucerless refugee from a set, gold-rimmed, a sprig of green visible under smudged pigment. As she sipped, she stood beneath the skylight, picking flecks of gummed-on blackout paper from the glass. Too early for whisky. Drink was becoming too important, especially since the end of war; that's when the hardest period of waiting had begun. Really, she should keep a clear head, but still the level of the bottle seemed to creep down. She uncoiled her plait. Corin loved the way it hung down her spine, tailed off just where her buttocks parted. She contemplated the snaky fair thing lying across her palm. Curious that it was part of her. As if to prove this, she yanked until it hurt.

Where *was* Corin? Home with Eleanor? Painting in a field or along the estuary? Or far away? 'Come,' she pleaded, 'come.' Against the walls and propped on easels was his recent work: landscapes with water, shining mud, footprints of birds and humans, distant human figures, dwarfed by skies. They were muted paintings, wet greens, mud browns, blacks, dark blues, shadowy greys, but if you looked there was always a streak of bright, the golden lining of a cloud, a watery gleam of lime, a dab of scarlet poppy.

She must have slept a little and woke to later light, feet on the creaking stairs, his voice at last. 'Clem! Christ almighty, you scared the crap out of me!'

Hands on hips, feet planted wide, he stared down at her, wide old man in ridiculous shorts. Paint on his blue Guernsey, long hair greasy, grey-stubbled chin. His knees were rough, shins woolly above sagging socks and broken sandals.

'What is it?' he said. 'You look like shit.'

For a moment she was dumb, staring up at him as he waited for her to speak. Once she spoke, everything would change, she knew that. It was like the moment before submerging oneself in a wave, or in sex, the moment of letting go.

'Edgar. Three months ago,' she said, and it was her sorrow reflected in his face that broke her. He knelt and enveloped her in the smell of lanolin and linseed and paint, his dear stinky old self.

'Why didn't I know?' she wailed. 'Three months! Shouldn't I have felt it here?' Wet-faced, she shoved him away and punched herself, hard, in the heart.

'Stupid fucking war,' he said. 'What a fucking waste. Christ. Poor Edgar. Poor, poor little sod.' And he pulled her back against him, banged her on the back till it knocked the wind out of her. 'Have a drink... Oh, you have. I need one. Have another.' He whipped his handkerchief from his pocket, and she buried her face in its Paisley warmth. Pablo miaowed, crept onto her lap, thought better of it, jumped down.

He picked up the cup, filled it, swigged, refilled. Side by side on the sofa they sat. His teeth were grinding. 'Shouldn't you be at home?' he said. 'Smoke?' Shaking her head, she dried her eyes, watched as he struck a match and plumed smoke.

Oh, how frightful she must have looked, but what did it matter? With Corin her face could fall right off because it wasn't about appearances or surfaces with him – ironic, surely, in a painter. A strange laugh hiccupped out of her. His hands were huge, rough-knuckled, paint seamed round the nails, safe hands somehow. *With him I am in safe hands,* she thought, or chose to believe. He turned, wound one hand in her plait, and kissed her, face softly prickly, smoky, whisky-tongued and for the first time in weeks they peeled away their wrappings and made love, and it was the best for so long, she rose right out of herself into the sensation – and then fell, as if dropped from an enormous height.

'Ha! I can still get it up then!' he said into her neck, a wet snuffling animal, so crude, and oh, how she did love and loathe his frightful crudeness.

'I can't believe we did that,' she murmured. 'It's the last thing...'

'In fact, sex and death are best of pals.' He disentangled himself. 'Need a slash.' She watched his dear, old, creased bottom as he went to the screen in the corner, heard him empty himself into what sounded to be quite a full bucket. From outside came the hooting of a barge. He returned and stood in front of her, arms folded above the concave belly which shadowed his penis, dew-dropped and wrinkled, sweetly shrunken now. 'Another drink?' he said.

'Better go.'

The infernal strap of her brassiere! She fumbled it tipsily, pulled on her vest, her crumpled dress, stumbled into her knickers. She knew grief was in store, a great barrage balloon of tears, but for now it was drifting ahead of her; in its shadow, still she could breathe.

As he pulled on his clothes, she wound her plait around her head, secured it with pins. There was no mirror here to check in, but she could tidy in the car, bathe when she got home. It was getting late.

'Aida needs to know,' she said, shocked to realise that the girl might *not* yet know. Surely her first impulse should have been to telephone her daughter? Edgar's sister. Shameful. Not a good mother, Clem. And wouldn't a good mother have sensed *three months ago* that Edgar was gone? Wouldn't she have *known*? Her mouth was so terribly parched. That awful feeling when drink begins to wear off and the only remedy is another drink. Down the stairs she stumbled, and stepped out into a glorious autumn afternoon in a country where the war was really over, and she had lost her son.

And now he's been officially memorialised, and his name will go on an engraved list, to be displayed for ever in St Mary's Parish Church. During the service, there was weeping, of course. Among the congregation were some shrunken men from local regiments, those who had come back remembering those who hadn't. There's one now, a wraith in a greatcoat, shivering by the porch. If she was another type of woman she'd go and speak to him, take his hand in hers. What if he knew Edgar? Painful though it would be, she'd like to meet someone who was there with her boy, learn something of what he went through. To *know*. If Aida were here, she'd do it; she's never backward in coming forward.

If only it had been she who'd phoned Aida on the day of the letter. She'd have managed it better than Dennis, broken the news more gently, insisted that Aida come straight home, and then this rift might not have grown between them all. Her own brother Ralph was lost in the first do. She knows how it feels to lose one's brother. But it was Dennis who phoned Aida at the Ministry. She took the news "sensibly", he reported, and Clem can just imagine the stiff way he would have put it and Aida's shrivelling away.

Corin approaches now, standing before her.

'Thought I saw you being dragged away,' she says.

'Forgot this.' He wags a trilby at her. She's never seen him in a hat, except occasionally, a mothy beret.

'He'd forget his head if it wasn't glued on,' says Eleanor, arriving at his side. 'Sorry for your loss,' she adds. Funny that a painter should marry someone so plain, Clem thinks, not for the first time. The woman is a perfect little dinky model of a woman, marred by rabbity teeth and watery eyes.

They leave, and she slides the flask from her bag. No one's

looking; she takes a fortifying sip, spirits for the spirit, and then Dennis is there.

'What *are* you doing on that wet seat? You'll catch your death. And flaming droppings everywhere. Good God!'

'Pigeon, I expect.'

'I say, you do look seedy, old girl.' He peers down at her with his most irritatingly doctorly expression. 'Let's get you down to the surgery for a once-over.'

'You make me sound like an old jalopy,' she says. 'And I'm perfectly all right.' The last thing she wants is him fossicking around inside. She stands too fast, and light-headedly is forced to let him steady her.

7

## STARLING

He spins back from a pyre in the jungle to a crowded London pub, as two brimming tankards are banged down in front of him. 'All right there, mate?' says Lammy.

'Yup. Cheers.' Their eyes meet bleakly as they chink glasses together and sup.

'You?'

Lammy grimaces, slurps, wipes his mouth with the back of his massive fist. Even in the few weeks since they parted at Liverpool, he's filled out. Still got gaps where he lost his teeth though, the beriberi did that. Thank Christ, thinks Starling, running his tongue round his own teeth, I managed to hang onto mine. Edgar lost a couple towards the end, spoiling his smile.

'The missus, she... Well... she don't understand.'

'Your wife doesn't understand you?' Starling chucks out an Edgar-like laugh but he knows what Lammy means. No one who wasn't there can possibly understand. Look at Mum, look at everyone who seems to think you can just keep schtum and put it all behind you. Best foot forward, all that crap.

'But you've got your kid,' he says.

'He don't know me from Adam.'

'He will.'

Lammy snorts. 'When Celia said, "Say hello to your daddy", he hid his face in her effing skirt.'

'Give him time.'

He flashes between the familiarity of the English pub, and the incongruity of being there. And with Lammy, who just now seems his only friend. His rock. The gentle giant turned up late on, in a posse of limping skeletons from another camp. It was Edgar who took to him first. He turned out to have a voice, and they'd sing together, Edgar's tenor dancing round Lammy's rumbling bass.

Starling and Lammy ramble on like men in a pub do, but there's more to it than that; there's a sort of relief, because here *is* someone who knows. They don't have to talk about it, and they don't talk about it, they just... *know*. Lammy happens to be unscathed, except for the teeth, and the pits on his legs. Maggots were used to eat the necrotic tissue of tropical ulcers. Great fat buggers they were. You packed them in and hoped for the bloody best, and in Lammy's case and others, they worked, but left craters too big for the flesh and muscle to fill. He's got one on his own calf, a furry dip in the flesh, like a mouse's nest. Edgar had no ulcers, but got everything else, till it was too much for his poor body to take.

Starling starts to get up to buy a round, but what with his one hand it's going to be tricky so without a word, Lammy takes his money, shoulders through the ram at the bar. It's Thursday night and men are on the loose, not a female face to be seen. Demob suits, work overalls, a uniform or two. Voices are a deafening wall, laughter splitting through, smoke nearly thick enough to lean against. Here comes Lammy back again, good bloke he is, hair streaked with grey, scar on his cheekbone.

'There you go. Handed over Everett's drawings yet?' Lammy says as he lowers himself down.

'Duty done,' lies Starling. His hand goes to the tin in his pocket. As he takes a swig of beer, his stomach tightens like a fist. 'Then I fucked off home.'

'What was it like?'

'Home?'

'No, you stupid bugger, seeing them. Everett's family.'

Starling takes out his fags and they light up. He did see Edgar's mum and dad on Sunday. He went to Seckbridge, meaning to call at the house, sure to catch them both in on a Sunday, but they were out. A woman answered the door, told him the doctor and his missus were at a memorial service. He found the church just as people were coming out, milling about in the graveyard. The memorial wasn't just for Edgar, that soon became plain, but it would have been the perfect chance to meet "the folks" naturally, hand over the bloody tin. They might even have invited him back for his dinner. The dad was surrounded, shaking countless hands – respected, you could see. That's what being a doctor earns you: respect. The mum, he couldn't see at first, then spotted her, sitting alone, boozing on a bench; that took him aback. He would have gone over, but she looked too sad, too cut off. No sign of the sister, that surprised him too. He could have gone up to the doctor like everyone else, shaken his hand; he was all ready to – but once again he bottled out. Pathetic. What if he can never do it? Will he spend his whole life trying, and failing? Why not just shove the tin in the post? Or chuck it away. Or keep it. No one would ever know. But he promised Edgar. The tin's starting to feel like a fucking albatross in his pocket.

'You all right, mate?' Lammy asks again.

'Sorry. Yup. Cheers.' Starling raises his glass, spills beer down his chin.

'What are they like then? Edgar's lot?'

'Just what you'd expect. Nice enough. Well-to-do, you know. A cut above the likes of us.'

'Speak for yourself.' Lammy grins. 'So, what you doing in the Old Smoke?'

'Been here a few days, stopping in a hostel.' Starling swallows beer that seems not to want to go down. 'Don't see eye to eye with my old man; no point hanging about at home.'

A man comes round selling winkles in paper cones, and the vinegary smell bites through the smoke.

Starling raises his eyebrows, starts fumbling for change, but Lammy shakes his head.

'Can't stand the fuckers. No ta, mate,' he adds to the seller with a grin, and the man pushes off.

'Good of you to put me up tonight,' Starling says. 'Hostel's full.' This is nearly true. Truth is, he hasn't been able to sleep there – and when he has, nightmares have woken him and others in the dormitory, and finally got him kicked out.

'What are mates for? What'll you do next?'

Starling swigs. He needs to get rid of the fucking tin before he can move on, that's the truth of it. But he will move on. St Thomas's have kept his place open, say he can start as soon as his sponsorship's confirmed.

'Best get back or she'll start creating,' Lammy says.

'She's nice,' Starling says. 'You're lucky.'

'She is, but... I dunno. Don't know her anymore.'

'Give it time.'

Lammy shrugs. 'Another half? One for the road?' He rises and Starling watches him go, a huge man, a head taller than most of the mob. He inhales smoke from the air. You hardly need to smoke your own fag in here. He tips back his head to stare at the yellow/brown ceiling, breathes the way he's been taught, right to the bottom of the lungs and lets it out slowly.

He will deliver the tin, course he will. He'll pull himself

together and do his duty. Fulfil Edgar's final wish. And then he'll be free. Able to move on, get straightened out, get rid of the parts of himself that are wrong. And be a regular man.

There's a tussle at the bar, and the barman shouts for order. Starling looks over in time to see Lammy shoved, the beer slopping. He's a mild man mostly, but he does have a temper. You don't see it much, but what with the drink and worrying about his missus and all. Starling sees darkness close over his face, sees him drop the full tankards, pull back an arm and let his fist fly, and then all hell breaks loose, beer, glass, yells, a pile of arms and backs, blood spurting from a split nose. It's over as soon as it starts, and then the police are there, and Lammy gets hauled away shouting like a drunk, though he isn't all that drunk.

8

## STARLING

Starling stands outside, head back, mouth open, tasting the air. Drizzle soaks his coat, his hair, hangs in a drip on the end of his nose. He swipes it with his sleeve. It's all gone quiet – move on, nowt left to see. Celia won't be too happy. Should he still go back?

He shivers, a deep malarial type of shiver, hopes it's only the damp. He finds his way back to Lammy's street. If he doesn't let Celia know what's happened, she'll fret. He owes it to Lammy to let her know. Beneath sulphurous streetlights, privet glitters. He looks up. No visible moon or stars. This is a patch that survived the Blitz. It's tidy suburban semis. Laburnum Villa is Lammy's, or at least he rents the ground floor.

He shuffles about on the doorstep before he dares ring the bell, and after a wait, hears movement. Celia's face comes round the edge of the door in a spill of light.

'What's happened to your key?' she grumbles before she realises Lammy's not there. 'Where's Horace?'

Starling gives an inadvertently melodramatic shiver.

'Well, *you'd* better come in anyrate, and have a warm.'

She stands back to let him in. He removes his hat and

follows her through into the little sitting room, tidy now, toys cleared away. She's combed her hair, and taken off her apron. There's even a trace of scent in the air – a good sign for Lammy. She's a slight redhead with a pointed face, a bit jumpy, like a pretty fox.

'Sit down.' She points to the low armchair by the fire, and folds her arms. 'So, what's the story then?'

'Cop-shop. He got in a scrap.'

'Oh my giddy aunt.' Her hands fly to her head.

'Wasn't his fault,' Starling says. 'He didn't start it.'

'Is he hurt?'

'Don't think so.'

'Thought the war might have knocked some sense into him!'

'What do you mean?'

'He's always been a bloody hothead.'

'Really?' Starling considers. That's not how Lammy strikes him at all. Yes, he might have the occasional flare-up, but otherwise he's steady. He tells Celia this, describes his staunchness, the way he kept their spirits up with his calm way of going on. 'You need men like that about you, men who keep things on an even keel.'

She sits down on the sofa crossing her legs, twisting one ankle round the other, gnawing a nail. 'Funny to hear about him from someone else! And you call him Lammy!' She jumps up, takes a bag from a cupboard, and settles down again. 'Might as well get on with this since he's not here.' She pulls from the bag some elaborately patterned knitting; explains how she's using unravelled sock wool to make a pullover. 'For his Christmas. Think! There won't be another jumper like it in the whole wide world!' She pulls a ripply strand of yarn from her bag. 'You know, he hasn't uttered a word about what he's been through, not one blinking word.'

Starling gives another shiver.

'Cold? Shove on some more coke.'

He gets up to rattle on a couple of lumps from the scuttle. A spray of coke dust makes a glittery fizz against the black throat of the chimney.

She knits in silence for several minutes, and he's lulled by the faint clicking of her needles. Frowning, she mutters as she counts and moves the yarn about. When she gets to the end of a row, she puts down the knitting and jumps up. 'Look, be a dear will you, and hold the fort while I go down to the cop-shop and see what's going on? Anthony won't wake up.'

'What if he does?'

'He won't,' she says. 'Honestly, you'll hardly know I've gone.'

Once the door's banged behind her, he gets up and roams: a wedding photo on the mantelpiece, Celia in a dress that shows off her tiny waist, clutching a bunch of flowers, Lammy enormous beside her; Lammy in his uniform; a snap of Celia holding a newborn bundle. Postcards are stuck in the frame of the mirror. There's one of Colombo; it's the same one he sent Mum when they stopped off there on the voyage home.

---

He wakes with a start to find Celia back, untying a headscarf, face shining with drizzle. 'Sorry to wake you! They're letting him cool off overnight,' she says, 'then they'll send him packing, no charges pressed seeing as how he's only just back from... Well, you know all about that.'

He watches her moving about, and she's like something from a dream.

The way she flits about, and jerks her head, she's like a finch. Fox or finch?

She frowns down at him. '*Years,*' she says fiercely, as if the word itself is an outrage. 'It's not natural to be apart for years and then... well... to be expected to just go straight back to being man and wife.' She flushes, turns away. 'If you know what I mean.'

In an awkward silence she twists her fingers together, and he notices her thin wedding ring, the stubby ends of her fingers, all the nails chewed off.

'Cuppa?' she says.

'Please. Mind if I...' He takes his Players out, shakes the box.

'Not for me.' She goes off out to the kitchen.

He lights a fag and lies back in the armchair, staring at the ceiling, fancy mouldings picked out in cream against the white. A solid house that sat here undamaged throughout the Blitz.

'Did you stop here all through?' he says when she comes back with the tea.

'Mum took Anthony down to Devon for the worst of it.' She puts his cup down on the edge of the hearth. 'I went till he was settled then I come back. Worked as a telephonist. Helped out in the WRVS. Kept myself busy, believe you me.'

She tunes in the wireless to a Glen Miller concert, resumes her knitting. It's oddly relaxed, considering they're strangers – the most relaxed he's felt since God knows when. He enjoys the domesticity: smoking, supping tea, watching the way she flexes a dainty foot in time with the music, the way she moves her mouth, silently counting stitches.

'Good cuppa,' Starling says, and he means it; it's just the right shade of brown, tastes proper, not like some of the gnat's piss you get fobbed off with these days.

'There hangs a tale! My sister married into the Lyons family, so she's sitting pretty, and some of it spills over onto me. *Us. Us* now. Me and Horace.' She says this as if reminding herself.

*"Chatanooga Choo Choo"* is on, and she hums and wiggles in her seat, feet tapping.

He smiles. 'You like to dance?'

Startled, she reaches over and switches off the wireless. 'As if I would...'

'No! I wasn't asking!'

She's gone dark red.

'Sorry,' he says. 'I only meant–'

'When I said about me and Horace, and... maritals, I wasn't meaning...'

'Of course not! I'd never...'

The silence prickles. Should he leave? But where would he go? She winds up her knitting, stows it away.

'Sorry,' he says again.

'No,' she says. 'It's me. I'm just too... It's pretty rum sitting here this time of night with a man I don't know, when I hardly even know my own hubby anymore. Do you know I've lived in this house *without* him ten times as long as *with*.'

'He's a good 'un,' Starling says. 'He saved lives. Saved mine.'

'How do you mean?'

He hasn't talked about this with anyone else and he won't, but something about this moment, this woman, brings it out of him and for once he lets the guard off his tongue. He tells her how they had to walk miles through the jungle every day just to get to work, fighting through bamboo and vines and God knows what else, whipped if they fell. If you could stand you had to work. If you were too ill, you didn't get fed. A morning came when, what with malaria, he couldn't stand, so couldn't work, so there was no ration. It was the only time in the whole three and a half years that he gave up. So many others had died, why not him? Nothing special about him.

The death hut was where men too far gone were put. That's where, on the third day he couldn't stand, he was slung by the guards. But that night Lammy had dragged him out, carried him to Edgar in the medical hut, and stayed with him – the two of them, Edgar and Lammy feeding him with rice water, coconut milk. It was their willpower, not his own, that pulled him through.

When he finishes, he's shivering, and she's bending towards him, legs twisted round each other, gnawing at a thumbnail. 'Lord bless him,' she murmurs. 'And bless you, Starling dear. You poor sods going through all of that.' She gets up, walks about, minutely adjusting the photos on the mantel. 'I can't make sense of it, you know? The silly bugger who goes to the pub and ends up spending the night in the clink, and... him... the man you just described. And you call him *Lammy*. That's funny. Makes him seem like someone different from what I know. He's Horace to me.'

'Course he is,' Starling says and, finding himself adopting his mother's tone, 'He's your Horace all right. Never stopped talking about you the whole time we were there.'

'Really? Well, thank you for telling me all that. And I'm sorry for thinking...' She gives a sort of smile. One of her front teeth is slightly crossed over the other. 'Have you got a girl?' she says.

He shakes his head, then hesitates. Best say yes perhaps, to smooth things over. 'In a way.' Because he could; he probably could get someone, a nice girl to talk to, to be with like this, maybe to dance with, to knit him a jumper out of unravelled sock wool. 'All a bit up in the air.'

'Go on.' She looks delighted, *relieved*, even.

But he can't think of anything more to say.

'Well, good luck to you,' she says in the end. 'Tell you what. If it all works out, you bring her round for tea.'

'I will.'

'Promise?' She yawns. 'Long day. Now, you'll be all right

bunking in with Anthony? Sorry we haven't got a proper spare room.'

What he wants to do is stoke the fire, go on sitting in the warmth and talking or hearing her talk till he falls asleep, and then have her watch over him the rest of the night.

*But play your cards right, Starling, and you could have a wife of your own.* He's never really pictured it before. Never seen the attraction. Mum would be so happy if he did. There might even be a nipper. That'd prove he's a man. The idea of a *woman* has never tempted him before, but the idea of a *wife* now, that's something different: comfort and understanding, someone clean of that filthy time, someone to hold and console him.

Once he's used the bathroom, she leads him to the child's room, dimly night-lit. Anthony's on the top bunk, face stern in sleep. He's big-boned, like his dad. There's a knitted gollywog and a bear propped at the end of his bunk, a *Beano*, and on his pillow a little toy tank. Starling picks it up and examines its miniature caterpillar tracks. Earlier, after a tea of macaroni and fried spam, Anthony had lined up all his vehicles and talked Starling through them, proud as any garage proprietor; the tank was his best, he said.

Gently, Starling replaces it beside the child's cheek and sits on the lower bunk, takes his shoes off, sits on the edge with head bowed. It's taken it out of him good and proper, breaking the rules and talking about Lammy like that. Talking about Edgar. Edgar who they couldn't pull through. Edgar who was put on a pyre and burned, that smell of roasting flesh. *No. No. No. Don't think.*

*They shoved the drunk man in the clink*
*So, he'd cool off and have a good think*
*And then I don't know*
*How the next bit should go*
*But we shouldn't have had that last drink.*

He undresses, and shivers into his pyjamas. Is it malaria or just the cold? He won't sleep, but still he gets under the covers to have a warm, stares up at the wire mesh above him that holds the weight of Lammy's kid. A door shuts. Celia settling down. Lucky bugger, Lammy is, to have her to come home to... when he comes home that is.

---

*Teeming beetles, little tanks, burning bones, the smoke, the stench, a shaking, a shaking,* and a voice hauling him out and up, into the light of a bedroom where there's a kid crying, a small face close to his own, a creamy female smell. 'Wake up you silly blighter, you're safe, it's just a dream, you're here,' and the flames recede, and the earth stills, and he struggles up to sitting.

'Oh, Jesus, oh Christ. I'm sorry.'

Celia kneels beside the bunk, and it all comes back, where he is. He's safe, safe but wet with sweat and shuddering.

Her hand is cool on his brow. 'You're burning up. Nightmare? Horace's had a couple of shockers since he's been back.'

'I'm all right, sorry, sorry.' Starling curls on his side, like a grub. 'Touch of malaria,' he murmurs, 'comes and goes.'

'Come along, Anthony, we'll leave the gentleman in peace; you can cuddle in with me,' Celia says and the boy, clutching his tank, eyes huge and wet-lashed, stares over his shoulder as he follows his mother out of the door.

When all's settled down again, Starling goes to the bathroom to pee and to splash his face. The floor's cold and he hurries, shivering in damp pyjamas, back to the tangled sheets, but he can't risk sleep. Instead, he reaches into his jacket pocket for the tin. Lammy and Edgar kept *him* alive, but he and Lammy couldn't do the same for Edgar. They let him down.

And now, if he fails to deliver the tin, he'll be letting him down again. It's all he can do for him now, and he will do it. He will take the tin to Seckbridge and give it to Edgar's parents. He'll say comforting things. He'll do good.

He gets a sudden urge to open the tin. Been tempted before but resisted. Edgar wouldn't mind though. It's only sketches. Skipper Brand British Navy Cut, dull green tin, dented, rusty, scratched. He has to jam it against his ribs with his left elbow to prise off the lid. When it opens there's a scatter of tiny bits and dust. Expecting to see a neat wad of sketches, it takes him a moment to comprehend. The contents of the tin are flakes and fragments and, he sees, a dead ant. *Fucking hell.* The ant must have eaten the drawings.

He gathers up the scraps, crawls closer to the nightlight and peers: leg, bird, waving arm, fish head. He returns each piece to the tin, but not the ant. That, he grinds between his finger and thumb till it's dust.

Last time he closed this tin, Edgar, stupid bugger, trapped the ant inside. All this time he's been carrying it round like something precious! A laugh wants to start, hard, jagged, but he keeps himself quiet, rocks to and fro, wet pouring down his face, clutching to his heart the little tin of ruin.

## 9

## CLEMENTINE

She toils over the mincer, averting her eyes from the greasy meat worming through the holes. The useless girl who's supposed to do for them this week has failed to materialise, and Dennis's spiv let him down, so she was forced to queue outside the high street butchers for half an hour for this paltry amount of... one shudders to think. But it will have to do; there's only the two of them, after all. Time marches on and still the potatoes to peel, the onions to chop, and all the dreadful tears they cause. When onions provoke tears, grief results, a recent discovery. Cooking's not only a bore, but also *hard*; another discovery. She never realised there was so much *thinking* to it, so much drudgery. If only she'd been more appreciative of Linda – hard-working, uncomplaining Linda, and her staunch "hubby" – while she had them. But they've moved to Yarmouth to be near their son, and fair enough, one mustn't grumble, but really and truly it is a catastrophe.

She pauses to rub her arm; the wretched mincer wrenches something in her shoulder. Not properly clamped to the table, it wobbles so that she must lean all her weight into it. Dennis is at the golf course, and the house aches with emptiness, around and above and below. Empty boxes of cold behind closed doors. She's unaccustomed to being alone in the house. Although she hardly used to count Linda as *company*, she was a constant unobtrusive presence, a low (and cheerful) hum in the background where now there's silence, but for the irritating chirping and chiming of all the bloody clocks – and her own sighs.

For twenty-five years The Beeches has been her home. Strange to think she's never been alone in it, or never felt alone, what with Dennis, the children, Mr and Mrs Hale who worked for the Everetts until they retired, then Linda and family and, early in the war, a series of evacuees.

Now it turns out that she alone isn't enough to animate the house, and the house itself seems well aware of the fact. Oh, but hark at the self-pity! So many people get sucked into that trap. She will *not* join their dismal league. *Pull yourself together, Clem.* Count your blessings: a comfortable home; a tolerable marriage; the children, think not about the loss, think of the happy years with Edgar. And be grateful for Aida, a trickier customer indeed, but a dear at heart. She might not have been here for weeks, but she's promised to come next weekend. That's something else for which to be grateful. She stretches her mouth into a smile to signal to her drooping spirits that all is well.

In her belly there's the dragging sensation that's become an almost constant worry. In ten days' time, there's an appointment with a chap in London. Dennis doesn't know. She can't bear for him to examine her, as he would (fingers where they haven't been for amorous purposes for years, thank heavens), to fret and pronounce on her condition.

It was on the night of the letter, after she'd fled to Corin's studio and they'd made love, that she began to bleed. And though menstruation had been over and done with for years, it seemed appropriate somehow, as if her womb was weeping. But the bleeding continued, and secretly she saw a man in Ipswich, who recommended a colleague – a female doctor, specialist in women's health – in Harley Street. Dennis thinks she's going to town to have her hair done and to lunch with Aida. Aida isn't actually available, of course, but the day is full up already: the appointment, an exhibition at the Tate, Christmas shopping. Apparently, Norway has sent a gigantic Christmas tree for Trafalgar Square. One must have a look at that, she supposes, though the thought of Christmas appals. One can't simply ignore it though. She owes it to Aida, to Dennis, to try and make everything as normal as possible. So, despite everything there will be trimmings, and pudding, and all the rest of the nonsense – only, for that she really will need help. Tomorrow morning, first thing, she'll get onto the agency again, or – extreme measure – try the Labour Exchange.

*Damn it all, now the mincer's jammed.* She squints into its maw, pokes with a fork, extracts a splinter of bone, and retches. Oh, how she loathes raw meat, and this smells less than fresh. It's getting dark. With a greasy finger she switches on the light, which illuminates the contents of the table like a dull still life. Painting the onions and potatoes, and even the meat, she would find perfectly possible. But transforming them into a cottage pie?

And then to top it all, there's the chime of the doorbell. She waits for Linda to answer, before remembering. In the hall she removes her apron, tidies her hair. What a perfect fright! It's a cruel mirror this, they should get another. No need to answer the door of course. But curiosity drives her forward, that and the prospect of novelty.

On the doorstep stands a young man.

'Mrs Everett?' He extends his hand. 'Friend of Edgar's. Just back from the East. I... I...'

She has a sudden wild impulse to slam the door in his face, but instead she inhales and takes his hand, thin and cold in hers. 'Do please come in.' A slight, dark, bespectacled chap, his outsized army greatcoat stands stiff around his body like the casing of a beetle. He stands as if stunned in the hallway.

'A friend of Edgar's you say? I expect you'd like a cup of tea?'

He nods, darting a curious, almost rudely intense look at her face.

'Coat?' As he removes it, she sees that he's missing a hand, and that under his appalling demob suit, he's utterly skeletal. He takes off his cheap-looking fedora and she sees a small, well-modelled head with thick, black, wavy hair pushed back from the forehead, thick brows that almost join, a pronounced widow's peak.

She's about to take him through to the sitting room and sit him by the fire, when she realises that the fire might have gone out. (Dennis can see to that when he gets home.) And the pie won't cook itself.

'Come and sit in the kitchen,' she says. 'It's warmer in there.'

He follows her through, and she settles him in Linda's chair, beside the range, while she fills the kettle. 'We've lost our help. She was a rock, been with us since she was a girl, she and her husband lived in. There should have been a help here today, but she didn't turn up, not so much as phone call, I ask you! So, I'm having to do for myself.' She hears her voice running on, querulous, self-pitying. 'But never mind,' she adds brightly, 'onwards and upwards!'

His steady scrutiny makes her nervous. 'Can I help?' he says. Through his spectacles, his eyes are huge, dark, and solemn.

'No, no, you sit tight,' she says.

'I used to help Mum with cooking and that.'

She detects a trace of the north in his voice, a trace of the common. He's so dark, one must wonder about a touch of the tar brush, too. Of course, his class *expect* the woman of the house to slave away in the kitchen. But they also expect a bit more skill.

'Perhaps you might chop the onions?' she suggests before remembering his missing hand. 'Oh, I'm so sorry...'

'I can peel spuds,' he says.

He hangs his jacket over the back of a chair. He's so thin that even through his shirt and pullover you could almost count his ribs. Did Edgar ever get that thin? Her lovely sturdy son. *No, no, no, no, no, no.* Chin up. A few more cranks, and the last miserable scraps of meat squirm out. Self-consciously, she scoops and scrapes the hideous stuff into a pan, brings her specs down from her hair to peer at the recipe.

He's moved across to the sink and, covertly, she watches him jam a potato against his chest with the forearm of the missing hand, and begin to peel. This poor soul was Edgar's *friend*, knew him as a soldier, as a prisoner, knew him, perhaps, up to his death. He will tell her things she longs and dreads to know – but somehow, she seems unable to speak. Her jaw has set solid. Move, Clem, pull yourself together. She forces her hand to pick up a knife and begins to slice through the papery onion skins, peeling them back from the white, releasing the juice of the nasty, pungent little onions. Still she can't speak, can't breathe. Goodness, she hasn't even asked the fellow's name! Shocked by this ill-mannered omission, she looks up and slashes the place between her thumb and forefinger.

With a pathetic bleat she lifts her hand, blood dripping onto the chopped onions. *Oh blast it!* She'll have to throw them away and start again, and her eyes are streaming so she can hardly see, and blood is getting everywhere. 'Do excuse me...' She makes for the door.

He follows and ridiculously, blindly, she feels an urge to

flee, starting up the stairs, beginning to feel faint, blood on her dress, she stumbles and falls, banging her head on the banister. Everything sparkles numb for a sickening second.

And he's there beside her. This is preposterous! A complete stranger in the house, seeing her in this state; oh, where the dickens is Dennis when you need him?

'Here. Let's get you sorted out.' He stoops over her on the stairs.

'I'm perfectly all right.'

'Don't be daft,' he says. Such colossal cheek silences her. 'What would Edgar say if I didn't help his mum, eh?' He grasps her wrist and elevates her hand. 'I know what I'm doing. Edgar and I worked together in the camp, you know.'

She glances at his sharp young profile. *A medic then?* 'Ah, perhaps he mentioned you... in a letter...' she remembers fuzzily.

'He wrote about *me*?' His face blazes with sudden alarming joy.

'Yes, he mentioned a fellow medic...' she says, 'great chum I think...' and the stairs start to rock, his head to swing in front of her eyes like a lantern. 'Oh dear... I really do feel...'

'Come on now,' he says, 'let's go and get you patched up.'

He helps her to the bathroom, where she slumps on the wicker chair, head between her knees. He kneels, holding tight her wrist to stem the bleeding. Once the faintness has receded, he binds the wound. He's wonderfully dexterous, even with his single hand, his concentration devout. The serious young face, the small head, so much smaller than Edgar's, so much more serious and intense. It's a deeply characterful face. Incredible that this is a friend of Edgar's, real, alive, right in front of her. So close. What was the name? It will come back. He looks so *young* though – and a completely different class of person than she'd assumed.

Once he's dressed the hand, he palpates her head. Young,

but still, clearly an excellent doctor; there's a gentle authority as he moves a finger, asks her to follow with her eyes, quizzes her about nausea or further dizziness.

'I'm feeling much better now,' she says, which is almost the truth. All she really requires is a good stiff brandy. 'And heavens, I haven't even given you a cup of tea! Come on, let's put that right. You go down and I'll get changed.'

Once he's gone, she changes out of her blood-spotted frock and takes a fortifying gulp from the hip-flask concealed in the dressing table before tidying her hair and, feeling rather foolish, adding a dab of lipstick, a spritz of perfume. What *was* the name of the chap? Something birdish and rhyming... Crowley! Roley Crowley! Of course!

She finds Crowley on the stairs, with a bucket of pink water, blotting blood from the carpet.

'Someone else can deal with that,' she says, wondering whom. 'Come on.' In the kitchen the kettle has boiled almost dry, filling the room with steam.

She removes the kettle from the stove and surveys the mess of bloody onions and repellent meat. 'Not my finest hour!'

There comes the sound of the front door, and Dennis's voice. 'Darling? Where are you?'

'Kitchen,' she calls, quite gaily, and smiles at Crowley while they wait for Dennis. He appears, red in the face from the cold (and no doubt the nineteenth hole) thick badger-striped hair pushed back from his forehead, carrying in a breath of raw wintery air. He takes off fogged spectacles and widens his eyes, taking in the stranger, the blood, the mess.

'This is Dr Crowley,' says Clem. 'I've just had not one, but two silly accidents!'

'Crowley...' the young man says. 'But—'

'Crowley.' Dennis extends his hand, and he takes it. 'How do?'

The young man stands there, allowing his arm to be pumped up and down by Dennis, eyes huge, mouth agape, looking almost half-witted.

'Pal of Edgar's,' Clem says. 'Don't shake his arm off, darling!'

Oh, but the poor boy does seem so terribly young and thin and bashful. Stunned to silence by Dennis's outrageous heartiness.

'Dr Crowley came to call on us, and then...' She indicates the bloody onions, her bandaged hand. 'And I made the most frightful ninny of myself! Cut myself, bumped my head. Dr Crowley took charge. Oh, doesn't that sound ludicrously formal? It's Roland, isn't it? May we call you Roland?'

He looks utterly bewildered. Shell shock or something like? Dennis widens his eyes at her and grimaces. Clem comes to the rescue. 'You could do with a drink I expect, Roland?'

'Yes, a good old stiffener, that's the ticket.' Dennis surveys the table.

'I was attempting a cottage pie,' Clem explains.

'Tell you what,' Dennis says. 'Chuck it all away and I'll go out for fish and chips, how does that sound?'

'Really?' says Clem. Dennis tends to consider fish and chips déclassé, excusable only on a seaside jaunt.

'The good companions,' he says, beaming at Roland. Clearly, he's spent a good long time at the nineteenth hole.

'I am sure we will be.' Clementine glances at Roland, hoping Dennis doesn't scare him away.

Dennis hoots. 'No, that's what Churchill calls fish and chips,' he says. 'The good companions.'

'Come on. We must offer Roland a drink,' she says.

'Naturally we must.' Dennis reaches his hand again. 'Friend of Edgar's, friend of ours,' he says gruffly.

Once Dennis has rekindled the sitting-room fire, he pours generous brandies all round, lights his pipe, offers cigarettes, but when they're settled an awkwardness descends. There's some attempt at small talk, which clearly isn't Roland's forté. He's ill at ease, fidgeting, sipping the brandy cautiously. (Oh heavens, he never did get his cup of tea!) He sits on the sofa, thighs crossed, such pitiful sticks, brown demob shoes (with a grey suit!), one foot wagging up and down, up and down, till she wants to grab hold of it. If only Dennis would go away and leave them to talk. He'd be more likely to open up, perhaps, without Dennis's emphatic presence. Oh, but her head is starting to throb.

'I've brought you something,' the boy blurts. He fumbles in his pocket and puts, into Dennis's outstretched hand, a rusty old tobacco tin. 'From Edgar. He asked me to bring it. It was his drawings of the camp, he put them in the tin, but an ant got in. There's not much left, but still, I thought you should have it.'

She lunges to snatch the tin from Dennis – to hell with manners – takes it to the corner, with the lamp. He was talented, Edgar, should have been allowed to go to art school, but always biddable, he did what was expected and followed in Dennis's footsteps. The time she wasted trying to encourage an artistic streak in Aida! She turned out about as artistic as a parsnip. *Why* did she not concentrate that attention on Edgar? Why did she not stand up for his wish to study art? A gulf of guilt opens in her. As she eases the lid off the tin it's as if her breastbone is being prised apart. She should have loved Edgar better. Here an eye, here a roof corner, here a fern, here a wing. Later, she'll study them properly, but for now, as if they are treasure, she tucks them back into the tin and returns to the fire where Dennis is puffing away.

'Might I see?' Dennis stretches out his hand, but she doesn't want the pieces out of the tin again, she doesn't want his big hands sweating on them.

'There's not a great deal there, we shall look at them together presently. 'But,' turning to Roland, 'thank you so *very* much. You don't know what it means to have even these tiny scraps.'

'He was... Well, out there he was... We were the best of *pals*.' His voice cracks and for fear of a scene, Dennis scoops up the conversation, steers it onto golf. 'You play, old man? I used to force poor Edgar onto the course. Hopeless!' And he takes them through today's game, hole by hole. Roland endures this with an unconvincing show of interest. He seems uncomfortable in the chair, squirming and fidgeting like a child, and so thin she wants, like a mother bird to feed him, to fatten him up, as his own mother must want to do. And she wants to hold him tight too, to keep him *still*.

Blood has oozed through her bandage, she notices, and the cut is stinging. Later Dennis will rebandage and she'll coax a sleeping pill. When, finally, Dennis reaches the eighteenth hole, she interrupts. 'Tell us about your family, Roland. They must be so relieved to have you safely home.' Now her own voice threatens to break. She swallows dryly, feeling sick, too much brandy on an empty stomach, and a bang on the head to boot!

Roland shrinks and twists painfully, and she and Dennis exchange alarmed glances.

'Wiped out in the Blitz, '42, direct hit.'

'Oh, my dear.' Clem hauls herself unsteadily up and goes to lay a hand on his shoulder. 'So sorry for your loss,' she says, echoed by Dennis. She thinks of last Sunday, *loss, loss, loss*, washing round the gravestones.

'As I,' says Roland stiffly, 'am sorry for yours.'

Clementine sits down, nods, stares at her hands, the neat bandage blossoming red.

Silence falls, in which a small collapse in the fire shoots a cinder out onto the hearth rug. Dennis gets up to stamp it out, and keeps stamping with unnecessary vigour.

'Which is also mine,' Roland continues, rather surprisingly. He stares down into his glass as he talks. 'Edgar and I, we were like that.' He lifts his hand, index and middle finger twisted together. 'We got each other through, you might say. After our MO died – cerebral malaria – the two of us took over. Edgar was brilliant. *Brilliant.* We had almost no supplies, you know, you should have seen how he improvised.' He stops and gulps, the suppressed emotion in his voice alarming.

'All right, old man?' Dennis sends her a pleading look.

'His work.' Roland holds up his sewn-together sleeve.

Clem shuts her eyes, presses her feet to the floor. The first operation she assisted on in the field hospital, back in the Great War, was an amputation. Forgotten for years, it comes back to her in a rush, the weight of the foot as it fell into the bucket. The shock of the severance.

'He saved my life,' Roland is saying. 'And that of many others. And even where he couldn't, he gave comfort.'

Clem closes her eyes.

'That's our Edgar,' Dennis says gruffly. He struggles with clearing his throat, before he stands. 'I say, old man, it's time to fetch the good companions, would you like some? And I dare say we could offer you a bed? I'd like to hear your thoughts on this new National Health nonsense.'

But Roland shakes his head and stands. 'Thank you. But I must go for my train.'

'Don't be a stranger though,' Clementine says. An idea occurs to her and jumps from her mouth before she can properly consider it. 'Why not come to us for Christmas? You've lost your folks, we've lost Edgar. One bird, two stones. We'd love to have you, wouldn't we, darling?'

'One stone, two birds,' Dennis corrects, sending her a furious glare before he says, 'Of course, most welcome.'

'And we'd love you to meet Edgar's sister, Aida. She's a bit... original. She'd take to you, I'm sure. They were thick as thieves as children, you know. You simply must meet her.'

'He talked about Aida a lot,' says Roland. 'What was it he called her? Diddy?'

Clem's hand flies to her heart. 'Yes! He couldn't say *Aida* till he was about five, and Diddy stuck.'

'They used to have a den behind the garage, and a secret cage of mice.'

'Bally things nearly froze to death,' Dennis chips in. 'Mrs Hale warmed them in the range, brought them back to life.'

'And Aida said...' begins Clementine.

'"Why's Mrs Hale roasting our mice?",' Roland supplies.

They are all standing in the hall by now. Clementine helps Roland on with his coat, her hands lingering on his shoulders.

'*Please* say you'll come on Christmas Eve.'

'I'll run you to the station,' says Dennis tautly.

'No, it's all right,' Roland says. 'The walk'll clear my head.'

'Promise you'll come?' Clementine says.

'I don't know...'

'*Please*.'

'Don't bully the poor chap.'

'Thank you,' Roland says, 'but–'

'That's settled then.' Deliberately, she cuts him off. 'We'll expect you on Christmas Eve. Don't let us down.'

She surprises herself, and Roland (and no doubt Dennis) by kissing him on the cheek.

They wave him off, then Dennis shuts the door, humphs himself violently into his overcoat.

'I'm going to sit down,' she says, shivering. Her stomach drags, her head aches, the hall has filled with wintery air.

'Are you off your bally head? Inviting him for Christmas! Practically dragooning the poor fellow!' Angrily he knots his scarf. '*Aida's an original, she'll take to you!*' he mimics.

'Just trying to be kind.'

'We might have discussed it! What will *she* say?'

'Oh, come on, darling,' she says wearily. 'You don't really mind, do you? His family all gone. And after all, a chum of Edgar's.'

'Well, it clearly doesn't matter *what* I think, does it?' He slams the door behind him.

She returns to the sitting room, hugs her arms, warms her bottom by the fire. A photograph of Aida catches her eyes, the angle good, so you can't see the spoiling jut of her nose. Dennis is right; she won't like a stranger being here at Christmas, might even use it as an excuse to stay away. Though you never do know with Aida. *Mary, Mary, Quite Contrary*. She might hate the idea, or she might be delighted. Best thing, probably, is not to say.

## 10

## AIDA

The hedgehog boot scraper with its idiotically cheery expression still stands guard by the door. So much changed, and still it grins. When they are all bones in the ground it will, no doubt, still be grinning on. She pokes the toe of one shoe between its bristles. Months since last she stood here. That seems an innocent time now, just after Hiroshima when they were all unbearably on edge, expecting news with every ring of the telephone, every knock on the door, every flap of the letterbox. Terrified, excited, jittery with anticipation of Japan's surrender, which they thought would mean Eddie's return. They were planning a party – not immediately, of course. Eddie would need time to recover. Ha.

Opening the door now feels like opening the cover of the book of *Before*. Before the war. Before they knew. The hallstand's the same, the smell the same, the rising stairs the same. Mummy coming to meet her, hands outstretched, is the almost same (though surely thinner?). They hug tightly, hang on a moment too long. Daddy's out, of course, it being Saturday, golf day, and that too is the same as always.

But really, of course, nothing's the same.

Standards have shockingly slipped. For a start, lunch is taken on trays on their laps by the sitting-room fire; unheard of! There *are* proper pork sausages from Daddy's spiv, which Mummy had to fry herself, there being no help. She looks worn out, almost scraggy, a sticking plaster on her hand, nails ragged and unpolished – and despite making a smiley effort, so *sad*. Talking about Edgar would be awful, though not talking about him is worse. Over their sausages they make conversation rather desperately, about general things, the weather, rumours about what's coming off rations, Princess Elizabeth – will she marry the dishy Greek? They might as well be strangers waiting for a bus.

The more she looks, the more details of difference she notices. The sitting room is messier, dustier; bits of clinker scatter the hearth; every surface is covered with haphazard piles of newspaper and books, slivers of unopened cards (Christmas and condolence). Oh, she really *should* have come home before. They should all have been pulling together. How desperately mean of her, to stay away. Mean and cowardly. "Cowardy custard" they used to call each other, she and Eddie: *Cowardy, cowardy custard, stick your tongue in mustard*. And once he did: she mixed an egg cup full of Colman's English and dared him to, and he screamed his head off, ran around with his yellow tongue sticking out, tears spurting from his eyes. She was always daring him to do stupid things, and he always did them, the little twit.

Clementine's gazing at her in an unbearably beseeching way. 'Tell me what you've been up to,' she says.

'Just work. I won't be able to stick the Ministry for long. It's utter *purgatory*.'

'Why not give it up, darling, come home for a while?'

'Maybe.' But she won't. She scans the room, messier than usual, yes, but still largely, comfortably, the same: wide, velvet-curtained bay window; piano lid jostling with family photos, and flowers, always flowers; Clementine's paintings, and, of course, in pride of place, her most treasured possession, a Murray-Hill landscape of wide, shining fields and in the distance a plough with its accompanying whirl of seagulls, white against a charcoal sky. Mummy has a soft spot for that mad old artist – but it is a good painting, even she can appreciate that. This is home, dear and familiar, and thank heavens it's here. Thank heavens it wasn't hit.

'Honestly darling,' Clementine says. 'I'm flailing about dreadfully without help. These girls I find to come in for a day or two are all hopeless. I can manage the telephone and a bit of tidying myself, but the laundry... the *food*.'

*You're a grown woman, you should be able to cook,* Aida thinks pettishly, but stops herself. *Be nice. Be kind.* 'What have you done?' She indicates the sticking plaster.

'Well now. There hangs a tale,' Clementine says. She puts down her fork and looks at her hand, stretching the web between her forefinger and thumb and smiling peculiarly. 'Let's clear up, and then I'll tell all.'

Aida nods, struggling to dispel irritation at the unnecessary air of mystery. Clearly, she cut or burned herself, probably while cooking, end of story. They take their trays through to the kitchen and Aida washes up, covertly watching Mummy make coffee. She's still well-dressed, of course, still beautiful, fair-grey hair plaited and coiled, an apron to protect her fine, loose now, blue wool dress. Aida carries the tray back to the sitting room. Rain slants tediously against the window, and she throws another lump of coal onto the fire, switches on a lamp.

'I'd murder for a slice of cake,' she says.

'Nothing left when I got to the bakers – except those rock cakes you can break a tooth on.'

'They would have done!' Aida kicks off her shoes, curls her feet underneath her. 'Now, tell all.'

Clementine scrapes drips off her cup into her saucer. 'Well, last week we had a visitor.' This isn't at all unusual – but the expression on her face is. Something pent-up, a suppressed excitement, which gives Aida a premonitory *frisson*. She waits while Clementine takes a leisurely sip, then leans forward. 'Enough of the suspense!'

'Oh Diddy, you're starting to sound quite *American.*'

'Am I?' She flushes.

'Well. Last Saturday, I was in the kitchen trying to make a cottage pie when the doorbell rang. Honestly, I was in such a fluster I nearly didn't answer. But I did and in he came, and... Well, the long and short of it is, he turned out to be a chum of Edgar's.'

It's like something hitting her in the diaphragm. An upper cut. She grits her teeth, takes a breath, *calm, calm.*

'I *know,* darling. You can imagine what a...'

They sit for a while, listening to the fire, a cascade of the half hour being struck from mistimed clocks all over the house.

'Ciggie?' Aida says.

'Not for me.'

With trembling fingers, Aida gets out her case and lights a Craven A, grateful for the bracing bite of smoke.

'From his....' Clementine appears to be searching for the right expression. 'From his *prison camp.*' Somehow, she manages to make this sound like prep school, and Aida puffs smoke impatiently.

'A close friend, it turns out, a young doctor. Roland Crowley.'

'Roland Crowley? Didn't Edgar mention him in that letter from India? Roley Crowley? Wasn't there a limerick?'

'Yes, the very chap!'

The coffee cup trembles in Aida's hand, and she puts it down.

'Oh heavens, Diddy, honestly, I made such a nincompoop of myself in the shock of it, cutting my hand…' Clementine indicates the plaster. 'And on the stairs tripping and banging my head. And he took charge, this Crowley. Rather marvellously. Came to my rescue if you like. The hero of the hour. And then Daddy came home, and we all had a drink.'

'Did he talk about Edgar?' Aida asks. Inhaling too deeply, she makes herself cough.

'He said what a first-class medic Edgar was. That he saved his life.'

Aida blinks hard to dispel a threat of tears, then she snorts. 'Sure it's the same Edgar?'

Clementine looks down at the plaster on her hand. 'This chap has a hand missing, and he told us that Edgar performed the amputation. Probably saved his life.'

Aida stares at her mother, the information curdling on the surface of her brain. 'Eddie,' she whispers.

'Yes.' There's a trickling as part of the fire collapses. The wind's getting up outside, wintery wild. 'He talked about how well they knew each other. Apparently, they used to talk for hours. Really got to know each other. Believe it or not, he even knew we used to call you Diddy!'

Aida clamps her jaws to suppress what threatens to be a howl. But a weird joy happens inside her too. A tough rooty thread of it, piercing through her guts. This is the first direct information they've had about Edgar.

'He's a nice enough young man.' Clementine puts down her cup, reaches for her mending basket.

Aida stubs out her cigarette, sensing a *but*.

'A northern accent. Also, quite dark… not *actually* a darkie I don't think… but a thoroughly nice chap, all the same.'

'What do you mean *but?*'

'A good egg, I'd say. Oh and…' Clementine forages in her

mending basket, holds up a filthy old tobacco tin. 'He brought us this. Apparently, he promised Edgar. Just some little scraps of drawings that he did in the camp though they've mostly been destroyed.' She hands the tin to Aida, who prises it open with her thumbnail, and tips the pieces into her lap. 'Apparently an ant got in,' Clementine explains. Tiny pencilled details: a duck, a fern, an eye, part of a hut, a wing.

Aida studies them, one by one, a lump in her throat the size of the moon.

'He was frightfully *thin*,' Clementine says with a shudder, 'quite skeletal, like one of those fearful Belsen photographs. Quite a shock to see. It brings it home…'

Carefully, Aida tucks each scrap back inside the tin. Her hands feel grimy, maybe some of Edgar's skin cells transferred to her own skin. She holds her fingers to her lips, and then gets up and goes across to perch on her mother's armchair, to force herself to embrace her. 'Oh Mummy,' she says. At her touch, Clementine seems to collapse, and the two of them sit and rock and weep as they should have done all those weeks ago.

But Aida's arm is at an uncomfortable angle, and soon the posture begins to feel forced, embarrassing. She pulls away first and returns to the sofa. They both dab their eyes and there's silence. The quarter-to chimes out, the tinkly mantel clock making Aida's teeth tingle as it did when she was a child.

Clementine tucks away her hanky. 'I must say, Diddy, I do wish you'd came to the memorial.'

Aida opens her mouth but can't even remember the excuse she gave. In truth, she'd spent the day in bed, refilling her hot water bottle, eating a bag of broken Marie biscuits and rereading an old Dorothy Dunnett. She lights a fresh cigarette.

'Sorry,' she murmurs at last. 'Hey, Mummy, shall we have a look at the letter about Crowley?'

'I haven't been able to bear to,' Clementine admits.

'Where is it?' Aida asks.

Clementine leans down to her mending basket and pulls out an envelope. 'I was waiting for you,' she says. 'Will you read it?'

Aida takes and holds the letter from her brother. She's read it before, but not for years. The envelope is cheap and flimsy, the postage a stamped blur, but you can make out the date: 13.1.41. Edgar's familiar, childishly rounded handwriting tears at her heart.

He never was much of a one for writing letters – usually he resorted to picture postcards with jokey scrawls or limericks, and once he was taken prisoner, apart from one official postcard, all communication ceased. This letter, three sides of paper, was by far his longest. It was posted in Bombay, where his regiment was stationed temporarily on its way to Singapore.

She unfolds the pages and clears her throat before she begins to read:

*'Dearest Mummy,*

*So much to tell! I don't know where to start so I'll start where I am. Bombay. I like what I've seen of India. With regards to the heat, it isn't very different at this season from England in the summer. Though the chaiwalas and fruit-pedlars who swarm around the camp lend a splash of very un-English colour.'*

She pauses, blinks; tears standing in her eyes make it difficult to focus. She breathes in smoke, taps ash. So *weird* to be speaking her brother's words.

Clementine leans forward, face eager. 'Find the part about Crowley,' she says.

Aida's eyes skim the details. He must have been sozzled to have rambled on so much – the relative prices of cigarettes, the bore of parades, the taste of Indian spices – until she reaches the relevant words. *'You'll be glad to know, I've found my feet here amongst the men, particularly a chum from St Thomas's – Roley Crowley. Good chap, a few years older than me–'*

'That is strange,' Clementine interrupts. 'He seemed younger than Edgar. At least, younger than Edgar would have been now.'

They stare at each other for a bleak moment, and then Aida resumes.

*'...but we are sympatico. Hope we'll be able to stick together. Makes all the difference to have a proper chum, don't you know? The name is rather splendid, isn't it? Of course, it's really <u>Roland</u>, but that spoils the rhyme. Here's an effort for Diddy:*

*A clever young medic called Roley*
*Who was never particularly lowly*
*Went to a temple*
*Swapped sausage for lentil*
*And turned out most frightfully holy.*

*Total tripe!*

'He's right there!' Aida says, hardening her voice. 'Definitely not up to his usual standard.'

'Go on, darling.'

Aida finds her place.

*'Total tripe! R's not holy at all, and in fact rather partial to a sausage! But he is as taken by the Hindu temples as I am. So much more fun than Christian churches. I wish you could see the colours and the interesting gods here. There's one called Ganesh with an elephant's head! I've done some sketches for paintings when I get home – <u>then</u> you shall see. We visited the aforementioned temple when we finally reached port and were granted a couple of days' leave. As well as sightseeing, Roley and I had a grand bust in the town; the bazaars are full of marvels. I'll buy a few trinkets and send them home if I can.*

*The mail hasn't come yet, but I'm hoping for letters from you of course. I miss you all but manage to keep a stiff upper lip. Hope you, Daddy and Diddy are all in good sorts. Send them my love and keep the best bit back for yourself.*

*Toodleloo for now,*
*Best love,*
*Ever your Edgar xxx'*

Carefully, Aida folds the letter, slides it back in the envelope and returns it to her mother.

Silence stretches between them. Aida finishes one cigarette and lights another. Clementine picks up her mending, an ancient camisole – lifts her glasses to her nose and begins to stitch – but soon the needle comes unthreaded and drops to the floor. 'Oh bloody, bloody *thing*.' She lets the camisole fall. 'Time for sherry I think?'

'Surely a bit early, Mummy?' Aida says. Her heart is beating strangely. She feels as if Edgar is somehow there now, hanging between them in the dusty air, conjured from his own words. 'I'd like to meet this Roley Crowley,' she says.

Clementine seems about to speak but does not. There's an odd pent-upness to her expression. Aida kneels to pick up the dropped camisole and needle. 'Hasn't this thing had it?' She holds up the frail, heavily mended piece of silk.

'You're right.' Clementine picks up the next thing in the basket, one of Daddy's Argyle socks.

'If only there were some *sun*,' Aida says. 'It's been so dreary lately. So *dark*.'

As if in agreement, wind moans in the chimney and the rain beats on the glass.

'Only a couple of weeks till the shortest day,' Clementine says. 'Draw the curtains, darling. You will be here for Christmas?'

Aida gets up to pull the curtain cords and swish the velvet, shut out the afternoon. Of course, they would have to stop talking about Edgar now, after bringing him so close. It makes her want to scream. She sighs. And of course, she shall have to come for Christmas, despite the vile idea of celebrating around

Edgar's absence. He wasn't there for the last four, but at least they were able to raise a glass to him, to know (or at least believe) that he was still in the world and would return. She watches her mother pour a sherry. She really has lost weight, dress loose over her hips and bosom, shins spindly.

'Any young men to speak of?' Clementine sits down with her tiny gold-rimmed glass, inclining her head.

Always the same question. And fair enough. No point mentioning the American. Though there have been many, the last boyfriend her parents met was the awful Brian Burk. As usual when he comes to mind, she scrubs at her mouth, to rid it of the tongue-memory. The parents would have conniptions if they knew what she's done with various men since, but then they're stuck in the dark ages, in their deadly marriage. Though what about Daddy? She feels a sudden surge of pity for her mother, all scraggy and innocent, not knowing what he's been up to.

'Yes, no,' she says.

'Which?' Clementine sucks on an end of cotton, and squints to thread it.

'Someone's been following me,' spills from her mouth entirely unplanned.

'What do you mean?' Clementine drops the needle.

'I think...' Aida sighs. 'Well, there seems to be this lurker. When I go home at night, once outside work...'

'Darling! Have you called the police?'

'No, it's not that bad. I'm probably just being silly.' She fashions a reassuring smile. 'Honestly Mummy, it's probably all in my head.'

'You *know* we don't like you living alone.'

'But actually, there *is* someone real,' she says, in an effort to deflect. 'Here, I'll thread it for you.' She stoops to retrieve the needle. 'He works at the Ministry – only more senior, a bit older. Neville Guthrie. Rather a dishy Scot. It's not *serious*, he's just nice company.'

'How much older?'

'Only a few years.'

Clementine gets up to refill her sherry, holds the bottle up to Aida.

'Go on then.'

'Have you told this Neville chap about the lurker?'

'Honestly, I don't really think there is one. I don't know why I even said it.' She threads the needle and passes it back.

Clementine clucks with exasperation. 'Honestly! *Something* must have made you say it.'

'No, oh I don't know. I'm a bit bonkers at the moment.'

Clementine frowns, studying her face.

'Can we just forget it please?'

'I *do* wish you'd be serious, darling! How on earth are we supposed to know whether to worry about you or not?'

'I'm grown up, Mummy! I don't want you to worry about me!' She accidentally knocks back the whole glass of sherry.

'What's his family like then? This "Neville"?'

'Don't know.'

'You don't *know*? Haven't you asked?'

'They're Quakers.'

That shuts Clementine up. She purses her lips, pushes her glasses up her nose, stretches the sock over a darning mushroom.

'Mummy,' Aida says after a while. 'When you met Daddy, was it... I mean, were you sort of, swept off your feet?'

Clementine smiles at her so gratefully that Aida shrinks. When she and Edgar had their snail farm, the snails would shrivel back their feelers if they touched them, and retreat into their shells; she gets that feeling now. Mummy's voice comes out all fat and warm and confidential, and she shrivels inside. 'Well darling, let me think. It *was* love, of course it was; he's a good husband, father, provider. But...' She puts down the sock, lights herself a cigarette.

'But what?' Aida's feelers come waving out again.

Pensively, Clementine exhales, her eyes gone oddly foggy. 'Once upon a time, I *was* as you put it, "swept off my feet".'

'Not by Daddy?'

'It was different with Daddy. More... sensible and sober.'

'What about...'

'Oh.' Her smile is sudden, and alarmingly radiant. 'He was Canadian,' she says, 'went by the name of Powell. We met in France, but...'

They hear the car draw up outside.

'In the war?'

She nods, glancing at the door and speaking quickly. 'Anyway, he died, I married your father and here we are, happily ever after.' She gives a bright, false smile. The front door opens, there's some banging about in the hall and Dennis bursts in, all black and silver, bringing with him a raw aroma of pipe smoke and rain. Aida rises and he squashes her against him, chill face, whisky on his breath. 'Darling Diddy,' he says. He holds her at arm's length to examine her. 'Do like the get-up.' He waves his hand at what she's wearing, a perfectly dreary frock that he must have seen a million times. 'Doesn't she look marvellous?' he says to Clementine. His eyes light on the sherry glasses. 'At it already, ladies?' He puts a hand to his forehead, makes a jokey pantomime of searching for a yardarm. 'Might as well join you.'

He seems no different. She finds herself sniffing for a wisp of perfume. But he's been on the golf course, for heaven's sake. At least that's where he says he's been.

'Aida's been telling me about–' Clementine begins.

'Top-up, ladies?'

'I just mentioned someone I met.' Aida looks daggers. The

last thing she needs is Daddy worrying about the lurker. What on earth possessed her to mention it? 'Mummy was telling me about your visitor.'

'Oh yes, Crowley. Not our sort, but a good sort all the same.'

'*Not our sort*! Good God, Daddy! And he was a friend of Eddie's. A close friend.'

He hands them both brimming sherries, and settles back on his armchair with his glass, takes out his pipe.

'Isn't anyone going to ask me about my game?' he complains, only semi-jokingly. 'Birdie on the fifth!'

'Spare us,' Clementine mutters.

Aida watches Dennis open his tobacco pouch and stuff his pipe. As a child she was entranced by the process, and the glamorous stink of it, the special words: *flake, shag, shank, dottle*. He'd let her help screw the tobacco into its tight plug, told her that each pipe has its own ghost, which is the taste when you suck it empty and cold. Sometimes, he let her taste the ghost before he filled the pipe. She thinks of the woman in Simpson's, the coy look over her shoulder, the teasing way he touched the end of her nose.

'Saw you in London recently,' she says.

'Really?' He smiles. 'Damned if I saw you.'

'Simpson's in the Strand,' she says. 'You were leaving. I only saw you as you left.' His eyes meet hers for an excruciating splinter of a second, then he concentrates on lighting his pipe, puffing away till there's a gurgle of tobacco juice. The hour begins to strike. He takes a gulp of Scotch.

'I expect you were with this Neville chap?' Clementine says. 'Diddy's been telling me about her new beau. A Scot.'

'Good chaps, the Scots. I met a–'

'I'll tell you what.' Aida jumps up. 'Why don't I start peeling the potatoes? In fact, I'll cook dinner, shall I?' Earlier she spotted some pathetic little pigeon breasts in the pantry, goose-pimpled and purple: they won't take much roasting.

'Oh, yes please,' Mummy says.

Aida bangs the door behind her rather harder than is necessary.

## 11

## CLEMENTINE

Clementine parks the car a little way from the studio in the dripping shelter of a cedar, but before she goes in, wanders down to look at the river. It's a lovely morning, unseasonably mild. Milky light gauzes the air and high tide laps glassy green at the moorings. Under a skim of mist, rusty leaves drift on the water. At breakfast she told Dennis an outright fib: that she was off to a Red Cross meeting. He didn't even look up from *The Times*. She doesn't like to lie, and as a rule avoids it. But needs must. Sometimes an untruth is necessary. Heavens, it's about the only way a marriage can survive – at least this one – and she needs, actually *needs*, to see Corin. To see him for himself, but also to show him the tobacco tin sketches, to tell him all about Roland Crowley, whose existence has set up a kind of agitated prickle inside her, making it hard to settle ever since.

The letter is still there, in her mending basket. Now that Aida has read it out loud, she's felt able to pore over it herself, examining every word. It's disappointing that there isn't more about Roland Crowley. Oh, if *only* she hadn't so rashly invited him for Christmas. Whatever got into her! Aida will not like it one little bit. Or will she? She did say she wanted to meet him – but at Christmas? This sensitive Christmas? She'd retract if she could, but they have no address for the man, not even a telephone number. Still, he may not come. She's more or less sure of it; after all, he seemed unwilling to accept, and he must have realised the invitation was offered in the spirit of the moment, not seriously *meant*. Almost certainly, he will not come. Though there is a part of her that hopes he will.

There's that beastly dragging in her abdomen again. London tomorrow – but she's read enough in Dennis's medical books to be able to self-diagnose a gynaecological cancer of some sort. Which means, of course, that she might be going to die. She'll wait until she knows the worst before saying anything; she'll wait till after Christmas. Strangely, she isn't the least bit scared.

The gauzy glitter has gone from the air now, the sky has become overcast and raw with the threat of rain. She hurries to the studio. When she mounts the stairs, she finds Corin bare-chested in shorts and socks, one brush clenched between his teeth, rapidly stippling viridian with another into the dark of a small riverscape. He nods with blank eyes, and she knows not to speak, silently takes off her coat and hat, settles on the sofa behind him. A paraffin heater flickers its blue flame, and the studio is warmly fuggy. His back is plump, shoulders grizzled with grey hairs, and in the groove of his spine, a slick of sweat. Pablo hops onto her lap and sets up a fervent purr.

Eventually, he removes the brush from his mouth, and wipes his brow. 'There.' She tips Pablo off and gets up to stand before the easel with him, and he slings a heavy arm over her shoulder. He smells pungently of his sweaty, gingery self, and there are speckles of green on his grizzled belly.

'Oh darling,' she exclaims. 'You've caught the very moment when it starts to turn, when it catches you here.' Her fist goes to her solar plexus. 'It's like the first breath of autumn or the first moment of dusk.'

He nods. 'That is what I'm after, but...' Frowning at the canvas, he removes his arm. 'Not there yet.'

'No? I think...'

Shaking his head, he picks up his palette, and with a tiny brush he adds one speck to the bottom right and stands back to look. His teeth grind and drops of sweat trickle down his chest. 'Fuck it, fuck it,' he mutters, peering forward. Then he darts his brush forward, drags the speck into a wriggle. And that's it! She laughs with delight. It's a reflection, perhaps of a street lamp at dusk, just at the very turn of the day, and it transforms the work. The painting seems designed around it now. That was the point of it. That wriggle of light.

'Thank fuck for that.' He sighs gustily, puts down his palette, crams the brushes in a jar of turps and turns to embrace her, but she steps away from his painty skin.

'You'll ruin my jacket!'

He takes a rag, rubs his belly, then pulls on a crumpled shirt.

'*Turn of the Day?*' she says. 'Call it that? Or just *The Turning?*'

He grunts. 'Not bad.'

'Shall we have tea?'

He nods and she busies herself with the kettle and the camping stove while he lights a cigarette, and slumps down onto the sofa. Painting exhausts him. It's physical, like a fight. Though she stirs vigorously, beads of powdered milk float in the tea. She'd never dream of drinking it like that at home! He lights a cigarette for them both, and they sit in suspended silence for a moment.

'What brings you here today, then?' he says.

'I missed you.'

'I was laid up.' He picks tobacco from his bottom lip. 'Missed you too,' he adds.

'Thanks for coming to the service. It really meant a lot to me.'

He says nothing.

She looks down at the scab on her hand. No need for a plaster now. There will be a scar. 'Aida came home at last, *such* a relief, so lovely to see her again... but before that, we had another visitor.'

He gets up and roams, glancing at his painting from different angles as she describes Roland's visit. 'And this is the tin. Look...' As she prises it open, he lands heavily beside her, holding out his hand.

She tips the scraps onto his palm. 'There was an ant trapped. This is all that's left.'

'Fucking hell,' he says. He picks a sketchbook from the floor, tips the pieces onto a blank page, reaches for the whisky bottle, holds it up.

'No,' she says. Then, 'Oh well, perhaps just a tot in my tea. One really should at least wait till lunchtime!'

It begins to rain, sleety drops that batter and slide on the skylight. He leans his face close to the page, examining the scraps, moving them about on the paper as if they're pieces of a puzzle. A scrap of face, a rather wonderful bird in flight, a corner of a roof, looks like bamboo. He breathes heavily as he studies them. Through her skirt she can feel the warmth of his thigh beside hers. Will he want to make love? Last time was months ago, the day of the letter. And the day the bleeding began.

Eventually, he puts down the sketchbook, and as if he's been reading her mind, takes her face between his hands to kiss her, begins to take the pins from her hair, letting the plait tumble down her back. She doesn't want to hurt his feelings, but neither does she want to make love. But then he stands abruptly, stares down at her with wide, confused eyes. 'Clem?' he says. 'Oh Christ,' and a hand drops to his side, scattering hairpins.

'What's the matter?' She jolts with alarm, glancing towards the door where he seems to be staring, thinking that it might be Dennis, but there's no one. Pablo yowls and lashes his tail and then Corin, the whole weight of him, collapses on top of her.

She struggles from under him. Maybe a heart attack? His eyes are closed, he's heavy as death but he isn't dead, there's still breath. 'Darling,' she says. 'Corin, darling, I'll run and phone, wait, just wait.' He's lying in a terribly awkward position, half on, half off the sofa, but he's too heavy for her to move. She grabs her coat, stuffs her plait into her hat and hurtles down the stairs. Freezing rain lashes her face as she runs along to a telephone box. She dials home and tells the latest hopeless daily girl to send the doctor to Sir Murray-Hill's studio. She doesn't say her name, and if the girl recognises her voice she doesn't say.

'Sir Murray-Hill,' the idiotic child says. 'How do you spell that?'

'Just tell the doctor. Say it's urgent. An emergency.'

When she gets back, she finds Corin still breathing, thank God. She manages to manoeuvre him into a more comfortable position, eases a cushion under his head.

'Go,' he murmurs, spit running from a corner of his mouth. And of course, before Dennis arrives, she must.

'Shall I ring Eleanor?' she says.

He says something, but it isn't clear. She kneels and kisses him, takes a last look at his greying face, his dear sturdy legs splayed on the floor and goes down to her car, sits in the driving seat, drumming her fingers on the wheel, biting her lip until she tastes blood. And then she drives home.

As soon as she enters the house, the help confronts her. 'I can't be expected to clean and cook and take messages,' she says. 'I've been run off my feet all morning.'

'All right,' Clem says weakly.

'So I'll be off then.'

The girl, a wisp of a child, her lip distended by a cold-sore, puts on her hat and leaves. Just like that. Clem stands open-mouthed in the hall after the door bangs. She should ring the agency straight away; she should complain. But instead, she removes her coat and hat, and goes into the sitting room for a stiffener. Two brandies she swallows in quick succession then collapses forward, head between her knees, tears running upside down into her hair. It's a trickly, tickly feeling that goes with the sound of rain on the windows, hissing down the chimney into the little fire. A sulky fire laid by a sulky girl. Eventually she hears Dennis's car arrive, hears the surgery door bang downstairs, hears his voice begin. He'll be up soon expecting lunch. Another drink and she'll pull herself together. In the kitchen she finds the sink still piled with breakfast dishes and nothing in the larder but bread and cheese, the bread stale, the cheese fit only for a mousetrap.

Dennis comes into the kitchen.

'The girl went,' Clem says, without looking at him. 'And I'm going to lie down. You'll have to fend for yourself.'

'What do you mean, "The girl went"?'

'Too much for her apparently.'

'Well, good riddance. She was a halfwit. I had to show her how to use the telephone! They don't know they're born, these days. Honestly, that agency is useless; you need to get onto the Labour Exchange. We need a proper live-in couple.'

'Oh, do we?' Clem snaps. 'I hadn't noticed.'

'What on earth's the matter with you?'

'Could I have one of those pills?' For the first time she dares to look him in the eye.

'Good meeting this morning?' He holds her gaze for just a bit too long, and her face fills with blood. 'By the way, I was called out to Sir Murray-Hill's studio earlier,' he adds, and picks up the bread knife, begins sawing at the crumbling loaf.

'And?' she says.

'Stroke. Lucky *someone* was there to raise the alarm.'

'Oh no,' she says weakly. The effort of acting is too much, and her legs give way. She sags down onto a chair, rests her chin on cupped hands. 'How serious?' she asks.

'Hard to say at this stage. He might pull through, though there's bound to be some sort of deficit.'

The word is like a soft and terrible wafer, *deficit*.

'Will he still be able to paint?'

'Ha! That'll be the least of his worries.' He slices a corner of cheese. 'I say, are you all right, old girl?'

'Well, I'm... shocked.'

'Naturally. Because you knew nothing about it.' He chews the morsel of cheese and pulls a disgusted face. 'And how *was* the meeting? Red Cross was it?'

She hesitates too long before saying, 'Just the usual.'

He gives a contemptuous laugh. 'You must think I was born yesterday! Oh, by the way, there's paint on your sleeve. I'm going to have a bite at the golf club.'

And off he goes. Yes, there's a smudge of white on her sleeve. She thinks of the magical wriggle of light, lays her cheek on the table, and listens for the slam of the front door. *Oh Corin, Corin, Corin*. Something sticky under her cheek, and from this angle she can see crumbs scattered like boulders across the grain of the wood. You can't blame Dennis for being angry. Why did she not simply say she had called in to see Corin after her meeting and found him collapsed? Why weave such a tangled web?

She sits up suddenly, with a sickening lurch of realisation. She's left Edgar's scraps behind. What a terrible, terrible mother! She can picture them on the sketchpad where Corin tipped them. She stands – she'll go and get them now. She stuffs a crust in her mouth, tries to chew but it's too dry, her throat has locked. The room swings arounds her. She must have drunk more than she thought. Rain batters the window; the drops slide, half gelid, turning to sleet, and she knows she's good for nothing this afternoon but lying down. Her eyes will barely focus. Corin will live. He will. He must.

She goes into the sitting room for another drink to take to bed. An afternoon cap. Tomorrow she'll fetch the pieces from the studio. Oh no, tomorrow is London and the specialist. She pours a glass, starts up the stairs, goes back for the bottle, and makes for her bed.

12
---
AIDA

Hand tucked into Neville's tweedy arm, she feels emboldened to stare into the lurker's doorway: empty. She rather wishes he was there to see her with Neville – a big, strong chap. The lurker himself seems rather a weedy specimen. And timid – after all, he's never even spoken to her, just harmlessly lurked. Should she mention him to Neville? It might arouse a chivalrous streak. But is he even real? Anyway, when she comes to think of it, she hasn't seen him for days.

Neville stands shelteringly behind her as she unlocks the door, and it's rather nice to feel protected. This is the first time he's consented to come in at the end of an evening. Usually there's just a pleasant, decorous kiss on the doorstep. But tonight, lingering looks over the rabbit paprika (lingering on her part, at least) make her think this might be the night. If they're going to be a couple, then there must be *something* physical. How can she possibly make a decision without trying him out? Ludicrous to keep oneself pure, and risk colossal disappointment on the wedding night. Even Dora and her Chris have given it a try and, judging by Dora's shining eyes when she kept schtum about how it went, it went well.

Once in her room she sees its crumminess afresh through Neville's eyes: cracked sink, tap dribbling through its rubber spout, hearth rug clogged with soot, but at least, since she'd planned to bring him back, it's not too untidy. Before leaving this morning, she washed the dishes, pushed the usual clutter behind the sofa, draped the lamp with a pink scarf to soften the shabbiness. Now she hangs his coat behind the door, switches off the cruel overhead light, and kneels to set a match to the ready-laid fire. Behind the drawn curtain in the alcove, the bed awaits, all plumped and freshly made.

On the sofa, she snuggles up to him, enjoying his broad-shouldered bulk, his comforting solidity. (Though it's a shame his clothes smell like an old woman's wardrobe. Not his fault though; it's his digs.) His sweater, intricately patterned with muted blues and greys and rusts, the colours of Scottish moors, she supposes, is exquisite, and his arm round her shoulders warm and heavy. He's quiet and she's tired after a tedious day at work, pushing the tea trolley, waiting for Neville (doing overtime) to finish and then the long meal, over which she did get just a teeny bit bored. If only he'd talk about personal things, reveal himself to her. Instead, he tends either to clam up or to spout brainily impersonal information or political opinion. Over dinner it was Nuremberg, Gurdjieff and the Beveridge Report. Her trivial mind would keep crawling off, noticing his handsome nose or distracted by gusts of laughter from the people behind her, straining to catch what they were saying. Does he have a sense of humour? He seems to find her amusing, but he doesn't often actually *laugh*. But at least when he's talking, she's prevented from chattering – it's the silences that set her off.

The food was a step up tonight, a better class of restaurant than his usual choice, but he munched through his rabbit paprika (delicious) obliviously. At least he wouldn't demand much skill in the kitchen. It's quite a husbandly thing to go on like that, she supposes, mind on higher things than mere sustenance. She can imagine their children raising eyebrows at each other, like she and Eddie over Daddy's politics or golf. And his heart's certainly in the right place. His politics agree with hers (or would if she were more political). But there must be a way into him, a way beyond his intellect and reserve. She smothers another yawn, sits up. Bad form to invite him in and then fall asleep!

'This is beautiful,' she says, running a finger over a row of patterns on his sweater. 'Who knitted it? Your mother?'

Minutely, he reddens and she wakes up at once, intrigued.

'Go on?' she says, and when he doesn't immediately answer, she feels a rising urge to babble almost as strong as her previous urge to yawn. 'None of my business, sorry, I can be nosy. It's beautiful work. Wish I could knit like that. No, I don't really, I wouldn't have the patience, and I'm hopeless. I knitted my share of socks for the boys, of course, but I pity anyone trying to walk in them!' She presses her lips tight to shut herself up. It's a loathsome habit this need to fill the silence. *Wait Aida, wait for him to speak*. She counts to twenty and then he does.

'My wife.'

'You're *married*?'

'Divorced. Well, in the process of.'

'Oh good golly! I'm so sorry, why on earth did you not say before?' Immediately, she forgives his reticence. Poor man. She nestles her head on his woolly shoulder. Somehow, knowing that he's married promotes him in her estimation; he's emotionally wounded perhaps, which accounts for his self-protection. She will bring him out of himself; the challenge rises freshly to meet her. She lifts her face for a kiss, but he doesn't notice.

'Thought I'd put the kettle on if you don't mind?' He stands. 'Ought to be getting back soon.'

'Or a drink?' she says. 'I've got some liqueur that Daddy brought back from somewhere. It's vile but I think we need a drink. God, I do hope wine will be back in the shops soon. They always manage to have it at home, Daddy's spiv's a marvel, but I haven't managed to buy a bottle since I don't know–'

'Tea will do fine.'

She presses her lips tight together – *don't chatter, don't chatter* – as she watches him fill the kettle. She ought to have jumped up to do it. Odd to have a man in here performing this domestic task. A soon-to-be divorcé though, which is rather thrilling. Hidden depths, he has, which happen to be her favourite kind. There's the usual hiss and smell of gas as the ring fails to catch, and then the small triumphant *whoomph*. He turns, a set look on his face, folds his arms and leans back against the sink.

'All right. I met Fiona at a camp in Scotland – Aviemore – a Socialist summer camp in '38. We fell in love, so to speak, married in '39.'

Forcing herself not to interrupt, Aida reaches for her cigarettes, holds out the pack to him, but he shakes his head.

'I've got my pipe.' He retrieves it from his coat pocket.

She lights up, takes a breath of smoke.

'At the outbreak of war, we parted, me to rural work in Wales, she – clever lassie – to Bletchley. Where she met someone else.'

'Lord!'

He shrugs, fiddles with the stem of his pipe.

'Sit down,' she says. 'I'll make the tea. *Sure* you couldn't do with a little nip of something?'

He sits down, shaking his head, smiles at her, bravely she thinks.

'Do light up,' she says. 'I like the smell of pipe smoke. Daddy smokes one. It makes me think of journeys, the car always billowing with it till you could hardly see out of the windows. He likes to drive with his pipe clenched between his teeth. Like this.' She snatches his pipe to demonstrate, and he snorts. Nearly a laugh. *Progress?*

The fire hasn't taken properly, and she forages under the sofa for a piece of newspaper, scrabbling around on gritty knees, and seeing the parcel that arrived this morning when she was rushing to tidy up. She'd forgotten! Her heart had hammered when she'd seen the big box with its American postmark – until she recognised Aunt Harri's scrabbly handwriting, and she'd shoved it out of sight. It's for Christmas and she doesn't want to think about Christmas yet. On her knees, she goes over to the hearth and holds a sheet of newspaper against it, until eventually it sucks inwards with the draw of flames.

'*She* knitted it?' She balls the paper and chucks it on the flames. 'Your ex-wife? And you don't mind wearing it after everything? God, *I* wouldn't.'

'Rather a waste not to.'

She brushes grit from her knees, notices a ladder in her stocking. *Damn.* 'Do you keep in touch?'

'My mother does. Fi lives in Devon now, has a wee boy. It's *all right,* you know, you needn't look like *that!*'

'Like what?'

'I didn't own her. She did the right thing. There are no hard feelings.'

'Do light your pipe, darling.'

But he puts it back in his pocket and gives her such an earnest look that she quails, and there's silence. The fire crackles, the alarm clock ticks, he clears his throat as if to speak but says nothing more.

'Did it come as a shock, or did you suspect?' she asks eventually. 'I mean was she that type?'

She shouldn't have said "that type". The expression hangs crassly in the air. Another long silence. Well, she shall just have to get used to them. An adult relationship doesn't have to be all chat, chat, chat. Mummy and Daddy can go for hours without a word. But suddenly she's pierced with longing for the American, no awkward silences there, and they used to laugh their heads off. At what, she can't recall. What will he be doing now? How often, she wonders, does she cross his mind? Or is it, for him, truly out of sight, out of mind? The alarm clock has an irritatingly fast tick, as if it can't wait to get to the end. The end of what though?

'I'd rather talk about *you*,' he says at long last.

'Smooth!' She laughs, but he looks deadly serious. 'Well, for a start *I've* never been married!' She picks up her cigarette, taps ash into a saucer. 'S'pose I shall have to think about it one day, but not yet.'

'How old are you?'

'Twenty-four. I know, I know, spinsterhood creeping up, the old shelf looming! Time I settled down; you should hear Mummy on the subject! How old are you?'

'Thirty-one.'

'Well, that must account for these nice lines.' She stubs out her cigarette and puts a fingertip on the fan of creases beside one of his eyes. As he smiles, she feels the creases deepen. 'Well, I'm going to have a drop of the vile liqueur,' she says. 'Sure you won't? Oh, I bet you'd prefer Scotch, wouldn't you? I wish I had some. Daddy's a great one for Scotch.'

'Not for me,' he says.

'I won't then,' she says, expecting him to say, "Go on", but he says nothing, only sits down on the sofa, stretching out his legs. Not as long as the lovely lanky American's legs.

He was the last man in here. Neville's are sturdier. A country type. Sensible. He'd make a good father; he's the right, reliable shape for it. She stirs the leaves and pours the tea, rattles half a scuttle of coke onto the fire, glances at the curtain that conceals the waiting bed. She tunes in the wireless, finds some jazz.

'Miles Davis,' he says, lifting a finger.

'You like jazz?'

'Some.'

'Perhaps we should go to a jazz club then? We could go dancing; shall we?'

He nods non-committally. At least he's tapping his foot now. What else can she do to help him relax? If he won't drink, she's at a loss. It occurs to her that Aunt Harri's box might contain something edible or quaffable. She retrieves it from behind the sofa, peels off and opens the card stuck on the box: Father Christmas on a glittery rooftop, and inside:

*Happy Christmas, darling niece. We're sending these goodies to your flat so you don't have to share! Save till Christmas. Will send a bigger box to The Beeches. Be strong this difficult year. We think about you, and poor dear Edgar, every day. Love from Harri and Gwen xxx*

Averting her face till she can control her expression, she stands the card on the mantel, saying brightly, 'Bless them! They live in California now, my aunts.'

'Oh yes?'

'I really *should* save this till I get back after Christmas, but let's just have a peep.' She lifts the box onto the table and rips it open. Potato-printed wrapping paper – Christmas trees with flaking paint, oh bless their loony hearts. Nestled inside, *hurrah*, a bottle of wine, jars of homemade jam and chutney, Lucky Strike cigarettes, a slab of Hershcy's chocolate and a

Christmassy tin of biscuits. The chocolate she pushes to the bottom among the packing straw; that is not to be shared.

'Wine?' She brandishes the bottle, but he shakes his head. 'Well, at least we can have "cookies" with our tea.' Aida opens the biscuits, big, fat craggy ones, only a bit battered by their journey overseas.

'I think you'd like my aunts,' she says. 'They lived nearby when we were growing up. My brother and I used to cycle along the river to their little cottage, or "wretched hovel", as Daddy put it. They'd be much more in your line politically – and mine – than Daddy's. He's a raving fascist.'

He stretches his eyes.

'Not *actually* fascist.' She blushes.

'What's his stance on Mosley?'

'You'll have to ask him. No! For God's sake don't! If you ever meet him, steer clear of politics, or he'll bore your ears off. And shock your socks off while he's at it!'

He's grinning at her now. He takes a crunch of biscuit. 'Delicious,' he says. 'And if I do meet him someday, I shall take your advice.'

She takes a bite, glorious, the taste of real butter and sugar, with a lavish studding of macadamia nuts and raisins.

They sip their tea, and crunch in an almost comfortable silence. 'Is this still Miles Davis?' she asks.

'Yes.'

'I don't know much about jazz – you'll have to teach me.'

He nods. She brushes biscuit crumbs from her lap. Their silence grows less comfortable. Why on earth won't the conversation flow? She makes a show of wagging her foot in time to the music, eyes straying to the box with its bottle of lovely Californian wine. The evening's turning horribly sad, and sober. What would he do if she pulled him up and tried to get him to dance? Would he run for the hills?

'Is it hilly where you come from?' she asks.

'The Borders is hilly indeed!' He smiles, and adds, 'It's bonny countryside.'

'Going home over the break?'

'Sleeper on Christmas Eve.'

'Oh, doesn't the Sleeper sound romantic?'

'*Sound* perhaps. The reality is somewhat different.'

'I'm off home on the twenty-fourth too. But without my brother it'll be...' She stops and sniffs, eyes threatening to fill.

'I know,' he says. 'Come here.' He puts an arm around her, and she snuggles her face into the jumper so beautifully knitted by the faithless Fiona, finding comfort for a moment. But he holds her so tensely he might as well be made of wood.

She pulls away with a twitch of irritation. If they're not going to make progress, he'll have to go. She sneaks a look at her watch. It's half past nine. If nothing's happened by ten, she'll kick him out. And give him up as a dead loss. There's not enough *spark* to him, she'll tell Dora. No *fun*. What a waste of an evening. She could have gone out dancing; goodness knows what she might be up to by now.

'Why didn't you go back to bonny Scotland after the war?' she asks.

'Friends in London.'

'Proper friends or Quaker friends?'

'Same thing,' he says, then, 'Well both actually, and I'm very involved with the party.'

'Labour?'

He looks flatly at her.

'*Might* have been some other sort of party,' she says. 'You might not have been talking about politics.' *Oh God, you're sounding like a total imbecile, Aida. Shut up.* 'Why aren't you still a draughtsman?' she asks. 'Must have been a lot of training, and then you end up in the bloody old Ministry of Food.'

'I haven't "ended up".' He sounds a touch testy now. 'And my old firm folded.'

'Surely you could get a job somewhere else?'

'Actually, I have my feelers out.' She thinks of snails. 'And I'm happy with what I'm doing, for the present.'

'*Really*? At the Ministry?'

'Taking each day as it comes.'

'*Really?*'

'Yes, really.'

She expects that at any moment he'll get up to leave, and she won't stop him. But then, without warning, he lurches in for a kiss, jolting her nose as their teeth clash.

Amazed, she kisses him back. Well, this is a turn-up! About time too. She kneels up on the sofa, puts her hand on the back of his neck, soft skin, the hair bristly at the nape. If only it wasn't for the mothball whiff... not his fault if his digs smell depressing... *Oh don't think about it, don't breathe too deeply.* She urges him down onto the sofa – hard work, he resists gravity – but eventually he's on his back, and she wriggles on top of him. In a moment she'll suggest moving to the bed. He groans, as if giving in to something, pulls the back of her blouse free from her skirt and his warm hands roam on her bare skin, and she unbuttons his shirt, kissing bits of skin as they become available though there's a thick woollen vest in the way.

She wanted this, didn't she? She wanted it, but something is missing. She dismisses the thought, kissing and moving against him, and soon his trousers are undone and he's pushing, hot and urgent, against her thigh.

'Hold your horses, let's move to the bed,' she says, but he seems content to carry on where they are. She starts to wriggle down her knickers, but he mumbles, 'No.'

'No French letter?'

And then he groans, and she feels warm wet on her thigh, on her underwear.

'Sorry,' he says, 'sorry.' He leaps up to fasten his trousers, looking stricken. 'Aida, for God's sake! I had no intention...'

'It's all right.'

'I'd better go.'

'No! Don't.'

'I'll be locked out.'

She pulls herself up. 'Just hang on a mo, then.'

In the bathroom, she peels off her sticky knickers, peers in the mirror into her own steamed-over eyes. He didn't so much as touch her.

He's in his hat and coat when she comes out and he bends, almost decorously, to kiss her cheek. 'Sorry,' he says again.

'*Please* don't apologise. It's all right. Better luck next time!' She cringes, face wildly flushing. 'Sorry, I only mean, oh God, I'll shut up. I'm sorry. I only mean it's all right. Honestly, it's all right.'

He puts a forefinger to her lips. 'Hush.' He takes her by the top of the arms and studies her face for an unnervingly long time, and then he says, 'I love you, Aida Everett.'

'What?' She gawps up at him, at his shiny, besotted eyes.

'And I don't say that lightly. See you tomorrow, darling.' He presses a kiss to her brow and leaves. She stands with mouth agape, listening to his footsteps descend the stairs, before she lights a cigarette and stalks about the room. *What?* Then she parts the curtain to peer down at the street. He's already gone. And there's no sign of the lurker either, just a cat slinking by, and old Gladys stumping along with her pram of lost toys.

She washes her face, cleans her teeth, pulls back the alcove curtain. This morning, she made it up with fresh sheets. Not a waste though – nice that it's clean and smooth just for her. Whatever's the matter with the man? He's been *married* for

God's sake. You'd think he'd just stumbled out of a monastery. Maybe, she wonders, as she unhooks her brassiere, that was the problem with his marriage? Brainy Fiona, the wonderful knitter, went off and found herself a better lover? Or maybe it was just nerves? Maybe he needs more time?

But *I love you?* Saying *that* then! How utterly *gauche*. What utter, crashingly poor judgement. Well, that has put the tin hat on it. It's never going to work. Her job now must be, very gently, to let him down.

How very comforting to button herself chastely into Eddie's pyjamas – the soft, thick cotton – and how luxurious to slide her legs between clean, smooth sheets. She reaches for the book Neville lent her weeks ago, Aldous Huxley's *The Perennial Philosophy*. It's been waiting in the bedside pile for ages. She gazes at its dreary cover, puts it down and picks up *Evil Under the Sun* instead.

# PART 2

## CHRISTMAS

*'A Christmassy sparkle is easy to add to sprigs of holly or evergreen for use on puddings. Dip your greenery in a strong solution of Epsom salts. When dry it will be beautifully frosted.'*
(World War II. Ministry of Food advice.)

13
---

AIDA

The first Christmas Eve since the war. The chilly carriage is crammed with muffled figures, coughing and sneezing; a stink of wintergreen comes from the man seated, too snugly, beside her. In the corridor stand soldiers, all khaki and kit-bags, returning to their families. Smoking, joshing, *alive* young men. Turning her face to the dark window, she huddles into her mothy old musquash. In the rack above her seat are presents for the parents only.

The woman opposite has a baby on her lap, she thought at first, but now she sees it's a pug panting under a mohair shawl. The woman whispers to the dog and smiles complicity at Aida, opens her mouth about to speak, but Aida snaps shut her eyes. Some Yank further up the train drunkenly roars out *"Frosty the Snowman"*; the wintergreen man lights a cigar; a real infant begins to squall.

The first Christmas since. The first Christmas without. If she'd had any say in it, they'd have skipped the whole business this year. She'd have stayed in London, gone out on the town with friends tonight, danced her feet off, drunk too much and stayed in bed tomorrow, reading, and demolishing the remaining treats in the Christmas parcel. But duty calls. And after all, it's only a *day*: breakfast, church, lunch, presents, walk, tea, games (only, probably not games this year). Plenty of booze at least, but keep an eye on Mummy. Will there be tears? Or will they brave on through, barely mentioning Edgar's name?

Two days actually: Christmas and Boxing Day and then back to London on the first train. And back to work. One bright spot: the lurker seems to have given up, and the clutch of nerves when she turns into Buttress Street is loosening (though she still finds herself twitching back the curtain, several times an evening, just to be sure). There is a thread of regret mixed with her relief though. Now, she'll never know who he was, or what he wanted. It was, at least, excitement of a sort.

The train's on time, a Christmas miracle, and once the other passengers have dispersed, she pauses on the railway bridge, gazes out into the darkness, breathing in the frosty breath of the river, the familiar hoppy tang from the brewery. So much crisper and fresher than stale old London air. A candle flickers from the window of a barge, and there's a harsh bird call, weird in the dark.

Daddy waits in the car park looking rather spiffy from a distance, lamp-lit pipe smoke wreathing him in silver. When she reaches him, he grasps both her hands in his leather gloves, peers at her through the glitter of their mingled breath.

'You got here, then. And all on time.'

'So I did!' You can always rely on Daddy to state the bleeding obvious; it used to madden her and Edgar, but now she finds it soothing.

'Everything all right at home?' she asks. Bloody stupid question! *Nothing's* all right.

He wobbles his glove in the air. '*Comme ci, comme ça.*'

'Really? What?' She wonders about the other woman.

'Oh nothing, nothing. Splendid to see you, Diddy.'

'Thanks for coming to pick me up.'
'We waited dinner.'
'No need!'
'Of course, need!'

Pipe clenched between his teeth, he starts the car and pulls out onto the road. Though blackout's been over for months, it still seems strange out here, to see light brazening out from windows and street lamps, the rich peep of stained glass from the church.

Puffing on his pipe, Dennis drives with both hands on the steering wheel, and they don't speak again until he pulls into the drive. Gravel spits as they swing in between the gateposts and pull up by the entrance.

'You go in. I'll put the old girl away.'

Aida opens the car door, puts one leg out, then turns back. His silence isn't unusual, but she feels suddenly rattled. 'How *is* Mummy?'

He removes the pipe and clears his throat. 'Rather unexpectedly we have a visitor; it's given her a bit of a fillip.'

'What kind of visitor? Who?'

'Go and see. I'll bring your bags.'

Aida steps out and watches him drive round the side of the house to the garage, subtly put-out. A visitor on Christmas Eve? But *she's* the visitor. She tips back her head to look up at the dark beech branches, between which the sky shows a frosty stipple of stars. But maybe it's a good thing, a distraction. It'll only be old Murray-Hill, or some deadly dull golf partner of Daddy's. *Please* God, don't let it be "a prospect" – though having mentioned Neville should have put paid to any danger of that. She'll play him up a bit even though he's a dead duck.

Before entering, she takes a deep breath, and experiences a sudden unexpected *frisson* of pleasure at being home again. This time opening the door is like opening the book not of

*Before*, but of *What Next*. She chuckles at the fancy. War is *over*, she reminds herself. It really *is*.

In the hall she removes her coat and hat, peers into the hall mirror, boofs up her squashed hair, freshens her lipstick. Mummy hasn't come bustling to meet her but jumps up when she enters the sitting room. 'Darling! At long last!' She engulfs Aida in warmth and perfume, then pulls back to touch her cheek. 'Oh my goodness me, you're freezing! Come by the fire. We've got sole fillets though I had to twist the fishmonger's arm. Pour yourself a drink, do. I've managed to get a new couple, the Jacksons, Elsie and Frank, to do for us over Christmas. I'll go and tell them to put the fish on; it's nearly nine and we ought to be eating or we'll never get to bed.' Giddy and hectic and overly rouged, she's clearly had more than a few sherries already.

'Daddy says we have a visitor?'

She nods. 'He'll be down in a minute.'

'Murray-Hill?'

She pulls her chin in, frowning. 'But you know he's...'

'Still?'

'You don't just bounce back from a stroke like that.' Her voice cracks.

'Are you all right, Mummy?' There are shadows under her eyes and she looks exhausted, seems to have diminished, even in the last couple of weeks.

'Perfectly all right. Pour yourself a drink. I'll only be a moment.' The door clicks emphatically behind her.

Aida arranges her presents, newspaper-wrapped, with the small pile under the Christmas tree, pauses to finger the familiar glass bells and baubles. German glass: there was a debate at the first Christmas of the war about whether it was patriotic to use them, but expedience won. Her favourites were the bells, Edgar's the twisted glass icicles. She tinks one with a nail, sets it rocking then goes to the fire to warm her hands. Clementine's been busy with the decorations; the card-crowded mantelpiece is twined with frosted ivy. As she picks up a Christmas card to read, the door opens. She turns, and drops the card, her mouth falling open. The person standing there looks like, surely *is,* the lurker.

'Happy Christmas.' He extends his hand. 'Aida?' The other hand is missing, she sees. He's a thin, dark, Mediterranean type, though his voice is northern, his shoulders narrow, spectacles a little askew. His hand remains extended. 'Aida? I'm a pal of Edgar's.'

'Roley Crowley?' she says faintly, taking his hand, thin, hot, in hers. There's a pronounced widow's peak in his dark, pushed-back hair. *Is* it the lurker?

'Oh, you wretches, you beat me to it!' Clementine sweeps back into the room. 'I wanted to make the introductions. Dr Roland Crowley, Aida, my daughter.'

Aida and Roland shake hands again for her benefit. *Can* it be him?

'What will you have, Roland?' Clementine pours sherries for herself and Aida. 'A nice stiff Scotch?' And the door opens on Dennis, rubbing his hands as he approaches the trolley.

Over a meal of consommé, sole meunière and stewed pears, the conversation jolts on broken tracks. The family avert their eyes as the visitor manages his food – thank heavens it's all soft – cutting with the edge of his fork and scooping American style.

The Jacksons, a homely young couple, he with the sort of limp that suggests a wooden leg, trudge humbly in and out. Aida recognises from Mummy's satisfied expression that they might well become a permanent fixture.

'Simply heavenly not to have to worry about the cooking,' she says. 'Dr Crowley arrived when I was making the most almighty hash of it in the kitchen!'

'You told me,' Aida says. *But you didn't tell me you'd invited him for Christmas*, she thinks.

'So nice to have a friend of Edgar's...' She stops suddenly, puts down her fork and takes a vast, unladylike gulp of wine.

'Californian vino,' Dennis says, 'the aunts sent us a crate of the stuff.'

'And dates and pecan nuts,' adds Clementine. 'We shall tuck into those after Christmas dinner.'

'They sent me some goodies, too,' says Aida.

Dennis asks Aida about her work, and the conversation moves onto family matters, which must be ditch-water to Roland, who nevertheless puts on a show of interest.

'Edgar told me all about the aunts,' he says. 'Didn't they breed dogs?'

'That was Gwen really,' Aida says. 'Massive great things. And they lived in a tiny cottage. Sometimes you could hardly see them for the dogs! Gwen's not an aunt by blood, but Aunt Harri's "friend".' She emphasises the word, widening her eyes at Roland.

'*Companion*,' Dennis insists. 'Harriet's husband was killed in the first do, leaving her with twins. I don't mind admitting I was worried, but she has the Everett grit – though you wouldn't think it to look at her – a tremendous spirit of get up and go.' Aida blinks. There seems to be a quiver in the air, wobbling the pipe and candle smoke that hangs above the table. Could something of Edgar, some last wisp of him, be here? *"Get up and go"*, Daddy often used to say when they were children, praising Aida for hers, chiding Edgar for his comparative lack of same. Edgar used to tease her about it. *"Run downstairs and fetch me a currant bun, Aida, with your famous get up and go."*

Elsie comes in bearing stewed pears and evaporated milk.

'Is that everything?' she says. 'Only we might be getting off now.'

'Very nice dinner indeed, thank you. That fish was done to a tee,' says Clementine. 'Just set the coffee tray in the sitting room, and then yes, you get off home. We'll see you bright and early. Oh, and Merry Christmas.'

'Hope you're paying them simply *oodles*,' Aida says, when Elsie has closed the door.

Clementine dents her brow at this lapse of taste. 'Fine young couple. Old-fashioned manners. We might have found our help, darling,' she says to Dennis. 'After New Year I'll see if they want to move in downstairs.'

'There are some dank quarters behind the surgery,' Aida explains to Roland.

'Not dank, delightful!'

'Would you live there?'

Clementine frowns.

'I like the frosty ivy,' Roland says. 'Is it sugar?'

'Heavens, I wouldn't waste sugar on that!' Clementine gives a hectic laugh.

'My wife is nothing if not artistic,' says Dennis proudly, and changes the subject to Roland, probing him about his background and training. It turns out he's from Sheffield, a scholarship boy, dragged himself up by his bootstraps, found himself a sponsor, qualified just before war broke out. Rather than go into practice, he signed up immediately and was launched straight in at the deep end in the jungle, practising, along with Edgar, with minimal equipment or drugs.

But Roland shifts uneasily during the interrogation, clearly uncomfortable and Daddy eventually lets him off the hook, wangles the subject round to his own med student stories, and Aida tunes out as she watches Roland. *Of course he's not the lurker, you idiot!* After all, she never really got a close look at that poor fellow, only a shadowy glimpse or the glow of a cigarette in the dark. He happens to be the same *build*, that's all. Mummy's right though; he does look frightfully young to be a contemporary of Edgar's, let alone older than him.

'How well did you know my brother?' she asks Roland, butting into Dennis's monologue.

He bangs down his fork, and glares. 'Please don't interrupt.'

'Sorry, Daddy. But isn't it vile that we barely mention his name?'

'We were great... pals,' Roland says quietly.

'There's a time and a place. This is the dinner table,' Dennis says.

'Really?' Aida mutters. 'We can't mention your son at the table?'

Clementine dabs her mouth on a napkin. 'Oh, *please* don't squabble,' she says.

Aida takes a steadying breath, forces a smile. 'Were you with him last Christmas?' she asks Roland.

He puts down his spoon and looks to Dennis. 'If you don't mind, sir?'

Dennis shakes his head, refills his wine glass, but still Roland hesitates, looking at each of them uncertainly, such soulful eyes behind the lenses of his glasses.

'Go on,' Aida says.

'Please do,' says Clementine.

Roland dabs his lips on a napkin before he speaks. 'Well, yes. The Nips gave us the day off. He was a good singer, wasn't he? We cobbled together a sort of panto.'

'What was he, principle boy?'

'An ugly sister.'

A painful laugh bubbles in her chest. 'Such a show-off!'

'Tenor,' Clementine says. 'He was a soloist as a boy, church choir.'

'All those tedious evensongs we had to sit through!' Aida

grins, takes a mouthful of sweet, grainy pear. 'An ugly sister, though! What a hoot!'

'I expect it kept your spirits up,' said Dennis.

'And who was Cinderella? Not you?'

He shakes his head. 'Not me, no. Lammy did the honours. Corporal Lambert. It was hilarious – Lammy's built like a barn door. The two of them sang.'

'What?'

'All sorts.' He frowns. 'Carols of course, they used to do "*My Grandfather's Clock*".'

'We used to sing that,' Aida says, and sings. "*Stopped short never to go again when the old man died*".' And she winces into a silence.

'"*Whispering Grass*",' Roland says, as if to rush over the pain. 'That was a favourite.'

'Oh, yes,' Aida breathes, adding greedily, 'Tell us more.'

'Really, Diddy,' says Dennis. 'Let the poor chap get his breath.'

Roland smiles, an unexpectedly lovely smile from his starved face. 'He told me he called you that.'

'Did he?' she said, then laughed. 'Did he Diddy!'

'*I* told you that, darling.' Clementine gives her an odd look. 'Let's move through for coffee.'

Aida notices an unsteadiness in Roland's gait, wonders if he could be drunk. She's a bit tight herself, come to think of it. All through the meal Daddy kept industriously filling their glasses, so actually they are all a bit tight as they issue through into the sitting room, where thanks to Mr Jackson, the fire blazes.

They settle round the hearth, and before he lights his pipe, Daddy offers cigarettes.

'Oh look!' Clementine gestures towards the coffee tray, a plate of little star-shaped biscuits, a sprig of holly in a jam jar. 'It's those little extra touches that count. Do hope they'll stay.'

'Pay them well and treat them well–' Aida starts.

'Now, now,' says Daddy, smiling at Roland. 'My daughter the socialist,' he says.

Roland smiles uncertainly. She wishes he'd say more. Crippled by shyness? He sits down on one end of the sofa, Aida, once Dennis has lit her cigarette, at the other.

There is a moment of quiet, the spitting of the fire, a gurgle as Dennis sucks his pipe.

'What did Eddie say about me?' Aida asks.

'Really, Aida! You're not the centre of the universe,' says Clementine.

But Roland smiles. 'Let me think. Oh yes, he told me about some Mexican jumping beans.'

'Oh goodness! The jumping beans!' She cackles, claps her hand over her mouth. 'Oh, Lord! Remember, Mummy?'

'How could I forget?' She's pouring coffee. 'Revolting things.'

'They started hatching out.' Aida shudders, recalling her horror as maggots emerged from one brightly painted bean after another, the screaming in the nursery – more from Eddie than herself. 'We didn't realise they had grubs in them. That's what makes them jump, you know.'

'What did you think it was?' Roland asks. 'That made them jump?'

'Magic.'

Dennis laughs scoffingly. 'Magic!'

Roland treats her to his smile again.

Clementine moves a low table to between Roland and Aida, for their coffee cups and the plate of biscuits. Leaning close to Roland she puts a hand on his shoulder. 'You can't possibly know how *lovely* it is for us to have you here,' she says, a creamy throb in her voice. 'A close friend of Edgar's, and now a close friend of us all. Isn't that right, Diddy, Dennis?'

'Hear, hear,' says Dennis.

Embarrassed, Aida picks up her coffee, spills a spot on her skirt. 'Damn,' she says, scrubbing at it with her sleeve. She notices the thin bones of Roland's thighs, the sharpness of his knees.

'Monopoly?' Dennis says. 'It isn't Christmas without Monopoly.'

'Monotony, he used to call it,' says Aida. 'Remember, Mummy?'

Clementine nods, eyes too bright, smile too tight, and there's silence while Dennis goes to fetch the game.

14

STARLING

He bolts the bathroom door and meets his own eyes in the mirror. Crowley! Fucking Hell! Screws his eyes shut, pictures the poor bastard, and his phantom hand feels the squeeze of hot, thin fingers. 'Keep up the good work, boys,' Crowley mumbled as he lay dying. Maybe his last words on earth.

Keep up the good work is what he wants to do. What he means to do. Christ Almighty. Without warning, all the lies come spewing out of him into the bog. When he pulls the chain, water rinses them away, and he stares at the printed trade name: *Venerable Crapper*. He snorts and tears come to his eyes. Edgar said their bog was called Venerable Crapper, but he never believed him.

He slinks onto the quiet landing, all hushed with muted lamplight. Back in his room, he crouches queasily against the wall. It's the mother's studio, a cold, blue room, with a high ceiling and a stink of turps. He'd hoped to stay in Edgar's room, which is just next door. Just through the wall. The mother did point it out – finger stroking the door – but she didn't open it.

Just the upstairs of this house is three or four times the size of his parents' two-up, two-down. On this part of the landing alone there are four doors all in a row: Aida's, Edgar's, the studio, the bathroom. On Edgar and Aida's doors hang nameplates, Aida's flowery, Edgar's blue with boats and sky. And that's just *part* of upstairs. To have so much *space*! To spend a childhood with mahogany banisters to slide down, as they did, Edgar told him – Aida one side, he the other – racing to the bottom. Envy gnaws: to grow up with all of this! But it wasn't all jam. Edgar said "Mummy" was more interested in painting than in her kids, and more interested in Aida than in him. He had said it as if he didn't care, but still, he had said it. Starling blinks, glimpsing a little lad in the doorway, hanging around, waiting to be noticed.

Earlier, the mother walked him round the house, pointing out her work, and that of a famous artist he's never heard of. He knows nothing about art, but can see that her paintings – "daubs", she calls them – are good. At least, they look like what they're meant to be, mainly flowers and fruit. What's the point of painting stuff like that? But one is really good: black-haired Edgar in sunshine, milk-haired Aida in shadow. They're exchanging glances, and she's caught something *live* about them. They look a proper handful.

Of course, he can't stay here. Roland fucking Crowley! What *is* he doing? Shouldn't have come. Should have taken the train north instead to surprise Mum. Not just surprise, delight. That's what he meant to do till he saw a bloke at St Pancras who reminded him of Edgar. Something came over him then, remembering how Mrs Everett begged him to come.

Hugging knees to chest, he groans. When they mistook him for Crowley, why the fuck didn't he put them right straight away? At first he was too bloody taken aback, dumbstruck, then it seemed too late. Didn't seem to matter all that much then, never thought he'd see them again. Edgar would knock the bloody daylights out of him if he knew. How stupidly moved he was when the mother said Edgar mentioned him in a letter. As if he would!

Crouched low on the floor, he makes himself as small as can be, groans into his kneecaps, stump trapped between thighs and chest, other arm tight round his shins, holding himself together. The Everetts might be snobs and boozers, but they are *Edgar's*, and they are kind. And *they* are grieving too. Did he think he could put things right by turning up here? Did he think he could come clean? It wasn't a lie at first. It wasn't his lie, nor his fault. It was their mistake. But by coming back, he's made it a lie, he's made it his fault. He pictures all the crap he's been coming out with all evening rushing down the Venerable Crapper's throat. Crapper. Yes. Crapper, that's what he is.

Leave. Wait a bit. Till they're all asleep, then go. Go home. See Mum. Please Mum. You can stay up there for good and all, you crapper. Stay where you belong.

*There once was a sweet whippersnapper.* Violent shivers now, malarial or is it just cold? Hard to tell, too much to drink, too much to eat, too much everything, too much, too much. *Whose bog was called Venerable Crapper.* Yanking a blanket from the bed, he huddles, crouched, waiting for the house to sleep before he makes his getaway. *He went off to war, to return home no more. And that was the end of the matter.*

---

The day after they mistook him for Crowley, he awoke feeling sick with himself, like there was a bloody great oily bird of some sort clinging to his heart. But it galvanised him too, made him determined to stop arsing about, wasting time. Demobbed now, nothing to stop him getting back to med school. So, he left the hostel that morning, set off down Catford High Street walking fast, a man with a mission.

Outside the phone box was a youngish bloke balanced on a crate, both legs gone, medals on his coat, a penny whistle sticking weirdly out of the mouth-hole of a red balaclava. *"Kiss me Goodnight, Sergeant Major"* he was tootling. It seemed a good omen, and Starling chucked him a penny. In the jungle, at the worst moments, Edgar and Horace used to launch into that one, mad grins on starved faces.

He went into the box and dialled. A girl's voice. 'Garstang Motors, good morning, how may I help you?'

'Would you put me onto Mr Garstang please?'

A crackling silence. '*Mr* Garstang? Do you mean *Mrs* Garstang?'

'No, Mr Garstang. Tell him it's Leonard Starling, will you?'

He heard, muffled, 'It's a bloke asking for Mr Garstang.' And there was a wait, before she came back on, clearing her throat and speaking more formally, 'I'm afraid I have to inform you that Mr Garstang passed away, a year past now. Heart,' she added.

He leant against the wall of the box. 'So, who's in charge?' The square of glass he was looking through steamed up, and the people walking past, the busker's red woollen balaclava, all turned to smear.

'Mr Garstang's brother-in-law Mr Bartlett's taken over the reins,' said the girl. 'Or should I say steering wheel?' A stifled giggle.

'Caller please insert another coin,' interrupted the operator, but Starling couldn't get his penny into the slot in time. 'Disconnecting you,' said the voice.

'*Please*,' he yelled, 'wait, I'm injured!' which startled the operator into giving him the moment he needed to get the penny in, the rest of his coins spilling onto the dirty floor.

'Put me on to Mr Bartlett please.' He crouched, receiver clamped under his chin, the cord only just long enough to allow his scrabble to scoop up the money.

'Putting you through.'

He commiserated with Mr Bartlett about the loss of his brother-in-law, before getting to the point. 'As you'll likely know I won the Garstang Medical Scholarship, due to start in September 1940, but I joined up. Mr Garstang was happy to defer the scholarship, said, "Be in touch the moment you get back, young man".'

He waited, but Mr Bartlett said nothing, so he went on. 'I was a POW. Far East. So only just back, you see? I'm phoning to confirm that I can take up the scholarship next year – before I re-register for med school. Don't want to jump the gun.'

Bartlett cleared his throat. 'Look here, young man...' A pause, the click of a lighter. 'As a matter of fact, this scholarship business has been a contentious issue. All well and good when trade's booming, but it hardly needs saying that these are thin times, thin times indeed.'

Starling stared through the glass at the beggar, still piping away.

'Whilst I respect all that Mr Garstang achieved in his time, what you must see is that there's a new man at the helm now, new start.'

Scratches on the glass, *PG loves GF*. The tune plays on and he thinks of Lammy's rich bass, his great grin. And how Edgar would throw back his head, laugh his donkey laugh.

'...And the scheme has been discontinued.'

'But not for those already *agreed,* surely?' The telephone box seemed to sink, that small square of concrete, and he went down with it as he spoke. 'In Mr Garstang's memory surely his current scholarship boys should continue?'

'Aye, and they are. But you haven't started, lad.'

'Because *I signed up*. I'd be almost through my training by now.' There's silence. 'If it wasn't for the war,' he finished lamely.

'If it wasn't for the war! Aye lad, well we could all say that. Now, new broom, clean sweep.' A woman's voice asked him if he was ready for coffee. 'New regime, so to speak, no fat you see, what with the economic state of play and Garstang's eccentric – *generosity*, let's call it – it's every man for himself, this day and age. I'm sure you understand.'

Starling dropped the receiver and left it hanging, stepped out into the raw morning. The beggar was still playing the same tune. The fucking rhythm of it got into his feet as he fled from the box. The sun was gone, and it was cold. Then what? Can't remember.

---

Now the clocks chime, all out of step. Doesn't it drive them mad? It's one o'clock on Christmas morning. So, that was the end of that. If Bartlett had come through, he'd have been on his way to being a doctor now, instead of being a... what? A disabled, unemployed ex-soldier like millions of others. A nobody. No, not nobody: a liar and a fraud.

Wait till you hear nothing for a bit, then scarper. Pressed against the wall, he nods off, jerks awake, listens to the noises of the house. Eventually he stands, makes for the door, but freezes when he hears a noise through the wall. Edgar's room. What's anyone doing in there? He strains to hear, even puts his ear against the wall, but there's nothing.

Once the clocks have finished striking two, he creeps out, stops by Edgar's door, peers at the painted sign, boats on blue water, birds in bluer sky. There'll never be another chance. He turns the handle, steps into the dark. Not quite dark, moonlight comes through the window. He stands with his head pressed against cold glass till his breath has fogged it over and then he turns, sniffs, trying to smell Edgar. When he flicks on the light he sees a shiny green eiderdown, a bookshelf, a Meccano crane, a chest of drawers. He kneels, opens each drawer, touching the folded pyjamas, vests, socks, pants. All clean, all waiting. In the wardrobe, more shirts, jackets, a tangle of ties. So many clothes! He touches everything, presses his face into rough and smooth cloth, snuffling for traces. He feels in the pockets of the trousers and jackets, but there's nothing. He studies the shelf of books, some medical – several that he has too – but more art books and poetry. Edgar used to recite poetry at night, kept him sane, he said. It was something they shared: Eliot, Hopkins, Yeats... And for Edgar especially, Hardy.

He takes a book, sits on the edge of the bed, lets it fall open where it wants to: *The Darkling Thrush*. Ah, he knows this one, had to learn it by heart at school. Memory rises to meet his mouthing of the words:

*An aged thrush, frail, gaunt, and small,*
*In blast-beruffled plume,*
*Had chosen thus to fling his soul,*
*Upon the growing gloom.*

The words set off detonations inside him; he closes the book and his eyes. The shivering has stopped. He takes off his shoes, lies back on the bed. A balsa-wood gull wobbles from the ceiling. Sleepiness comes over him, and he gets under the eiderdown. He'll rest, just for a bit, in Edgar's bed. When the clocks strike three, he'll hop it. The pillows are deep and soft, and gravity pulls him into the mattress, which is not too soft, it's just right, and he thinks of all the nights that Edgar slept here, all the dreams and all...

15
---

## AIDA

After church, the Christmas constitutional along the river path: unthinkable to do anything else, whatever the weather, which happens to be disappointingly mild for Christmas. The sky's watery, the breeze damp, the river stand-offishly green. Aida smooths her silky square scarf into the collar of her musquash. Beside her, Roland wears an army greatcoat, his cheap fedora tilted so that you can barely see his face.

The parents are walking ahead. 'What a *find* they are.' Her mother's voice drifts back. 'Even *Mr* Jackson – Frank – had his sleeves rolled up at the sink. Fancy!'

Daddy grunts as he skirts a puddle.

Aida raises her eyebrows at Roland, who grins disarmingly, dipping his chin. Of course he's not the lurker! But just to remove any niggle of doubt she will ask. Naturally, the answer will be no, and she'll be mortified – but then she's always putting her foot in things. Best to jump in with both of them and get it over with. Talking about putting her foot in it, she's broken a record today by doing so at the crack of dawn when she got up to visit the WC and was startled to find him at the top of the stairs, bag over his shoulder, very much in the attitude of "burglar with swag making getaway".

'Happy Christmas!' she said, and he whipped round so fast she was afraid he'd tumble downstairs.

'Same to you,' he said, stepping back from the brink.

'Not making off with the family silver, I hope?' she said, and then, 'Oh God, I don't mean that!' Flushing utterly beetroot. 'I mean what are you up to at this time? I don't mean "up to", I mean why are you up? I mean...'

Dennis rescued her by appearing on the landing, tying his dressing-gown cord and yawning. 'By Jove, you're up bright and early,' he said. 'Season's greetings, and all that.'

'Merry Christmas, Daddy.' She hugged him gratefully.

When she turned, Roland was slinking back into the studio. *Had* he been meaning to escape? He'd have been marooned in Seckbridge – no trains till tomorrow. Odd. She likes that – he's something different, unexpected, certainly – and a friend of Eddie's. As Eddie's sister, it's no more than her duty to befriend him. And he really is rather dishy. Not handsome exactly, earnest and speccy and so *slight*, small of skull, delicate of build. Like a bird – funny that he's called Crowley! Possibly, he's not terrifically *manly*. Behind the specs, rather smeared this morning, his dark, almost *Indian* eyes are soft and hurt, intelligent. And there's something about the empty shirtsleeve, stitched so neatly, that touches her heart. Perhaps he's shy? That could account for his urge to bolt. After all, he's spending this significant day, this first peacetime Christmas, with utter strangers – you can hardly blame him.

She points things out as they walk. He's not a chatter, but seems interested enough. Across the river there's Sutton Hoo, where the Viking ship was discovered, where she went on a trip from school. She tells him about the aunts, generally chatters on until a sudden yawn engulfs her and she crams her gloves against her mouth, yawning till her eyes are watering: terribly bad form.

'Tired?' Roland says.

'Sorry. Couldn't sleep,' she says. 'By the way, I saw your light on last night. Couldn't you?'

He gives her a sideways look. 'Don't sleep much,' he says.

Two grumpy girls in matching hideous crocheted hat-scarf-and-mitten sets stomp past, a few steps ahead of their parents. Aida laughs. 'Unwanted gifts, methinks!' she says, then feels a catch in her throat. Spotting these was something she and Edgar used to do on the Christmas constitutional. (You got one point for any obvious Christmas present, but five for an obviously unwanted one. Those girls would have scored her a ten.) Funny how Roland's presence seems to provoke these silly memories of Edgar, suppressed till now.

'By the way, were you about to bolt this morning?' she asks, but he refrains from answering.

She yawns again. 'Sorry!'

He smiles, a lovely smile that smites her, (smites!) like a shaft of light. She's feeling hazy and lazy after rather too much wine and a poor night's sleep. Normally she sleeps soundly in her childhood bed, but last night couldn't settle, aware of Edgar's empty room on the other side of the wall. And in the next room, Roland. After a sleepless stretch, counting back from a hundred in threes, remembering the words of poems – quite a lot of *Hiawatha* – tricks that usually work, she gave up, put on her dressing gown, and crept out onto the landing. All quiet. She went into Edgar's room, stood hugging herself in its chilly neatness. Never neat when Edgar was in it, now it has taken on the tidy air of a museum. The books, the balsa seagull that stirs in the slightest breeze, the Meccano crane he built when he was twelve and refused ever after to dismantle. His books, mostly medical or poetry; he wasn't one for novels. *"What's the point of a made-up story?"*

For several years, till they grew out of it, he and she had a Christmas ritual. She was posted to stay awake till the parents' bedtime, waiting for the creak of Daddy's feet, which came with a whisky smell and the weight and rustle of a bulky stocking arriving on the end of the bed. And she'd count to a hundred before creeping out, lugging her stocking to Edgar's room, shaking him awake. Somehow, he had no trouble falling asleep on Christmas Eve – which she could never understand. And they'd open their stockings together, her cold toes tucked into the cosiness of his covers, and then, with toffee or tangerine in their mouths, crayons and cars and doll's house furniture strewn across the bed, they'd snuggle down and sleep.

Last night she stood shivering and winding the winch of the crane, raising and lowering the string with its bale of matches that must have been dangling for fourteen years. On his desk stood a shiny anatomical model, a head and torso, that Edgar dubbed Norman, insisting it was male, despite it having no genitalia and an androgynous face.

'How do you know it isn't a girl?' she asked him once. He was sitting under a lamp, a textbook open on his desk, cramming. The model, standing on its shelf, caught the light glossily, looked halfway glamorous.

'Call it Norma if you want,' he said with a shrug.

'Maybe it's a *homosexual*,' she said, daringly, having only just learned the word.

'Homosexual doesn't mean not being a man,' he retorted.

'Hermaphrodite then?' she said, and he hmphed.

Norma is a becoming hermaphrodite with a mild, cheery expression and lustrous pink torso. You can remove the casing from half the head, to reveal the skull, eye socket, and a section of brain. And you can unclip the outer chest to see what's packed in beneath. Sometimes he'd let her unclip the ribs and remove the heart, the lungs, the liver, the spleen, the pancreas and all – but she could never fit them back again.

Last night, having a sudden brainwave, she carried the model downstairs, rolled it in a page of *The Times* and hid it behind the Christmas tree. It was on her way back up that she'd noticed a line of light under the studio door.

She catches his arm to steer him out of the way of a child wildly wobbling on a new bicycle, a father haring behind, bellowing, 'Stop, Susan! You'll end up in the bally brink!'(One point.)

She laughs. 'Eddie and I used to race our bikes along here,' she says, watching the father catch up with Susan before she tips into the river. They've stopped by a moored boat, a *putterer,* Daddy would call it, a dirty tub piled with crates and coils of rope. 'Eddie had a boat,' she says, 'just a tiny thing, *Harebell*, he loved that boat more than anything.'

'I thought he called it *Speedwell*?'

She hiccups a laugh. 'Crikey, you do know your stuff! Some blue flower anyway, and of course she was painted blue. He redid her every year. Always mucking about in her.'

In the angle between the moored boat and the bank float feathers, straw, a fishbone, all rainbowed by a sheen of oil.

He nods, but says nothing, walks on, eyes down, missing hand tucked protectively inside his coat. She's talking too much again. The parents are quite a way ahead now, pipe smoke billowing in Dennis's wake.

She manages to stay quiet. Interestingly, it's not the awkward kind of quiet that happens with Neville. She sighs. Before he left for Scotland, he gave her a wooden spoon with a thistle carved on its handle, tied with a tartan ribbon. She shouldn't have accepted it. But there has not yet been time or opportunity to let him – gently – down. Poor old Neville.

A swan glides past, a pure and almost startling white against the green water. She really must confront Roland about the lurking. No, *confront* is not the word. Just calmly bring it up. But how does one do that?

'Do you mind me asking about your hand?' she says instead, and quickly, 'Don't, please don't say if you don't want to...'

He untucks the arm from his coat, holds out his jacket sleeve, stitched across the absence. 'Crushed,' he says. 'We were dynamiting a ravine. I got off lightly. A couple of others were blasted to kingdom come.'

'Oh my God, I'm so sorry,' she says. She stops and stares at him, then turns and walks quickly, quailing inside, suddenly hot. She peels off her gloves and shoves them into her pockets.

'I wish it would snow,' she says desperately. 'It shouldn't be like this on Christmas Day, should it? Lord, I'm hot in this wretched fur.' She plucks at the musquash, feeling a babble rising. 'It's not very Christmassy is it? Not like a Christmas card. Where are the snowy cottages and reindeer? Where are the snowmen? Though I did see a robin earlier, but then you're always seeing robins, aren't you?' She presses her lips together. *Shut up.*

The tide is starting to ebb; mud glistens like chocolate blancmange. The parents are well ahead, and they are holding hands! Normally, the two of them scarcely touch. A display for Roland's benefit?

A heron clatters down, lands on a post in the water. Edgar had an odd passion for herons. It fidgets itself into position, cocks its head. To hunt for fish, of course, but it does seem to be trying to catch her eye. What if Edgar is sending her a message via the heron? What if he's actually inside it? A silvery feeling travels up her spine. *Don't be fanciful, Aida; there are always herons!*

'I wanted to ask you...' she begins, turning pointedly away from the bird.

He tilts the brim of his hat, waits.

'Someone has been... tailing me.' She cringes. Lord, what a way of putting it! *Tailing!* Like a third-rate spy movie.

He shifts from foot to foot, slides a finger beneath one of the lenses of his specs.

'I mean of course it *wasn't* you... *of course* it wasn't, but someone seemed to be following me, and it gave me the heebie-jeebies, though he seems to have stopped now in any case, and he might *not* have been following me anyway, it just seemed that way and he happened to look a bit like you, in build anyway, I didn't see anything else, so I have to ask, before we become friends, which I hope we will, you see that? I'm sorry.' Her face burns, and she can feel blotches rising on her neck. She catches his sleeve. 'Roland, I'm sorry. If you get to know me better, you'll realise what an absolute twerp I can be. Look, another robin!' she says desperately. She points at the little bird, which has landed on a gatepost. 'It only needs a sprig of holly in its mouth!'

They're approaching the end point of the walk, a platform jutting into the river, where ducks and geese gather clamourously to be fed. Feeding the birds is a vital part of the Christmas ritual.

'Listen.' She tugs his sleeve again. 'Can we forget I said that, please? *Please?* I really am the most colossal buffoon. Edgar always said...' But she tails off, seeing his expression, the way his face has gone the colour of cardboard. A great beast of a swan comes scything down, feet ploughing the water in front of it.

'*What?*' she says.

He hangs his head.

'It *was* you?' she shrieks, causing Clementine to peer back over her shoulder.

'I...' he begins, but nothing follows. He looks puzzled, dazed even, his eyes burning. 'Since I've been back I...'

But they're too near the parents now. Ducks and geese flap and squawk as Clementine flings crusts. Sparrows hop hopefully nearby, and Aida empties her own paper bag for them, stuffs it in her pocket and walks off. She goes to stand on the other side of Clementine, heart flustering, ears beating with blood. Dennis is monologuing about swans, the rise and fall of numbers, indeed statistics are available in the museum, if anyone cares to know. Once all the paper bags are empty, as is the tradition, they turn for home.

'Roast goose.' Dennis rubs his gloves together, smacks his lips.

'Now we've all worked up an appetite,' Clementine says.

Casting a look back at the brutish squawking geese, Aida takes her mother's arm, and pulls her on ahead. What on earth should she think? What excuse can there possibly be? Should she tell Mummy? No, not now. Don't upset her now. It will keep. And anyway, before she says anything to trigger Roland's banishment, she needs to understand. She deserves a proper explanation. Her mind boggles painfully to accept it: the lurker and Roland are one and the same? She has to force herself to tune in to Mummy, who's talking about poor old Murray-Hill. 'No more lessons for me,' she says sadly, 'not for the foreseeable future. Possibly never.'

'Oh Mummy! I'm sure that's not true. And anyway, you don't need lessons; you're brilliant as it is.' Aida squeezes her arm.

'I miss him most dreadfully,' is the startling reply, and they walk along in silence for a while.

'I didn't know you knew him all *that* well,' Aida says. 'I thought he was just your teacher.' She looks back at the two men, solid Daddy and slight Roland. The *lurker*.

They pass the heron, poised in absolute stillness on its post, and the boatyard where the *Speedwell* (or *Harebell*?) probably still huddles under a tarpaulin. They nod and exchange greetings with other families out for their Christmas constitutionals. Aida looks back over her shoulder again to see Dennis pointing something out to Roland, imparting some vital information, the history of the Deben barge, perhaps.

'What do you make of Roland?' Clementine asks suddenly.

'Seems nice enough.' Aida watches the muddy toes of her boots as she walks. 'Doesn't it seem a bit odd to you though, Mummy, the way he's attached himself to us? I mean Christmas of all days!'

'But I *invited* him, darling! He hasn't *attached* himself. In fact, I rather twisted his arm.'

'Did you?'

'I thought...' She sniffs and dabs at the corner of each eye with a finger of her glove. 'With... well you know... gone.'

'Edgar, you *can* say Edgar!'

'Oh *why*?' This is almost a wail. 'Why *him*? Why couldn't it have been – Roland for instance? His family was killed in the Blitz, no one would have missed him.' She stops, gasping and breathless. 'Oh, what a terrible thing to say!' She slaps at her own face with her glove.

'Mummy!' Aida grabs her hand. '*Don't.*' She turns to look back – the men seem safely deep in conversation. 'Come on,' she says. Although she despises people who say "buck up", she almost resorts to it. Today they must buck up, play the game, best foot forward, all that cheery guff. 'The more the merrier, I suppose,' she says. Come on, let's speed up and get spruced for lunch.'

Once she's changed, lipsticked, perfumed, she goes down to the sitting room for a sherry. A smell of roast goose permeates the house, making her stomach rumble. When she opens the sitting-room door, there's Roland alone, hunched by the fireplace, thin and miserable. He looks up and starts as she enters. She closes the door behind her and folds her arms.

'So?'

'Please.' He holds out his hand.

She stomps over to the fire. 'I need to know what the hell you were up to, and it had better be good,' she says. 'Otherwise, I'll tell them. I'll tell them you've been following me and scaring me, and Lord knows what Daddy will do then.'

'Oh *Aida*. Diddy...' He meets her eyes beseechingly.

'Don't dare call me that!'

He takes a breath, seems to stiffen his spine before he speaks. 'All right. I wanted to see you first, before I met the rest of the family. To meet you. Because I loved Edgar so much, and you two were close.'

*Loved.* Flames leap and crawl among the logs. Aida glances in the overmantel mirror at the back of his black hair, her own pale face, and staring eyes.

'Why didn't you *speak* to me then? Lord! All that hanging about like a stray dog!'

He exhales, runs his fingers through his hair.

'Go on,' she snaps.

'You see... can we sit?'

She flumps down onto the sofa, and he perches on the arm of Daddy's armchair. He leans forward, forearms on his thighs. One hand, one sewn cuff.

'Spit it out then.'

'Edgar talked about you all the time. I had this tin of drawings that he did, a tobacco tin, and he'd asked me to give them to you.'

'I know. I've seen it. Me personally, or the family?'

'Don't know for sure. It's not easy... I'm having trouble settling down, you see, acclimatising, even *thinking* straight. I keep doing, saying, things I don't mean; it's all a mess in here.' He knocks on his brow, as if it's a door.

Without offering him one, she reaches for a cigarette, fingers trembling as she lights it. 'Go on.' She draws in the first hit of smoke.

'At first, I thought to give you the tin, being nearer; that was my plan. But... I lost my nerve.'

She taps her cigarette on the rim of a cut glass ashtray, notices a trace of her coral lipstick on the paper. 'You must have lost it several times then,' she says dryly, 'before you most bizarrely found it, and turned up here.'

'I know it sounds...'

She crosses her legs and pulls on her cigarette. 'What an *utter* chump you are,' she says.

'I don't know why. I just could not seem to... and then I got the feeling I might be unnerving you.'

She snorts. 'Did you?'

'So, I gave up that plan, and came here.'

'You didn't think I might be "unnerved" when I saw you here too?'

He hangs his head. His thick black brows are drawn together, his fingers rake through his hair. 'I hoped you wouldn't recognise me. I never meant you any harm. Honestly Aida.' His eyes are huge and dark; he seems close to tears.

She lights him a cigarette, careful not to smudge it with her lipstick.

The door opens and Daddy enters, hair slicked back, smelling of Brylcreem. 'Not drinking yet!' he says. 'By Jove, we must put that right.' He lifts a decanter and a bottle. 'Roland, old chap? What's your poison?'

She watches Roland's thin face, the baby-smooth brow with its sharp widow's peak, the dark eyes under the lenses of his specs, and it's as if she can see right into him. She knows he doesn't really want a drink, but feels obliged to say, 'A Scotch, sir, please.' The ninny! She does wish he'd stop saying *sir*, though Daddy, of course, is lapping it up. There's an almost sore place inside her now where the anger was, sore on his behalf, the great, soft, utter clot. Wincing, smiling painfully, she shakes her head.

'Coming up!' Daddy rubs his hands and gets down to pouring the drinks.

## 16

## CLEMENTINE

Clementine hauls up the stairs, legs warping like Plasticine, an awful dragging in her innards, an awful tearing in her heart. What on earth possessed her to invite the wretched chap? And more to the point, what possessed him to come? Rather than help fill the gap, he's a constant reminder, salt in a wound. And it's clearly upset Aida. Dennis was infuriatingly right. An impulse was all it was, drunken, probably. No, not actually drunken, never drunken, but *loosened*, become uninhibited. And he should have realised that; he should have read the situation. Perhaps it's a class thing. He doesn't know the code. Oh, so, so, so much on the mind, so much. Edgar, Corin. Her hand strays to her abdomen, and this too.

She removes her skirt and blouse, dons her Christmas frock, worn on this day only for the past six years at least, shabby, mended from a candle burn, threadbare under the arms, but still her favourite. It's deep-pink shantung silk, looser round the hips and round the bust, now, than it was. Unwinding her plait, she captures stray wisps, pins it back into its crown-shape – stops to rest her arms midway. As she raises them again, she feels the silk give way. Damn. She should find another, but no, just keep your arms down. She sprays Shalimar on her neck and wrists – Dennis buys this for her every year (no doubt there's another bottle waiting under the tree) – and searches for the lipstick that compliments the dress. Coty, Peony Pink, her best lipstick, only the merest stub now – she's managed to last it the whole war – but it's nowhere to be found. She casts about her dressing table, scrabbles through a drawer of scissors, and tweezers and tubs of this and that, frowning. When last did she wear it? When did she last care what she looked like? Lately, she hasn't bothered much with lipstick except for a smear of Vaseline, perhaps, or of the serviceable tawny colour she found in Boots.

And then it comes back to her. The last time was the day of Corin's stroke. Perspiration beads her brow. Dabbing with a handkerchief she remembers, in a flash, that she was wearing her dreadful old gaberdine that day, a mild day, too mild for fur. The gaberdine, of course! The lipstick might be in its pocket. She hurries down to the cloakroom. And the key too! The studio key! If that's there, then she can retrieve Edgar's scraps. Scraps of Edgar himself is how, ridiculously, she's begun to think of them, and not an atom more of him must be lost. How could she have forgotten the gaberdine? Is she losing her marbles now, as well as everything else? All the searching for that wretched key and the gaberdine never even crossed her mind. She rustles through the coats: Aida's old green thing, Dennis's overcoat, golf stuff, a gardening jacket she uses for pottering, till she finds the gaberdine, and in its pocket – *oh, thank heavens!* – both the lipstick and the key. Over and over, she's rifled through all her other jackets, feeling down into the linings, tipping out her handbag, searching the car, even raking through the gravel of the drive. She sags against the coats with relief. The key is found! A Christmas miracle, she thinks, or near enough.

In the hallstand mirror she smears her lips peony, smudges

them together, and stretches a smile. If only she could go *now*. At the first opportunity she will. A few days after Corin's stroke she drove back to the studio, only to discover that the key was missing from her purse. That day's become a charcoal scribble in her mind, the deep throb of panic and fear, and the need to appear normal, though whatever "normal" is has begun to elude her. Whyever didn't the gaberdine cross her stupid mind? It's Dennis's fault, all his coats piled on top. He is a man of many coats, different weights of tweed and cashmere for golf, for visiting patients, for town, for travelling. Several times she tried – and failed – to gather the courage to ask Eleanor for access to the studio. Unlike Dennis, Eleanor has always known about the affair – it simply wasn't in Corin's nature to lie. Not *affair,* that makes it sound sordid. Eleanor was prepared to put up with them being together once a week (she had shut up shop on their sex life, as Corin used to say, hooting at the expression) on the understanding that it didn't disrupt the marriage. Now, a tacit protocol seems to have been established: Clem can ring occasionally and ask after Corin, and that is that. No visiting. And she hasn't dared ask for access to the studio.

And now that Dennis knows about her malady (no hiding it in the end) he treats her like an invalid, and she feels semi-captive. He tried to stop her walking this morning, but as she pointed out, Aida would have questioned it and Aida is not to be told, not yet, not till they have the whole picture. So, he held her hand as they walked, as if she was an invalid or an imbecile.

Now Clem, pull yourself together and get on with Christmas. Set an example for the girl. Everetts don't wallow; they put their best foot forward. If she's learned nothing else in all the years, she's learned that. What a state she was in after the Great War, allowing herself to collapse, to have an actual nervous breakdown when poor Edgar was born. That time is so hazy now she wonders if it *might* have been possible for her to pull herself together then, to snap out of it? But in any case, now she *can*. She *can* keep up a brave front. For appearances' sake, she can, and she will.

Before entering the sitting room, where Dennis's voice is chuntering on over the clink of glasses, she pauses. Marvellous roasty smells emanate from the kitchen; she will try and muster some appetite, some *joie de vivre*. Absolutely no wet-blanketness allowed today, Clementine.

'At last! What *have* you been doing?' Dennis is puffing on the fat cigar (*"Castella, rolled between a Cuban hussy's thighs, ha-ha!"*) that he always enjoys at Christmas. She accepts the proffered sherry, opens her mouth to smile, and feels it fill with smoke.

---

At lunch she watches Aida, who appears unusually fresh and pretty. The girl has an attractive face, though she twists her mouth and scowls too often, and she's so pale, pale eyes and skin and hair, paler than Clementine herself whose skin has – or had – an element of cream to give it a bloom. Not only does Aida seem to have got over her earlier grumpiness and accepted Roland's addition to the party, but she's acquired a sort of glow, smiling away, eyes lit up – eyes on Roland. *Hmmm*. Roland himself is subdued, polite, clearly ill at ease. He eats very sparingly, poor young fellow. Perhaps after all, it's not such a bad thing to have him here?

The food is superb; Bless the Jacksons, bless Dennis's golf club spiv. They pull crackers, don paper hats, and eased by wine, the conversation flows like a stream over an aqueduct, smooth and frictionless, above an abyss. All right if no one looks down. Even the pudding, which was not quite the standard Christmas pudding (impossible to get the fruit), is tasty enough: a thick black lump of something involving prunes, jauntily sprigged with holly. By the time lunch is over, and the Jacksons have gone home for their own Christmas, her head aches and her cheeks are fatigued from so much smiling.

In the sitting room Dennis rescues the fire and twiddles with the wireless: time for the King. Not until after the King's speech are presents exchanged. The Everett way. How the children used to hate this wait, chafing and fidgeting every year until – to Dennis's disgust – she would relent and give them each one gift to unwrap before lunch.

In a cupboard upstairs are four years' worth of presents wrapped for Edgar, saved for his homecoming. Each Christmas she sent socks and tins of Spam and pears, jars of Marmite, useful things (never received), keeping back the real presents for his homecoming. It's becoming almost agony now, to keep a smile on her face. The muscles are beginning to cramp. She presses a finger into each cheek to help them rise, to drag up the corners of her lips.

They all stand and raise glasses as the King begins to speak. Dennis solemn – appearing, as he always does, almost liable to salute – the young ones going along with it. Aida adopts a dreadfully arch expression, which does her no favours. And then they all sit to listen. As the speech crackles out into the room, Clem finds herself unexpectedly moved. Tears spring to her eyes, as the King draws to his conclusion. 'This Christmas is a real homecoming for us all – a return to a world in which the homely, friendly things of life can again be ours.'

A spasm of grief twists inside her and she dabs her eyes, gulps back the brandy.

'Hear, hear,' says Dennis, voice choked, and Clem smiles at him, feeling a rare pang of fondness.

'*Now* can we have the presents?' says Aida, and Clem and

Dennis laugh. Bless Aida; it's the tradition that, after enduring the speech, she makes this demand.

Aida hands out the presents: for Clementine, a pretty scarf, some pearl studs, Shalimar. Aida seems delighted with a new cardigan, talcum powder, stockings, the latest Agatha Christie and a pair of rather ghastly porcelain geese (chosen by Dennis); Dennis gets his usual socks and gloves, and an Evelyn Waugh from Aida. Roland appears startled when handed his present, a fountain pen (gifted to Dennis by a grateful patient). The young man weighs the silver-barrelled pen between finger and thumb (thank heaven he's still in possession of his right one) gives it an experimental wiggle, as if signing his name in the air.

'I'm sorry,' he says, 'for not bringing presents.'

'Don't be daft, old man,' says Dennis magnanimously.

'What's that behind the tree?' Clem notices a bulky, newspaper-wrapped object. 'Where on earth did *that* come from?'

Aida jumps up. 'It's to Roland from E – I mean from all of us,' she says and busies herself lugging it out and thrusting it at Roland, but she's clumsy and the thing slips out of its wrappings and drops, scattering heart, liver, lungs and ribs. The emptied anatomical model lies face-up on the carpet mildly smiling.

Gorge rises to Clem's throat. She's always loathed the thing. Dennis bought it for Edgar as a boy, in his campaign to turn him towards medicine. That year the children squabbled all through lunch about whether it was male or female. The torso ended prudishly above the groin so you couldn't tell. When Aida said the word "genitalia" at the table, Dennis almost had a conniption, knocking over his glass of wine, rising horrified from his seat, paper crown askew. 'Genitalia at Christmas luncheon!' he'd bellowed, sending the children into stitches. They liked to quote this back to him when he was being his most stuffed-shirtish.

Chalky-faced, Dennis smooths his moustache, but says nothing, and Clem rather agrees. It's a colossal cheek for Aida to gift it to Roland without discussion; besides, a qualified doctor hardly needs such a childishly rudimentary learning aid. It might even be construed as an insult. Dennis stands to pour another brandy, lifting the bottle to each. Only Clem accepts. Really, it does help smooth the edges.

'Thank you.' Roland sends his gaze to each of them in turn, almost ludicrously sincere, those dark, foreign-looking eyes.

'Eddie would want you to have it.' Aida kneels to scoop up the organs and tries to fit them back in. Roland says, 'No, I think you have to get the liver in first. Look.' He drops to his knees on the hearth rug beside her, and Clem and Dennis exchange pained glances at the two of them, the fair and the dark heads so close together.

'Look, this comes off too.' Aida lifts a section of the face and pops out an eye, revealing the empty socket. Sharply, Clem snaps her gaze away.

'Anyone for Monopoly?' says Dennis.

'Perhaps later,' says Clem.

'In that case.' He stands and yawns hugely, beating his hand against his mouth like a Red Indian. 'A spot of postprandial shut-eye would fit the bill.'

'Would you mind,' says Roland, 'if I follow suit?'

'No dear, you go and lie down,' Clem says, relieved. She looks at Aida, hoping she might buzz off somewhere too, so that she can slip out in the car, make a dash to the studio, be back before she's missed.

But, 'Shall we make a start on the washing up?' Aida says, when they're gone.

'The Jacksons will deal with that tomorrow.'

'Yes, but Mummy, if you want to keep them, you mustn't

treat them like skivvies. I'm sure they'd appreciate it if we at least made a start.'

Clem groans. Of course, she's right. 'Perhaps later on.'

'Or leave it for Daddy?' Aida grins at her own preposterous suggestion.

They sit in the quiet for a moment, the only sounds the ticking clock, a creak and flutter from the settling fire.

The anatomical model stands beside the hearth. Clem gestures. 'You might have consulted us.'

'I thought you hated it?'

'Yes, but it was...'

'*Edgar's,* yes. But Mummy, he isn't *here* anymore. He wouldn't mind Roland having it.'

Clem focusses on the end of a glowing log, almost white hot, watching the spidery lines where the wood will soon disintegrate. She's never tried to paint fire – it would be a technical challenge to capture that constant movement and change. Corin would be able to – or would have been able. She tries to remember if he ever painted fire. Perhaps a distant bonfire? Yes, in an early painting of the Bawdsey marshes. The end of the log crumbles, whitened pieces flaking away, causing a ribbon of sparks to flutter up the chimney.

The two women are quiet for a lulling moment till Aida asks, 'Can I have another look at Eddie's tin?'

Clem closes her eyes; it was only a matter of time before the girl asked, of course. She sighs. 'I took it to show Corin – Sir Murray-Hill,' she says, 'and that was when he had his stroke. In the panic, I'm afraid it got left behind.'

Aida sits forward sharply. 'Lord, Mummy! You were actually *there* when he had his stroke? Good golly!'

Clem swallows hard. She removes her paper hat, and screws it into a ball, watching her knuckles pop out like ivory marbles. She forces her hands to soften.

'But surely you've asked for them back?'

'I don't feel I decently *can,* with all Lady Murray-Hill's got to deal with.'

'But why should *she* mind?' Aida's voice has gone shrill. In one smooth movement she stands up, and arms folded, looks down at Clem. Her paper crown is round her neck. 'What does Daddy say?'

'Nothing. You know what's he's like. I haven't mentioned it.' She does count herself lucky that Dennis has never asked to see the pieces. Sometimes his pragmatism works beautifully in her favour. To him they will be nothing to go getting maudlin over.

'We have to get them back!'

'I *know,*' she murmurs. 'I would have gone and got them, but I lost the key to the studio. And then this morning, as luck would have it, I found it.'

'You have a *key* to Sir Murray-Hill's studio? Why?'

'It's a spare in case he got locked out or something. Can you put another log on the fire, darling?'

Aida eyes her sceptically. 'Why *you,* though? It's miles away. And you don't know each other *that* well, do you?'

'Well, anyway. The log?'

Aida picks one from the basket and throws it carelessly into the hearth, causing a tumble, a dimming of the blaze. 'It'll catch in a minute,' she says, hopefully. The two women sit staring at the screwed-up paper on the floor: the presents, glasses, ashtrays, the face of the model, with its sickly smile.

'You could throw some of this mess on,' Clem says.

Aida begins gathering and screwing paper into balls. She rips off her paper hat and throws that on too. 'Well, since you've found the key, why don't we go now?'

'Daddy wouldn't like it. I thought I'd slip out tomorrow.'

'No, Mummy, *now.* Or else *I'll* go. Give me the key; remind me where it is.'

Clem looks up into her determined face, at the familiar set of her jaw. Aida always got her way as a child – still does. 'I might be a bit too tipsy to drive,' she says.

'Then I'll drive. I'm actually better at driving after a drink.'

Clem hauls herself up. It is an idea, Aida a sort of alibi, forcing her hand. 'We can say we went out for some fresh air.' She follows Aida out into the chilly hall where they pull on outdoor shoes and coats.

'Why not simply tell the *truth*?' Aida says as they step out into the fresh dark chill. She gets into the driving seat and starts the engine.

'I think Daddy might find it a bit *rum* that I've got a key,' Clem says carefully, lowering herself onto the chilly leather seat. 'And it *is* a bit odd now I come to think of it.' She manages a strained laugh. 'I really can't remember how it came about. There must have been some occasion, and then we forgot all about it.' She turns away from Aida's sceptical eyes to peer out at the lit-up flashes of beech trunk and gatepost as they turn onto the dark road.

'Yes, but why–'

'I'm thinking you might have rather a soft spot for Roland,' Clem deflects, and Aida shuts up, swings the car out onto the deserted road.

'He's a darn sight better than Brian Burk,' Clem says.

Aida laughs. 'God, Mummy! That's not saying much!'

'I'm glad you didn't settle for him!'

'Fat chance!' She changes gear confidently. Driving ambulances in the war has given her an easy, nonchalant driving style that Clem envies. 'Pompous arse.'

'Diddy!'

'Well he was, wasn't he, even then? Lord knows what he must be like now.' She looks over her shoulder and turns. 'I expect he was *born* middle-aged. Anyway, I don't know if I'll "settle for" anyone.'

'Of course you will.'

They skim along the dark empty main road; here and there is a glimpse of lit-up Christmas trees.

'Anyway, I've only just met Roland,' Aida says.

'You seemed very anti this morning.'

'Which way is it now?'

'Straight along and turn left... That's it.'

'We might have got off on the wrong foot.'

'The wrong foot? How? Stop along there.'

'Here?' Aida brakes by the dark bulk of the warehouse building and jumps from the car. Clem tilts back her head. Thin moonlight filters through river mist, glints on the damp wooden wall.

'Come on, Mummy.'

Clem gets the torch from the boot of her car. Aida shines the torch as they go up the dark rickety stairs, and on the keyhole as Clem unlocks the door.

'Gosh, we're like burglars!' Aida says.

'Shhh.'

They make their tentative way up the stairs. And when they reach the studio Clem clicks the light switch, but nothing happens. Must have been cut off. Aida swings the beam, slicing through the darkness. 'There's nothing here,' she says. Clem, breathing in the ghost of the smells of turps and linseed, has already seen. The long space is empty; a thinner darkness shows the open skylight. The space is utterly freezing and dark and empty, and it stinks of cat.

'Someone must have cleared it!' Aida says. 'What a pong though! Yuck.'

'Shhh,' says Clem. She wants to listen, to experience the space, but Aida *will* fidget and chatter on as always.

'Why shhh? There's no one here! Look, let's drive to the Murray-Hills now we're out. And explain. I could go to the door if you don't want to. Say "Happy Christmas, and can we have Eddie's drawings back?" Why should *they* want them?'

There comes a touch against Clem's shin, and she jumps. 'Give me the torch.' And when she shines it downwards, there at her feet is an emaciated Pablo, mewing silently.

'Oh my God,' says Aida. 'Look at the poor thing.'

'Must have got shut in.'

'We'll have to take him.'

'I don't know.' But Clementine stoops to lift the creature, who was such a grand cat but weighs almost nothing now, whose fur is cold against her face, and he sets up a loud mechanical purr.

'We'll take him home and give him some goose,' Aida decides. '*After* we've been to see the Murray-Hills.'

'No.' Clem makes her voice firm. '*Not* on Christmas Day.'

Aida tuts and sighs. 'But we can take the cat?'

'I suppose we must.'

Aida reaches for Pablo, and gives the torch to Clem, slashing light through emptiness again.

'All right then. But we'll go tomorrow?' Aida nags. 'Promise?'

Clem shines the torch around. Everything gone: the paintings, the easels, the furniture. Left are splashes of paint on the floor, a cleaner space where the sofa used to be. Under the cat-stink, the ghost of linseed and turps; wetness glistens where rain has dripped through the open skylight onto a scatter of bones and feathers. Pablo must have been out on the roof, catching birds. The building's too high for him to have jumped from the roof, so he was trapped. Poor Corin; he must surely wonder what became of him.

'Come on then, Mummy, let's get this poor puss home.'

'One minute.' Clem closes her eyes to be here for this one last moment. This studio is more to her than just a room. It's where, for more than twenty years, the realest, most natural and passionate part of her has lived. And now that is all over. If Aida were not here, she'd sink to the floor and wail.

But Aida's already making for the stairs. Clem follows her daughter down, locks the door for the last time, and into her pocket she drops the useless key.

## 17

## AIDA

Thank God that's over. The first Christmas without. Over and done with. Only Boxing Day to get through, then back to London. Still dressed, she flops onto her bed, shoes on, toes pointing at the ceiling like the toes of an effigy. Daft thought. Sitting up, she kicks off her shoes and falls back again, fingers plucking at tufts of candlewick. That poor starved cat! It might have died if they hadn't rescued it. A sweet kitty, skin and bone, though... like someone else she knows. A grin stretches her face, a peculiar sensation when she's flat on her back. Supine grinning. Fancy a cat living at The Beeches! Daddy never allowed pets, though she'd have murdered for a dog. Eddie too. They campaigned for years to no avail. Once they kept secret mice, once they were allowed stick insects, but the jar got overturned, invisible eggs scattered in the carpet and for weeks, tiny insects turned up in the folds of the curtains, clinging to the leaf-patterned wallpaper on the landing.

'Just a stray we found on our walk,' Mummy said, when they arrived home with the yowling Pablo, and shot Aida such a look that she bit her tongue. *Why lie?* Mummy drank steadily for the rest of the evening, an evening that concluded with a game of charades, such a mistake to insist on going through the motions like that. Eddie used to excel at charades, revelled in dressing up, was a hilarious mime and mimic. Poor Roland though, clearly there's not a theatrical bone in his body. He's too shy, *too honest* for play-acting. Too honest altogether. After all, he *could* have lied. If he'd denied being the lurker, she'd have believed him, was all too eager to believe him. Those eyes, so solemn, like the eyes of a bushbaby, designed by Mother Nature to tug at your heartstrings. Though there's no design to *him*. He's just what he is. His attempt to act out "Many a slip 'twixt cup and lip" was excruciating.

Too vulnerable, too honest, too nice. NO. Do not even consider it, Aida.

She swings her legs round to sit up. It's chilly in the bedroom. Mummy was three sheets to the wind of course – ha! That would be a good one to act out, she wouldn't have had to do a thing! – and Daddy steered her upstairs at ten o'clock. Whatever must Roland have thought? As if with relief that the day was over (surely an ordeal for him too) he followed them upstairs, disappointing Aida, who wasn't in the least bit tired. Or only tired of the charades. But ha! Hadn't the whole bloody day been a charade?

She lights a cigarette. Smoking in the bedroom is forbidden, or was, but there seems no point in petty rules like that anymore. Exhaling smoke brings a whoosh of sadness, and along with it a curious stab of crossness. By dying and doing it so ridiculously late in the war, when it was all *over* in Europe for God's sake, Eddie has spoiled Christmas for ever. Spoiled everything for ever. Will there *ever* be a year when his absence doesn't scream? When they'll feel properly light-hearted again? And it's not just happening in this house. All over the country, all over Europe, all over the world, people will have spent the day trying to celebrate around a void.

Her loot is piled on the chest of drawers. Shame Roland didn't bring anything – she'd like to have something from him. Edgar might have brought back exotic presents from the East, silk scarves, curved-up slippers, opium pipes? She blows out a sad plume of smoke.

The geese stand back-to-back. *Really, Daddy!* Designed for a sitting-room mantelpiece in a home she has yet even to imagine. They're too fragile to take back to London, wouldn't last five minutes anyway; she's always smashing things. Butterfingers. She turns them to face each other. Gormless expressions. Probably cost a bomb. Daddy will have called in at the little antique place in town, half-cut after golf, bought the first thing he saw. Wherever they stand in future, these gormless geese will remind her of this: the first Christmas since.

Will Roland stay in their lives? He evokes in her the most alarming feeling of tenderness, even *motherliness,* and that's not something she's accustomed to feeling for humans. Cats, maybe. How satisfying it was to rescue the artist's cat. Pablo, ha! She pulls her nightdress from under her pillow, silky flesh-coloured stuff with ecru lace. But the material is slick and cold to the touch, causes a shiver. It's comfort she needs tonight so she puts on a pair of Eddie's pyjamas instead, just like the ones she wears in London – winter pyjamas, thick, soft winceyette with a pale blue and white stripe. She pulls the cord tight round her waist, rolls up the sleeves. Strangely, the legs are not too long – though Eddie was taller, he had a longer body and shorter legs. Once, as children, they stripped and stood in front of the parents' wardrobe mirror to compare their bodies. Eddie's skin was yellow and pink, his tummy round, chest broad, legs short and sturdy while she was long-legged, thin, her skin blue-white. And of course, between the legs there was the greatest difference. Solemnly they took turns to kneel and examine one other. She was privately relieved not to have such untidy protuberances. He said she had a sideways smile.

Now she puts on her dressing gown and slippers, creeps downstairs to warm some milk. Light still showing under Roland's door. Is he reading? What does he read? She'll start the Christie tonight. Nothing like a cosy murder to send you off. Warm milk and a new book with its new smell. Pablo, shut in the kitchen, winds round her ankles, his purr incredibly loud. She pours him a saucer of milk. On her way back upstairs, she pauses outside the studio. Still the light, but not a sound. She's tempted to knock... but no. All down the landing she can hear the rumble of Daddy's snore. However does Mummy stick it?

Back in bed, she pulls the lamp closer, and snuggles childishly against her pillows with the milk and a rubbery slab of prune pudding filched from the pantry. It's not exactly *lovely*, but it's sweet and comforting. She chews and slurps and opens the book, but after a chapter or two, puts it down; there's nothing *wrong* with it, the usual set-up of suspects-to-be on the lead-up to a murder, but her mind won't latch on. It skitters about, glaringly wide awake. She drains the milk, picks at the skin that clings to the rim of the cup. Sleeping is *hard*. The falling-off part. Once she's dropped off she can sleep for England; it's letting go that's the problem. Often, just as she gets to the brink, she springs awake again, heart pounding. "Go over every detail of your day" is a trick someone told her, "remember every tedious detail and *bore* yourself to sleep". But she doesn't want to do that tonight. She tries *Hiawatha... but admit it, Aida, you're too aware of Roland, only two walls away, with only Edgar's empty bedroom between you like a sort of chaperone.* Beside a man, curiously, she can sleep like a baby. The American slotted in so well behind her, his long body a hot bolster, his arm pinning her down till she felt the safest she's ever felt.

Roland intrigues her. Might as well admit it. Even the lurking is fascinating. He's a puzzle. A qualified, experienced doctor, who looks about twelve. (Be fair, eighteen!) She snorts. No, but he looks very young; perhaps it's an effect of starvation? The lurker! (His explanation more or less convinced.) He's a pal of Edgar's; that trumps everything.

She wriggles across the bed, against the resistance of the tight-tucked sheet, nearer the wall of Eddie's room. As children they used to tap messages to each other in morse code. Can she remember it now? Absent-mindedly she taps E.D.G.A.R. Weirdly there's been not a single tear all day. Could she weep now? She tries, but her eyes stay dry.

And then she stiffens, hearing a creak, sits up, straining her ears. There's movement in Eddie's room! She springs up, grabs her dressing gown, goes out onto the landing and listens. Nothing – but light shows under the door and when she opens it there sits Roland, fully dressed but for his shoes, on Edgar's bed.

'How dare you!' she hisses. 'Get out.'

He looks up at her dazedly, blinking his bushbaby eyes, stands up, replacing his specs, pushing back his hair.

'Sorry,' he says. 'Just wanted...'

'What? Wanted what?' But he looks so unutterably lost that her temper fizzles out. 'What? A good snoop?' He seems unable to speak. Softly, she closes the door behind her.

'I wasn't snooping,' he says.

'First a lurker now a spy!' Shaking her head, she fights a smile. 'You really are the most colossal idiot, aren't you?'

'I... guilty as charged,' he says. His sudden grin is unexpectedly lovely. He does look so *very* young, so very thin.

'Why are you *dressed*?' she says.

He shrugs.

'You sleep in your clothes?'

'Sometimes.'

'Lord!' She wanders across to Edgar's crane. 'Did *you* have Meccano?' She winds the winch to make the bale of matchsticks rise.

'I had a little set, once. Nothing like that though.'

Silence, but for a faint mechanical squeak as she lowers the bale.

'He made this when he was about twelve. He was so proud he'd never take it apart.'

'Will you tell me more about him? As a lad,' says Roland.

She turns, noticing the silky skin of his neck above his collar. 'Like what?'

'Don't care. Anything.'

She kneels to lug a box of sketchbooks out from under the bed, sits beside him, opens one. 'Oh crikey, look! It's me!' A page of tiny sketches of herself in different poses. The day comes back to her. He was driving her crazy, following her about with his pencils. 'I must have been nine or ten. Here's me fishing, skipping, just standing – look how the wind's blowing my hair.' They'd been on holiday in Norfolk, a warm breeze, seals on the sand. And yes, sure enough, she turns the page to reveal seals and boats, the parents in the distance, herself again in profile carrying a bucket and spade, dress tucked into her knickers.

She would never have had the courage to look at these on her own, but showing them to Roland makes it possible and, seeing through his eyes, she's proud – amazed at how good they are. Some of the simplest sketches are just a line or two, and yet the way they suggest movement is almost magical.

Roland reaches across her to turn the page. Fish in a bucket. A sea urchin. A starfish, seaweed, a mermaid's purse. The fingers of his right hand are beautifully slim and sensitive. But the left ones are gone, the whole hand, gone. Whatever must that feel like? Wincing, she regards her own soft hands, the nails messily painted a peachy pink. She passes the sketchbook to him and watches him continue to flick through: boats, birds, trees, a sketch of Mummy at her easel, pages of clouds, a flying kite.

'He never wanted to be a doctor, you know,' she says, round a sudden lump in her throat. 'But Daddy wouldn't hear of him going to art school. Oh yes, he had to join the family firm. Damn Mummy for losing those sketches.'

'What?'

'Yes, the ones you delivered. She took them to show someone and forgot them.'

'*Forgot* them?'

'Well, not forgot, but...' She notices his sharp cheekbone ridges, the hollows shadowed under the bleak lightbulb. The tender feeling isn't exactly lust; it feels more nuanced than that. His lips are finely shaped, there's almost a cupid's bow. And on his chin, the dimple. *What would it be like to kiss him?* The thought startles her. 'Actually, Mummy and I went out to try and get them back when you were having your postprandial, but no luck.'

'Oh?'

'We *will* though. Don't worry.'

He shrugs.

'Anyway, there are loads more sketchbooks here. Tomorrow, we'll get them out, shall we? Have a proper look?'

She feels him shudder, becomes aware of his leg close to hers on the bed. Through the twill of his trousers his thigh bones are thin as walking sticks. 'Did Edgar ever get this thin?' She puts a hand on his knee, making him jolt with shock.

'Sorry.' She pulls it away.

Silence. His socks are navy-blue wool, mended and worn through again to reveal a sharp edge of toenail. Someone darned them and needs to darn them again. She wonders who.

'An ant,' he says.

'Sorry?' She thinks for a daft moment that he said, "an aunt", that he was reading her mind.

'An ant got in the tin with the sketches.'

'I know.'

'Got everywhere, the buggers. Ants and God knows what else, flying things, biting things. Swarms sometimes so you couldn't see, in your lashes, in your eyes.' He takes off his specs, scrubs his fist so hard against his face that she winces for him.

'Lord,' she says softly. She can sense him trying not to shiver. 'You should get to bed. Hot water bottle?'

But he hunches over his knees, and she can hear a frantic clicking in his throat. She's tempted to put her arm round his shoulders but doesn't dare.

'The nights are the worst,' he mutters. 'The bed's too soft and the dark too... *dark*... and when I start to drop off, I never know... I...' He turns his head to send her a fearful look. 'I don't want to *scream*.'

She twists a finger in her hair until it hurts. What to say? What can she do to make him feel better? She goes to Eddie's wardrobe, hesitates for just a moment before opening the door. There are his clothes: cricket whites, old school blazer, flannels and twills, and tweeds, all expecting him to wear them again. Poor ignorant clothes. They don't know. From the bottom she brings out his slippers and, overcome by an impulse, kneels and lifts each of Roland's feet to slide the slippers on. They are moccasin-style suede slippers, fur-lined, worn shiny at the heels and toes, worn to the shape of Edgar's feet, bigger and wider than Roland's. He says nothing. She's about to make a quip about how ludicrously biblical she feels in this position, but when she looks up his eyes are closed.

'Why don't we creep down and raid the kitchen?' She scrambles to her feet. 'That's what we used to do if we both couldn't sleep, me and Eddie.'

He opens his eyes and blinks. Looks blankly at her.

'Come on!' She pulls him to his feet, and they creep past the snores and tutting clocks, downstairs to the kitchen, which is warm from the range. She forages in the larder, pulls out leftover goose and roast potatoes, and the rubbery pudding, black and shiny as tarmac. 'Warm milk?' she says. 'Or cocoa, or tea – or whisky?'

He looks like someone waking from a dream. 'Your mum brought me in here when I came before,' he says. 'She was trying to make a pie.'

'She told me. She can't cook for toffee. Shameful, isn't it? To depend on other people, in this day and age. Sit down.'

'Can *you* cook?' he asks.

'Well, not really. But I intend to learn. When I... if I ever have a family, I will do it *all* myself. Cooking, cleaning, all of it. I might not *even* have a nursemaid.' She's surprised when he laughs, and there it is, Eddie's laugh, a sort of seesaw bray.

'What's so funny?'

He shakes his head.

But of course, he won't have had a nursemaid. And women of his class did for themselves without a second thought. Well done, Aida; foot in mouth again.

'Scotch,' he says.

She goes through to the sitting room where, in the faint gleam of the fire, Norman/Norma smiles benignly. She pours two tumblers from the decanter and carries them back.

He sips the whisky, light reflecting in the lenses of his specs so she can't properly see his eyes.

She picks up a crunchy roast potato; oh they are delicious cold.

'I really shouldn't wear his slippers,' he says. 'What would your... your folks think?'

She shrugs.

'Anyway, they're too big.' He shuffles his feet around to demonstrate.

'Up to you. I'm in his pyjamas.'

He stares at her over the rim of his glass.

'I find it comforting to wear them.' She flushes under his intense scrutiny.

'Can I see?' he says.

She sticks a leg out.

'No. I mean all of them.'

'All of the pyjamas?'

He nods, eyes huge and grave, and she gives a nervous giggle. 'Don't you think that sounds rather... I don't know... lurkerish?'

'No!' He half laughs and bangs down his whisky glass.

'Shhh.'

'I mean I want to see the *pyjamas,* not you.'

'Thanks very much!'

'Sorry, that sounds...'

'Crikey, this is weird.' She laughs warily. The whisky is making scrambled egg of her brain. She rarely drinks it, and this is the proper stuff, full strength.

'What I mean is...' he starts but gives up.

She pulls off a greasy shred of goose. 'Aren't you going to eat anything?'

'It's nice to be near his things, his family, his... *world.*'

She ponders this. 'Of course. Though for the past few years, it *hasn't* actually been his world, has it? *You've* been more his world than us.'

'But that wasn't real life.' A frown etches intense lines between his brows. 'It was what we had to survive to get *back* to real life.'

Goose slides down her throat, with the burn of whisky. 'Which not all of you did,' she points out miserably.

He stares into his glass, which is already empty.

'Another?' She dashes out and into the hall, pauses to take a deep breath. Holly round the hall-stand mirror, a Christmas card toppled to the floor. She *could* cry now, she could howl, but at the same time, exhilaration blasts through her. Such a strange brew of feelings she can hardly contain them. Her heart patters. She's *excited*. In the sitting room the Christmas tree looms darkly against the wall. Norma/n beams. She sloshes whisky, and the peaty smell catches in her throat.

'Let's do a deal.' She hands Roland his drink. 'I'll tell you about Edgar before the war, and you can tell me what you knew of him in, in the *prison camp*.' She winces at the prissy way these words come out.

'You don't want to know.'

'But I *do*. I *really* do. Look, I'll go first.' She feels silly now but obliged to continue. She cuts a tiny slice of pudding – doesn't really want it – divides it into minute pieces. 'But I don't know where to start.' The whisky smells repulsive now. She pushes the glass away, runs a fingernail down a groove in the wooden table, searching for something to say. 'He was my best friend,' she says, 'odd thing to say about one's brother, but it was true. Daddy was hard on him, expecting much more of him than he did of me, not really approving of him or ever praising him when he was always praising me. And I was the naughty one. I deserved not to be approved of sometimes! But he didn't hold it against me. Some brothers would. Oh Lord, I need a ciggie. You?' She runs through to the sitting room again, fetches some, hurries back. Moving helps use up her fidgety energy. *Fidget britches,* they used to call her, *tomboy, little madam*.

'It's as if,' she says as she bursts back into the kitchen, 'In a queer sort of way, it was more like I was the boy, and he was the girl.' She lights the ciggies, and hands him one.

'Oh, I did *love* him so much. How am I going to live all the rest of my life without my brother?' Her voice mangles, a tear escapes and she scrubs it away with her fist, pulls on the cigarette till the end flares. 'All right, that was my side of the deal.' She brings a hanky from her dressing-gown pocket and dabs at her eyes. 'You tell me something now.'

18
---

## STARLING

Gorge rises in his throat as he stares into the greasy cavity of the goose. Inside Edgar's slippers his toes clutch at flattened fur. The way she's sucking in smoke as if it's oxygen makes him queasy. She stands in front of him, too close. Is she flirting or just being natural? Think of the skin under the pyjamas. A girl's skin, a girl's forked body. The chair hurts the bones of his pelvis. He stands, moves away from her, goes to the stove, a massive iron thing, squats down with his back to it. The warmth presses into his spine and his hips sigh with relief. He slides further down into a froggy squat, hoping to Christ he doesn't fart.

'You all right down there?' She hands down his plate with its scraps of goose, his whisky.

'We got used to squatting or sitting cross-legged,' he says. 'No chairs.' And as if to demonstrate, he sinks right down and crosses his legs, Buddha-like.

'Golly. Yes, you see that's just the sort of thing I want to know.' She drags her chair closer and sits down. Her slippers are velvet, smart, red and gold. He thinks of Celia's tatty ones. Celia the pretty fox. Lucky Horace, with her to come home to. Aida looks more like a hawk, the way she's peering at him over her beaky nose. A hawk hovering over a shrew.

She offers him a smoke, but he shakes his head. She lights one for herself. 'What were the rations like?' she asks.

'Not much... Rice, lizard...'

'Lizard!' she almost shrieks. 'Lord!'

He blinks at the memory of the weevilly rice mixed with shreds of whatever they could get: snake, slug, monkey, bits of the greens some men managed to coax from the ground. Tiny amounts in their shrunken guts.

'Eddie used to eat like a horse.' She blows out smoke, begins to gnaw her thumbnail.

'Fruit sometimes,' he says, 'the Nips gave us fruit and veg now and then, bamboo shoots. They were starved too so most things they kept. Sometimes guava, yam, jungle spinach. But in the end there was nothing but filthy rice.' He runs his tongue round the inside of his mouth, still scarred from vitamin-deficiency ulceration.

'Poor Eddie.' She's almost whispering. 'My poor brother.'

They stay quiet for a bit. She's hunched over her knees, hair hiding her face as she gnaws a nail. 'Thank you,' she mumbles. 'I do want to know this.' When she crosses her legs, her knees are too close to his face, and he shuffles a bit further away.

'Your turn,' he says. The stove is like a warm body behind him. Did Edgar ever sit like this, on the floor, feeling this same warmth against his spine? He liked the kitchen he said, he liked Linda, the housekeeper. The starved cat curls into his lap, its purr a warm buzz against his bones. He strokes its triangular head, feeds it a shred of goose. It licks the grease from his fingers, tongue rough, purr loud. Aida stays quiet, unusual for her.

'Go on,' he says.

'What do you want to know?'

'Love life?'

She sniffs, examines her thumbnail. 'He wasn't a great one for girls.'

'No?' He studies her expression.

'Not that I knew of, anyway.' She's fiddling with a bit of pudding now, rolling it between her fingers.

He gulps down the dregs of his whisky. 'The only one I ever heard him mention was Enid,' he prompts.

'Crikey yes! I'd forgotten. Enid! He never brought her home though. They were at med school together.'

*"Wasn't a great one for girls." Is there any meaning in that?*

'Wild oats I expect! He said something about her once, what was it?' She swallows a pellet of pudding, frowning as she thinks.

'He told me she expected him to marry her,' he prompts.

'No!'

'"Not bloody likely", he told me he said.'

'I can just hear him saying that.' She laughs sadly.

It was the first camp after Changi, when they'd still had some flesh on them, some energy. His first knowledge of the jungle: the tough, tangling green, the heat and biting swarms, the deafening whoops and screams from out of the green, such complicated green, it tangled your brain. They were clearing land for the railway. It was killing work and many died. But this was early on. He didn't know Edgar well. They were hacking with machetes, through vines as thick as their thighs. Someone asked Edgar if he had anyone waiting for him at home. He, sweat running down his chest, stopped for breath, mentioned Enid – a good sort, but there'd been a misunderstanding. 'She thought I'd marry her, till I set her straight.' Pulling a face, he turned unexpectedly to look at Starling. And there was a moment then, a meeting of eyes that seemed charged with meaning, but what was the meaning?

'Really?' Aida shakes her head. 'He never breathed a word

to me! Oh, I know what he said! She was a big girl, apparently, but she had a little girlish way of going on, coy or arch or something, that grated on him. "Why do girls have to be so affected?" he said.'

Yes, he can imagine Edgar saying that.

'Do you think *I'm* affected?' she asks. He shakes his head. She wants something from him, it's clear. They want something from each other. But it's something neither can have, because what they both want is Edgar.

'We had a wedding once, in the nursery,' she says with a giggle. 'Linda helped us. I had a veil made from a lace curtain. Eddie had a daisy in his buttonhole. Linda made us a special cake and iced it white. We both promised that when we were grown-up, we'd marry no one except each other. Silly!'

Her knees, in Edgar's pyjamas, are still distractingly too near his face.

'He was always talking about you,' he says. 'It was always, Diddy this or Aida that. Didn't you drive ambulances?'

'Mmm. I loved it. I suppose that's odd?' She crosses a leg over her opposite knee. The trouser leg rides up and he sees a fluff of pale hairs, fine as thistledown. 'Diddy!' She snorts. 'When I was a baby, I called him Eggy!'

He snorts and the cat twitches irritably.

'Oh, that's not the best of it!' She grinds out her fag, shakes the box at him, and he takes one. 'When we were... I don't know, fourteen and sixteen, perhaps, he was reading Freud... Aunt Harri sent him Freud and me Jung for Christmas. I hardly touched the Jung, but he read them both. He was going through a pretentious phase. He started calling me Id and of course I called him Ego! Aida – Id – Edgar – Ego, do you see?'

Starling rests his head back against the warm stove. She's giggling, her cheeks pinked up, her pale eyes shining. His eyes snag on her legs again, the soft pyjama cotton. Oh, he'd like to hold them, hold on to her legs in those pyjamas. *Cradle* them.

'Tell me something about *you* now,' she says suddenly.

'Me?' He stubs out his half-smoked fag on the greasy plate.

'Yes, Dr Crowley, you!' Her voice sounds drunkenly fond, as she leans forward smiling. He shrinks back against the stove. Forgot for a moment who he's meant to be. *Get a grip, Starling. Christ. Get out of here.* The cat jumps off as he stands, staggers, catches hold of the table. She steps closer as if about to hold him. But the door opens, and in comes Dr Everett.

'I say,' he says, 'what's all this?' He surveys the food, the tumblers, the two of them so close together.

'Sorry sir,' he says, stepping back.

'No need for sir!' Aida says. 'It's Christmas, Daddy! We're only having a nightcap.'

He folds his arms across his belly. 'You woke Mummy up with your shenanigans.' He gives Starling a look. 'She says time to call it a day.' And, as if the house agrees, clocks begin to chime all over the place.

'Up to bed now, children,' Dr Everett says.

'Night, night, Childe Roland, sleep tight,' says Aida, grinning at him from the top of the stairs. He goes back into the studio, pulls back the curtain, and presses his forehead against the glass. Cold and hard and fogging up. *You can't do this anymore. Can't keep it up.* His conscience rises in him like a light. He hasn't done any harm. Not really. He's given comfort. But it's enough. It's the end.

He stuffs his things into his bag. He will take the pen, but not the anatomical model. Irrelevant to him now. He slinks downstairs, pulls on his coat, pushes his feet into the elastic-laced shoes. There's a pad of paper and a pencil on the hall stand, and he writes a note:

*Thank you for your hospitality. I can't tell you what it has meant to me to have spent Christmas with Edgar's family. I am sorry to have to leave so abruptly. All best wishes for 1946, Roland.*

He leaves it folded beside Dr Everett's place at the table. Outside, he gasps in freshness, as he sets off for the station. Odds are he'll have to wait all fucking night for a train. But who cares? This is good, Starling. Decisive. Once you're home, think again, start again. Find a job, a wife, it doesn't matter about the other thing. You can forget Edgar now. Forget those feelings. You can live a decent, ordinary life. From now on that's what you do.

19

---

AIDA

At dawn she rises, shivers into underwear, stockings (laddered, damn it), skirt, twinset, and packs her bag. There's a train at eight. If she hurries... She creeps to the bathroom. Of course, it's letting the side down; the parents will go bats. And what about *him*? Last night there was a moment of... *something*... or the potential for something, at least. If only Daddy hadn't... *Tenderness* as well as attraction, a disconcertingly squashy kind of emotion, but how mortifying it would be to have *feelings* going on in front of her folks. If she stayed, Mummy would be sickeningly alert all day, interpreting, signalling with her eyebrows, with tilts of her head. She'd engineer for them to be alone, and then burst in on some pretext to see the result.

No, that's not on. See Roland in London, let the thing, whatever the thing turns out to be, play out there. She will not *pursue*, no, rather wait for him to look her up again. Which he almost certainly will. *Almost*. And if not... well, cross that bridge, et cetera. No need for him to lurk this time. *The thought of that!* She watches her brow dent as she brushes her teeth; such thin skin, it shows every blush, and wretched bruisy patches under the eyes whenever she's the least bit tired. Why on earth couldn't she have inherited Mummy's famous complexion? She spits into the basin, wipes her mouth, dabs on lipstick, smudges rouge.

She knocks on the parents' door, hears the bleary kerfuffle of them waking. From downstairs there's the dim sound of breakfast preparations. (Bravo, Jacksons!)

She gives them a moment, before opening the door. 'Only me,' she says.

'Diddy,' Mummy murmurs, pulling herself up in bed, and yawning.

'Off out?' Daddy reaches for his bedside glass of water, throws his head back and gargles before he swallows.

'I'm going back to town,' she says. 'It's been lovely, but...'

Dennis begins to object, but Clementine cuts him off. 'I think we all managed rather well, considering.' Her plait snakes greyly over one shoulder of her crumpled white nightgown as she squints up at Aida. There's a stuffy smell of alcoholic breath, talcum powder, embarrassingly human fustiness.

'All things considered,' Dennis agrees. 'But I thought we'd have you for another day at least, Diddy.' He pushes out his bottom lip in a mock sulk. 'Tell you what, stay today, and I'll drive you back first thing tomorrow – or tonight?'

'No, Daddy. Sorry. I need to go and clear my head – and think.'

'I'll run you to the station then.' He gives a great histrionic yawn and swings his legs out of bed.

'No, I'll leave my case here and walk. You could drop it next time you're in town?' She thinks suddenly of the other woman and holds his eye.

'Can do, will do.' He looks down.

'What on earth will we do with Roland, all on our own?' Clementine says.

'You invited him!'

'He's sure to be taken aback. You and he seemed to be...'

'*Don't.*' Aida kisses them both. Mummy grasps her hand for a moment, then lets it go.

'I'll be back on my birthday,' she promises. 'And I'll ring on the 31st.'

---

The streets are still and damp, and the hard heels of her shoes clack smartly along the pavement. Her lungs expand with fresh, damp air. She stops to peel a beech leaf from the toe of a shoe, wondering how Roland and the parents will spend the day. Roland the cuckoo, the substitute, the curiosity. That wet, hurt look in his eyes sometimes, it twists something in her belly. Is it a sort of maternal feeling? Once, during the Blitz, an ARP warden dug a baby out of a collapsed house and handed it to her. No sign of the parents in the rubble. They were buried (probably dead). The baby, grey with grime, squirmed in her arms, its wet, heavy, almost black nappy soiled and stinking, and she felt not compassion or tenderness, only a kind of revulsion at its animal struggle and its blind, wet, ruthless face. She worried then that there was something wrong with her, that she was unnatural, the type of woman who fails to have maternal feelings. She never played with dolls but populated the doll's house with snails and beetles instead. *Poor baby,* she thinks now, trying to kindle a motherly ember. It will be about four, now: *please let it be happy, wherever and whoever it is.*

Outside the station, she stands on the railway bridge, watching the dawn light gleam on mud. A heron throws a priestly shadow, there's a bicycle fallen in, deep footprints leading to and from the bank where someone (presumably) tried to rescue it. Boxing Day morning: strange to be out and alone and heading away from family. It makes her feel mature, a sad woman of the world standing on a bridge, elated yet wistful. She leans her arm on the rail, posing, like a film star. Though when the train comes chuffing in, she childishly enjoys the commotion beneath her. She and Eddie used to race to the station to do exactly this, getting thrillingly whooshed in steam as they pelted the roof of the train with twigs or conkers.

The platform's deserted when she descends and boards the train, walks along the corridor peering into the dim carriages, looking for an empty one. A few lumpish people huddle down, a big pram and a mother with a snotty-looking brood. In one carriage sit German prisoners of war in their pea-green uniforms, in the next a lone figure. She passes, pauses, goes back and stares. *What?* She peers through the glass until he feels her eyes, turns and, visibly, flinches.

She opens the door. His glasses and hat are on the seat beside him, his hair rumpled and flopping over an eye. He pushes it back in what is already becoming a familiar gesture. His chin is dark with bristles.

'Bolting after all?'

'Are *you?*'

*The cheek of him!* 'Hardly,' she says coldly, and then with an edge of sarcasm, 'Mind if I join you?'

He shrugs and she settles herself opposite him. There's no lighting in the carriage and in the dimness he looks yellow, sickly, as if he hasn't slept at all. He puts back his specs.

'You've got a smut on your face,' he says.

She takes out her compact and yes there is a smut, of course there is. If you stand in the steam, that's what happens. So much for her film star moment. She dabs with her handkerchief and closes her compact with a cross click. And then they sit in silence until she says, 'Bad form to walk out on your hosts – they'll be expecting you to be there for breakfast.'

'And you,' he says.

'They're *my* folks! And at least I said goodbye. I explained.'

'I left a note.'

'Didn't see it.'

'Wasn't for you.' He seems different, surlier, more northern.

'So?' she says.

He removes his specs, and without them his eyes look naked. His thick eyebrows are chaotic from his rubbing hand. 'Yes, bad form,' he mutters. 'I'll phone later and apologise. It was just…'

She might as well have stayed at home! After all, with Roland gone, they could have had a quiet day reading, sherry, a game of cribbage. And now the poor parents will feel deserted and – she starts as she realises – they might even think that she and Roland *planned* to take off together. She'd put money on it that Mummy will think that.

She begins to contemplate jumping off and returning home, but before she can decide the train starts to jerk and chug, flakes of ash whirling past the window. He replaces his glasses, reaches for his cigarettes, offers her one, but it's too early in the day. She looks away as he struggles to light it.

'It was just too much,' he says at last, on an intake of smoke. 'Being in the bosom of the family.'

She blurts a laugh. 'It's hardly a bosomy kind of family!'

His smile is wry, barely a smile at all.

'*Do* ring them, won't you?' she begs. 'Their feelings will be hurt. I hope they don't think we planned this. A Boxing Day bolt.'

He opens his mouth to speak, but says nothing.

'I jest,' she says. She looks at his kit-bag. 'Where's Norma?'

'Who?'

'Your present! The model.'

'Couldn't carry it.'

'I shall have it sent on.'

He nods, head tilted, blowing smoke and she enjoys the smell of it in the chilly air.

'To where?' she asks. He affects not to hear. She removes her gloves, gnaws on a rough edge of nail.

'Well, anyway, as it turns out, we're rather in the same boat,' she says. 'It was too much for me too, going through the motions like that.'

He nods slowly, pressing his lips together, really looking at her, *into* her almost.

'Though it was nice having you there. It helped, really. Someone to talk to – about Edgar. And the parents seem to dote on you.'

'Dote,' he repeats, grimacing as if the word tastes bad.

Another silence. A flock of something – pigeons? starlings? twists tight, then scatters above a ploughed field.

'I'll need your address for Norma. Shall we see each other in London, do you think?'

The question still hangs between them when the guard comes to sell them tickets.

'Liverpool Street,' they say at the same time, each fumbling for money.

'Change at Ipswich the both of you,' the guard says.

'How long's the wait?' Roland asks.

'Half an hour. Rum old day to be travelling.' The guard looks between the two of them, and winks at Roland, before he shuts the door.

'Well, anyway, it's nice to have a travelling companion,' she says after a gap, and cringes at how prissy that sounds. Bare trees across dun fields, red-brick cottages, wads of wet cloud scud by.

He says nothing.

'It was nice talking last night,' she says. 'After I went to bed, I was trying to remember one of Eddie's limericks.'

He nods, reluctantly drawn. 'He was a champ at them.'

'We used to compete – he was so quick though, wasn't he? This is one of his.' She runs through it in her head before she clasps her hands in her lap and begins.

*'There once was a young girl called Cerys,*
*Who nothing could ever embarrass,*
*Till the bath salts one day,*
*In the bath where she lay,*
*Turned out to be plaster of Paris.'*

He snorts. 'Ours were much bluer than that!'

'Do you remember any? Tell me one, do!'

He shakes his head.

'Why not? Because I'm a girl?'

'Yes.' He meets her eyes, oddly.

She snorts. 'What are you, Victorian? *Nothing's* too rude for *me*.'

He sits back. 'Nothing's too rude for *you*?' He whistles as he exhales a plume of smoke. 'Quite a claim, that.'

The damn flush again. She feels fury rising inside her. Who does he think he is? 'What I mean is,' she says, 'I'm not a prude. I'm a modern woman. I worked through the war. The things I saw on the ambulances! It'd take more than a dirty limerick to shock me! For God's sake, Roland! Do you think I'd shatter? I grew up with *Eddie,* remember! He could be filthy.'

'True.'

'But not *only* that.' She feels suddenly defensive on Edgar's behalf. 'He was terribly witty. He was the wittiest person in the world.'

'No argument there.' He inclines his head, as if studying her. 'You're different.'

'What d'you mean?'

'Away from your *folks*.' He says "folks" mockingly.

'I bet you're different away from *your* folks,' she retorts, before remembering his loss. She claps a hand to her mouth. 'Whoops. Sorry, big bloody foot in it again.' But he only shrugs. 'You must tell me about them someday,' she says.

Silence. A miserable huddle of cottages in the midst of a big wet field hurtles by.

'Anyway,' she says. 'Aren't we all different with different people?'

He gives her a wry look, shuts his eyes.

'Why are you being so beastly?'

No answer.

'Not *really* different though,' she muses after a long silence. 'But we have different aspects, don't we, slightly different versions of ourselves with different people? I don't mean false beards and identities, or *fraud* or anything like that!'

Silence again. Still the closed eyes. Has he fallen asleep?

'Actually, I always thought it would be rather fun to be a spy!' she says. Oh, how childish that sounds. How annoying she's being; she's even annoying herself. But she can't just leave him be. Clearly, he's tired of her. *Do not chatter, Aida.* She takes her book from her bag, but her eyes won't stay on the words.

Quiet but for the battering rhythm of the train. Grey outside, black lace of trees against the sky, corduroy-ridged fields lancing by.

She fidgets with her bag. She's starving, in need of coffee, but of course there's nothing on the train. All she has is a couple of sticky humbugs. She offers one to him, but he shakes his head. And they're rattling on. Ipswich soon. Unlikely anything will be open till Liverpool Street.

'Where are you going to work?' she asks. 'Hospital or general practice? Do you have a practice?'

He gets out a box of Players and, daring the intimacy, she

takes them from him, though he wasn't offering, and lights two, gratefully inhaling double smoke before she hands his over.

It's ridiculous that she hasn't even got her own ciggies on her, that she didn't bring supplies from the house, a hunk of bread and cheese or something. No forethought. Once again. He's staring out of the window, miserable as all hell, by the look of it.

'Go on then,' she says, in desperation. 'I dare you. And if I'm shocked – which I won't be – it'll be my own fault.'

He turns his head and looks at her at last with a curious, rather cold, smile.

'Go on. I *dare* you to shock me. I actually want you to shock me.'

'All right...
'*There was a young doctor called Everett,*
*Whose cock was the size of a leveret,*
*When doing the job,*
*It was bit by a dog,*
*And a surgeon was called in to sever it.*'

He sits back in his seat.

'There. I win,' she says. 'Not shocked at all. It's actually rather funny.' She forces a giggle though really she is, if not *shocked*, unexpectedly upset. No one wants to think about their brother's "cock", dead or not. 'Cheeky rhyme,' she adds breezily.

She meets his eyes, and feels locked in to some sort of challenge, but one she doesn't understand. It's as if she's got into an argument in another language and doesn't know how to win. He's clutching his handless arm, ciggie in the corner of his mouth, squinting against the smoke, sort of huddled round himself inside the outsized overcoat. More silence stretches between them. Her mind scrambles for a way to rescue the mood.

'Let's have a big slap-up breakfast together at Liverpool Street?' she says. 'On me.'

He picks up his hat, and flips it onto his head, tugs down the brim. 'I'm stopping off in Ipswich, visiting a pal.'

'But your ticket...' He's lying. He paid straight through to Liverpool Street. Even asked the connection time.

The train's slowing. His face has closed to her now, eyes avoidant, expression neutral, bored or worse, *cold*. He stands and shoulders his bag. She wants to say something to fill the silence that gapes between them now. *What's the matter? What has she done?*

'It really was very clever,' she says, embarrassing herself with the needy sound of her voice, 'you must have had the most tremendous fun, the two of you, rhyming away together...' Words pour from her mouth like bubbles. 'I don't mean *fun*, oh God, of course it wasn't *fun* out there, foot in mouth again! As you might have noticed, I have foot in mouth disease.' Oh, it's excruciating but she can't stop, rattles on and on, stuffing the silence with froth.

The train stops and they step down onto the platform.

'Enjoy the rest of your journey,' he says, rather formally.

'Be in touch?' she says, 'You know my address.' The blood rushes to her face again. 'I mean... well you know where I live. Aren't you going to give me your address?'

Expressionless, he salutes the brim of his hat and walks away. She watches him dwindle, a slight reed of a man, bent to one side with the weight of his kit-bag. He fails to look back, and she shivers in the chilly cheerless morning.

What went wrong between them? Why is she such an absolute ass? He must think her an utter fool. Such a *girl*. Why couldn't she hide her shock? No, not *shock* – *grief*, a fresh stab of it, thinking of her brother like that and all right yes, there was a minor degree of shock, shock at the crudity. No need, surely, to be *quite* so crude? Surely he could have chosen a different limerick? It was disrespectful. Was it? To herself? To Edgar? Men's humour. He warned her and she, oh so pathetically, helped him prove his point.

But it was his cold expression that really hurt.

## 20

## STARLING AND AIDA

Fucking hell. He'll have to hang around now, freezing his nuts off, wait for her connection to leave then get the next one, God knows when, find somewhere to lurk till then. *Lurk!* Oh, Starling, what a fucking crapper you are.

He stamps away from the station, follows the river, finds himself at the docks, bombed to kingdom come of course. Shrivelled fireweed drips in the ruins; there are even the start of trees pushing up through the ruins of a warehouse. Gulls swoop and mock round a crane towering rusty against the grey.

Oh, fuck it. Her poor face fighting not to look upset; truth is, he upset himself. Nice, she is, interesting; he likes her and judging by the way she looks at him, she likes him too. Maybe they could be something together? Maybe *she's* the type he could marry. Smart. Funny in her way. He could be part of the family. Train to be a doctor still, step into Edgar's shoes. His toes remember the flattened fur in Edgar's slippers, and clutch inside his boots.

NO. You can't do that because it is all a lie. You are a lie. You're a lying crapper. And you upset her. Edgar would punch your lights out.

More wrecked warehouses, the Customs House still standing, building work, reconstruction – nothing doing today though. In the dock, a rusty half-sunk hull, oily rainbows on the surface. His stomach writhes, hungry but bloated from yesterday's feed. A sudden vision of Mum's roast potatoes. Paper hats, cotton-wool snow on the mantel for her glass animals. She'd have done him proud, she promised, if he'd gone home. Why didn't he? Why is he such a fucking crapper?

He stomps uphill into town, past shut shops and solicitors, building sites giving off the same burned stench as everywhere. He walks till he aches, shoulder dragging with his rucksack, invisible hand throbbing like a cartoon hand, ballooning bigger with every step. He walks till he's utterly done in and then he turns, plods back towards the station.

———

She peers through the frosted glass of the Ladies' Waiting Room once more. And at last, oh yes, there he is, back again, just as she guessed. *Pal in Ipswich my flipping foot!* To think he's prepared to miss his train, and hang around for hours, just to avoid her. Why the hell didn't she board her connection? She'd be nearly there by now instead of frozen and starving in this stupid waiting room. What a feeble waste of time. Boxing Day, too!

She goes to the door, ready to confront him. Rude! Ungrateful! And that doesn't begin to cover it! But she stops. He's made it plain he's had enough of her. The way he looked at her… Oh Lord, it makes her squirm. Is she so unbearable to him? Most men would… but he's not most men.

She goes to huddle by the tepid stove. Tears smart in her eyes, and her stomach groans. It's his fault she's hungry; her predicament is all his fault. Two hours she's been here, and there's still more than an hour to wait. Her eyes roam to the empty chocolate dispensing machine, the cigarette machine with its *Out of Order* sign, the closed buffet hatch with its peeling posters: Walls Have Ears, Cadbury's Chocolate, Bile Beans. If she'd got on that train, she could have been dancing by this afternoon. She jumps as the buffet hatch shoots up and an old man with a patch over one eye peers out. 'Refreshments?' he says.

She springs up, fumbling for her purse. Over his shoulder she can see another hatch opening into the Gents' Waiting Room.

'Do you have sandwiches? Cake?'

'Only these.' He opens and shakes a tin of dubious-looking biscuits at her. 'It's done me no good getting here today, I can tell you, but I have to open up an hour before the train's due. Double time, it being a bank holiday.'

'So glad. I'll take one. And a cup of tea. Do you have ciggies?'

'Fives of Woodbines. Sure?' He frowns at the biscuits. 'I reckon they'll be stale.'

She takes her tea, Woodbines and a biscuit, and returns to the stove, a little fortified. Nothing to stop her going out on the town when she gets back. There's a Boxing Day dance at the Palais. A few gins and she'll dance the night away. Dance this whole diabolical Christmas away with it.

Tea drips onto her lap each time she lifts the cup. At least she has the waiting room to herself and it's not *utterly* freezing. The wall clock is stuck at ten to five. She lights a ciggie and looks out at the platform. Empty now. Either he's gone off again, to see his so-called "pal", or he's in the Gents' Waiting Room. What an idiotic situation! Smoke snorts from her nose. She could go in there, and... but *no*, Aida, *no*, leave the poor beggar in peace. He's made it plain he doesn't want to be with you. Or was he just upset? Did she unwittingly upset him? She searches back but can't think of anything. That stupid limerick. Edgar, oh Edgar, with your smutty jokes and your smutty friends.

The biscuit has gone soggy in the saucer. More sawdust than anything, but there's a trace of musty sweetness. The man puts the wireless on. It crackles and hisses before resolving into the news: something about Germany, something about football, something about twins born at midnight on Christmas Eve and called Mary and Joseph, poor little buggers.

Is Roland listening on the other side of the hatch? Is he too drinking weak tea and eating an ancient biscuit? He'll suppose her in London by now, and good riddance. But she will not take it personally. He's damaged. There's something raw about him, something bewildered. He needs time alone. And he needs patience and love. Put yourself in his shoes. Enduring Christmas with strangers when his own folk are dead. And whatever must it have been like in the jungle? Look at the way he crouched last night, like some kind of savage. But he's far from savage. A smile drifts to her face, and a warmth blooms through her. The word "sweet" arises, not a word that often applies to men, in her experience. It's been a long time since she's felt so drawn towards a chap (not counting the American, but that was nothing like this). This strong feeling of... *tenderness* is disconcerting. Last night she'd thought... there did seem to be reciprocation, a tentative start of something. Surely, she didn't imagine it. Or is it just because she's Edgar's sister? Clearly, he was very close to Edgar.

She sniffs sharply, pulls hard on her cigarette. Think about something else. Neville for instance. It occurs to her that he too is, in his own way, a sweet man. She said she'd phone him when she got home. He'll be back tomorrow. Oh, the dreadful evening when he declared his love! She gives a shivery little laugh. Poor man. She'll let him down gently, kindly, stay pals even. They can still go to the flicks and so on if he likes.

She takes out her Christie, decides to start again. She's been looking forward to reading this, but there's too much *real* going on. "*White Christmas*" fights through a crackle of interference. If only, instead of being terrified of the lurker for those idiotic weeks, she'd faced up to him. Priceless that the lurker turned out to be Roland! Maybe they'll laugh about it, one day. If only she *had* confronted him then, well that would have been a different story. There wouldn't have been all this absurdity. Well, she'll hold back now, keep out of sight till he's on the train, then for the second time in one day, burst into his carriage! Maybe one day they'll laugh about this too. They'll tell their children the batty story of how they met.

Now you're really getting ahead of yourself!

She finishes one cigarette and lights another. Best get more or she'll run out before Liverpool Street. Ash skims the surface of the cooling tea. The green dress with the amber beads will be perfect for the dance. Plenty of drinks, plenty of dancing, lights and warmth and laughter. Why not invite Roland? He might, of course, say no (probably will) but she can take the knockback. Play the long game. If he says no she'll let him go – for now. There will be other opportunities. If he hasn't fallen for her yet, then she'll just have to make sure to grow on him. He's not in his right mind now, something like shell shock, she guesses. And grief, of course. There's always grief.

A couple of stout women with walking sticks and rabbit coats enter the room and frown at her, make a kerfuffle of sitting down and wiping their noses. They are enormous and old, and almost identical, even to their green felt hats. Twins?

'Refreshments?' the man says, sticking his head out of the hatch.

The twins ignore him, both sitting with giant handbags on their knees.

Aida dowses her ciggie in the biscuit-slurry in her saucer

and goes to get another pack, peering over the man's shoulder. There are voices, but she can't see the speakers. 'Does there happen to be a young man in there?' she asks, nodding towards the Gents' Waiting Room.

'There's quite a few of 'em.'

'Trilby, specs, with a missing...' She holds up her hand, wincing as she does so. What a way to describe him! 'Nice-looking,' she adds, and flushes.

'Dark fellow? Little?'

'That's him.'

'Want me to fetch him?'

'No thanks.' Smiling, she settles back down by the stove and tries to concentrate on the Christie, though she can't stop her eyes flicking to the stopped clock, can't stop a ripple of excitement. Not long now till the next train.

---

Liverpool Street. *At effing last!* He gazes up at the iron struts of the roof. Light comes through the glass, and with a flutter of pigeons, his heart lifts. *Relief.* The first good feeling since God knows when. Now he can be himself. Be *Starling*. Forget the farce. It's too hard, probably illegal. Impersonation. Is it a crime? Regrettable behaviour, at least. Thinking about that hurt flinch in her eyes makes him flinch too. But she'll get over it. She's better off out of it. The absence of his hand throbs as he strides along the platform, avoiding people, porters, prams, and luggage. You'd think Boxing Day would be quiet, but no, and there are soldiers on their way to somewhere, a platoon of them gathered, smoking, under a patched-over bit of glass roof.

The plan: back to Horace's place, if they'll have him, and then tomorrow, home. At least Mum'll welcome him, and he can live cheaply, find some sort of work, consolidate. That's a comforting word and he mutters it as he leaves the station: '*Consolidate.*'

And then a hand catches his arm.

'You see I simply couldn't leave it like that,' she says. 'Won't you come and have some lunch with me? My treat? I don't know about you, but I'm ravenous.'

Gone dumb, he hesitates too long. Tries to speak but nothing happens.

'*Please* Roland? I know you must think I'm an idiotic goose.' In the light coming through the dirty glass, the end of her nose is red, her lips chapped, and her eyes shine with what might be tears. Can't believe that he can have such an effect on a *girl*. 'And a twit,' she adds. 'And a twerp. And a clot.' Her eyes beg him to smile, and he nearly does. He could just walk off again. But she looks so *sad*. It'll only be an hour or so more of his life, and truth is he could do with a drink and a bite to eat.

'You must have been waiting here for hours.'

'No, I was on the same train as you. Come on.'

'What?' But she says no more, grabs his arm, drags him along to a hotel, not the sort of place he'd ever dream of entering, but she breezes in there like she owns the place, enquires about lunch and next thing they're through the plushy entrance and into a bustling dining room. A waiter seats them, hands them menus. Sir and madam, he calls them, making him want to laugh. When she asks for menus, there's a sort of bossy ring to her voice that makes him cringe.

This is his chance to come clean. A better way to end it. Tell her the truth. See if she still wants to buy him his dinner – sorry, *lunch*. But a waiter's waiting, pencil poised. Might as well have some grub now he's here. They have the 2/6d menu of the day: soup, trout, ice cream, nothing that'll take much cutting up. She orders a bottle of wine. He feels embarrassed, the way she takes control. The waiter's face might be trained to be expressionless, but what's going on behind it? *Wait till you've eaten, Starling, then set her straight.*

While they're waiting, she goes off to "wash her hands" and comes back with fresh lipstick, a tentative smile. Her eyes search his face. What's she searching for? What does she want?

The wine is thin and sour, and he gulps it back while she tells him how rather than take the first connection, she waited in Ipswich, intending to collar him on the train, but chickened out.

'Then I saw you walking away,' she says, 'and I simply couldn't let you go. And now here we are!' She smiles and he smiles back, glad she's cheered up. *But NO,* Starling. No more deception. Just come out with it. Say: *I'm not Crowley, that was a lie, but it's not a lie that I was a friend of Edgar's.* There. It would take no more than two seconds. And then she might just walk off, or throw her wine in his face, or... what? But however she reacted, he would be out of the dark, and into the light. Free of the lie.

But she natters on about her work, her friends, a nervous sort of nattering as if she's scared to stop and let him speak. The soup's a watery Brown Windsor, which his stomach accepts, along with the tiny soft portion of fish. There's a hubbub of noise in the dining room. It's warm and the wine eases his shoulders. He's tired after a cold night at the station, walking and huddling on the platform, where the minutes passed slower than any he's lived before. Where he kept so still that a mouse paused on the toe of his boot. He did manage a few scraps of shut-eye on the train, but not enough. Now he could happily slide under the table and snooze. She's warmed up, eyes bright, cheeks pink, telling him about Edgar as a child, how he rescued a baby thrush, and kept it as a pet for years.

'He even let it peck toast from between his teeth.'

*I'm not Roland Crowley, that was a lie, but it's not a lie that I was a friend of Edgar's.*

But he does want to hear more about Edgar, and he doesn't want to spoil her mood. All he has to do is sit here, listen, smile. They'll finish lunch and he'll tell her the truth, and then they'll part. And that will be the end of it.

But after lunch she pulls him into the bar. 'Let's have another drink,' she says, 'come on!' There's a pianist, a lanky, handsome boy. Starling stares: a beautiful jawline, eyes closed as he plays, long, black fingers moving on the ivory. He feels a stab of lust – oh no, please not that, not now. Sleepy, jazzy notes roll from the piano.

'Let's get pie-eyed,' Aida says, and the way she grins, the way she tilts her head, brings Edgar sharply to mind. If Edgar were alive, perhaps *they'd* be here together, the two of them, getting pie-eyed on Boxing Day afternoon. Why not stay a bit? After all, there's nowhere else to be. Before they leave, she'll know the truth.

The afternoon slides past in smoke and some weak cocktail she keeps ordering, and afternoon turns into evening, then night. A space is cleared for dancing. A drummer and a trumpet player join the pianist. The music gets into your bones. He keeps losing himself, then waking to find himself now seated, now pressed close to her slim body on the dance floor, smoke and perfume in her hair but on the skin of her neck, a babyish soapy smell. She's nearly as tall as him and eyes shut, the slow notes of the piano tumbling round them, he lets himself pretend that she is Edgar; after all, this *is* the closest to Edgar he's ever going to get.

## 21

## AIDA AND STARLING

Even in her arms it's as if he's made of smoke, as if, when she lets go, he'll dissolve. The thought of returning alone to her cold and messy flat is unbearable. Tonight, quite simply, she *cannot, will not,* be alone. Too late to track down her friends – and anyway, it's Roland she wants tonight.

He's not a practiced dancer, but he learns fast, his body responding to her movements. *Bliss.* At the end of a lovely shimmery boogie-woogie, she forces herself to let him go, nips out to ask the concierge to call a taxi. Although she half fears he won't be there when she returns, there he sits, legs crossed, smoking, gazing at the pianist, which, in order to avoid her eyes, she assumes, he's been doing since they arrived.

He looks up at her blankly as if he's forgotten who she is. Poor man, he's clearly had it.

'Come on,' she says, and he stands unsteadily, too many gin slings.

It's drizzling outside; halos sparkle round the lights and street lamps, a smeary blur of dark and light. 'Something I want to say...' he says.

'Let's get out of this rain first.' She pulls him towards the waiting cab. His eyes dart down the street as if about to run, but she keeps hold of his hand as they climb in, and the car pulls out into the traffic.

'How about I rustle up some supper?' she says, mentally ransacking her cupboards. Unfortunately, she's already scoffed most of the hamper goodies – though there's still the wine. 'There isn't much: a tin of Spam, do you like Spam? Or pilchards? Lord, aren't there always pilchards? And I've got spuds. I could make chips. Oh, and I've got a bottle of wine. From the aunts.'

'The aunts,' he echoes. 'Those aunts. Edgar was always...' He trails off, removes his hand from hers.

She knows how to get his interest back. 'Oh, good golly!' she says. 'I'm having *déjà vu*... me and Eddie in a taxi coming back from somewhere or other – a dance – and he made up this limerick... Let's see if I can remember...' She closes her eyes. *Come on, come on,* 'Oh yes, something like:

'*She returned from the dance in a taxi,*
*Whose seats were remarkably waxy,*
*Though she gave a great heave,*
*When trying to leave,*
*She was stuck to the seat by her jaxie.*'

That elicits a laugh, thank goodness.

She grins. 'The best limericks are at least a *bit* rude, don't you think?'

He's back with her again. Clearly, the thing to do is to keep on about Edgar, and she doesn't mind that. Lovely to be able to talk about him without upsetting or boring anyone. She tells him about the deals they made: how he'd do her homework if she made his bed; he'd mend her bike if she made treacle toffee.

'We were quite... what would you say? Transactional children,' she says.

'Transactional,' he repeats. Perhaps a hint of mockery in his voice.

The taxi draws up round the corner – gas mains still up – and she pays the fare. What with lunch and all the gin, that's her weekly budget blown; she'll have to dip into her rent if she's going to eat. Of course, Daddy would give her a sub, but she prefers not to ask. Prefers to be independent. Roland could at least have offered to pay for *something*, though. Is he mean, or simply hard up? As if reading her mind, he says, 'Sorry, short on cash. Wasn't expecting to be out on the town.'

'You can jolly well pay me back next time!' she says, sneaking a look at his reaction to "next time". But he's turned away, adjusting his hat.

'I don't live far,' he says, 'I'll leg it from here.'

'You're not going yet?' They stand facing each other under a flickering street lamp, which makes her think of a movie jittering to the end of its reel. 'At least walk me to the door!' In Buttress Street they stop. The shopfronts are dark, the street silent but for a dripping gutter. Drizzle hangs in the air. He's standing in front of the doorway where he used to lurk. Does he realise? She watches him tilt back his head to look up at the window of her flat. Yes, he does. It gives her a shiver – but there's nothing to fear from Roland. He's entirely harmless, honest to the point of gormless, she thinks, suppressing a grin.

'At least come in and have a cup of tea,' she urges.

'I'll come in for a cuppa and use the toilet,' he says, 'then I'll be off.'

'Charming!'

She can feel his eyes on her as she unlocks and opens the door. Inside she picks up a couple of muddy trampled cards – not for her – shoves them on the hall table, and leads him up the stairs, past her neighbour's door, ashamed of the dinginess and the stink of old cooking. Inside the flat he stands in his hat and coat, arms by his sides, looking appalled, and she doesn't blame him. It's a mess; she didn't have time to so much as wash up before she left. Greasy plates beside the sink, shoes and scarves and cards and books and letters strewn all about. A plate with a brown pear core and the foil from the Hershey's chocolate. A greasy frying pan containing burnt fried bread. A smell of damp and mice.

'The bathroom's through there.' She cringes at the thought of the stockings and knickers left to drip over the bath, the cracked and dirty basin. While he's in there she turns on the geyser, piles the dishes in the sink, turns off the main light and throws the pink chiffon over the lamp to soften the edges of everything. She fiddles with the wireless, finds a mushy sort of concert on the Light Programme: better than nothing. She's kneeling and setting the fire when he comes back, and she's acutely aware of him behind her as she screws newspaper into twists, arranges kindling and coals.

'Shall I put the kettle on?' he says, and she's reminded suddenly of the Neville debacle. Was that only a week ago?

'Or wine?' she says.

'I've had enough,' he says.

'But it *is* still Christmas.' She smiles over her shoulder at him.

He shrugs and grins back. Something about the sparkle in dark eyes, you don't get with light ones. It's like an ember catching – and in fact the fire takes obediently, instantly improving the atmosphere of the room. There's a damn good draw on the chimney: about the one good thing about this flat.

He removes a shoe from the armchair and sits.

'You like drink,' he observes.

'Oh, come on! It's Boxing Day!' She retrieves the bottle from the hamper and holds it up. A garish-looking bottle, *American Dare, Red Wine*, takes the corkscrew to the bottle, pours it into her only two glasses, keeping the cracked one for herself. 'Bottoms up.'

He sips cautiously, eyes straying round the room. She takes a gulp. The wine is harsh and bracing after all the sweet cocktails. Reasonably disgusting.

'Like tarmac,' she says. 'I'm starving. Sure I can't tempt you to some Spam?'

He shakes his head, smiling. 'How can I resist?'

'I can resist anything except temptation,' she says, hearing her brother quoting, as she knows, does he. Their eyes meet, and she peels hers away, aware she's a bit sozzled and must take care. *Do not throw yourself at him, Aida.*

'Shall I make chips?' she says. 'There's chutney too. Bless Aunt Harri. She's a prodigious preserver of anything that grows. Hope you'll meet her – and Gwen.'

'*Prodigious*,' he repeats. 'You do remind me of Edgar with your fancy words. Say it again.'

'Prodigious.'

'No, like you did the first time.'

She repeats the sentence, with the same slight ironic inflection, as if mocking herself. She's never realised that she does that but he's right, she does sound like Edgar; she flushes with a tremulous pleasure.

'He wasn't such a chatterbox though, was he? I'm sorry; I can't help it. I try not to. It always got me in trouble at school. Do feel free to shut me up.' But he doesn't, and she gabbles on ten to the dozen about jellies and jams, chutneys and sauces, idiotically listing damson, greengage, bramble, plum and for God's sake, beetroot. *Oh, shut your face, Aida.*

Kneeling, she retrieves potatoes from the cupboard. She's never made chips before, but surely they're just spuds cut up and fried? She peels and chops, cleans the frying pan, melts lard and once it's gone runny, tips them in with a couple of thick slices of Spam. From the hamper she takes the chutney. Green tomato.

When she looks round, his eyes are closed.

The news comes on: U.S. War Loans; U.N. talks on atomic weapons; a lost wedding ring found in someone's Christmas stuffing.

'There'll be something jollier in a minute,' she says. 'What kind of music do you like?'

'All sorts. Piano.' He opens his eyes. 'I like watching people play the piano.'

'I can play,' she says. 'Though you wouldn't want to watch *me*! I'm all fingers and thumbs. Oh God, sorry!' Blushing furiously, she peers into the frying pan. The Spam has started to sizzle, but nothing seems to be happening to the chips at all. 'I'm so sorry, Roland. Bloody foot, bloody mouth.'

He's silent.

'Eddie had all the flair. I have no flair at all.'

'Don't call me Roland,' he says suddenly.

'Why?'

Silence.

'Why?'

He shrugs. 'Forget it. Call me what you like. And everyone has some sort of flair.'

'Do they?' She considers. 'What's yours then... Roley? Is that better? Is that what he called you?'

He reaches for a cigarette, and she bites her knuckle, itching to help him light it.

'I suppose I might have a flair I haven't discovered yet,' she says. 'There are probably people who die, never having found their flair. What a sad thought.'

He looks as if he's miles away. Bored? But then he begins.

*'There was a young lass with fair hair,*
*Who supposed she was lacking in flair,*

*Till one day her talent,
Became abruptly apparent,
A talent remarkably rare.'*

She laughs with delight. 'Oh, it's just like being with Eddie! Well not *just* like... I wonder what it *will* turn out to be though. My flair.' Could it be sex appeal? she wonders. Though she doesn't seem to be appealing to him. And she thinks of Neville, and a similar conversation so recently. And the sex debacle. Anyone would think she was a tart.

Roland closes his eyes. The way his hair grows back from his forehead, the widow's peak, the dark waves seem just about perfect.

'Maybe you can help me discover my talent.' She kneels, and very tentatively puts her hand on his knee, feels a flinch, withdraws it. It's like trying to tame a wild animal! 'We can help each other, can't we? I mean, comfort each other.'

'Something's burning,' he says.

And he's right. She jumps up. The Spam has scorched on one side, though the chips remain stubbornly limp. Still, she dishes them out onto hastily dried plates, and blobs on some chutney. They sit with plates on their knees; Perry Como croons *"Till the End of Time"*; and she rattles on. The quieter and more distant he becomes, the more she gabbles. He eats half the Spam, but barely touches the chips.

'Sorry,' she says. 'There's obviously more to chips than meets the eye.'

'My digestion's all mucked up,' he says.

She bites into a chip, limp and greasy but still raw in the middle, puts down her fork. 'Edgar had *such* an appetite,' she says, remembering the way he used to wolf down his food, always demanding seconds and if possible, thirds.

'We used to talk about food a lot, in the jungle. *This* would have been a luxury,' he says, indicating his plate.

'Well at least it's not lizard!' She laughs too hectically.

He says nothing.

'If you aren't finishing that?' She indicates his Spam. When he shakes his head, she leans over, and forks it onto her plate. 'Waste not, want not,' she says, idiotically. It feels weirdly intimate to be eating food from his plate. Doris Day now, *"Sentimental Journey"*. Neville comes back into her head, tapping his foot to the music last week, sitting just where Roland's sitting now. This is like a strange replay of that evening – with added Spam. She snorts. Lord, she must really be sozzled. But what a different feeling that was, trying to force herself to want him. Quite the reverse with Roland.

'I suppose I might be said to have a flair for dancing,' she says. 'I certainly love it. We could dance now?'

He puts his plate on the floor, takes off his specs, and rubs his eyes. 'Headache,' he says.

'Would you rather the radio off then?'

He nods and when she switches it off the sudden silence is like a douse of cold water. She picks up the plates, wondering, *now what?* What she'd really like to do is hold him. But might she frighten him off? So nice when they were dancing, he felt so *right*.

'Aspirin?'

But he appears to be asleep, and she dares to go and peer more closely at his face. Smooth eyelids fringed with thick black lashes, thick brows that grow almost together, dents from his specs on the sides of his straight nose, delicate lips, a deeply scored groove above. His skin is olive, he badly needs a shave, the bristles make a dark, silky shadow. His eyes snap open, and she jumps back.

'Just checking you were still breathing!'

He frowns, that lost look again as if he really doesn't know where he is. 'I should go.'

'Why not stay? I don't mean like that! I could make you up a bed on the sofa?'

He hunches over his skinny knees, sighs then looks up. 'I'd rather sit up,' he says.

'All night?'

'I'll be off at first light.'

'Me too. Work.' Before he can change his mind, she goes to the cupboard, face throbbing with heat. She can't read him, but he's staying, he's staying with her and that must mean something, surely? Lord, how desperate she seems, even to herself. Cheap even. Never has she been like this. It's mortifying. She gives him one of her own pillows, and a sleeping bag. 'Eddie's,' she says, unrolling the green padded cotton. 'Boy Scouts!'

He puts out his hand, strokes the material.

'He wasn't a natural Scout,' she laughs, 'he was dragooned into it. And me into the Girl Guides. Lord!' She rolls her eyes, but he's not looking at her, only at the sleeping bag, which he holds foolishly in his arms as if it's a child. His eyes, unguarded by his specs, have a blurry warmth to them and she feels a corresponding glow inside. How nice to be able to please someone. 'What else can I get you?' She wishes she had milk she could heat for him, or *cocoa*; how heavenly that would be.

'I'm all right,' he says.

She takes her pyjamas into the bathroom. Eddie's pyjamas rather. In these she'll be perfectly decent. Her hand strays towards her lipstick and perfume. No, that would seem absurd, but she does spend a moment tidying her hair, such beastly boring hair, and removes the worst and droopiest of underwear from the airer. Too late, he's seen it all, but *still*. Her face is drunkenly flushed. *'There was a young fellow named Roland'*, she begins as she brushes, but no, he doesn't want to be called Roland. Roley then. Easier to rhyme anyway. She grins idiotically as she spits out the powder, picks up the scourer and Ajax, and gives the basin a clean as she composes. When she's ready she goes back through and clears her throat.

'*There was a young fellow called Roley,*
*Whose socks were most awfully holey,*
*When mended with hemp,*
*They gave him the cremp,*
*And he lost all his sense of controlly.*'

She dissolves into giggles. 'Sorry!'

He's got the sleeping bag draped round his shoulders. He opens his eyes and smiles. Oh, such a smile; it seems to shift her internal organs. She stands looking down at him with her arms folded.

'Controlly?' he says. 'Cremp?!'

'Well, it's late!'

'You *are* like your brother,' he says.

'Actually, so are *you,* in some ways.' There's a silence so tight it almost creaks. 'Didn't you want to tell me something earlier?'

'Not now,' he says, nodding at the pyjamas. 'His?'

'Yup.' She twirls foolishly. The moment stretches tautly. 'Well, goodnight.' As she moves towards her bed, she hears him stand up, feels him approaching, and she stops. It is as if all the hairs on her body and head are aerials stretching towards him. She swallows, mouth dry, turns to face him and he steps back. Impulsively, she rests a hand on his cheek. 'Night-night, Roley,' she says, feeling an absurd urge to call him 'dear'.

As she turns away again, his arms come round her from behind, and she feels warm breath on the nape of her neck. He begins, softly, to run his hands down the thick brushed cotton over her hips and thighs, and her whole skin turns electric. She can't breathe, hardly dares to move, for fear of breaking the moment. And then she turns in his arms and kisses him, a deep kiss, though he's tentative and pulls back a little. She begins to feel foolish, about to end the moment herself, but suddenly a strength is in him, and he gets hold of her, and his kisses are hard and probing, but not expert at all, a part of her notes, while her mouth reciprocates. 'Stop, stop,' he mutters, most weirdly, between kisses. But she doesn't stop, doesn't want to stop; she wants him, of course she does, and he kneels in front of her, undoes the knot of the pyjamas and lets them fall, and she sees that his eyes are closed. And she pulls him up and to her, undoing him, his eyes still shut... and though he persists in saying 'Stop, stop, stop!', love is made. At least that's how it feels to her, actual *love*, though it's so fast and inexpert and there's no French letter, no words of love, there's nothing careful, no caresses or sweet nothings. He groans and shudders, and they stop. Now is the time for sweet nothings. He's obviously inexperienced. *Well, he's been a POW for years Aida, what the hell did you expect? You might be the first for* years. She wriggles out from under him, stands, pulls up the pyjama trousers.

He sits on the edge of the sofa, head drooping. 'Sorry,' he mutters, voice thickened as if he's on the verge of tears.

'Don't be daft,' she says. Yes, there are actual tears standing in his eyes. 'No need to be sorry. I'm *happy*.' It's only partly a lie. Happy but puzzled, she'd like to add. She bends down to kiss his brow, a weirdly motherly gesture. Next, she'll be ruffling his hair or spitting on a hanky to clean a smut off his cheek! Nervously she laughs. 'Though that did come as a surprise.'

'You wanted it?'

'Well... yes.'

'I didn't mean...'

'Shhh.' She holds a finger to her lips, shivers, feels wetness trickle down her leg. Back in the bathroom she washes. Without the boiler on the water is only tepid, but she doesn't care. They've made love! She and Doctor Roland Crowley have made love! It wasn't wonderful but it was *significant*. Catching her own eye in the mirror, she quails remembering the mortifying scene with Neville. What a tart she truly seems to be. *But no, Aida, that was different. You didn't, don't, couldn't, can't, love him. And in any case, that's all over.*

When she returns to the kitchen, she finds Roland in hat and coat. Again, she recalls Neville. *Oh Lord.*

'Don't go,' she says.

'I'm not going to sleep. I might... shout out.'

'I don't care. We can sit up all night, we can play cards or anything, or we can just talk... or if you want to sleep, I don't mind at all if you shout. I'll be here.'

But he's heading for the door. He turns, and somehow gives the illusion of looking into her eyes without actually meeting them. 'Please don't think I had any bad intentions towards you and your family.'

'My *family*?!' she shrieks. 'What are you on about?!'

'*Edgar's* family,' he says, hoists his bag over his shoulder, opens the door and leaves. Numbly, she listens to his feet clumping down the stairs. She hears the outer door slam shut. And when she goes to the window, she sees him slope away down the street, just as she used to spot him out there lurking.

---

He strides off down the street, heart thumping: *you fucker, you fucker, you fucker, you fucker.* His feet slam into the road. It comes to him that he could end it. Walk to the river and end it. She shouldn't have come so close to him, should not have stood in front of him like that in Edgar's pyjamas. No. You can't put the blame on her. *You fucker, you fucker, you fucker, you fucker.*

This morning, he nearly got away, nearly saved himself. No one has done wrong here, but him. Has he the balls to jump into the water? In the jungle, Edgar, starkers, washing in the river, got swept away. No one there to see, no one knew where he was. The Nips thought he'd escaped, but that was absurd; there was nowhere to escape to, they were deep in the jungle. To escape would have been suicide.

His feet begin to drag. Two days later, helped by some Chinese women, Edgar returned. He was punished by being buried to his neck and left in the sun all day, guarded so that no one could offer shade or water. By the time night fell his eyes were swollen shut, his neck limp. He looked dead. Starling and Lammy had to dig him out. He was still alive, but only just. He recovered, but never quite. Something had gone from him, never again so ready with a quip or a limerick. How would Aida like hearing that? She thinks she wants to know, but she does not.

He's reached the river now, and leans over the concrete parapet to watch the dark flow. Cold and peaceful. No, not peaceful. It's just black water. No one's about to stop him. If he went in now, there would be cold and then beautiful, beautiful nothing.

He tries. He starts to scramble up, but as soon as he gets on top of the parapet he's scared of falling, and gets back down. He walks away from the river, fast. After all, he only did what men do to women. And she wanted it. She could have pulled away. There was no force. And it was natural. Man and woman. That's what it's all about. Man and woman like in the Bible. Like Mum and Dad, like Celia and Lammy.

Why then did it feel wrong?

He keeps walking, in the end almost walking in his sleep. No real sleep for nights now. And he never even told her the truth about who he is. And he does actually like her. She makes him laugh. She reminds him of Edgar – but she's herself, too. And he likes that self. If it wasn't for the fucking lie. If it wasn't for the fact that he's homosexual. As he thinks this, he clocks that he's admitted something. He's homosexual, a bender, a pansy, a poofter, a queer.

Can he settle for that?

He calls up the thought of Celia, the idea of *wife*. That's what he wants, isn't it? What about Aida as a wife? If they married, he'd become part of Edgar's family. If it wasn't for the lie, might that have been possible? What if, he feels a surge of extra energy, begins to walk faster, what if he goes back to her flat tomorrow, tells her the truth? He could just come out with it: "*My name's Leonard Starling. I'm not a doctor, but a one-handed, poor nobody who lied to your parents, and fucked you last night while thinking about your brother. Will you marry me?*"

He snorts. No fucking way.

# PART 3

## PAPER AND INK

*To discover the truth in one's own heart, one's first weapon of choice must always be the pen. Writing and Discovery.* (E.P Crowley 1936.)

# AIDA

15b Buttress Street
    London
    SE6

6th January 1946

Dear Roland,

Since you (no doubt deliberately) failed to give me your address, this is a ridiculous enterprise. However, I will go utterly fruitcake if I don't express my feelings somehow, so I will write to you regardless of the fact that I am not writing to you. Or that I am writing to you, but you are not receiving my missives. (Or missiles.)

Who knows, perhaps you'll emerge from the woodwork one of these days so that I can present you with my scribblings (rantings)?

Here's a limerick just for you:

There was a young doctor called Roland,
    Who sadly had only one hand,
    He seemed nice as pie,
    Or was it a lie?
    Do please help me to understand.

I'm not angry about what happened, but I DO really, really, REALLY need to understand. You seem to veer about, where emotion is concerned, and I am confused. There were moments when I thought ~~that you like~~ Suffice it to say, I'd like to see you again. Apart from anything else, you're a precious connection to my brother and I hope at the very least, that we can be pals. I phoned Mummy and asked her for your number, but she says you never gave it. And that strikes us both as extremely rum. Mummy says she did ask you, but looking back, realises that you always managed to obfuscate.

They (the parents) were, unsurprisingly, upset that you left without a word on Boxing Day. Your note was, and I quote, 'Inadequate to the task,' – Daddy's words – not to mention 'bloody rude,' (mine). In an effort to smooth things over I went home for my birthday (4th Jan in case you're interested, which you are not). Mummy and I decided to visit the old artist, Sir Murray-Hill, (he's had a stroke) and see if we could get Edgar's scraps back. But his wife more or less sent us packing. She said anything left littered about would have been thrown away. 'Any old rubbish,' she said. And she only let Mummy have <u>five minutes</u> by his bedside and wouldn't leave the room. He has difficulty speaking. Very upsetting, Mummy found it. So, the best thing is to accept that the scraps have gone. I'm so sorry, after all your efforts (rather unorthodox in parts!) to get them to us. However, as they say, worse things happen at sea. (How do they make that out?)

Back at work now. Appalling weather, isn't it? Is the sun on strike like everyone else? The Ministry is a beastly place, and the news re food is grim. No end to rationing in sight. It will get worse before it gets better. Lucky we had such a good feed at Christmas – thanks to Daddy's spiv they tend not to go short. I, on the other hand, have been living grimly on pilchards, and an apparently newly invented fish called barracuda. I don't know if you've come across it? Don't bother; it's worse than pilchards. ~~Though maybe not lizard!!!~~

Well, that's all for now.

Affectionately yours,

Aida. X

15b Buttress Street
London
SE6

6th February

Dear Roland,

There is something very particular, and rather urgent, that I need to speak to you about. I don't know what to do. Oh, hell's bells. Since I'm not sending this to you, I might as well come straight out with it. I think I might be pregnant. The curse is late, but I have no other symptoms, so it might <u>not</u> be that. If I am, then clearly we must meet and talk about it. Never in a million years would I say this in a real letter, but there's a possibility that ~~I might love you. You bring something out in me.~~

I've never wanted a child (and truthfully don't want this one) but I'm too scared to do anything about it. I know a girl who got pregnant twice and had both of them stopped. The first time was all right, but after the second she nearly died, and now can never have a baby.

I'm surprised that after our day and night together, and the closeness I thought we <u>both</u> felt (and what happened at the end of the evening, of course) that you haven't even had the courtesy to write and see if I'm all right.

Surprised is not the half of it! Did it never <u>occur</u> to you that I might get pregnant? Aren't you a doctor, for Christ's sake?! I know you're suffering some kind of shell shock or whatever it is, but still, this is VERY BAD behaviour. <u>Appalling</u> behaviour. In fact, I'm feeling so angry that I don't know if I even do want to see you. Edgar would punch you in the face. ~~And now you've made me cry.~~

    I never ever want to see you or even think of you again.

Yours with deep loathing and simmering resentment,

Aida.

15b Buttress Street
   London
   SE6

15th Feb

Dear Roland,

Mummy came to town to see a doctor yesterday. We met for tea in Lyons, and over toasted teacakes, she told me that she's got to have an operation. It was a shock, but when I think about it, she has been looking seedy. She assures me she'll live.

She mentioned an idea we talked about some time ago, of making a memorial to Edgar since we don't have an actual grave. Daddy will pay for something, she says. I wish you were reading this; you might have an idea of what he'd like.

I didn't mention Neville Guthrie to you. He's a chap from work, who I have been out with from time to time. He's a decent sort and seems to have fallen for me. I'm not in love with him, but he's not <u>impossible</u>. Yesterday afternoon we went to a Quaker meeting together. We sat in a circle, and one of the friends (as the Quakers refer to themselves) gave a little talk about being a beacon of light in these hard times, about generosity of spirit. I thought of you and your <u>un</u>generous spirit. (How can you simply walk away and never even see if I'm all right?) And then we all sat quietly. The Quaker way. The room was freezing, everyone muffled up and sniffling. Some "friends" were quite conventionally dressed, but there seemed to be a lot of very long rough scarves about, hand-woven in eccentric colours. I bet one "friend" made them for everyone for Christmas. Pools of water on the floor from tramped-in snow. I'm surprised it melted, it was so cold, clouds of mingled breath all smelling of Vicks.

The idea is that you wait for the spirit to move you to speak. I sat there waiting. I kept looking at Neville, but he was sitting with his gloves between his knees, looking down. Someone kept sneezing, and someone passed wind. I almost got the giggles. If Edgar had been there, we wouldn't have been able to control ourselves. (We got the most frightful giggles sometimes, and used to get sent down from the table.)

I had to think of awful things to stop myself. Awful things. ~~Never seeing you again, for one.~~ But then I began to cry. Tears just came out and ran down my face. Neville reached for my hand. How nice to have someone to comfort one. I could be that to you.

In the end someone got up and said a sort of prayer, and then more silence. I began to get used to it after a while. A full silence is better than empty preaching, I thought, and wondered if it was the spirit moving me to such profundity! Should I get up and say it? But it was the end of the silence by then. Afterwards, there were cups of tea and chat, which was disappointedly banal. All rather odd people, but odd in a nice way, I thought. The sort of people the aunts would like, particularly a lady called Christabel, with wooden jewellery and a tuft of beard.

Why am I writing all this to you? Well, of course, I'm not.

Cool regards,

Aida

15b Buttress Street
London
SE6

1st March

Dear Roland,

Why the heck am I saying "dear"? Am I going truly batty? I can't believe my stupid body would do this to me. But it wasn't MY body alone. That's rather the point.

At work this morning, I was on tea trolley duty, the only virtue of which is that it affords one half an hour away from the desk. Anyway, as I was making the tea, I suddenly felt nauseated by the smell, which usually I barely notice. And that, along with the fact that the curse still hasn't come (nearly a month late now), makes me think that I must really have fallen. ~~If only I were brave enough to have it stopped~~.

I've been trying to get Neville to sleep with me again; we have only once been together in that way, and it was a fiasco. He doesn't believe in sex before marriage. It's not a Quaker belief, just a personal preference. That might explain the mortifying shambles when we tried before and gives me some hope that if we <u>were</u> to marry, he would pull his socks up, so to speak! He's nice enough and smitten enough (I flatter myself) that he <u>might</u> not even mind if he knew the brat wasn't his, but easier all round if there's some ambiguity.

He's nice-looking. I like his nose and the colour of his hair. He has tiny ears, and big, capable-looking hands ~~though I loathe his thumbnails.~~ He carves wooden spoons. One of his front teeth is grey, but otherwise his teeth are good. God, sounds like I'm describing a horse! I wish he'd drink a bit more; it might make him more ~~interesting,~~ ~~fun,~~ relaxed.

The other thing is that Mummy's going into hospital next week, and I don't want to worry her. Would I confide in her otherwise? I don't know. She likes to think we can talk about anything. She always asks if I've seen you and is baffled that you haven't kept in touch. 'Not so much as a proper thank-you note,' she says.

And that is REALLY bad form, Roland. I thought you said you were going to write and apologise?

Sometimes, I try to picture you, in order to work out what it was about you that I liked so much.

I'm not normally a worrier, but I'm worried now: about Mummy and my own predicament, and whether to try to marry Neville.

Yours uncordially,

Aida

15b Buttress Street
    London
    SE6

5th March

Ruddy Roland,

I can't go near tea or coffee and have started throwing up, and my chest is itching, so that is confirmed.
    BLOODY BLOODY BLOODY HELL.

# STARLING

2 January 1946

New diary. New Year's resolution – keep it up. Collins diary, Christmas gift, smart, a-page-a-day and ribbon bookmark. Fountain pen from Edgar's old man.

Last "diary" was scraps of paper started in Changi and carried on for months, even in the jungle to start with. Felt important to record the days. There was much scribbling and sketching. Did we think we were so important?

In Changi I wrote stuff about work, friends, rations. Rice. 'Rice and shine,' Edgar said of our miniscule morning ration. After that "diary" was found, and I was beaten, I stopped bothering. But now, clean white pages, pen in hand. A silver-plated Parker – best pen I'm ever likely to touch.

Mum was overcome when I got home, insisted on hashing up another Christmas dinner. Why the hell didn't I spend Christmas at home? If I had, none of it would have…

Don't write the bad things, the lost things. This is a new year. The war's over. The lost things are lost. Like the hand. Gone things are gone, people too. If there was a way to wipe the brain, the memory, would I? Start all over again with a clean slate? It's what Mum said when Big Ben rang out from the wireless. 'A new year, Lennie, a clean slate.'

5th January

Writing makes thoughts last. Dangerous. If anyone were to read. If <u>you're</u> reading, please stop. But who'd want to? Write what the hell you want, no one cares. Write what the hell you want, and later, burn it.

Think about going back to being Lennie, instead of Starling?

7th January

The old man found me a job, starting tomorrow. 'Paper-shuffling,' he says. Pleased as punch when he told me. 'Earn your keep, son.' 'Prospects.' One-handed paper-shuffling is a trick I can learn. I'll do it for Mum. Just me being here pleases her. I let her cut up my food, light my fags. She's knitting me a pullover. (Reminds me of Celia, and the jumper for Lammy.)

Forget medicine, you crapper. You can't study that at night school. Who do you think you are wanting to be a doctor?

Screamed my bloody head off last night. Woke with Mum saying, 'There, there.' Black looks from the old man at breakfast. Scarpered off out of it after dinner, tramped through the hills, to the reservoir. Sun low, water like new pennies. Met an old bloke fishing beside a sign that said, "Fishing Strictly Prohibited". Coloured flies in the rim of his hat. Nose swollen (rhinophyma?). He was grubbing in a tin of maggots as I passed, and the sight stopped me in my tracks. Maggots in ulcerated wounds can eat the pus, dressed with leaves and strapped. Hurts like hell, but often works. If the stink goes away, the maggots will be fat and still.

He spoke. 'You all right there, lad? Drop of tea left in flask if you want it?'

I sat with him, though the light was going and there was a long walk back. The tea was bitter black. In a bucket, he'd some brown trout and gave me one, wrapped in newspaper. He asked about my war, and when I told him he put a hand on my arm and said, 'God Bless.' His own three lads were lost in France. 1940, 1941, 1942. In order of age. He used to bring them fishing here, he said. Our eyes met and stuck as if we were daring each other not to scream. We sat for a bit, water lapping against concrete. Then he sighed and threaded a hook with maggots and heaved up and cast his line.

I stood. Ashamed. There I was, miserable as all hell while this man had lost so much yet stayed cheerful. As I left, he wished me a Happy New Year and I said the same.

What I've done with Aida, spoils how I can think of Edgar. That pure feeling was the only good thing that came out of the whole shitshow. And it went both ways. It <u>did</u>. I'm <u>sure</u> it did. It wasn't all one way. But he'd ~~fucking~~ kill me now.

What if I write to Aida? If I write to the Everetts? The worst thing is Aida. Even after I lost control, she was <u>nice</u>. That slays me. She wanted me to stay. After all that, she wanted me to stay. But not <u>me.</u> It was Roland she wanted.

10th January

Meant to write daily, but resolutions are made to be broken. Work dull, answering phone, recording sales. If I play my cards right, I'll soon be allowed to receive payments. Be still my beating heart. (As Edgar would say.)

Along with me in the office are Nancy Smith and Mr Broadhurst, and through a pane of glass, Mr Ramsay the boss. Don't have much do with him. Nancy's nice. She shows me the ropes. Mr Broadhurst's about fifty, dandruff shoulders, hearing aids that whistle.

'Thank God for a bit of life,' Nancy said. We were on our break. She's dark-haired, dark-eyed, red-lipped, what Mum'd call fast. 'Do you like dancing?' she asked. She goes three times a week. 'Trouble is I keep wearing through my shoe leather!' When I said no, she asked me to the pictures. So, I'm meeting her outside the Odeon, Saturday night. At least it's something to tell Mum, who's always on at me to go out, have fun. I heard her telling a neighbour I was meeting "a young lady from work". Of course, she wants grandchildren. If only I wasn't the only. If only my sister hadn't died. She might be living round the corner with kiddies now, calling her Gran, keeping her company. But there's only me.

2nd February

Nance, done up to the nines, reeked of scent. We saw 'Madonna of the Seven Moons'. I thought of Aida as we sat in Odeon. During the film I felt N's hand searching for mine, but it was the wrong side. She clutched my empty cuff, then snatched her hand away. We both sat stiff for rest of film and when the end came, she was lost for words. We stopped at the Red Lion for a drink. I bought her a Martini, had a pint of ale. She wanted to know if I preferred Phyllis Calvert or Patricia Loc. Which was more my type. She thought the film far-fetched: 'as if anyone could have a dual personality.' 'People can be different with different people,' I said, and felt sick. Isn't that what Aida said? 'Well yes,' Nancy went on, 'but that's not the same as different personalities.'

She sucked smoke through lipstick. I swigged beer. 'You could <u>want</u> one thing, but <u>need</u> something different,' I said. 'Deep!' she said and giggled. She took out her compact, patted her hair. 'How's your love life?' she said. I told her I had a girlfriend in London. She looked put out at that, but only for a minute, then asked her name. 'Aida,' I said. She lit a cigarette and crossed her legs. Plump, nylon legs that made me think of pork chops. Her eyes were roving round the bar.

I had to get out of there. 'You all right?' she said. 'I get these heads,' I said. 'I'll walk you home.' But she got up, waved to someone. 'A friend of mine over there,' she said. 'You toddle off and take an aspirin, I'll be all right. See you at work.'

Why can't I be normal? ~~Went in Three Tuns for a pint and met a chap and we went out back. Grey-haired, pin-striped,~~

~~married~~. As I walked home, snow swirled in my eyes, blotted me out.

9th February

Getting on all right at work, though a trained monkey could do the job. Things were stiff with Nance for a bit, but we're pals again. She tells me about her conquests (many). Mr Ramsay approved my attitude, and offered to send me on a bookkeeping course, two nights a week. The old man triumphant. 'My son,' he keeps saying, 'my son, singled out.'

'Good old Lennie,' Mum said, so proud. 'Now we just need to find you a nice girl.'

Thought I could be myself at home. Who was I kidding?

15th February

~~Five now. The Three Tuns is the place. I've learned how to catch an eye, when to follow. It works. It's a relief and a release. But I do not want to be like this.~~

The light this time of year makes me sad. It's stretched too thin. Everything's worn out, gutted. Grey faces, patched-up windows, broken this and that everywhere. Sad crocuses pushing through dead grass. In the jungle we wished for the cool of England, for mist and rain, and snow and damp. But here it is, and it is dismal.

Thinking about Horace and Celia. Their clean, honest little life. That's what I want. A life like that. Above board. No secrets. A wife, kids, home, and hearth. And <u>love</u>. At home, I'm not at home, because I'm not what they think. Mum's pleasure that I'm here makes me feel bad. Dad's occasional grudging approval riles me up. And we both know what he's wondering.

Mum asked about Nancy; would I be seeing her again. 'I see her every day at work. That's quite enough!' I said. 'What you want's a nice lass,' she's always saying. 'A nice sensible lass to settle you down, look after you.' The old man flapped the paper, said nothing. I took the dogs out the back to cock their legs, had a smoke, went to bed. Can't sit in at night. Mum knits, the old man does the pools, reads the paper, goes out for an occasional pint. He never invites me along, not that I'd go. I read a bit, fidget, walk the dogs, or go out alone and end up sometimes not alone.

AIDA

15b Buttress Street
London
SE6

10th March

Ruddy Roland,

Mummy has had her op: a hysterectomy, and various other parts have gone too. She looked tiny in the hospital bed but was beaming bravely. I tidied her hair, and with a dab of lipstick she looked halfway herself. Daddy says she has "an odds-on chance". I'm not sure what that means exactly, but it sounds better than odds-off. He's in a frightful state.

Just before I met you, I happened to see him with another woman. I meant to confront him at Christmas, but you distracted me. I never said a word about it, but after visiting time yesterday, he took me for a drink. We talked about ordinary things, nothing difficult. (No mention of Mummy, believe it or not!) Anyway, on my way back from the Ladies' I caught sight of him from a distance and realised that he's still fearfully handsome (for his age) with his thick black and white hair, and brown eyes. Distinguished. He was smoking a cigar and sipping whisky, and I had the dreadful thought that if Mummy were to die, he'd most certainly marry again.

I hadn't planned it but, 'I saw you with a woman,' I said as I sat down, and he choked on his smoke. 'Before Christmas, in Simpson's in the Strand. Small with a blue hat.'

'The restaurant?' he said, which for him counts as a joke, but I didn't so much as smile. He said nothing for simply yonks. The cigar smoke was making me queasy. I sipped lemonade, and my lipstick made a sickening smudge on the glass.

'Ah yes, that must have been Mrs Keppell,' he said at last. 'A friend.'

'Does Mummy know her?' I asked.

He looked daggers. 'Mummy knows I have "friends",' he said. 'I advise you Diddy to be a good girl and mind your own business.'

I had a good mind to storm out, thinking of poor Mummy lying there with half her innards gone for a burton.

There was a man propping up the bar and when he turned, I saw his face was terribly scarred – burned, I suppose, the skin so thickened it looked as if his eyes were peering through leather. His friend was on crutches. Poor damaged goods out for a pint. Made me want to blub. I keep blubbing these days.

'I love your mother deeply,' he said quietly after a time. 'And the things between us are stronger than the things that get between us.'

I was taken aback. I've never heard him say anything even remotely wise. Usually, the best he can do is state the bleeding obvious. I wonder if I could stand up and quote him at the Quakers?

Kind regards.

Aida. (Kind!!)

15b Buttress St
    Etc.

23rd March

R. R.,

Just struck by the shocking thought that I'm going to be a parent. That seems a different thing from going to have a baby, somehow. More solemn and important. This thing inside me might still be alive in eighty years!

15b Buttress St

30th March

Dear R.R.,

Visited Mummy, who talked about nothing but Edgar. It's only the second time I've seen her properly cry, awful with her thin face and hospital smell. (Must take in her Shalimar.) We plan to make a memorial for Eddie when she's up and about. What would he want, I wonder? A little statue or something?

    Went to Quakers with N. and thought about it, but the spirit neither moved me to speak nor sent me a brainwave. Daddy's pearl of wisdom didn't seem relevant, so I kept schtum. I prayed for Mummy, and the quiet was soothing; it didn't make me want to laugh this time.

Best regards,

Aida

The usual

1st April (Fool)

Dear R.R.,

Must stop writing this rubbish. You are not worth the paper and ink. Neville's going to be the brat's stand-in daddy. He came back to mine after the flicks. We saw 'Sentimental Journey', which made me cry. (All this bloody blubbing not like me at all!) He walked me home. I asked him to change the fuse on my wireless. I can perfectly well do fuses myself, but it was a good ruse, and the fact that it had popped the night before seemed like a sign.

Once he'd changed the fuse, we kissed, properly, and he started to get flustered. He asked for tea. I made a cup for him, trying not to breathe in the smell of it. Even the smell of the kettle heating on the stove has started to get to me, even the smell of the gas.

'Aren't you having one?' he said.

I couldn't stomach so much as a glass of water.

We sat on the sofa together, but I couldn't seduce him while feeling I was about to vom.

He was wearing rather good tweed trousers and jacket, and a Fair Isle pullover. Good dress sense is something to add to the list of positives. The clothes are on the worn side, of course. However many coupons would a Harris tweed suit be these days?

'I've made you something.' He produced from his pocket a wooden spoon, the handle of this one carved in the shape of a bird. The grain in the wood is like speckled feathers; he's polished it till it has a golden gleam.

'You made this for me?' I said, nearly in bloody tears again!

'It's a song thrush,' he said and leaned in for a kiss, but I had to run to the bathroom to be sick. When I came back, he was standing, wringing his hands.

'You all right?' he said. 'Tummy upset? Should I leave?'

I nodded. 'Sorry,' I said.

'Can I get you anything before I go?'

I shook my head.

He buttoned his coat. 'See you at work.' He started going down the stairs. I picked up the spoon and pressed my fingers against the pointed beak of the thrush. Having been sick, I felt a little better. I went to the door and called him back.

'I'm expecting a baby,' I said.

He sat down on the sofa, still in coat and hat, gawping up at me.

'How?' he said. 'Not from...' He waved his hand.

I sat next to him. I hadn't decided how much to say, how honest to be, how far I could trust his goodness and besottment. (I know that's not a word.) Also I suppose, R.R., there is still a tiny shred of me that is hoping you will come riding in on a white charger with a cast-iron excuse for your silence. (See what you've done to my metaphors.)

'Must have been.' I peeled away from truth, with a dizzying sort of lurch.

'But surely none of the... the stuff got near the...' He was making such ridiculous gestures with his hands that it nearly killed me not to laugh.

'Must have,' I said.

'Oh, my darling.' He stood up and held me tight. His coat buttons hurt.

I sent him away then. Utter self-disgust. I feel sicker

about my lie than I feel literally sick, which is saying a great deal.

(Not your) A

Dearest Roland,

What if you're dead? That is a logical explanation for your silence. I sobbed till my pillow was a swamp when this occurred to me. How did it not occur before? An accident? A murder? A jungle disease catching up with you? Malaria, something like that?

Suddenly the baby became precious to me because it is a surviving part of you. I hope it's a little boy with black hair and a widow's peak. A little boy who will grow up to be a doctor, but only if he wants to be; he could be an artist, if he prefers, or a farm labourer or an engine driver or a teacher or a poet or a road sweeper. (Or, if a girl then a female version of you, dark and quick, a little bird.)

Shoddy of me to have been dishonest with Neville. But it's the best thing. How many women before me have told lies in order to protect their children? You could even call it <u>honourable</u>.

I'm determined to find out whether you're alive or dead, Roland.

With love,

Aida

15b Buttress St
SE6

7th April

Dear Roland,

A letter from the American. I never mentioned <u>him</u> to you. We went about together before Christmas, and he loved me and left me, as they do. I never expected to hear from him again. I liked him very much indeed. More than I meant to. When he left, my heart wasn't broken, but it was dented. And never a word since, as with you. Is it something about me that causes men to run for the hills?

I could hardly believe my eyes when I saw the airmail letter by the door. Someone had trodden on it, a muddy footprint across my name and address. I thought it might be from Aunt Hari, but no, the writing was wrong. At once, all thoughts of Neville dropped away. I ran upstairs, though I was already going to be late for work. If he wants me to go to America, I will, I was thinking. And it occurred to me that I could tell him the baby was his. It would admittedly have to be rather a late baby – only by a few weeks though. The upset of the voyage might slow the pregnancy down – medically feasible?

I made myself sit down and take a deep breath before I tore it open and unfolded the flimsy paper. What finicky writing he has. It was written in pencil. Once I'd read it, I screwed it up, bawled, was sick, then went to work.

Neville very nice, but the fact he fell from my thoughts at the mere sight of an envelope is hardly a good sign.

Love,

Aida.

Usual

10th April

Dear R.,

I was shocked when I got to the hospital this evening. Mummy had taken a turn for the worse – an infection. She was lying very still, hardly managing to speak or smile. If she dies, there will only be me and Daddy left, and we will never hold together. That is a selfish and unworthy thought. I rang him. He's in touch with Mummy's consultant. He sounded very grave.

Cried at work. Neville kind but couldn't face him.

Dora went with me to see Onions, and he sent me home.

A x

Dear God, if you let Mummy recover, I'll be good – no more sex outside marriage – and I'll tell Neville the truth about the baby.

Dear R.,

The American, it turns out, is a married man with three children and now a fourth on the way. He apologised for failing to mention any of the above, says I am "a swell girl", and wished me well. No return address.

There was a young idiot gell,
    Whose lover thought she was swell,
    Now she's up the duff,
    And if that's not enough,
    She's certainly heading for hell.

A

Usual

15th April

Dear R.,

I explained to Neville about Mummy, told him I was spending the weekend at home. Of course, he was fine and decent and said he'd see me next week. 'We have a lot to discuss,' he said. It's only a matter of time before he proposes. He's taking a week's leave to visit his family in Scotland soon, and suggested very tentatively, that I might come.

Scotland. I've never been.

A

Usual

20th? April

Dear R.,

Daddy and I visited together this evening to find Mummy a bit stronger. Glory be! Thank you, God. (Now I must keep my part of the bargain.)

I took her a bunch of tulips, and held her poor hand, which was a normal temperature again. Daddy produced a letter from Mrs Murray-Hill (who'd heard Mummy was in hospital). The letter said that her husband has made a slight improvement and is getting some movement back. The letter included a card that he'd done for Mummy, rather a sad sort of scrawl – meant to be a flower? And the handwriting drooped across the page like a collapsing line of washing. It bucked Mummy up no end to have it though. Sir Murray-Hill was quite a famous artist in his day. Don't suppose he'll paint again, not seriously. Shame. Mummy was quite the devotee.

Afterwards, Daddy and I went for supper, and not a word was said about Mrs Keppell or marriage or Edgar. I asked him how one would know if a doctor had died. He laughed at me, guessing I was thinking of you, Roland, and said he'd make some enquiries. If you are dead, I would like to know for sure before I commit myself thoroughly to Neville. Daddy dropped me home and gave me five pounds! Not sick once today.

Must I keep my side of the bargain? I'm sure God would understand.

A

# STARLING

28th February

Went to Three Tuns last night, usual drill. He went again. He went out first, I waited a bit, then followed. He was in bogs as expected. We got in a stall and locked the door. But then a banging on door. Thought my bleeding heart would stop. Was he a plant? They do that, police, "picking pansies" they call it, but it wasn't that. He was scared shitless, worse than me, blubbing and muttering about his wife and kiddies.

'Police. Step outside please, gentlemen.' There was a small window, high up. It had to be me, lighter and younger. If, when he opened door, he was alone, he'd be all right, nothing proven. I stood on his shoulders, squeezed through, dropped into a gap between back wall of the pub and gents. Dim voices, then quiet. Complete dark. Couldn't see a fucking thing.

Only way out was up. Felt like hours it took, to climb back to window, braced between walls. Kept falling, and having to try again. Thought about not trying. My bones would never be found. What if there were other bones under here, pansy bones, I thought? That spooked me enough to keep trying. Window only apparent when someone turned on the light. In the end, I got out and legged it, would have sprinted if I hadn't twisted my ankle. Got home covered in scratches, torn clothes, lost specs, so now half blind while I wait for new ones. Said I'd been chased by a dog, had to jump over a wall. Not too far from truth. Dad passed no comment.

Never again.

7th March

Had to fork out for new specs. Scratches healing. ~~Fucking~~ browned off.

15th March

Evening class started. Other students mostly (about sixteen). Kids, bored by the war. Hit it off with one of the mature ones. She reminds me of Aida. Sort of direct and unfussy. (Red-haired, freckled, snub nose, large bust, physically nothing like, it's the manner.)

She raised an eyebrow at me at a daft remark from one of the babies as she calls them. Full-beam smile. We talk after class about the state of the world, Nuremberg, Ireland. She's clever. A wife like that, someone you could talk to... Maggie's her name. Engaged to a copper(!)

Dreamed about Edgar. Nothing bad, just that he was here. A few times back then when our eyes met, I ~~thought,~~ wondered, do you feel the same? When he was dying, I nursed him, washed him, held his hand. There was no cure for dysentery. He knew what lay in store. He got so thin, so hot, skin burning dark, eyes sunken, writhing, too weak to get to latrine. Did my best to keep him clean. He knew when the end was near and told me where his tin was buried.

When he died, I kissed his lips.

I never got dysentery: only malaria, pellagra, only ulcers, only a lost hand.

Sometimes I think he felt the same. Sometimes I think he'd have been disgusted. Or maybe he'd have understood, but kindly turned me down.

I have to live the rest of my life never knowing.

19th March

A new resolve. A late new year's resolution. I WANT TO BE A GOOD AND PROPER MAN. I want to want women. I do like them, enjoy their company more (when I think about it) than most men. But I don't feel sexually attracted. That's the <u>only</u> problem. If I could fix that, I'd be happy. It feels good to be clear about this. I will fix it.

A homo who wants to go straight,
    Has hell of a lot on his plate,
    Try as he might,
    The process is shite,
    But how else can he find a life mate?

I <u>will</u> clear my conscience with the Everetts, particularly Aida, starting with Aida. I'll write. Tell the whole truth. Try out:

Dear Aida,

    The reasons for this letter are twofold: 1, to apologise for my behaviour on Boxing Day. You were nothing but kind. I took advantage of you in the worst possible way. 2, I am not Roland Crowley. He died in '44. Nor am I a doctor, but I had been about to start med school in '39. When I visited your mum to return the tin, she assumed I was Roland Crowley. I never said I was. But I should have put her right. And then it was too late to put it right.

    I felt sick at the deception. I should not have come for Christmas. As soon as I got there I knew and tried to get away. When you saw me on the stairs on Christmas Eve, I was trying to leave. I ~~was horrified to see you on the train~~ did my best to lose you on the way back to London. I should not have gone home with you on Boxing Day.

I don't expect you to forgive me or to ever want to see me again, but I want you to know that I like you very much. I would like to see you. Should you be able to find it in your heart to forgive me, then please write.

Yours…

Fuck it, that won't do.

1st April

All Fool's Day. Fool or not, appointment with Dr Bailey next week. How to face him? He's known me since birth.

Last week a bout of malaria meant a day off work. Sweating and shivering under a sheet, Mum fussing with tea, hot water bottles, aspirin. To close my eyes was to be back in the jungle, crawling with lice, mosquitos. Edgar nursed *me* then. As after the amputation. He quoted Thomas Hardy to me. One about love, "Woman much missed how you call to me, call to me." He read that. Meant as a message?

Can love that's never spoken be called love, or does it need to be spoken to be true? But if it's never spoken, it can never be broken. If I were a poet, I could make a poem of that.

Better not spoken, not tested nor spoken,
    Or better to blurt it and risk?
    Better to live on not knowing, not growing,
    Or risk all as the cost of the tryst?

He did once say "My Darling Starling". Was it only because of the rhyme?

April 7th

Caught Nance crying in kitchen at work. She's up the duff. Means to get rid. Face hard and blank when she said that. She was pressing her stomach against the sink. 'Why not have it?' I said. A nasty laugh she gave. 'How many reasons do you want? First off, my Dad'd skin me alive.' She was counting on her fingers. 'Second off, I don't want to be tied down yet or <u>never,</u> third off, I don't quite know whose it is. Oh yes, judge me. I know I'm a trollop.' That word made me laugh, and her too. 'Well, that's what my granny would say,' she said. She suddenly hugged me. 'You're a good mate,' she said. 'The only man I can talk to without it turning into you-know-what.'

12th April

Appointment came up. Twenty-minute wait felt like hours. Mums with prams and kids. A bloke with a bandaged foot. One with muffled-up ears. As I sat there I thought, what if I was the doctor behind that door? I'd have been a good doctor, I know I would. But let it go, Starling, you crapper. That's not for the likes of you.

When I finally got in, old Doctor Bailey hauled himself to his feet, and shook my hand in both of his.

'Leonard. Good to see you, lad. I was sorry to hear what happened to you. Good to see you back.'

'Lost a part in the process.' I waved my empty cuff.

'Your mother said. Your poor mother, in here with her nerves nearly every week while you were gone. I was as relieved as she was when she heard you were coming home.'

He sat down behind his desk. He's got fatter since I saw him last, lost hair, grown jowls. When I was a nipper, I thought of him like God. Wanted to be just like him. Family doctor.

'Sit down, lad.' I did. 'Well then, what can I do you for?' (usual joke).

I couldn't speak, and he waited, tapping his pen.

'Still getting fevers – malarial,' I said in the end.

'How often?'

'Just now and then.'

'Let's have a look.' He heaved himself up, lifted my specs off, and pulled down my lower lids. 'No sign of jaundice.'

'And getting pain here…' I pointed to where my hand would be.

'Let's have a look-see then.'

I don't normally show the stump. Had to struggle out of my jacket and pullover, sit in my vest to show him. He held my forearm gently in his big hands and tears wanted to come.

No one has touched me there since Edgar.

'Nicely healed,' he said, and told me what I knew. 'Phantom pain doesn't happen in the site of the missing part, but in the brain, which thinks it's still there. It will die down over time.'

'Thank you,' I said.

'Anything else?' he said.

'No, thank you.' I put my clothes back on and stood.

'I hear you're training to be an accountant.' He laughed. 'Nothing gets past me! Your mum's pleased as punch. Do you know, I remember you as a solemn little lad standing just where you are now, saying you wanted to be a doctor like me!' He smacked himself heartily on the chest.

'I did.'

He scratched his head. 'Bless me, of course. Didn't you get Garstang sponsorship?'

'Yes.'

'You got a place?'

'St Thomas's, but they've stopped the scholarship, so I'm scuppered.'

He shook his head. 'Well, that is a crying shame,' he said. 'But look on the bright side, Leonard. Accountancy's a good solid job. Not such arduous training either!'

'Thank you.' I made for the door but stopped. If I didn't speak then, I never would. 'There's something else,' I said.

He nodded, as if that's what he expected, that and pointed at chair. I sat down. Words stuck in my throat.

'Spit it out, lad,' he said, looking at his watch.

I swallowed. 'I'd like to get married, and all the usual.'

'Ah.' He smiled, leaned forward, and patted me on knee. 'Go on.'

'It's just that…'

'Spit it out.'

I closed my eyes. 'I don't like girls in that way.'

When I dared look up, he was nodding. 'Don't worry, lad, after all you've been through it can take the libido time to recover. Clap eyes on the right young lady, and all will spring into action, don't you fret.'

'No. It's men I…'

He didn't move, but something behind his face changed.

'You're confused,' he said.

'No,' I said. Now I'd started it was a relief to go on. 'I've always been like that. It's boys I like, men. But I don't want to. I want to want a woman; I want to marry, and have kids.'

He picked up his pipe, stuffed and lit it. You could hear a baby crying in the waiting room. 'Well, that's half the battle,' he said. 'The other thing is stuff and nonsense.' He puffed smoke. 'Immaturity is what it is. Boys will be boys, and all that. Not uncommon in the immature male, trust me, Leonard.' He tapped the side of his nose. 'Your true invert never grows past it, but you're better than that. I've known you since you were a nipper – before! – and there's nothing wrong with you. Nothing at all. You go out there, doctor's orders, find yourself the right girl and it will all fall into place. Understand?'

I nodded.

'And don't breathe a word of this nonsense to your mother. With her nerves…'

'Of course not.'

'And now I must get on.'

'Thank you.'

'Don't worry, lad,' he said. 'Just follow my orders and you'll see. Nature will take its course. I'll be delivering your first baby before you know it, just you wait and see.'

Three Tuns.

26th April

Tried to write to Aida again. Failed again.

Went with Nancy for her "little op". It was a house in Earl's Court. Left her there and walked in park. Bus tickets and fag ends blowing round in circles. Back just in time to see her totter out.

'What I need's a drink,' she said and clutched my arm.

Nearest pub was White Lion. Bought her a cherry brandy, which she tipped straight back, and I got her another. She looked different. No make-up except some lipstick she must have put on after. Prettier without the eye stuff. Looked like a sad child, in her mum's high-heels and lipstick.

'Eternal damnation for me then,' she said. She's Catholic, or was: 'No point in it now, is there?'

I lost God in the jungle. Before that, had the normal watery sort of English Christianity. Out there some men got more religious, others lost it. What kind of god would allow this? etc. The Japs gave us Sunday afternoons off, unless it was forfeited as punishment (often as not). But when we had afternoon off, our Chaplain, Hunter, would put together a service: prayers and hymns, which we shouted with gusto. More patriotic than holy I think. The services were when we did funerals, saved up from the week. It was a rare week when there were none. Edgar was one of five. For sanitary purposes the bodies were burned. ~~The smell, the smell. The worst thing when you're starved, the smell of meat smoke. The horror when it makes your mouth water~~.

Nance asked me about my girl. 'Not seen her lately,' I said, 'but soon.'

'Lucky cow,' she said. 'She doesn't know how lucky she

is. No bloke has ever been as kind as this to me.' And she reached over and touched my knee.

I said nothing.

'If I didn't know better, I'd wonder if you wasn't a pansy,' she said suddenly.

I choked on my beer, and she giggled, seeming more like herself.

'Listen. If you was, it wouldn't bother me. I've nothing against that sort of carry-on. But I'm sure your girl knows better!' she said. 'Oh Lord, I feel queer. One more then back to beddy-byes for me.'

I went on the bus with her and walked her home. She held my arm but kept stopping to sit on a wall.

'Bleed too much and you call a doctor,' I said.

'If that happens I'm to say I did it myself. She told me what to say I did.'

'We don't have a telephone in the house, or I'd say ring me...'

'What, are you a doctor now?'

'Actually, I was a medical orderly in POW camp,' I said. (Whyever didn't I just say <u>that</u> to Mrs Everett?)

'Really?' She gave me a look, then clung on to my arm.

'I'll take you home.'

'No, stop here. I'll tell Mum I've got a tummy bug and bad time of the month.'

I left her at her corner. Scared for her, too restless to go straight home. ~~Walked about till I found myself at Three Tuns. A miner, nice lad. The last time~~.

27th April

Nance back at work, quieter than usual, but all right. I thought afterwards, what if I'd offered to marry her? What if I'd told her I was queer, then we could each live our own lives, bring up the kiddie like a married couple? But too late now, the deed is done, and in any case, I couldn't live with her; ~~there's not enough sense or intellect.~~ I couldn't love her the way I might be able to love a woman like Aida or Celia. Women who hold their own.

There must be a way to be happy.

3rd May

Found a number in a phone box. Trixie. Climbed three flights of stairs, to the top of house. Ordinary house with an ordinary smell of soup, and she was ordinary, and that helped. £5. But then she called me "my duck" like Mum does. Started off all right, even got stiff, but couldn't make it work. It was the perfume, the greasy stuff on her cheeks… and all the flesh, folds and folds of it, till you didn't know where you were. I shrivelled up. She didn't mind, said it often happened, said did I want to 'try again'. But I felt a panic coming, sweat and shakes, almost <u>tears</u>. Total fucking humiliation.

~~Back to Three Tuns instead. Same miner. Again. He asked my name. I lied. Cried after. Never again. I will not be that man.~~

# AIDA

15b Buttress St
    SE6

21st April

R.R.,

Who the hell are you?
    Apart from being a bloody liar and a fraud?
    It took Daddy one phone call.
    I thought something was fishy. You are too <u>young</u>. We've been over and over it, Daddy and I. I've never heard him swear like that. I feel dirty, violated, mortified, utterly, utterly stupid. Who am I pregnant by?
    We shan't tell Mummy. Not till she's better, if ever.
    You and your bloody bushbaby eyes. If I had a doll of you, I'd stick pins in those eyes. You are a bloody bastard pig. I hate you. And I am a fool and a tart. And you recognised that, and you took advantage.

~~Stupid oh stupid Aida,~~
    ~~Believed every word of the bleeder,~~
    ~~She even felt love,~~
    ~~As warm as a glove,~~
    ~~Now she's cast in the role of a pleader.~~

Why am I bothering to write to you? Well, of course, I'm not. The YOU I'm writing to does not exist.

I've felt the baby move.

R.R. Go to Hell.

R.R.

You seemed so sweet. You made me feel something I have never felt before.

STOP IT. STOP IT. STOP IT. STOP IT. STOP IT. STOP IT.

15b Buttress Street
London
SE6

3rd May

Dear Lying Bastard,

Glorious spring weather yesterday. In Neville's office, the window was open to the birds and the traffic. Deliberately, I left him till last, pushed the trolley into his office and shut the door behind me. I had the truth in mind and meant to blurt it before I lost my nerve. He was in shirtsleeves, bent over his desk. He turned his face up to me. Sunshine on the tips of his lashes.

'How are you feeling, darling?' he said.

'Better today.' I handed him his tea. 'Stewed I'm afraid.'

'Come here.'

I stepped round the trolley. He grated his chair back, and patted his knee. Obediently, I perched.

'I've something to say,' I said.

'Yes, we do have quite some parleying to do, don't we?'

'First let me speak,' I said, but Onions came in then. Looked at us aghast. We might as well have been writhing naked on the floor. I leapt up, took hold of the trolley handle, and was rattling off before he could utter a word.

'What's up with you?' Dora said when I got back to my desk.

I described the scene, and she tittered behind her hand. 'Going well then?' she said. 'You haven't said much, lately. Thought it must have fizzled out.'

'On and off,' I said.

'On now, clearly.'

Onions put his head round the door and scowled at me, seemed about to speak, thought better of it, and withdrew.

Dora and I raised eyebrows, grinned, and got on with our work. I watched her busy hands, as she sorted papers, the teeny flicker of her ring. Her hands are childishly tiny, and her feet size three, but the rest of her is average. Apart from the covetable nose.

'How's Chris?' I asked after a while, and allowed her to tell me about his football team and recent wrangles with her future in-laws about the wedding. 'Less than a year to go!' She's banking on an end to sugar rationing so she can have a three-tier cake with real icing. Her sister was married last year, and her miniature cake was enclosed in a cardboard hatbox iced with plaster of Paris. 'I'll settle for nothing less than the real thing,' she said. 'Do it properly or not at all.'

I can just imagine her as a mother – coming out with such things, sensibly managing life, making everything just so. Myself, I cannot imagine doing any such thing, yet it is all hurtling towards me like an out of control train.

Or am I on the train?

Since the night at my place, N. and I haven't spent much time alone. Once, before the theatre, he gave me a cup of tea in his Charing Cross flat. It's a proper flat with separate rooms, light, a view of trees. Tidy, but for wood-chippings on the carpet; it smelled of mothballs, accounting for his miasma of old-woman's wardrobe. Everywhere, piles of books and papers: Greene, Huxley, Gurdjiev, the Beveridge Report, The Manchester Guardian, a cryptic crossword part-complete. On that occasion there wasn't time for amorous activity, and on each of our outings since, we've kept busy. He's walked me home, but dropped me at the door. We kiss and hold hands. He's not a bad kisser. By tacit consent we've avoided situations that allow for sex.

(continued on 4th)

So, yesterday N. and I coincided our lunch-breaks and walked by the Thames. We found a bench in a niche overlooking the river. A chain of barges laden with scrap metal was gliding along, and seagulls perched on the palings, eyeing our sandwiches. I was chatting away about something when he interrupted me. 'Will you marry me?'

This was hardly a surprise, but still.

'I need to tell you something first,' I said. Unwisely, I threw a scrap of crust to a gull, and caused a kerfuffle. We hid our sandwiches till they'd gone, then we sat in silence. He waited. I like that about him – that he'll allow silence, that he'll peacefully wait. I thought it awkward at first, but I'm getting the hang of it. A Quakerish sort of peace. I can be quiet, but as soon as I stop trying not to speak, out it blurts, as if the words have been queuing in my throat. I don't even necessarily know what they're going to be. But this time I did know. I meant to tell him the truth.

On the next bench, a woman sat holding hands with a man in a wheelchair. The rug over his legs hung empty from the knees. She was laughing and chatting, pointing things out to him. His head was turned away, so I couldn't see his expression. I thought she might be trying too hard.

Neville's eyes were on me, so I turned back. I would keep my bargain with God, I thought, even though I only half believe in him. I did try. I even started.

'This baby,' I said.

'Would be happier if its parents are married,' he said firmly. 'We'd be a family, Aida. You, me and...' He nodded towards my middle. And he looked so lovable at that moment. So dependable. It did seem stupid to spoil it. And I didn't want to hurt his feelings, not when his feelings were so good.

'So, yes or no?' he said.

'Suppose so,' I said. It felt as if something inside me had broken off. But it didn't hurt.

He stood, he paced, he sat, all the time grinning and shaking his head. Eventually he sat down on the bench, lit a cigarette, put back his head and breathed out a huge happy gust of smoke. It amazes me that I can make him so happy. I glanced at the side of his face. His jawline is good, strong. A handsome man. A catch.

'When do we expect it?' he said.

'August or September I think.'

He reached into his inside pocket and brought out a tiny box. 'My mother gave it to me.' He handed me the box and when I opened it, I was stunned into silence. White gold, a single large diamond surrounded by a halo of tiny ones, utterly exquisite. 'It was a great-aunt's. She married an Austrian aristocrat, and left it to my mother, but her fingers are too big. She wants my future wife to have it.'

He took the box back, pulled the ring from its white velvet cushion. 'May I?' He slid it onto my wedding finger. It fitted perfectly. A good omen? I tipped my hand this way and that, admiring the extravagant sparkle, and kept my truth all buttoned up.

Ax

STARLING

2nd May

Out of the blue, a letter from Dr Bailey. He hopes I've come to my senses, but if not, the following might be of interest. The following was information about a "relevant" trial at Wharncliffe Hospital, seeking suitable subjects.

My heart went flip.

What must it be like if what you love is legal?

~~My love is dead. I saw his body burn~~.


5th May

First, tests of heart, lungs, blood, then an interview. The two men – Doctors Shine and Blackstick – fired questions, noted answers. No effort to put me at ease. The opposite, I'd say. Dr Blackstick was tall, face like a slab; Dr Shine, porky, bald, birthmark covering one cheek. Shine the more hostile. This research, they said, was not widely known about. If I was accepted on trial, I'd have to sign a confidentiality document.

'The treatment's known as aversion therapy,' Dr Blackstick said. 'Do you know what that means?'

I nodded.

'We need to be sure you can cope with a certain amount of discomfort and unpleasantness. To facilitate conversion, it's necessary to obtain a state of maximal physical and emotional crisis.' He was looking at me, hard. I met his eyes. He said that aversion therapy has been successful in treating alcoholism and transvestism. He told me about Pavlov's experiments with unconditioned and conditioned response in dogs, and how they were extending the theory towards curing humans of "degenerate tendencies". The trial they're conducting uses two methods of stimuli, he said, chemical and electrical. I'd be on the electrical strand. They were watching for my reaction. I kept my face still.

'Any questions?' Shine asked.

'Will it <u>work</u>?' I said. 'I don't care what it takes as long as it works. I don't want to go through it for nothing. I read in The Lancet that there's a cure.'

They looked at each other. 'You must understand that this is a <u>research</u> experiment,' Shine said as if to an idiot. 'A <u>trial.</u> By that very definition there can be no guarantee.'

'I think <u>I</u> know what you're referring to,' Blackstick said. 'In a trial in the United States, there has been a proven but limited level of success. One subject in particular, habitual sodomite imprisoned twice for degeneracy, is reportedly now a contentedly married father of three.'

'That's the one,' I said. 'And that's what I want out of this.'

'No guarantee,' said Shine.

'Yet there is hope.' Blackstick smiled.

After the interview, Shine left the room and Blackstick gave me a questionnaire and waited while I completed it. I felt like a kid sitting an exam, but an exam where the wrong answers are right.

1. Have you ever had sexual relations with a man? If yes, on how many occasions?

Yes. About ~~5.~~ ~~8.~~ 3.

2. Do you have sexual fantasies about kissing or intimately touching men?

Sometimes.

3. Do you have masturbatory fantasies, leading to orgasm, about committing sodomy?

~~No. Yes. No~~. Not exactly.

4. Do you have sexual fantasies about kissing or touching a woman? If yes, on how many occasions?

~~No~~. 1.

5. Do you ever have masturbatory sexual fantasies about sexual intercourse with women leading to orgasm?

No.

6. Do you ever have fantasies about intimately touching or kissing a woman?

~~No. Yes.No.~~

The questions were easy but difficult. It's not as simple as yes or no. For each, I wanted to say more. When they say "intimate" do they only mean sex? But sex isn't the only sort of intimate. I wanted to write that. I want to have intimate (more than sexual) times with a woman. Talking, laughing, holding hands, eating with, sleeping beside, being a family with. It's only the sex side of things that needs curing.

Blackstick smoked while I filled in the questionnaire. He sat with legs crossed, reading. The book was 'Three Men in a Boat'. It was making him smile. When he saw me noticing, he put it away. When I'd finished, I handed him my paper. He asked me to wait. I lit a fag and stood by the window looking out at the hills, the folds between them hairy with bare trees.

When Blackstick came back he said, 'We conclude that you're a suitable subject. But I will need your assurance that, however unpleasant, you'll complete the process.' He waited for me to nod. 'The research is ongoing,' he told me, 'but one of the subjects has withdrawn. Could you make yourself immediately available? You'd need to arrive on Sunday…'

'This Sunday?'

'… and the initial intensive period will take five days

beginning on Monday. After this you'll be required to attend one afternoon a week for a further month, and then once a month thereafter until completion of follow-up, which will be this time next year. And after that there may be periodic follow-ups to gauge the longevity of the therapeutic process. From a legal point of view, you'll be quite safe. Your name will never be recorded in our findings, your identity will not become known to the police.'

He watched my face as I took all this in. It was the timing that was the main problem. Sunday was only three days away. What would I say to Mum and Dad, or work?

'You're a most suitable subject,' he said. 'Sound of heart and lung, of distinct degenerate tendencies, yet with a serious and genuine desire to rid yourself of such.'

'But I'll need a week off work.'

He nodded. 'Illness and follow-up medical treatment is a common excuse,' he said, 'and we can support this with a doctor's letter. We do need your decision today. Shall I leave you a few moments to decide?'

'No,' I said, fast. 'I'll do it.'

He nodded. 'Excellent. In that case, come with me.'

I followed him down a corridor. Dark wood, dark pictures in dark frames. It was a posh bit of the hospital. He walked with a limp. I wondered what he did in the war, but didn't feel it was my place to ask. We went down three lots of stairs to the basement. Here, the walls were tiled, the floors green lino, squeaky when you walked. We turned a corner and went into an office. A white-coated man turned to greet me. I'd seen this man before. He recognised me too, though he showed no sign.

'This is Colin Frost. He'll be looking after you,' Blackstick said. 'Frost, meet Subject 24.' We shook hands awkwardly.

'Subject 24 will be taking part in the programme

beginning on Monday morning. Arrival Sunday afternoon. Medical checks and paperwork complete.' He turned to me.

'I'll leave you in Mr Frost's capable hands.'

And he left the room. Frost turned away to pick up his pen. He was a tubby, sandy man I'd seen in Three Tuns.

'Don't I know you?' I said.

He ignored that. 'Now, there are a few details to get straight, signatures and so on.' His voice was Welsh. He took me through protocols and instructions, and had me sign papers, but never met my eye. I was too knackered to say more then. Knackered and confused.

10th May

Treatment starts tomorrow. I've the week off work, a letter from Blackstick's secretary. The ailment not specified, but serious enough for urgent treatment. God knows what anyone thinks. I was tempted to tell the truth to Nancy, who had tears in her eyes, wanted to come and see me in hospital. But lies come thick and fast. I am honest at heart. At least, I was. Mum and the old man think I'm off to Leeds on a training course. 'Isn't that marvellous, duckie! Proves just how much they think of you.' Her pride hurts more than any of the old man's looks.

    Don't expect to sleep tonight. Took the dogs for a walk in the rain. Passed Three Tuns, but didn't go in.

11th

~~There was a young man with proclivities,~~
    ~~That were damned as a sort of depravity,~~
    ~~Wanting to marry,~~
    ~~He took a deep breath and he,~~
    ~~Now fancies more female-shaped cavities~~.

Wrote to Aida. Shoving the letter in the box felt like throwing a grenade.

Dear Aida,

My name is not Dr Roland Crowley, but Leonard Starling, trainee accountant. The rest I'll tell you if we meet. I'm living in Sheffield but can get the train down to London on any Saturday you say.

Yours,

Leonard Starling

(More or less that.)

AIDA

15b Buttress Street
London
SE6
12th May

Dear Roland,

Home for the weekend, went to see Mummy in the convalescent home. She was in a nostalgic mood. It's the same building, she told me, where she spent her lying-in period after Edgar's birth. (Mine too presumably, but it was only Eddie she mentioned.) It's beside the Deben; you can hear the boats passing. It was a day of lemony sunshine and flitting birds.

Mummy talked about the shock of producing a son. She'd been sure the baby was a girl. 'The wrong baby,' she said. Gave me the chills when she said that, and with a sort of foggy look in her eyes. 'What do you mean?' I said, but she clammed up.

On the walk back I saw two herons. It strikes me that I have never seen a baby heron.

A

15b Buttress Street
SE6
14th May

Dear R.,

So, I am engaged. (And I must remind myself you are not reading this.) After work it was drizzly cold (what a damn miserable spring), and N. and I went to Lyons for tea. He had his arm around me as we walked along, and I felt owned. Do I mean owned? No, I mean... <u>safe</u>, looked after. Love will come in the end. Don't Mohammedans have arranged marriage based on sensible considerations, marriages that often flourish? The ring means I am spoken for – it makes me jump to see it. I'm to meet his parents soon. We'll take the sleeper to Edinburgh on the 31st and I'll return alone on the Sunday, while he stays up and has his holiday.

And then, of course, it's his turn to meet my folks. Hope Daddy will behave, refrain from political ranting. On the telephone I told Mummy (home now) that I'm engaged. Of course, she's delighted. The strength of her delight made me quail. I feel dead in my heart. Or rather, <u>distanced.</u> 'The Scottish chappie?' she said. I didn't tell her about the baby. I meant to, but somehow didn't. In any case, it will be obvious before too long. There's a curve already, and everything's growing tight around the bust. Mummy started talking about a wedding in spring next year, but it'll have to be sooner than that!

R.R.

    Mr Starling!?

    Your letter has exploded my plans. I shall write back.

    ...Shall I?

25th May

Dear R.R.,

No, don't be ridiculous, Aida. <u>Think</u>. You're marrying Neville in 4 weeks. Registry office booked, Mummy's even bought a hat, so what is the point? What is the point in seeing him? Who even is he? <u>Starling?</u> What sort of a name is that?

Dear R.R.,

Somehow it helps to be writing to you.

Had to tell Mummy about my condition – the only way she'd accept that the wedding must be so soon.

'A hole-in-the-corner affair then,' she said, clearly disappointed. On the other hand, she has been understanding; she seems not so much shocked by the pregnancy as by my secrecy. 'But you've been so ill, Mummy,' I said. Perfect excuse.

(Though had she been fit as a fiddle, I still may not have confided before.)

'A grandchild,' she said, with a sort of wistful pleasure. I'm glad that I can give her that. We both hope it'll be a boy. Of course, Edgar will feature somewhere in the name. (Can't think of a girl form for Edgar that I like. Edwina sounds weasel-ish.) Becoming a granny will take her mind off her own ailments. To think that the parents will become the grandparents. And myself and Neville, the parents. Move along, all change, we're all on the same train, heading the same way.

Edgar would have been chuffed to have a nephew.

Aida.

27th May

Dear Starling, (Real draft letter!)

Got your letter, but too late. I'd already found out that you're not Dr Crowley. Daddy made enquiries.

I'm flummoxed. It is all too queer to take in. I don't understand, and don't suppose I ever will.

However, I will meet you, as I have something to say.

Shall we meet in London? Let me know a suitable date.

Cordially yours,

Aida

15b Buttress Street
SE6
20th May

~~Dear Starling~~ R.R.,

It's not the same if I call you Starling. Can't think straight. I am used to writing to Roland. The <u>you</u> to whom I am addressing these letters is clearly not <u>you</u>, and they are clearly not <u>letters.</u> But I can't seem to write any other way now. I've never kept a diary, thinking them dull and dutiful "did this/did that/sausages for supper", etc. But I have liked this writing. Wish I'd taken part in mass observation now. It turns out that writing helps me think. The secret is to address the words to someone else. In this case, someone who never existed.

You are a habit. You really are the lowest form of vermin.

Not to mention a spanner in the works, the works being my plans. The wedding's arranged, a tiny affair. No fuss please. Get it over with. Afterwards there will be some sort of lunch, and no doubt Daddy will spout platitudes. Later, Neville wants a bigger celebration with his family in Scotland. By then I'll be a <u>wife!</u> Obedient?

I do wish he had different thumbnails. They will keep catching my eye. If only he had funny toenails instead then they could stay safely hidden in his socks.

We're searching for a new flat but will manage in N's at first. It's nicer and nearer work than mine.

Unfortunately, the Saturday you suggest we meet is the same date as my proposed visit to Scotland. I told Neville a bare-faced fib about Mummy needing me at home, so he's going on his own. Disappointed, but he didn't object. He's a saint. He has that sort of saintly patience, anyway.

I'm anxious about meeting you again, of course. But I must get it over with before I wholeheartedly settle into wedding preparations. I'm still on the platform, yet to board the train. At least in my heart. Though I know it's the right thing to do, and N. is an absolute brick.

We went to a Fabian Society meeting the other night. I do think he's right about socialism – it's the only way – but the antics of <u>this</u> government are not making the grade. I wish I had a more political brain. I try, but my mind insists on trivia. The discussion was about state-funded nursery-age childcare, but all I could seem to think of was the hair of the woman in front of me, which was a wonderfully bright red. Dyed, I'm sure. Henna? It has given me an idea.

15b Buttress Street
London
SE6
23rd May
Dear R.R.,

Dora came shopping with me for my wedding outfit. Mummy wanted to come, but Daddy says she's not yet strong enough. She sent me all her coupons though. I ordered a grey georgette dress, generously sized, and a half-veiled velvet hat to match. Dora thinks it "all rather drab". The outfit was the first I tried. 'Don't you want to look around a bit more?' said the shopgirl. She and Dora ganged up in their disappointment. But the net veil is silvery, the colour dove-grey with a trace of blue. The dress fits nicely and is elegant, I think, and suitably muted for a hole-in-the-corner affair.

What she doesn't know is that for the wedding, I'm going to henna my hair. It was only a vague plan until I went into the chemist for olive oil (earache) and spotted, on the counter, lovely exotic packages of henna. Bright red hair with the grey and silver will be spectacular.

We went for tea in Selfridges. Odd to be sitting across a café table with Dora, rather than a desk. We ordered sandwiches and fondant fancies, and she drank her way through an entire huge pot of tea, while I sipped water.

'So, you've overtaken me,' she said. It only occurred to me then that she might feel put out. <u>Her</u> wedding has been a subject of conversation ever since I've known her, and now I've leap-frogged her. And there was my extravagant ring flashing away, eclipsing hers. Two young women, shackles on our fingers, signs that we were soon to be wives. The inevitability made me feel rebellious. I was picking apart a cake covered in sticky yellow. I don't know what the flavour was supposed to be, pineapple, perhaps? I can't remember what pineapple tastes like, haven't seen one for yonks.

'But it's different for you,' I said. 'You're in love; it's what you want.'

She stopped, with her cup halfway to her lips. 'Isn't it what you want, then?'

My face went hot. 'Of course it is.'

'Aren't you in love?'

I said nothing. She frowned, shook her cigarettes at me.

'No thanks.'

She lit her cigarette in her neat little way. 'What do you mean then?'

'Just the rush of it, just… Neville.'

'You're lucky. The steady sort, he'll be a good father.'

I've let her suppose that the baby is his, and still she thinks it's good of him to marry me!

I can't wait for the whole business to be over and done with. Once it's done it's done, and I will not have to think anymore.

15b Buttress Street
London
SE6
29th May
Dear R.R.,

The wedding is hurtling towards me. Less than a month. And my meeting with ~~you~~ Mr Leonard Starling. Though perhaps, after all, we should not meet? Shall I cancel? Yes. No. Yes. No. No I won't. Not yet. If I did, I'd only change my mind. I could simply fail to turn up. Yes, I like the idea of Mr L. Starling travelling down to St Pancras, which must take some hours from Sheffield. In my mind's eye I see him waiting, even clutching flowers? Ha! The second hand of the station clock jerking forward, as in a movie, his anxious face in close-up watching and wondering. Eventually it will dawn on him that I have stood him up. (I can hardly remember his face, though I know I liked it. I do recall bushbaby eyes and a widow's peak.) And off he'll go, never knowing that he's to be a father. Which is, after all, for the best.

Yours truly, Aida.

Dear Mr Starling,

Tomorrow, we meet. Or do we? It goes round and round in my head. What is the point? The wedding is nearly here. This month! Seeing you will only stir me up. But I need to have you in front of me, in order to put you behind me.

And you should know about the baby.

I won't write again. Not to you or to the non-existent Rotten Roland. Once I've seen you, he will vanish like smoke. I'll miss him. He's become a sort of confidante, pen-pal, imaginary friend and enemy.

Yours cordially,

Miss Aida Everett (soon to be Mrs Neville Guthrie)

Lord!

# STARLING

20th May

Hard to write. Shaking still. But I will record. The aim is to dehumanise. I understand that (which is not the same as being able to bear it). Though I did. Bear it. Five days, twice a day. Naked in a dark cell with an electric grid on the floor. At intervals, projected onto all four walls, a photograph of a naked man, slim, handsome, well-endowed, half erect. Accompanying the image, a shock through the floor. No escape. Hated that man by the end. Suspect I was being spied on through an aperture in the wall. Stood with my back to it, and did my best not to scream. No arousal when the photo flashed up, only fear. Excruciating shocks sent me into spasms, like being hurled through the air, convulsions, a taste of bloody metal. Each time I got up as soon as I could and stood and shook and sweated and shivered. Tongue bitten and swollen, blood running down my chin. When the picture appeared, I felt dread. At some point, the pattern changed. Sometimes the image was there without the shock, but still the same amount of dread. And that is how it works.

'Come on now, 24,' Mr Frost said, opening the door after the first time. And the same routine after every other. After I'd dressed, he took measurements of heart and blood pressure, asked questions about my degree of arousal, physical and mental sensation. All my answers he noted down. He wrote with his left hand. I wanted to ask him about the naked man. Some fate, to be used in aversion therapy.

Sometimes Blackstick questioned me too. Never saw Shine again. After each session, Frost took me to a room with a sofa and table. The table was piled with manilla files. He brought me tea and biscuits, said to relax, look through the files, find something attractive to focus on. Each file contained pictures of happy families – mother, father, children – or pictures of naked or nearly naked females. The females were young, mostly white, but some with darker skin. I leafed through but felt no more than if it was one of Dad's seed catalogues. I was still shaking, tongue massive and painful. Wondered was I being watched? In case, I stopped at one, a fair one, not as fair as Aida, but something a bit similar.

I understand <u>how</u> and <u>why</u> aversion therapy should work. The theory. Perhaps it has? No urge to return to Three Tuns. No urge to do anything, other than stick my head under my pillow.

'What's up with you?' Nancy said when I got back to work. 'Is it cancer?' and questions, questions. My head ached, and my hand shook. 'Leave the lad alone,' said Broadhurst. I could not look anyone in the eye, though to my surprise, Mr Ramsay patted me on the shoulder. I think rumour has spread that I am having some sort of radioactive therapy.

28th May

A note from Aida sent me into a spin. I'd given up expecting it. Or even wanting it. Had I? Have I? Scared. Scared of everything. The naked man flashes in my head and in my dreams, and I wake up sweating. I see him buried to his neck like Edgar in the burning sun, ants feeding on his tears.

We're meeting at St Pancras on 9th June. A summons, it feels like. All of the above, and now a summons to meet a woman. The only one I've done it with, though that's all a blur.

I await proof that it's worked. Haven't felt like looking at men but notice no extra feelings for women. No sexual feelings at all. Since the end of the treatment, I've walked miles to avoid the Three Tuns. My feelings about Nance and Maggie have remained the same. My evening-class marks have been high; there's a prize awarded each year for the best student, and I'm in the running. That only makes my heart sink. To be the best at something I don't care about seems a bad joke.

2nd June

A bright spot. Had a drink with Frost. Colin, I can call him now. At the end of the trial, he suggested it. Surprised me. Met Sunday at the Duke of Norfolk out in the Peaks. Fine day. We sat outside with our pints.

'Good of you, by the way, not to say anything. Appreciated,' Colin said, once our chit-chat had run out. I realised that was the point of this, but I was pleased he said it.

'So, it was you, at Three Tuns?'

'Indeed.' Colin was looking into his pint. 'Rum do, you must have thought?'

Over the road was a beech tree, starting to green up. Made me think of The Beeches, and Edgar and Aida.

'So, are you?' I asked.

'I am indeed.'

We were stuck for words then for a bit. Across the road a bus stopped, and people with knapsacks and sticks got off. A young couple came towards the pub door. She smiled. I thought this then: I am sitting in public with another homosexual man. I looked at Colin. His head was tipped back, eyes shut, legs stuck out, feet crossed. I looked at his trousers. No feeling of attraction happened. Does this mean the treatment has worked? Though I wasn't attracted to every man before.

'How can you do that job?' I said.

He took out his fags, offered me one.

'Just a job,' he said. 'I'm a nurse.'

'Just a job!'

'Important work,' he said. 'You wanted to take part in the trial, I believe? Wouldn't dream of inflicting that on anyone otherwise.'

That shut me up for a bit.

'But must be hard to see people suffer.'

He nodded. 'But for a result they desire.'

'Don't you want not to be?' I said.

'Not to be queer?' He was quiet, scratching his chin. 'Once,' he said in the end. 'Not now, so much. It's what I am. It's in the grain of me.'

In the grain of you, I thought. I drunk down some beer. 'But don't you want to marry, settle down, all that?'

To be able to talk about it! To have a queer friend! And

he is a friend. A new friend, first I've ever been upfront with. I felt something like happy.

A woman was dragged past by a huge dog.

'That's going to pull her over,' I said.

He was still thinking. 'I am settled down,' he said at last. 'My friend, Fred, he's a nurse too, works on the wards at the Hallamshire. We share a flat. We've got a cat. Not a brute of a dog like that. Why do people? We bump along quite happily.'

The calm way he said this! It was like a sudden light blazing in my mind. I could hardly think straight. 'Good,' I managed to say. 'But don't people…?'

He knew what I meant. 'Sometimes. You have to have a hide like a rhino's. We're both good rhinos.'

'What about your families?'

He frowned at that. Took a swig. 'Mine have washed their hands of me. His are all right. They'd sooner we were different, of course, but they go along with it.'

'How long?'

'Met in '44.' Looked at his watch then. 'Bus due any minute.'

'I'm going to walk back.' I was full of a rushing sort of energy.

'Sure?'

We left our glasses on the windowsill.

'Good luck to you,' he said, and we shook hands. 'I hope you get what you want from life.'

'I'm going to try.'

I saw him onto the bus, watched it drive away, then took the steep path down through a field of sheep to valley bottom. As I walked along my invisible hand was clutching the air. The river was rushing brown under the new leaves. Spotted a kingfisher flash past. Green fire.

Confused as all hell now. What if I'd met Colin before? Colin and Fred in their flat, with their cat. Would I want that? But then there's Horace and Celia, the way they are, normal in the eyes of the world, the way I want to be. Wanted to be. That's what I went through the trial for.

Don't know what to want, anymore.

# PART 4

## MODERN MARRIAGE

*The reality is that a certain candour is necessary between marriage partners, but to what degree must be delicately judged. Sometimes the most successful marriages come seasoned with a sprinkling of half-truth.* (The Etiquette of Modern Marriage, Doctor P.D. Pullen. 1946.)

## 71

## AIDA

She hurries out of the hammering rain into the puddled shelter of St Pancras. As arranged, he's waiting outside WH Smith, and her heart jerks like a bad dog on a lead. He's early. So is she. According to the station clock, it's not quite noon.

What is the point of this? Now the wedding plans are underway, what really is the point? Her shoes are soaked, probably ruined. They're her nicest ones; *why wear your best shoes, Aida?* Through the high glass roof, the rain-light wavers greyly. Shaking out her brolly, she tilts back her head to see pigeons sheltering on the iron struts, and rain spearing through cracks in the glass.

Half hidden by a pillar, with pigeons chuntering above and water puddling round her feet, she watches him. Crowds of people flow in and out, a restless shifting; sometimes she can see him, sometimes he's blotted out. How long, she wonders, will he wait? She could still leave. Perhaps to see him from a distance is enough. And then to let him go.

He wears a different coat: a belted gaberdine, with a dark trilby. Several times he adjusts the tilt of his hat, craning his eyes up to the clock. Light glints on his glasses, his serious young face. She'd forgotten that serious expression, and the *slightness* of him. Compared to Neville with his broad shoulders, this fellow seems almost elfin. Why is she here? There's still the notion that she should tell him about the baby, that he deserves to know. But does he? After all he's done, does he deserve anything?

As she watches, he lights a cigarette, flicking the lighter, already grown more adept at the one-handed technique. Silly little chap, so serious, and such a fraud. She tries to kindle anger, but the sticks are wet. Instead, maddeningly, she feels a part sensation of opening in her heart that has been screwed up tight for weeks. And she does, after all, need to hear his explanation. Even if *he* deserves nothing, *she* deserves that.

So she walks towards him. He starts when he sees her.

'Not expecting me?' she snips.

'Thought you mightn't come.'

'Very nearly didn't.'

They stand motionless for a moment, taking each other in. The busy station heaves around them.

'Are you hungry?' he says. 'Lunch? Or a drink? Of course, I'll pay, after last time.'

She blurts disbelieving laughter. The nerve of him, to refer straight back to 'last time' like that!

'Sorry, I meant, I only meant...'

The crowd is parting round them like water round wreckage. Strings of tension pull in his jaw; there are shadows under his eyes. His specs are smudged, his face cleanly shaven, a couple of black bristles missed at the corner of his mouth. She'd forgotten the length of his lashes, the thickness of his brows, the beloved widow's peak. *Beloved?* Where did that come from? NO.

As they leave the station, she puts up her umbrella; there are brollies everywhere, jostling like a herd of wet beasts. Rain bounces from the pavement, making a walk impossible. A walk would have been preferable – walking is better for talking – but they must go in somewhere and besides, she needs the loo, as usual these days. They pass the hotel where they lunched on Boxing Day, where they danced. Is he remembering? She darts a sideways look, but between his pulled-up collar and pulled-down hat brim, his face is hidden.

'Here?' He stops outside a milk bar, 'or do you want a drink?'

'This'll do,' she says. 'I haven't long.'

They step inside. He removes his hat and wipes his steamed-up specs, she shakes the drips from her brolly. The place is painted red and white, crowded, noisy, steamy, smoky.

'What can I get you?'

She chooses cocoa before pushing her way to the Ladies', where she sits on the WC, face buried in her hands. Feelings are only *feelings*, Aida, made of nothing corporeal. How can something made of nothing be so blasted strong?

Outside the cubicle she unties her headscarf, tidies her flattened hair, colours in her papery lips, peers into the cheap warped mirror at her cheap warped face.

He's sitting in a sort of booth. It's all attempting to be very American. The staff wear jaunty red costumes, and the drinks come in saucerless beakers. He has black coffee, and has bought a couple of lurid buns. Within the clatter they make a bubble of silence. His hat lies on the table between them, spangled with rain. He takes out cigarettes, offers her one; she shakes her head. She plans to wait for him to speak, to let him stew, but by the time he's smoked half his cigarette she can stand it no longer.

'So?' she demands. 'What have you got to say for yourself?'

He clears his throat, takes off his specs, and begins to spin a tale, or the truth. She has to strain to hear him above the hubbub. Sipping the watery cocoa, she watches his coffee grow cold, its black surface becoming flecked with ash. The coffee is the colour of his eyes. His face seems more in focus to her than any other face she's ever seen. Every detail is sharp, distinct. He lights another cigarette from the end of the first. She picks pink icing off a bun, fishes out a minute currant.

The story is farcically plausible. She'd forgotten how northern his accent is. His lashes really are incredibly long and silky. Her hand creeps between the flaps of her coat and to her belly. Please let the brat inherit those lashes.

'When your parents assumed I was Crowley I should have put them right, of course I should, don't know why I didn't.' He shrugs miserably.

Sipping her cocoa, she studies his thin and elegant hand, so different from Neville's spades. Mr Starling's thumbnail is the proper oval shape. On the back of each finger, a few black hairs; the skin is olive, greenish veins just visible. Poor missing hand. She feels a surge of sadness. As she dips a bit of bun into her cocoa, she notices her engagement ring, the show-off glitter of it, wonders if he has.

'All right,' she says at last, 'I can *just* about see how that could happen. But then you came for Christmas! As an *imposter*. Why did you do that?'

A girl in a yellow raincoat bumps into the table. 'Whoops, sorry.' She giggles, and her eyes snag on Roland, no, *Leonard Starling,* and she pauses, simpering, though he doesn't seem to notice. Aida feels a leap of possessiveness.

'That's all right,' she says coldly, and the girl pulls a face and moves along.

'Your mum insisted,' he says.

'She could hardly *force* you.'

'I know.' He seems genuinely baffled by his own behaviour. 'Maybe I thought I'd be able to put it right? I did *want* to put it right.' Deeply serious eyes, crinkled brow. *Almost* certainly, he's telling the truth. His story is both too dull and too nonsensical to invent. 'And Aida.' He meets her eyes so acutely that she flinches. 'I wanted to meet *you*. And your mum, she wanted us to meet.'

'Yes, believing you were someone else!'

He looks down, finally takes a sip of coffee.

'Anyway, why didn't you simply speak to me *before,* instead of doing all that ridiculous lurking?'

A shrug of the thin shoulders.

'And why didn't you at least tell *me*? At Christmas, you could have explained to *me*, even if we'd kept the parents in the dark.' She almost wails this; thank heavens it's such a noisy place.

'I got...' His brows draw together again. 'I got sort of *stuck* in the lie, and it got worse and worse. The longer I said nothing, the more impossible it got. I tried to leave. Remember you caught me on the stairs on Christmas Eve?'

She blinks. Yes. And she had made that crashing joke about the family silver.

'And after Christmas dinner when you and your mum went out, I tried to go, but I bumped into your dad. I *did* leave on Christmas night, slept at station.'

'You were there all night?' She recalls finding him on the early train after she too had bolted. Bolted, partly (and farcically, as it turned out) away from *him*. Feelings shift and jostle inside her as she searches his face for signs of plausibility and sincerity. Ciggie pinched between his lips, he picks up and replaces the specs that give him such an earnest, clever look, yet make him appear younger, a touchingly earnest schoolboy.

'How old are you?' It occurs to her to ask.

'Twenty-three.'

'I thought you seemed too young to be...' She tails off,

considering. 'But on Boxing Day, we spent all that time together! Why not tell me then? You even came back to mine!'

There's a shiver between them at this, a wobble in the smoke and steam.

'I'm sorry.' He sniffs, grinds the end of his cigarette in the ashtray. His face seems to seal itself off from her, a film over his eyes. 'Your letter said you had something to say?'

Yes, that is the excuse for this encounter. It strikes her that if *he* deserves to know, then so does Neville. And she will tell him, before the wedding, she *will*. Give him a chance to call it off if that's what he wants. Why are you *really* here, Aida? She evades Starling's eyes, glances round at the wet, mostly youngish, frantic folk. The war's over and they are free and flirting in the modern Yankee-style place, a flock of hectic, chittering birds. One girl with red lipstick tilts back her head, and blows perfect smoke rings. The clatter of chat, of teaspoons and cups, is deafening. Against the steamy window, the sun is glittering now.

She sees him notice her ring at last. 'Yes. Engaged,' she says, and registers the slight crumple of his expression. 'Batty weather,' she goes on. 'Proper mad-March-hare weather even though it isn't March anymore. Are you going to eat that?' She indicates the other bun, and when he shakes his head, she lifts it to her mouth. 'Well, Mr Starling,' she says, before she takes a bite, 'Now I know who you're not, perhaps you'd better tell me more about who you are?'

## 72

## STARLING

'The rain's stopped,' he says. There's a light feeling; he's glad to have told the truth. She knows who he is, yet still she's here, eating cake. 'Walk?' he says. She's still here, but she's getting wed. That whopping stone on her finger! Out of his league. Even if there was a chance, it's gone. Is that a relief?

She wraps the remaining cake in a hanky, knots her headscarf under her chin, and they push through the crowd and out into the dazzle and sudden heat.

'Congratulations,' he thinks to say.

'Let's go to St Pancras Gardens,' she says. 'Know it?' She leads the way. He looks at her shoes, wet suede. Why the hell wear suede, in this rain? His trouser turn-ups are wet too, but inside his sturdy demob shoes, the socks are dry. Thoughts rattle irrelevantly like a tin of dried peas. He watches her legs as she walks slightly ahead, slim calves in seamed nylon. Should he find this stirring?

'It's called the Hardy Tree,' she's saying. He gazes at the tree's roots tangled with broken gravestones; root and stone merge like something in the jungle. How mixed up everything is. Memories mix and merge till he hardly knows what's true.

Sometimes he thinks Edgar kissed him; sometimes he knows it never happened.

'Why the *Hardy* Tree?' he asks.

'Apparently he worked here, as a cemetery assistant.'

'*That* Hardy? *Thomas* Hardy?'

'The very same.' She points at an information board, but condensation has got behind the glass, fogging the words.

'Edgar liked his poetry,' she says. 'Me, I prefer the novels; give me a novel any day, though the poems are nice too. I can't stand *Tess,* though. Know it? *Of the D'Urbervilles*. When the note slides under the mat! And the ending. Lord! Excruciating! Fate. If you really believe you're fated, then you're done for. We have to be able to choose, don't we?'

Raindrops on leaves shine and scatter, and his non-existent hand clutches at nothing. 'Woman much missed, how you call to me, call to me,' he mutters.

'Oh, crikey! Eddie used to quote that.' She walks round the tree, pokes at the stones with her toe, wanders off. There's a sundial guarded by four little iron dogs, all beaded with rain.

'Once, I came here with a G.I.' she says. 'He'd never even heard of Thomas Hardy.'

'Your fiancé?'

'No.' She gives him an evasive look. 'I'm marrying a Scot actually. Neville.' The diamond glitters and she holds out her hand, raindrops all around like more diamonds, in the trees and everywhere. 'In two weeks' time, I'll be Mrs Neville Guthrie. I'm supposed to be in Scotland this weekend, meeting his folks.'

'Why aren't you then?'

She gives him a look.

'You didn't not go because of this?' he says incredulously, but she's wandered off again, and he follows her to a bench. Using his hat, he brushes the wet away, and they sit looking at the sundial. Its shadow points to somewhere after two o'clock.

'You don't seem very happy about it,' he says.

'Not fearfully if you want the truth.' She twists the ring round and round her finger. Her gnawed nails are painted pink.

Wet white petals stick all over the wet path. A tree drips. A blackbird sings, and sparrows squabble in a puddle. She takes out the leftover bit of bun and throws crumbs. In silence, they watch the creatures peck and scrabble.

'Why do it then?' he says.

She snorts, says nothing for a while, turning and turning the ring. He gets the stupid notion she's unscrewing her finger. She fidgets about, crossing and uncrossing her legs. She seems to be waiting for something or gearing up for something. A uniformed nanny pushes a pram past, frowning at their bench as if she has a right to it.

'Did you have something to tell me?' he says in the end.

She gives a sudden wild laugh. 'God! I keep forgetting you haven't read the letters!' Pigeons are bullying the sparrows now, and she kicks out a foot, causing a scattering. The nanny with the pram moves on.

'Letters?'

She laughs again, more bitterly.

'What letters?'

'Oh Lord, how I wish my brother were here,' she says. Her shoulders lift as she begins to sob.

He puts an arm round her, and she lets him, leans into him. He enjoys the feeling of holding her, of being the *stronger*. His ghost hand strokes her arm, and then she lifts her face close to his and he wonders if she wants him to kiss her, but before he can decide, she's jerked away.

'*He'd* know what to do.' She takes out a hanky and blots her eyes. Angrily blows her nose.

'About what?'

'I'm expecting a baby.'

There's a fracture in the moment, the light and the wet, and the blossom and the birdsong.

'Hence the wedding. Shotgun. Or as my mother would have it, a "hole-in-the-corner affair".' She gets up, begins to walk fast, past the sundial and the little iron dogs, past the graves and the church. She's forgotten her umbrella; retrieving it, he hurries after her and catches her arm. She stares at the umbrella, as if she's never seen it before.

'Are you all right?' he says. 'What can I do?'

'What can *you* do?' They're standing under a dripping tree. The sky is darkening again. 'Must get these wretched shoes off,' she says, 'I'm going home. You can come if you like.' Her eyes meet his for a flinch. He thinks of all he's gone through to be the man for this moment, possibly, if that's what she means. But perhaps it's not. After all, she's not only engaged, but pregnant. Do women still want sex, in that condition? Surely that can't be what she means? And in any case, could he?

'I've a train to catch,' he says, 'but...'

'In that case.' She stalks away.

There's a bus coming, and she jumps onto its platform. He hesitates, then chases the bus, jumps on too. Upstairs is blue with smoke. She's sitting at the front and shows no sign of noticing when he sits beside her. Wet branches batter the windows. He pays for them both when the conductor comes.

She mutters something he doesn't quite catch.

He sits ramrod straight trying to make it be anything other than, 'It's your baby.'

The bus stops again, and a young woman with an empty wicker shopping basket climbs the stairs and sits on the opposite front seat.

'Say that again,' he says at last.

'It's your baby,' she says, far too loud. The woman across the aisle tilts a greedy ear.

'Don't misunderstand me,' Aida says, 'I want nothing from you, only for you to know.'

A child! His child! The front window is a sheet of glittering light. He wants to scream, "I am a father. I'm to be a father!" The information runs through the cells of him, changing every one, charging him with energy. First thought: tell the old man, shout it in his face. *I am a father, I have fathered a child.*

'I want nothing from you,' she repeats. 'Not now, not ever.'

He turns and looks at her. Yes, now that he knows, he can see an extra fullness in her face, a sort of plush look. His eyes flick downwards but can make out nothing under her raincoat.

'*Mine,*' he says. 'Are you sure?'

'Boxing Day.'

He blinks and blinks.

'And as I said, I'm marrying Neville, so there's no need for you to do anything or even say anything.' She sounds doubtful now, regards him worriedly. 'Look, next stop coming up. Get off, will you? Run away and get your train.'

'No,' he says.

The woman with the basket leans towards them, looks about to fall off her seat. He turns his body protectively towards Aida. 'If it's my child you should marry *me,*' he murmurs.

She dabs at her eyes and nose, folds and puts away the handkerchief in a decided way. 'No. I told you. I'm marrying Neville. It's all arranged.'

The bus stops and starts, loading and disgorging, the bell rings, rain splatters the window. They sit without speaking and eventually she stands, rings the bell, and they go downstairs.

The bus has set them down on a corner he doesn't know. She puts up her umbrella, points across the road. 'You can catch a bus over there.'

'Can't I come in for a cup of tea?' he says.

She stands for a moment, frowning, then sighs. 'S'pose so.'

He follows her down an alley and over a makeshift path that crosses a bombsite, weeds and brambles all dripping wet, reaching her street from a new direction.

Once inside, she goes straight to the bathroom, and he fills the kettle. Boxing Day – that means she must be over five months gone. Obstetrics is not a subject he studied closely, though there was a cardboard pregnancy in an old book. It was an illustration of a woman at full term, naked but for wisps of material across her breasts and hips. You could lift a flap and see the tight-packed foetus, the blue twist of umbilicus, the liver-like placenta. You could see the way the woman's organs were distorted to accommodate the pregnancy: bladder flattened, stomach squashed upwards. Lying on his bed on Sunday afternoons while other boys played footie in the street, medical books were his comfort. Longing to be a doctor returns like a punch in the gut. That longing got him through his miserable childhood, got him through the jungle.

'Are you all right?' Aida says, and he realises that his teeth are gritted so tight, he can barely open his jaw to answer.

She sits down to take off the shoes. 'Ruined.' She kicks them aside, wriggles her nyloned toes. There's a ladder in her stocking, extending upwards from a mend. He notices her slippers under the table, and fetches them for her. Looking at him satirically, she pushes her feet inside them, gets up to make the tea. At Christmas, didn't she kneel to put Edgar's slippers on his feet? Is that what she's thinking? He goes to look out of the window, down at the doorway where he used to wait. Too cowardly to ring the bell like any normal person. Normal man. But he's to be a father. To father a child, surely is to be – in part, at least – a normal man?

'Sit down.'

He sits on the sofa, and she beside him, each with a cup of tea.

'Mind?' He gets out his fags.

'Go ahead.' She puts her cup and saucer on the floor, turns to face him. 'Since you're here,' she says. 'Can I ask you something?'

He nods, but she doesn't speak at once. Her eyes close, and she lets her head fall back; her neck is the whitest thing he's ever seen. Her body must be *so* white. He can barely remember. How vulnerable she is with her neck stretched back like that. How trusting. Even after all. To make love to her now. Could he? Is there an urge?

He draws in smoke, breathes it out slowly. 'Marry me,' he says.

She snaps her head up, shifts away from him. 'Are you joking? You buggered off out of my life after, well, you know, for months. You can hardly expect–'

'I don't,' he says quickly. 'But–'

'And the lies!' She hacks out a laugh.

'But–'

'But nothing.'

Her blouse is loose over a pleated skirt; now he can see the swell of her abdomen, a button straining at her chest. He wants to put a hand on her belly, but like a Keep Off sign, the bloody great ring glitters on her finger.

He tries to look away, but she's become fascinating. His kid inside there. A kid who will, he thinks with a rush, also be Edgar's kin.

'Is it even true that your family was all killed in the war?' she demands.

'No.'

She laughs unexpectedly. Not a nice laugh. 'What a terrible liar you are,' she says. 'To think I pitied you! Poor little orphaned Roley Crowley!'

He says nothing, blood hot in his face.

'Tell me about them,' she demands. 'Your folks. Anything I should know?'

'Like what?'

'I don't know. Anything.'

'I want to be part of its life,' he says. 'My kid, baby, he or she...'

'I'm sure it's a he,' she says.

'Can you tell?'

'Of course not!' She's grinning now. 'And you, pretending to be a doctor!' She hoots, then her face goes serious again. He's never known anyone shift emotions so fast. 'You're dropping.' Pointing to his fag. 'There's an ashtray over there.'

He gets up for the ashtray. Square, heavy glass, Senior Service, it says on every side. He remembers it from that night, from Boxing Day night, though he barely remembers anything else. Weak cocktails, a black pianist, her clutching onto him in the back of a taxi. A curtain half-open shows a rumpled bed in a poky alcove. The sink is piled with plates. He sits down with the ashtray by his foot.

'What are they like?' she says.

He stubs out the cigarette. 'The old man's a factory foreman, retired. Ordinary. Bit of a bastard. Mum...' He hesitates. 'Mum's half-Egyptian. Adopted by a captain and his wife after the First War.'

'Really!'

'The captain might have been her dad... but he and his wife died when she was small, and my grandparents adopted her, brought her up to forget "all that darkie nonsense".' He parrots a remembered voice.

'Egyptian!' She looks thrilled. 'So my baby will be part Egyptian!'

For some reason this riles him. 'Only a fraction.'

'An eighth?' She works it out on her fingers. 'If you're a quarter?'

He shrugs.

'What does she look like then? Your mum.'

'I take after her.'

'Egyptian,' she whispers, hand on stomach, diamond flashing.

'Marry me,' he says.

'No.'

'Why?'

She laughs at this. 'How many reasons do you need? Now, will you do something for me?'

'Anything.' He leans eagerly towards her. 'I'll do anything.'

'Scram.'

'What?'

'Buzz off. Please.'

He sits stiffly, rises, sits again, stands. She has her head tilted down, that long nose, pale bedraggled hair. Not beautiful or even attractive in this moment, but she has his baby inside her and he feels something rise in him, something like love. Nothing to lose by saying it.

'I love you.' Never has he said this before. Not the simple trotting out of those three simple words.

She glares up at him. 'Don't insult me.'

He picks up his hat and coat. She stays hunched over herself, waiting. Is she even breathing? Flat hair, laddered stockings, nylon toes. Is this his last sight of her?

'I'll go, but...' But he can't supply a but. He stands in silence for as long as he can bear it, and then leaves.

Outside, the shower has passed, and the sky shines like wet tin. Everything shines, and a blaze of light travels through him. *A father*. There's time before the train to stand himself a drink.

## 73

## CLEMENTINE

Elsie tucks the corners of the sheet under the mattress with wondrous dexterity, Clem notices as she tries to wrestle an incalcitrant pillow into its slip. Many years ago, Dennis dubbed this room her studio, but never has she found it conducive for painting. Here her paints are stored, that's all, along with art books, and a jar of brushes splayed like queer, dull flowers. It's become a useful spare room for a single person who doesn't require double sheets, which of course, lightens the load for Elsie – who is looking at her curiously. Clem realises she's cradling the pillow like a baby.

'It's all right, Mrs Everett,' Elsie says. 'I can do this. You go and sit yourself down.'

Clem positions the pillow, gives it a gay plumping punch. 'You *are* good,' she says. 'I'll go and see to the flowers.'

Elsie snaps the top sheet through the air. Before she goes down, Clem watches it float neatly and obediently into place.

She descends the stairs, deflated. Now that she's trying to be obliging with the help, ('Helping the help?' Dennis mocks, and inevitably, 'Why get a dog and bark yourself?') she finds herself subtly undermined. *Not good enough.* But one mustn't grumble;

the Jacksons are a godsend, and her experience of doing for herself was nothing short of disastrous. Aida has instructed her not to patronise the Jacksons. As if she would! 'Just treat them like human beings, and pay them well,' Aida said, 'no need to be unctuous.' This last when, (for Aida's benefit) she was rather too gushing with her thanks.

The bed is for the fiancé, Mr Neville Guthrie. Though the circumstances aren't ideal, with a baby already on its way, her heart gives a little leap of anticipation. Yesterday evening there was a programme on the wireless about sex, someone arguing that it's best to try before you commit to a lifetime... and though the argument against was virulent, she heartily agrees. Healthy that sex has become a topic for discussion. Even *Dennis* took news of the pregnancy surprisingly well. 'As long as they do the decent thing,' he said, adding, 'Of course, it remains to be seen what this *Caledonian* chappie is made of.'

Alone in the morning garden, Clem takes a deep sigh, tilts back her head to gaze at the dizzy blue sky. This is a momentous day, and whatever he's like, she's determined to welcome Neville Guthrie into the fold. Dennis is under strict instructions to be genial. Yes, the fellow may have got Aida into trouble, but they can be modern and broad-minded. (Yet what a relief that they're getting married! Even in this day and age, it will make everything so much easier.)

Irises for the table, those gorgeous yellow-throated purple ones – she pauses to admire – and roses for the guest bedroom, and Aida's. Dennis is set to pick the pair of them up from the station at half past seven, and Elsie to make a fish pie. Clem trails down the garden to the shed, which Mr Jackson (Fred, rather), isn't in today. He goes out to work elsewhere, doing the garden only at weekends – keeping it splendid all the same. She breathes in wood and string, a dry, wholesome loamy smell, as she fetches a trug, secateurs, canvas gloves. Cutting one's own flowers is a reliable pleasure. Now she wanders among roses, some blousy pink, some a tighter, velvety cream, inhaling their warm sweetness, gentling them in the wicker trug. She's feeling dreamy, almost romantic. The roses' sugared-almond colours make her think of weddings. Oh, such a shame that there won't be a great beautiful fuss of a wedding in the family. Two children, and only one hole-in-the-corner affair to show for it. No wedding ever for Edgar. *No. Don't think like that; don't go out of the light.*

As if to escape, she walks briskly to the pond, where the fish rise like ghosts, expecting their flakes of food. She perches for a moment on a garden bench, remembering the view through the window of the hospital when she was at her lowest ebb: the wintery London sky, spires, birds, wires, the occasional plane. When it became clear that she wasn't going to die, there were days when she gave in to the despicable sentiment of self-pity. 'Feel sorry for yourself and no one else will,' she used to say to the children in their sulks. Was that unkind? Goodness knows, she's tried her best to be a good mother.

Would a good mother tell Aida that Dennis isn't her real father? It's never mattered before. Does it matter now? She gazes at the snipped roses, pulls the gloves off her hot hands, drops them in the trug. When she thought she was dying she did consider telling the girl the truth. But telling would only cause upset, make them – Aida and Dennis both – view her differently. It would cause an awful kerfuffle, just at this happy moment in Aida's life.

'Mrs Everett!' Elsie's voice comes sharp from the kitchen. 'Telephone. It's Mrs Murray-Hill.'

She hurries in through the kitchen, drops the trug on the hall floor, terrified to take the receiver. He could be dead. Corin, he could be dead. Not today, *please*. Not yet. She raises the black receiver, it seems to take an age, to her ear.

'Hello? Mrs Everett speaking.' Eyes closed, she steadies herself against the hall stand, dread surging, mind spinning at a million miles an hour, wondering how she'll get through the weekend if he's dead, thinking of cancelling, thinking…

'My husband has asked to see you,' Eleanor says crisply. Clem exhales, dizzied, watching the sag of her own white face in the mirror. 'Will that suit you?'

She's almost panting, heart skittering its relief against her breastbone. 'How is he?' she manages.

'Up and about. Not the same, he won't ever be the same again. But he's got something for you. I said I'd have it delivered, but no, he insists on seeing you, stubborn old fool. If you could call in at about three o'clock, just for a few minutes? Visitors tire him.'

'Today? Oh no.' She watches dismay etch itself on her face. 'But today I can't. You see–'

'It will have to be today. I'm taking him to Devon for a few months, leaving tomorrow. We might even stay there. No matter. I'll have it delivered. Probably for the best.'

'No, no, I'll come…'

'Three o'clock then. Goodbye.' A vehement click, then silence.

On her way to the sitting room, Clem trips on the trug, spilling roses on the carpet. Alive! Up and about! And she's going to *see* him. She kneels to gather the roses, thorns piercing her fingertips. Of course, it's the worst possible timing, but the children aren't expected till this evening, and she won't be out for long. She might still have time for the flowers, and if not… well… not.

He'll want her to have a painting, she expects. Perhaps *The Turning* with its exquisite wriggle of light, which she will treasure for the rest of her life. Will Eleanor leave them alone, just for a moment, just for one embrace? Like a sun-warmed rose, her heart expands.

---

Eleanor greets her, unsmiling but perfectly polite, and ushers her through the shadowy house into a sun-filled conservatory. Here sits Corin in a wheelchair (*stupid, stupid, she never expected a wheelchair*), parked beside a wicker table.

'Here we are then,' Eleanor says. Her hair is in iron curls, cheeks mottled and flushed, fluffed with powder, clothes covered in a voluminous apron. 'As I said, we're off to Devon in the morning,' she says. 'My sister's a nurse, and we're going to stay close by. I've parked him in here, as everything's upside down inside. I'm rather busy packing and so on, as you can imagine, but he *would* insist on seeing you, wouldn't you dear? So here you are.'

'Thank you,' Clem murmurs.

He's *lesser*, that's the word that comes to her. Her burly, sturdy, beautiful, messy man has shrunk. His hair's cut short, he's cleanly shaven, he's wearing a collar and tie, the collar loose against a bristly withered neck.

'If you don't mind then?' Eleanor says. 'I'll get on. Ten minutes.' And she leaves them in the humid dazzle of the space, the overwhelming reek of geranium and tomato.

'Oh, my darling,' Clem says, when she's gone. She draws a wicker chair close and takes one of his hands, holds it in both of hers. It's curiously cool, the nails clipped neatly short, the skin shiny. She's never seen him so clean before; in the studio there was always splattered paint and turps, his unravelling sweaters stiff with pigment. Only ten minutes, and she doesn't know what to say. 'I wanted to see you before, of course, but...' But she stops; it's bad form to blame Eleanor, who has the burden of him now. 'She said you were up and about.'

'A bit.' His nod directs her gaze to a walking frame. 'Can't much...' He gestures to his face, and a trail of saliva escapes from the corner of his mouth. He struggles for his handkerchief, and she lifts it for him, dabs the wet away.

'I'm so glad you're alive,' she says.

The stroke has pulled one side of his face down, and thinner now, the shape is different. It's hard to find Corin in this man, and she has an urge to wail. Under the conservatory smell there's another basic and depressing animal one.

'I can't tell you how much I've missed you,' she says. 'That awful morning...'

In his eyes she finds him at last, in the cloudy greenish hazel. It's the same *him* there inside, the same spark of bright. A tear escapes one of his eyes. No telling if it's a tear, or to do with his condition.

'We've got Pablo,' she says suddenly. 'He's settled in beautifully at The Beeches.'

He makes a crooked smile. 'I wanted here, but...'

'Well, he's Lord of the Manor there!' She cringes at her jovial tone. 'Aida's getting married. Already expecting, I'm afraid. Cart before the horse, of course!'

'You all right?' he says, and she wants to climb inside his eyes, into the warmth of him; she leans closer.

'Yes, all better now. What a pair of old cronks we are!'

She wants to hold him, and she wants to run.

'For you.' With a nod of his head, he gestures to a small frame, propped with its face against a potted fern.

'So glad you're making paint...' She picks it up, turns it to face her, and stops. Not a painting. It's a drawing with collage, and the collage is composed of Edgar's fragments. She almost drops it, then sits with it on her knee, staring at what he's done. Pencil lines fill the gaps between the scraps, so that a detail of roof in Edgar's hand becomes a hut in Corin's, an arm becomes a man, a wing becomes a bird, a branch a tree. Words won't come.

'Hope... you don't... mind?' he mumbles.

Clem peers at him, seeing a wretched stranger who stole her dead child's work. Anger begins to rise, but when she blinks she sees her lover, the soul of him still there, still in the eyes, and she sees how he's rescued the last remnants of Edgar. He's *completed* them.

Before she can muster herself to speak, Eleanor bustles in. 'Ah, good. That's one thing to tick off the list then. Now?'

Clem stands, the frame tight under her arm. 'Goodbye,' she says to Corin and then, despite Eleanor's presence, she bends to kiss him on the brow, closes her eyes and rests her lips there for a second longer than appropriate. 'Thank you for letting me see him,' she says, allowing a drip of acid into the word 'letting'.

'Let me know, please, how he is,' she says, on the doorstep.

Eleanor nods, non-committal.

In the car, Clem sits with the collage on her lap, a sharp corner digging into her hip, rests her exhausted brow on the steering wheel, closes her eyes. Too leaden to drive, too overwhelmed to cry, she simply sits and waits until she can find it within herself to move.

74
---

## STARLING

The train leaves Sheffield on time, but close to Doncaster, it stops. No explanation for the delay. The third-class carriage is packed. A baby sets off bawling and its shabby parents – kids themselves – struggle, till an old biddy reaches out her arms. 'Give him here,' she says.

'*Her*,' mutters the mum, handing over the screamer. The old woman stands up with the baby on her shoulder, rocking and crooning. Soon, he'll have one of them. Whatever Aida says it'll still be his kid, see it or not. But he can't not. Can he? He can't not have anything to do with his own kid. It's not natural. The baby-rocking woman stands between him and the window, blocking his view. He shuts his eyes. It's up to Aida. The rest of his life is in her hands. He'll keep on trying to the very last, and if she says yes, she and the kid will be his life.

With a bristle of irritation, he thinks about Nance, who pulled him into the kitchen at work yesterday.

'Up the duff,' she said, 'thought I'd tell you first.' She picked a teaspoon from the draining board and started drying it, drying and drying, avoiding his eyes.

'*Again?!*'

'Handing in my notice on Friday,' she said. 'Wally wants me to put my feet up.'

He stared at her white face, lipstick dark as a scab.

'Don't look at me like that!'

'*Wally?*'

'He's not bad,' she says. 'A bit long in the tooth, but he's got a house. Nice. Chingford. Quite the gent.'

He felt like slapping her. After last time, you'd think she'd have learned her lesson. All the effort he put into helping her with that, and now look. 'Is it what you want?' he said.

She did meet his eyes, then. 'But it's not about what I want, is it?' Hard edge to her voice, glitter in her eye. 'In the end, we just have to do what we have to do.' She hurled the teaspoon into the sink.

He got out his Players and they both lit up.

'I'd ask you to the wedding,' she says. 'Only, Wally might think it a bit rum, me asking a bloke. He's the jealous type, see.'

'What's he like?' Starling asked.

'Bit of an old coot.' She puts her hand on her stomach. 'You've got to grow up, haven't you?' she says.

He thinks about this. Grow up. Yes. Maybe.

'He'll take care of me,' Nance said. 'No more Mister bleeding Ramsay. No more "Yes sir, no sir, three bags full, sir". No more getting up at the crack of dawn. Oh, don't look like that, Len.'

'Like what?'

'It's written all over your face. Disapproving.'

He forced a smile. 'It's up to you, Nance. Good luck to you. Hope you'll be happy. You and your Wally.'

'Don't you worry, I'll make sure of that,' she said, sounding anything but sure.

He sighs and opens his eyes; there's a bloke in the corner of the carriage looking at him. Must have been there all the time, hidden behind a newspaper. He's youngish, green eyes in a narrow, crooked face. Attractively crooked. The baby sets up wailing again, and the bloke grins at Starling.

'Smoke?' He leans across and shakes a packet of Senior Service.

'Would you mind not smoking in here?' says the woman holding the baby. 'Sorry love, I've got to get off my feet, been on them all bloody day.' She hands the parcel back to its mum. Starling gets a glimpse of its furious wet red face. The train lurches forward, begins to pick up speed.

'About effing time,' someone says.

Crooked-face gets up and goes to stand in the corridor, raises his eyebrows and the fag packet, an invitation. To escape the wailing as much as anything, Starling follows him out.

'Johnny,' says the man, holding out his hand. 'Bloody kids, eh? What a bleeding racket.' His handshake goes on a second too long. His eyes are long, leaf-shaped. It's only his nose that's crooked, looks like it's been broken and mended wrong.

'I've got one on the way,' Starling says, accepting a fag, breathing in the novelty of saying this along with the smoke.

'Well, hope it turns out quieter than that little bugger!'

They smoke in silence, watching the grey-green of a rainy June flow past the window.

'So, you're a family man then?' Johnny holds his eye for too long. Starling blinks. How the hell does Johnny know to try him? What gives him away? He's not even queer anymore. Though there's temptation. Why not? Just this one last time. The man nods down the corridor towards the toilet, turns, looks back over his shoulder. To be on a train is not to be anywhere. It would hardly count if he did. There's a powerful urge to follow Johnny down the corridor; suddenly he's so hard it hurts. He squeezes shut his eyes. Yes or no? If yes, does that mean the torture was a waste of time? Colin comes to mind. The straightforward handshake, the straightforward look in his eye. A respectable queer. You see, you could go that way, Starling. And on a train isn't anywhere; you could just try, just do it. Just once. Like a test. Backs of houses flash past, washing, lilac, a kid on a wall waving.

'Sorry.' He goes back into the carriage to endure the wailing babe.

---

Horace opens the door, shakes his hand. 'Come in.' He's in his dressing gown and slippers. 'Celia's gone to bed.' He takes Starling's coat, leads him through to the sitting room, where the fire burns low, and an airbed is inflated and neatly made up.

'Sorry to be so late,' Starling said. 'The train.'

'Bloody trains. Tea or anything?'

'I'll just have a smoke and turn in. Don't want to keep you up.'

Horace shakes out a couple of cigs, lights them, heaves back into his armchair. He looks done in. The tiles of the hearth make a tidy car park for miniature vehicles, military one side, civilian the other.

'Celia all right? And the kiddie?'

Horace grins proudly. 'Chip off the old block, it turns out.'

Starling nods, glad for him. 'Work all right?'

'You?'

'Bookkeeping. Training that is.'

'Thought you were all set on the medical lark?'

Starling fills his lungs deeply with smoke.

'I'm thinking of Africa – the groundnut business,' Horace startles him by saying. 'Tanganyika. Jobs there for the taking. The nut army they call it.' He laughs. 'Nut army, eh?'

'With Celia?'

'The whole kit and caboodle. Paradise it is out there. Wall to wall sunshine.'

Starling forces a smile. Don't go, he wants to say, I've few enough friends.

'Why don't you come?' Horace says. 'There's a fortune to be made.'

'I've started training now,' Starling says weakly, and they sit in silence for a bit.

'What brings you down then?' Horace says in the end. 'Not seen hide nor hair of you for months.'

Starling sighs. 'Sorry. Been busy. A girl.'

'Aha, so that's it.' Horace grins. 'Wearing you out, is she? You do look knackered.'

'Sorry.' Starling removes his glasses, rubs his eyes. 'Knackered is right, but it's not her. Long day, that's all. Long day, long week.'

The door opens, and Celia puts her head round. 'Hello stranger!' She comes in, and her embrace wraps him in a sweet, sleepy smell.

'Thought you'd dropped off,' Horace says.

'Sorry to be so late,' says Starling.

'Haven't you offered a cup of tea, Horry?' She yawns and stretches.

'He did.'

'I did.'

'You look worn out. What brings you down?'

'That's what I asked, and he said a girl.'

'Oooh.' She rubs her hands, foxy little face lighting up. She's all shiny with face cream. 'Come on then, fill us in.'

She perches on the arm of Horace's chair, and easily his arm goes round her waist. It's how it should be, man and wife, and though Starling feels a pang of envy, he's glad for them that they've found their way back.

'I *know*!' Celia jumps up. 'Why don't we have a drop of that elderberry wine? That'll loosen your tongue.'

'Don't see why not,' Horace says.

'Horry's sister makes it by the gallon. Pea pod too, dandelion, all sorts. Most of them are disgusting, but the elderberry's all right.'

Horace gets up and pours it out into sherry glasses, and they all light cigarettes.

'Now.' Celia sits in her own chair this time. The firelight shows the light hairs on her shins. 'Go on then.' She leans forward, eager for him to speak. Last time he sat here, she was knitting, the radio playing, and it was the first cosiness he'd felt since being back in Blighty. When he remembers himself back then it's a mess, a scribble, a blur. It's hardly like remembering himself at all.

'Did you finish the jumper?' he says.

'Fancy you remembering that! It's a bit on the tight side, isn't it ,Horry?'

'Not if I pull my stomach in.'

They all laugh, puff on their fags. The wine has a wholesome stickiness like cough syrup, and coats his teeth. They're still waiting, or Celia is.

'She's...' he begins, but something stops his tongue.

'Don't tell me,' Celia says, holding up a finger. 'In the family way?'

He blinks.

'It's written all over your bloody face!'

'Well...' No point denying it, and in fact he feels a little swell of pride as he nods.

'You dirty dog.' Horace grins, lifts his glass.

'Who is she then?' Celia says. 'What's her name? How do you know her? How far gone is she? Getting wed?'

'Hold your horses, love!' Horace turns to Starling. 'Sorry

mate. She's like the effing Gestapo when it comes to other people's love lives.'

'Just taking an interest,' she says. 'Is it the girl you mentioned before? Ida, was it?'

'Aida,' he says. 'Good memory.'

'It wasn't that long ago!'

Abruptly overcome with weariness, Starling closes his eyes. It feels like a long time ago, like another age, when he sat here with her that evening, Horace cooling off in the clink.

He opens his eyes. 'Thing is,' he says flatly, 'she's marrying someone else.'

'But it's *your* kid?'

'Lucky escape?' Horace suggests.

Celia frowns. 'Don't say that.'

Starling blinks. You *could* see it like that. For Aida, if he melts away, maybe it would be just that. A lucky escape. She can settle down and be a wife to someone else. Someone who properly wants her. Someone who can afford a fucking great diamond. Would she ever think about him? If the baby looks like him, she'd be reminded every day. Let it be a dark Egyptian-looking kid. Or let it have a look of Edgar. Both of them. A mix.

'Do you love her?' Celia asks.

'In a way.'

'In a *way?*' she shrieks. 'You didn't say that to her? Blimey! No wonder she's marrying someone else!'

'I do, but...' But what can he say? I'm queer? No. And even if he did say that, it wouldn't be true, or not the whole truth. He doesn't know anymore what he is. The metallic taste of electricity sizzles in his teeth, the image of the naked man flashing on a wall. He runs his tongue round his sticky teeth, takes a gulp of wine, thinks of Johnny on the train. He can resist. He did.

'You all right, mate?' says Horace.

'You have to tell her you love her,' Celia says. 'You have to win her over. It's only right if it's your sprog.'

'I did tell her.'

'Tell her again then. Keep telling her. And for God's sake don't say "in a way"!'

Horace chuckles. 'Calm down, love.' He makes a see-what-I-have-to-put-up-with face at Starling.

"I hear you're joining the nut army,' Starling says, to change the subject.

'Tanganyika,' she says. 'Doesn't that sound exotic? Wall to wall sunshine.'

'That's just what I said,' Horace says.

'Pays twice what Horace can make here. We can save for our own house.'

Starling smiles, and stifles a yawn.

'Come on, missus.' Horace stands, and pulls her up. 'Let's let the man get some shut-eye.'

'It's good to see you again,' he says. 'Thanks...' He gestures at the airbed.

When they've gone, he pulls the blankets off the bed, wraps himself up on an armchair. First thing tomorrow he'll go to Forest Hill to see Aida.

Or should he, rather, let her be?

## 75

## CLEMENTINE

She surveys the empty teacups, the remains of a scone, a wasp pestering the jam dish. Sun glints on the plated teapot, makes dazzles of the sugar cubes in their cut glass bowl. Tea on the lawn, just the three of them, felt almost normal this afternoon. The first airing for the wicker chairs, which spend the winter in the garage, little wisps of cobweb still caught in their weave. Dennis has wandered off somewhere, and Aida gone to the "loo" as she's taken to calling it, leaving her cardigan draped half on, half off the chair in her typically sloppy fashion.

Such a shock when she arrived yesterday evening with her hennaed hair. 'Thought it would jazz me up,' she said defensively. Not only is her hair orange, but every fingertip, and a map-shaped mark on her neck. She did it herself, just before coming down, apparently. Clem, already exhausted, had been rendered speechless. The clownish colour looks utterly preposterous. She might as well frizz it up and stick a red nose on. Thank *heavens* it's only to be a tiny wedding. Whatever will the poor fiancé think? He'll be here this evening – though they'd expected him yesterday. His non-appearance was something of a relief, and the evening passed in such a blur that she barely remembers it. Perhaps she shouldn't have drunk so much brandy, or begged that marvellous pill from Dennis. This evening will be better, though. She's looking forward to meeting the chap – the engagement ring is spectacular. A ring fit for a princess. And in fact, Aida mumbled something about Austrian aristocracy. 'Well, you've certainly landed on your feet,' Clem said, much to her daughter's obvious irritation. It has certainly notched their expectations of the fiancé up a peg or two!

She pushes the blanket off, feels it crumple round her ankles. A white butterfly alights briefly on the grass, and with it there comes a sudden incongruous blast of exhilaration, of gratitude, for *not* having died in the winter, when she came so close to the brink, for being, astonishingly, *alive*. To be alive in the garden in early summer, the sun warm on her living arms! Is this heartless in the light of everything? If so, so be it.

High in the branches of the beech a pigeon coos; the pond shines greenish hazel, like a kind, familiar eye. It feels underhand to have hidden the collage, but for a while she's keeping it to herself. One day it will hang on the wall, probably in the sitting room; she has a spot in mind. Eventually, no doubt, it will become a thing, just another thing that like any other thing, will hardly be noticed. A twitch in her fingers means the first urge to paint for months (a still life of the remains of afternoon tea?). Pablo stalks past, tail erect, and she smiles. *Corin.*

Aida returns, and flumps down on her chair. *What a fright!* The hair is the colour of rust, and looks flat and stiff – has she even rinsed all the henna powder out? It causes her skin to look even paler than usual. And there's a little spot on her chin. Always contrary, she's outdone herself this time. As fidgety as ever, she waggles her foot (scuffed shoe), picks up and sets down her cup, turns and turns the beautiful ring.

Nails all bitten to kingdom come. Neville's absence must partly account for the fidgeting. Perhaps she's nervous about his reaction to the hair? One can only pray that he has a sense of humour.

'I wonder if we might find a rinse to tone it down, darling?' she dares to say.

Glowering, Aida tucks a strand behind her ear. 'I like it.'

'Well, it's certainly... lively,' Clem says.

Unexpectedly, that makes the girl grin; pretty teeth she has, neat and square. Since her arrival she's been glum, uneasy, monosyllabic, flinching at every mention of the wedding. But there's so much to plan; even for a small affair there must be *some* of the lovely folderol. Flowers for instance, dress and cake. Is there to be a bridesmaid? As a wedding present, they're paying for a honeymoon in Ireland, a surprise to be announced this evening. Surely, *that* will please her? And once Neville's arrived, she'll have to buck her ideas up. (If he doesn't take one look at the hair and turn tail.)

After tea poor Dennis slunk back to the surgery, baffled, disappointed by Aida's surliness, and clearly upset by the hair. Now, neither of the women speak. There's the sound of water trickling down the kitchen drain as Elsie prepares dinner, and a chitter of sparrows. Aida fidgets, scratches her leg, fiddles with her hair, twists her ring.

'What's wrong, darling?' Clem says at last. Oh, the blackbird is singing sweet and silvery, fluting its dear little head off.

'Nothing.' That grumpy expression, familiar since her babyhood. There's a photograph of her in her pram, a pretty lace-edged sun bonnet framing comical ferocity. Such a mercurial baby. A memory attaches to the photo: after it was taken, little Edgar hurtled the pram round the lawn till she laughed and shrieked. They were such a pair. Losing her brother must have broken her heart. It's hard to keep in mind that the grief belongs to other people too.

'We're having duck,' she says, 'shot by a golf pal of Daddy's.'

'Yum,' Aida says dully. She examines her nails, chews an orange cuticle.

'Darling,' Clem says, 'do tell me what's the matter.'

'Just a mo.' Aida gets up, stalks about the garden, pinching lavender between her fingers and sniffing them. She stoops to peer into the pond, her cotton dress stretching taut round her thickening middle and bust. New clothes are definitely in order. Since Neville only has a modest salary (though the ring suggests family money), they can help with clothes and so on for the time being. Perhaps it's simply money that's the problem? Perhaps Aida is gearing herself up to broach the subject? Or perhaps she's nervous about introducing Neville. Well, whatever the chap is like, they will make him welcome. (Only, please God, don't let him be too hopeless.)

She lights a cigarette, savours the bite of smoke. Soon it will be time for sherry, the best moment of the day. Since the illness she's been strict about not drinking till six, or half past five at the earliest. But this is a special occasion.

Pablo goes to rub against Aida's shins. She picks him up, buries her nose in his fur, then settles with him on her lap. At first he struggles, then submits, melts, purrs as she strokes his long back. There's a stab of light from the diamond in her ring. Clem looks down at her own engagement ring, loose on her bony finger, sapphire and a more modest diamond, alongside the plain wedding band.

'Off to meet the train,' Dennis calls from the back door, and soon there's the slam of the car door and the sound of the engine starting up.

'Let's go in and get ourselves spruced up,' Clem says. 'We're so looking forward to meeting your Neville.'

'Oh, he doesn't care about that sort of thing.' Aida hunches forward. The cat jumps off and stalks away, settles himself on the stones beside the pond, irritably flicking the tip of his tail. 'Look Mummy, before he comes, I want to ask your advice about something.'

Clem draws on her cigarette, tickled. It's so rare for Aida to seek advice. Usually, she prefers to plough her own stubborn furrow, whatever the outcome. And look at this outcome! The tight cotton of her dress is grubby. The girl should change to something fresh: a bit of lipstick, a dab of scent (not that anything will compensate for the hair). They'll meet the menfolk, pour drinks to herald this new phase: Aida as an adult, and soon-to-be wife and mother.

The girl's hand has gone to her belly. 'The thing is, it's not...' she stops and takes a deep breath, '...actually Neville's baby.' This said, she winces and shuts her eyes, as if awaiting an explosion.

Clem opens her mouth and closes it again, sits motionless as this startling information sinks in. Several possible reactions occur. The girl looks so anxious, almost woebegone, pasty under the orange straggle.

'All right,' Clem says carefully, tapping ash onto the grass. 'Is he aware of this fact?'

Minutely, Aida shakes her head.

Clem clutches for what to say. A pigeon coos, the wasp circumnavigates the rim of the jam dish, from the road at the front there's the sound of a big vehicle, a lorry perhaps, grinding by. *Concentrate, Clem.*

'Are you planning to make him aware?'

'That's what I want to ask you, Mummy.'

Elsie comes out to clear the tea.

'Lovely scones. I don't know how you do it,' Clem says.

Elsie, loading her tray, says, 'They have to be fresh; that's all there is to scones, no secret.'

'Do you know what I think?' Clem says, once Elsie has gone. Aida looks up, almost hopefully. 'I think we should move inside. It's starting to get chilly; don't you think? Spruce ourselves up, and pour a little sherry.'

'But Mummy...' Aida wails.

'And then we'll carry on talking. Come on. There's plenty of time.' She holds up an arm and Aida takes it, helps her up, though really, she's perfectly capable herself. It's rather nice, sometimes, to be helped. Being ill has taught her this. What to say? What to say? Aida's bombshell has set up such a clamour inside her. They enter the kitchen, and she stops to chat with Elsie, to admire the duck waiting in its roasting tin.

---

She lets her dress fall to the floor, dabs talc under her arms, puts on her old primrose-yellow dress, far too big now, but still a becoming colour. As she leans in to powder her brow, her chin and nose, and colour in her lips, she meets her own eyes, stretches them in acknowledgement at her surprise. Perpetually crotchety, contrary, *Mary, Mary, Quite Contrary* Aida, who's never struck her as having much in the way of sex appeal, clearly must have some! She sprays perfume onto her elbow creases, damn that crepey old skin, and goes downstairs, through the dim hall and into the sitting room, where the sunshine that sieves gauzily through the net curtains is like a dream. Yellow roses glow in a bowl on the piano; the soft burnished sheen of the wood gives her a sudden urge to forget all this, to sit and play.

'All right, Mummy?' says Aida, anxiously following her in.

She hasn't changed her dress, or even, apparently, brushed her hair.

'Don't you want to...'

'He doesn't mind what I look like!'

'I very much doubt that!' Clem makes her way to the drinks trolley. 'Men appreciate one taking a bit of trouble, and with that hair...' but she catches Aida's scowl, and stops. 'A drop of sherry?'

Aida shakes her head. 'I'd sooner have soda water.' And she makes a great squirty business of working Dennis's syphon.

'Remember how you two used to fight over who was going to top up Daddy's whisky?'

'I expect I usually won!' Aida smiles. Her nose looks more in proportion with her slightly filled-out face. If it's a girl I hope she doesn't get that nose. Stop it, stop it. Clem pours and takes a welcome gulp of *Fino*, tops up her glass before sitting down.

'Look, forget what I said, Mummy. Anyway, it's *my* problem.'

Silence, though there's the sound of cars on the road, and birds. She's tempted to go along with this. But you can hardly leave it there, Clem. A good mother would not leave it there. She lights another cigarette. Since her illness, Dennis allows her ten a day, but she's lost count, and these *are* special circumstances.

'Do you mind me asking whose it is?'

Aida goes to the window, pulls the nets aside, and peers out. 'We'll hear them arrive.'

'I *know*.'

'Someone you care about?'

'Let's just say that the person wouldn't make a suitable husband.' Aida seems suddenly panic-stricken. 'Mummy, I feel as if I've suddenly been parachuted into making grown-up decisions. I'm not *ready*.'

'No one's ever ready,' Clem says slowly. 'I certainly wasn't.'

Aida bites her thumbnail, swings a foot in its scuffed shoe.

'It sounds as if you're being sensible,' Clem says and Aida looks at her, for once, as if she's worth listening to. She smiles, warmed. 'I'm glad you feel you can confide in me,' she adds. 'I am, after all, your mother.'

Aida gives a hectic laugh. 'I know *that*! It's fatherhood that's the question!'

Clem starts and blinks, holds a globule of sherry on her tongue before she lets it slip down. 'I knew someone once,' she says, letting her eyes rest on the roses, 'who had a child, not her husband's, and never told a soul. She decided it was for the best and it *was* for the best, as it turned out. I'm convinced of it. The father loves that child, and the child loves that father. Would either of them be happier if they knew?'

Aida gazes at her, eyes narrowed, almost as if with suspicion. Another steadying sip. The girl does not know, *cannot* possibly know. And Clem will never tell her. There, that's the decision made, for good and ever.

'As long as you're sure he'll make a good husband, as long as you love him and really want to marry him, then no harm done. *Or* you could tell him, and risk seeing him bolt.'

'But the thing is, I don't think he *would* bolt, Mummy, he's such a decent sort.'

'He'd think *differently* of you though. In the future it might come back to bite you.'

The sullen look, the shrug.

'If you really want my opinion, I think you should keep schtum.'

'But Mummy, that's so horrendously dishonest!'

Clem takes a deep breath, and her eyes go to the drinks trolley.

'Well, in the end it's up to you,' she says with forced

patience. 'I've said my bit.' She closes her eyes against the yellow dazzle of the room.

'I wish smoking didn't make me want to vomit,' Aida mutters.

From outside comes the crunch of wheels on gravel. Aida leaps to her feet, white-faced, looks in the mantel mirror, finally shows some vanity by clutching in a panic at her orange hair.

## 76

## AIDA

She pelts upstairs, locks the bathroom door behind her. Bloody Mummy! Being told to do something you're already going to do is maddening. In the mirror her face is mulish. Grow up Aida; you are with child. What an expression! She giggles as she flannels under her arms – pregnancy has given her sweat a funny, soupy smell. Imperial Leather soap has such a reassuring scent. Cradling the sudsy bar in her hands she sniffs, almost tempted to take a bite. But get a move on. The hair hasn't come out thick and vibrant and sleekly red like the woman at the Fabian Society. More like orange string. Still, can't be helped. In the bedroom, she drops the frock, finds an old school skirt with an elastic waist, and a (rather virginal) sleeveless broderie anglaise blouse, voluminous before, perfect now. She does a sarcastic twirl before the wardrobe mirror then meets her own eyes: *Why are you doing this? Allowing this?*

From below she hears the front door open, and the sounds of greeting, then a hush. They will have moved into the sitting room, making a beeline for the drinks trolley, of course. How will abstemious Neville take that? This time last week she was with Leonard Starling. Not a word since. She thought... Picking up her hairbrush, she sinks onto the bed. In the evenings, again and again she's found herself at the window of her flat, looking down at the dark doorway, yearning for her lurker.

'Aida!' comes Daddy's voice, and she shakes herself back into the now. She brushes her hair, still grainy with henna, clips it back from her face and, feeling rather like an actress stepping into a role, descends the stairs.

In the sitting room, Mummy and Neville stand by the drinks trolley, posed like actors themselves. Neville holds a whisky-soda.

'In your absence we've introduced ourselves,' Mummy says. She looks Aida up and down, and gives an annoyingly satisfied nod. 'A teensy sherry? Goodness me. That blouse hasn't seen the light of day for years!'

Neville stares at her with his mouth open, then snaps it shut.

'Hello darling.' With horrific self-consciousness, she approaches him, kisses his cheek. He squeezes her shoulder, and smiles. She's pleased, relieved, to feel a surge of fondness for him. See, he can cope with her, even with the hair. How very odd to see him here though. He belongs at work, in London. Certainly not *here*.

'It's rather startling, isn't it?' Mummy says.

'Preposterous,' Daddy says. 'You look like a tart.'

'Now, now.'

'And not even a very good tart.' Daddy hoots, and Neville throws Aida a panicked look.

'How was your journey?' she asks.

'Jammed like sardines.'

He lifts a strand of hair and makes a quizzical face. 'It's um... jolly,' he says.

Daddy snorts. 'Mr Guthrie's been telling us all about the Ministry,' he says.

'Neville, *please*,' says Neville.

'That must have been a thrilling conversation,' Aida says, and Mummy sends her a look.

'Shall we sit?' says Mummy. 'It's a shame you missed tea in the garden, Neville.' She hovers for a moment, to mark her first use of the name. 'Such a glorious afternoon, wasn't it, dear?'

'Yes,' Aida concedes. 'Good trip home?' she asks Neville.

'*Very* much so.' He gives her a mysteriously significant look.

The parents take their usual armchairs, and Aida and Neville sit self-consciously side by side on the sofa. He's wearing blue corduroy trousers that she hasn't seen before, and polished brogues. He puts his whisky-soda down on the occasional table. She snatches her eyes away from his thumbnails, examines her ring.

'Aida barely tells us a thing. Fascinating about the American wheat situation,' Daddy says, 'very fascinating indeed.'

'I'm afraid we're in for bread rationing before the summer's out though,' Neville says.

'No! For glory's sake!' Mummy says. 'Whenever is it going to end?'

'It's these bally payments to the Germans,' Daddy says. 'Bloody Atlee, and his bleeding heart brigade.'

Aida holds her breath waiting for Neville's response. He can't say he wasn't warned. He stands, as if about to pronounce and she catches her breath, half in dread, half thrilled, but he only says, 'I've brought you a present. Just a wee moment, it's in my bag.' He goes out to the hall.

'A present! You shouldn't have!' Mummy widens her eyes at Aida in a pantomime of approval. He comes back and hands her two of his spoons, larger versions than Aida's, the handles carved into herons. At the sight of Edgar's bird, Aida blinks.

'Salad servers,' Neville says.

'*Far* too lovely to use.' Mummy runs her fingers over the wood, lifting her reading specs to examine the carving.

'Neville makes them,' Aida says, feeling proud.

'You *made* them!' Mummy shakes her head in exaggerated disbelief. 'Well, I never did.' She runs her fingers over the grain of the wood.

'Let's see.' Pipe stem clenched between his teeth, Daddy heaves himself up and reaches for one. 'Splendid,' he says. 'Splendid.' He puts it on the table and settles back, legs crossed, head back, savouring his smoke.

'Quite the artist then,' Mummy says, and this leads them onto her work, and she takes him on a little tour, pointing out some of her paintings – and the Murray-Hill. In front of her portrait of her children, they pause. Neville takes and squeezes Aida's hand. Young Edgar, never to be old Edgar, bright-eyed and ruddy-cheeked. And they turn from the painting, and with forced gaiety, and not too much artifice, the evening runs on. Neville manages well, chatting away with Daddy, quite man-to-man, avoiding any further foray into politics.

'I'll go and see what's happened to dinner,' says Mummy.

---

Over the meal – consommé, duck, gooseberries – Aida winces as the subject of the National Health Service comes up. Daddy thinks it a dangerous socialist idea, typical of this bolshie government, imagining hordes of malingerers leaching the wealth, filling hospital beds with minor ailments, reducing the status of the doctor to a government serf, and so on. Once again, she half expects, and might enjoy, fireworks, but Neville steers the conversation onto the golf course. Clearly, he has taken heed of her conversational warning. Aida leans to him, feeling a surge of genuine affection. Daddy, incredulous to hear that he, a Scot, has never played golf, offers to take him round in the morning and give him a few pointers.

'That bally course,' says Mummy. 'I hardly see my husband at weekends, Neville.'

'Except last weekend.' Dennis smiles at Aida, who flinches as she realises what's coming next. 'I expect Mummy told you about Aldeburgh? I thought her well enough for a little trip.' He looks at his watch. 'This time last week we were eating fish and chips! Splendid, wasn't it, darling?'

'We stayed in the most extraordinarily squalid boarding house,' Mummy adds. 'But the sea was marvellous. That light. You forget.'

'Of course, there's still barbed wire all over the shop.'

'But it was a tonic. All that fresh air.'

'Yes, she mentioned it,' Aida says tightly. She can feel Neville's eyes on her as she stares down at her knees. As far as he's concerned, she was here last week, pandering to Mummy. Now she'll have to concoct another lie. Suddenly she's overcome by a wave of weariness, and she yawns, covering her mouth, yawns till tears come to her eyes. They all look tactfully away, and there's silence. If they were already married, there'd be fond references to her condition, but as it is, the baby is an elephant in the room. An elephant in the womb. The thought makes her snigger.

'What's the joke?' says Daddy, and when she doesn't answer he blunders on about the mileage and the petrol shortage, asks Neville about the Borders, Edinburgh, his folks. Seeing the strain on his face, Aida says, 'Shall I show you round the garden?'

Outside, the air is cool and fresh on her hot face and arms.

'Sorry about my father.'

Silence.

'All right. I suppose you're wondering where I was?'

He folds his arms, awaiting her explanation.

'I was intending to come home,' she says, 'but then Daddy sprang this going away idea on Mummy, and it didn't seem worth telling you. And I was feeling measly, and simply couldn't face the journey all the way to Scotland just for the weekend.'

'No need to have lied,' he says stiffly.

'I know. I know. I'm a chump. I simply haven't got your good impulses. They're not bred into me. I get into such muddles all the time.'

'All you have to do is tell the truth.'

'I know. From now on, I will. I promise. Cross my heart and hope to die.' She crosses it with her finger, but he's still frowning.

'And the hair?' He lifts a strand between his fingers. 'You must know I prefer girls with natural hair.'

'It'll grow out.'

From the roof, a wood pigeon calls *what a to-do, to-do, to-do*, over and over.

'What *were* you doing then?' Neville asks. 'Last weekend?'

She says nothing, feeling an impulse growing inside her, an itch of recklessness.

'You won't meet my folks till the wedding now.' He gives a mildly exasperated shake of the head. Good God! *Never* has she met anyone with such an even temperament. What would it take to make him rant and rave? If he knew that this time last week she was with the baby's father, being proposed to, being tempted to accept, would he be as forgiving? Abruptly it all feels too much. The lie. The size of the diamond on her finger. His gullibility.

'It's not your baby,' she says before she can stop herself. Reckless and wrecking.

Silence. The sound of a pan being scraped in the kitchen. A dog barking miles away. And *to-do, to-do, to-do.*

'Or at least it might not be,' she adds.

Still nothing. She dares not look at him.

'I can't marry you without you knowing that.'

Will he walk away, or will he stick out the rest of the visit for the sake of appearances? A bee bumbles past, a bird flutes high in a tree. The expression "my heart is in my mouth" strikes her as accurate, and she swallows hard.

'Never for a single moment did I believe it was,' he says.

'What?'

'I'm not mentally deficient, Aida.'

She gapes at him.

'But I don't care. I love you.' He pulls her to him, and her knees weaken with relief. And she's impressed that he's not as gullible as she thought. Oh, it is nice to be held by a big man, and she does like the bulk of him (and when he moves out of the digs perhaps his clothes will cease smelling). 'And the baby,' he says into her hair. 'I hope it goes without saying, I'll consider it my own.' She allows herself to be held, glad that her expression is hidden while she gets it under control. 'I am glad you told me of your own accord though,' he adds.

'So can we just go on as before?' she says, not quite believing that her bombshell has turned out to be such a dud.

'Does anyone else know?' he says.

She shakes her head. A good dud though, good that it's a dud.

'Am I allowed to ask whose it is?'

'A Yank,' she says, stepping back. 'A G.I. He's gone home. Even he doesn't know.' She frowns at herself. It's as if these days, she really doesn't know what she's going to say next.

He nods; this is satisfactory to him, it seems. Pablo stalks through the garden, lifting his paws like a jungle cat, and she turns to follow him, feels Neville behind her. The sun is low and their shadows long. *Why lie, Aida? You were telling the truth up to then; why not tell the whole truth?* His shadow seems to go straight through her.

They're standing by the pond now. Under the glossy surface there are glimpses of orange fin and tail. Water lilies are fisting into bud. Birdsong seems melodramatically loud.

'Now,' he says, 'I told you I had a meeting – that's why I didn't make it last night.'

'Didn't matter. Mummy was shattered anyway. We were all in bed by about nine!'

'You remember a conversation we had, oh, months ago now?'

There's the sound of laughter from a garden nearby. Such a glorious evening, all pink and warm and fragrant at nearly ten. 'We have had many conversations,' she points out.

'You asked me about returning to draughtsmanship. Well, an iron I've had in the fire has come to fruition, so to speak.' She winces at the mangled metaphor. 'I've kept quiet till now. Didn't want to go getting your hopes up.'

'Hopes?' The corners of her mouth are suddenly too heavy to lift.

'Myself and a pal are setting up a firm. Guthrie and McKiness – or vice versa, still to be decided.'

'Oh.' She swallows, dreading his answer. 'In London, or...'

'No, daftie. At home. Peebles.'

'Peebles?' As she repeats the queasy-sounding word, her heart plummets like a broken lift. A goldfish splashes, rises to the surface, its mouth creating dark little nothings in the glossy water.

'It's everything I hoped.'

'But I assumed we'd stay in London.'

'I was going to announce over dinner, but thought I'd tell you first. What do you think?'

'Marvellous.' Her voice and her smile are wooden. 'Jolly well done, darling.'

'Shall we go and tell them now?'

Goosepimples rise on her arms, and she resists a shiver. More greedy little holes in the water. 'Not yet.'

'We'll rent a cottage to begin with, but my plan is to build our own house. I've a plot in mind — lochside views, bordering a forest. We can design it together. You shall have whatever you want.' Tangerine light seems to be leaking from his hair into the tired sky. Bats are beginning to flit. 'And we'll be near my family for help with the bairn – we needn't go into too much detail there. They're longing to be grandparents, and will assume that they are.'

He stops to watch her expression, which she makes suitable. The diamond on her finger feels heavy enough to pull her arm out of its socket.

'But what about *my* folks?' she says.

'It'll be a wrench, I know. But we can make it work. They can visit, we can visit, as often as you like.'

'Need to spend a penny,' she says. 'Wait there.'

She bolts into the house, through the kitchen where poor Elsie is labouring in the dreary smell of carbolic, bumps into Mummy in the hall. 'Everything all right? What a good egg he is,' she whispers. 'Rather dishy too. And barely any accent to speak of.'

'Oh, for God's sake!' Aida runs up the stairs, and into the bathroom again. It's cooler now. The open window lets in the sound of the bloody bore of a pigeon. She presses her brow against the nubbly frosted glass. Neville stands out there waiting. Neville so good and nice and trying so hard. And trying so hard because he loves her. A proper, handsome, decent ungullible chap who loves her and will love the baby. There's a perfectly good future mapped out for her now. Lochside views. Bordering on forest. Perfectly safe and secure. She's landed on her feet. Her fingernails cut into her palms, and the baby wriggles and kicks.

77

---

STARLING

He lifts one foot, and then the other. The doorway stinks of piss. At his feet, a pile of fag ends. Sunday afternoon. He's been here (lurking, she'd say) on and off since Saturday morning. A last trip to London. A last shot. He thinks of a dog, waiting, waiting, waiting, not for a dead master, but for whatever his future might bring. Probably nothing. When she turns up, odds on she'll send him packing. Next week she'll be wed. And that will be the end of that. But he will have tried. He's paced and lurked, gone off, come back. A ginger cat winds round his ankles from time to time. Pigeons strut and peck. The woman from the sweetshop came out and asked his business, threatened to phone the Old Bill if he didn't give over, but he managed to charm her. Ended up with a bag of aniseed balls, sucked each one right down to its tiny seed.

An old biddy wheels a pram about all day, singing *"Green Grow the Rushes Oh"*. Her coat shines with grease, her shoes are split, the pram piled high with what looks like rubbish, but turns out to be stuffed toys she's rescued from bombsites: teddies, rabbits, pandas, an elephant. All grey with filth. Sad heap of snouts, paws, tails and floppy ears.

When he paces up and down the street, *I'll sing you one oh, green grow the rushes oh* runs through his head. *One is one and all alone and ever more shall be so.* He doesn't know any more of the words, so it's the same ones over and over till it drives him crazy. Now and then he goes to a café on the high street to use the bog or have a cuppa.

If it hadn't been for Thursday, when he met Colin and Fred and someone else, then he'd be more desperate. Truth is, he's in two minds. Two minds at least.

Last night, once he'd packed in waiting, he went back to Catford, took Horace out for a pint. Propped up at the bar, Horace told him that Celia had had an affair with a Polish airman while he was a POW. 'Nearly finished me off when I found that out,' he said, 'but she said I ought to know if we was ever to get back on a proper footing.' His big face crumpled as he spoke. 'Her telling me the truth meant a lot. You have to look at it from her point of view,' he almost pleaded. 'She wasn't to know if she'd ever see me again, was she? It was just a bit of comfort when all's said and done. Poor bugger got shot down, so that was the end of that.'

'No, you can't blame her,' Starling said, though he was shocked, felt personally let down by Celia. She was what *wife* meant. It was what he'd been aiming for. And if wife meant that... It all fed into his feelings from Thursday till he hardly knew which way up he was. But he tried to banish that from his head as they balanced on barstools, nursed their pints, got back onto the subject of nut farms and Tanganyika.

It's gone three now, and his train's at six. Another couple of hours. This is your last try, Starling, your last roll of the dice. If it wasn't for the baby, he wouldn't bother. 'Not off down to London again, Lennie?' Mum said, with a hopeful smile. She'd twigged there was something going on, and oh how glad she'd be if she knew what. And how glad he'd be to make her glad.

He lights another fag, and allows himself a luxury now, a think about Thursday night... a think about what he's been trying all day not to think. It *is* like luxury going over it, or like a tease. A complication. After work on Thursday, he met Colin for a cuppa. Colin brought Fred – a twitchy little bloke with round specs, sparse hair, a comical smile. Comical take on life altogether. Colin and Fred joked and laughed, and teased each other like any couple, as if it was normal for two men to be like that. Lymington's café turned out to be a place their kind can meet up. Funny he'd walked past hundreds of times. A good place, clean, nothing shady about it. Buns in a glass case, sandwiches cut to order. Homely soul behind the counter, friendly enough, keeping her nose out.

A friend of Colin and Fred happened along. That was Colin's phrase, but Starling wonders, did he *really* "happen along"? The friend, Peter, wore a suit – not demob – a nicely cut suit, his voice a cut above too, like someone off the BBC.

They shook hands. 'Col's mentioned you,' Peter said.

*Never mentioned you,* he didn't say.

'What's your line, Leonard, is it?' Peter said. 'Len, Lennie, what's your preference?'

'I prefer Starling.'

He nodded. 'Then Starling it shall be.'

Starling blinked, a bit dazzled. 'Trainee bookkeeper,' he said. What if he could have said doctor or medical student? Peter's smile was slow to spread. Fascinating, the way the lips stretched, making his dark moustache bristle. His eyes crinkled, a dimple appeared. To make Peter smile became something he wanted straight away.

'You?' Starling said.

'Teacher. Juniors.'

'Bet that takes it out of you.' Lame remark, but he was rewarded with another slow smile.

They got to yarning about all sorts. Turned out Peter wrote poems, a couple published in *Quarterly Review*, said he'd send Starling a copy.

'What kind of poems?' Starling asked.

'Arty-farty ones,' Fred interrupted, 'way above your head, old mucker,' and he punched Starling's arm.

'You don't know what's above his head,' Colin said. 'Our Starling's a dark horse.' And they all laughed.

*Our Starling* – that warmed him right through. 'You're right. Limericks are more my line,' he said, heart rising with Peter's smile, with the *ease* of it all.

'Don't sniff at the limerick form,' Peter said. 'Hang on.' He held up a finger, cleared his throat:

*'The limerick packs laughs anatomical,*
*Into space that is quite economical.*
*But the good ones I've seen,*
*So seldom are clean,*
*And the clean ones so seldom are comical.'*

'True!' Starling's laugh has a painful edge – how Edgar would have thrown back his head and brayed. Edgar would love Peter, he was sure, and the feeling would be mutual.

'Old chestnut. Can't claim credit,' Peter said.

Starling began scrabbling for a limerick, but his mind had gone blank. Peter looked at his watch. 'Meeting,' he said. 'Must love you and leave you. Delighted to make your acquaintance, Starling. Toodle-oo.'

He took Starling's hand in his, and the smile spread as their eyes met. Only a second too long, a split second, but it had meaning, and it set a crazy pulse hammering right through him.

'Well,' Fred said when Peter had gone. Starling heard Colin snort, and with some effort, pulled himself together.

A teacher. A teacher with a dimple in one cheek, black hair, inky fingers. A teacher who not only wrote poems, but had had some published. Who even appreciated limericks.

'You must come for your tea. Come on Saturday,' Fred said. 'We'll ask Peter too, shall we, Col?'

'Make a party of it,' said Colin.

Nobody said whether Peter was queer, and he couldn't ask. Are you just supposed to know? There was something in the air, a prickling. Of course he was... but maybe not.

'Sorry. Can't do Saturday,' he had to say, and had to walk away, walk fast, pace and pace, pace anywhere but near the Three Tuns. Didn't sleep a wink that night. Nearly went back on himself. He could have rung up Colin, said, "Yes, I'll come. Please ask Peter too." But he didn't, and Saturday night is over by now. And what would have happened? Where would he be? And who would he be, if say, Peter had been there, and they'd hit it off? If Peter was queer, and liked him? Inky fingers, slow smile, dimple, poetry. Last night he couldn't sleep, thinking about what might have occurred. Now he's shattered.

He thinks about Peter, and he thinks about Aida. He thinks about giving up the chase. But for the baby, he would. *His* baby though. Inside her. Can't not try. Not in good conscience. For Mum's sake as well as his own. A grandkiddy is what she wants. So happy that'd make her. Happier than anything in the world. And she deserves it. No prospect of that if he got together with Peter. And he could never introduce Peter to her, never take him home. It might kill her if she knew what he was. Her precious Lennie. No grandchild, instead a filthy secret to keep for the rest of her life. Only shame and being ashamed. And the old man would fucking kill him. If only his sister had lived. If only Mum's happiness wasn't up to him alone.

But if Aida says no... It's her decision now. This is a fork in road. Which way he goes depends on her. Another hour and a half he'll give her. He begins almost to hope she won't come.

And then at quarter to four she does, not alone; her fiancé (he assumes) trots along behind her, tall, red-haired, carrying both their cases. She's wearing a mac and an orange hat. Of course, the fiancé's there, what did he expect? He watches them go inside. He'll wait. He'll keep on waiting till five. Then it will be over.

He cricks his neck staring up at window. Nothing, but then the curtain moves. She looks straight down at him then her face vanishes. He lights a fag, fingers shaking, keeps looking up, bloody crick in his neck, but nothing more. What's going on in there?

After a bit, the door opens, and she beckons. He slopes across the street for his telling-off. It's not a hat, but her hair! She sees his expression, and scowls, a hand going up to it. 'I *know*,' she snaps before he can speak. 'Come back in half an hour. In the meantime, make yourself scarce.' And she shuts the door in his face. He leans his forehead on the bubbled varnish. *Orange hair!* And then he walks away, goes down the alley onto the bombsite, alight with buttercups and dandelions. Smashed glass glints in the sun.

Well, he'll see her then. And get to say his bit. The last throw of the dice. What she decides, decides his future.

In half an hour to the minute he returns. This *is* the right path to take, isn't it? Right direction. Right for how it looks to everyone. Right for Mum and the old man and Dr Bailey. Right in the eyes of the world. Eventually her face appears at window, and she beckons. He crosses the road, waits by door.

'Go on then.' She folds her arms. 'Say what you've come to say.'

'Can I come in? I've been on my feet all weekend.'

She widens her eyes. 'All weekend?'

'Since first thing Saturday.'

'Lord!' A streak of hair is like a scratch on her cheek. 'You idiot!' Her smile is quick: quick to come, quick to go, not like Peter's, which has more thought behind it, the lips wide and plush under the neat moustache, while hers are thin and pale and dry.

'Was that your fiancé?'

'Mr Guthrie. Yes.'

'He coming back?'

'Not tonight.'

'You sent him off?'

She says nothing. The red hair makes her look more washed out than ever; the shadows under her eyes are bluer than her eyes. In the end, she sighs and turns, leads him upstairs. The sound of someone's radio, organ music, a smell of Sunday dinner, of something burnt. He checks his watch – only half an hour if he's to catch his train.

'Lord. I am so flipping tired.' As soon as they're in, she flops on sofa, kicks off her shoes, curls her feet underneath her.

'Mind if I...' He nods towards bathroom. As he pisses he sees orange stains in the basin, on the bathmat and the towels. Dye all over bloody shop. *Slut*, his mum would say if she could see. Keeping things nice is what a woman ought to do, she'd say. Does he think that? He thinks about his idea of *wife*. How would two men together be around house? He wonders about Colin and Fred. Who does the housework, or do they both?

When he comes out, she's got her eyes closed. He sits beside her. No one speaks. He wants to put his hand on her stomach. The ends of her fingers are orange, her nails bitten and there's that bloody great ring.

'Henna?' he says.

'Yes, Sherlock.' A pause. 'You weren't out there all night, I hope?' she says.

'No,' he says. 'I did get threatened with the police though.'

She giggles sleepily.

'And I did meet a lady with a pramful of toys.'

'Gladys. God told her to return them to the children, she says.'

They're quiet, thinking about this.

'Any chance of a cuppa?' he says in the end. 'I haven't all that long.' He looks at her alarm clock; it's stopped. He gets up, puts it right by his watch, and winds it. There's still twenty-five minutes. Odds on train'll be delayed anyway, usually is. What if when he gets to station, he phones Colin? Says how about next Saturday for tea instead? Says why not ask that Peter?

'I'll put kettle on.' He fills it, and lights the gas.

'Say your piece then,' she says.

All of a sudden, he can't be bothered. 'You know what it is,' he says. 'What's the point?'

'You've waited all weekend to say *that*?' She blinks at him.

'I'm done in.'

She snorts a laugh. 'Well then, Mr Starling, if you're not going to say your piece, I'll just have to say mine.'

## 78

## AIDA

All weekend! Lord! All the time she was having tea with Mummy on the lawn, waiting for Neville, all that time in the hot and the birdsong and butterflies he was here, lurking. While she slept, while they sat round the dining table, while she rested her head on Neville's shoulder on the train, lurking. Poor, poor, little Leonard Starling. Leonard Starveling is how he looks, with his stick-thin limbs. He may have filled out a bit since Christmas, but still, he's awfully slight. You could fit two of him into Neville's frame – one in each trouser leg! And heaven knows, Neville's hardly fat.

He'd expected to stay, at least for dinner. Cod roe on toast she had lined up, though she's not hungry, only tired. If Starling hadn't been there, perhaps she would have let Neville stay. He did look crestfallen when she sent him packing, but he went without complaint; he always did what she asked. A lamb. So solicitous. A solid prospect (the parents). A catch. 'Clever old you,' Mummy whispered when they left. And look at how happy he is to take on the child, knowing the truth (well, some of it). A generous man. A good one. And not as gullible as she thought, either, which increases her respect.

'I'll have to go for the train soon,' Starling says, and she switches her attention back to him. Sunshine slants through the window, showing the dark stipple of his bristles – he needs a shave – the gloss of his thick brows. 'Say your bit then.'

A lock of hair has fallen over his specs, and he pushes it back. Something different about him from last time; there's not the pleading in his eyes, there's not the desperation.

'Sit down,' she says. 'I'll make the tea.'

'Goodbye?' he says as he sits down. 'Is that it?'

Aida spoons tea into the pot. On her last day at the Ministry, she purloined a fat A4 envelope full of tea leaves and rather than eke them out, she decides the situation calls for a good strong pot.

'Don't fret. I won't bother you again,' he says. 'Though I'd like to know about the baby. When it's born. Will you write?'

'Is that all you want, then?' There's a constriction in her throat.

'You know what I want,' he says rather curtly. The annoying little clock tuts off the seconds.

'This time next week I'll be married,' she says. 'I'll be on honeymoon. Ireland. A week in Dublin, a week in Cork. No doubt we'll kiss the Blarney Stone – though Daddy said, "*Heaven forfend!*".' As she talks, she twists the ring, takes it off, puts it back, gnaws at a stained and ragged nail. 'And then we're moving to Scotland. The Borders. We're going to build a house beside a loch, beside a forest. The baby will be brought up Scottish. It can swim in the loch. It can climb the trees. We can build it a swing.' She's beginning to sound mad now, she's well aware, and he says nothing, which is fair enough. What does she expect him to say?

She rattles on. 'Neville was a conchie you know. *Imagine* the courage that takes. He's in the Labour Party, he might even up end up standing for parliament one day. He's principled, and serious. Not like us.'

He frowns at that, she notices.

She pours out the good strong tea. Now she's over the sickness, she's begun to really enjoy it again. There's even a little bottle of fresh milk brought from home. *Small pleasures.* She sits beside him on the sofa, her old school skirt navy blue beside the grey pinstripe of his skinny legs.

'We'll live near Neville's folks. I'd rather live near mine. Still, one can't always get what one wants, can one? Not precisely what one wants.'

Considering this, he inclines his head. 'What do you want then?' he says, and she finds herself flummoxed. What *does* she want?

'If you could have anything?' he prompts.

'If I could have anything?' She turns the ring, and the diamond flashes. 'Well, not to be in this predicament, I suppose. To get into a time machine and travel back to Boxing Day, and to be more careful.' She gives a mirthless laugh. 'What about you then?' she says. 'If you could have anything.'

His dark eyes meet hers, and her heart feels squeezed.

'I know you say you want to marry me,' she says, 'but that's only because of the baby, isn't it?'

He keeps his eyes on hers but doesn't answer. There's a clear fingerprint on one of his lenses.

'Isn't it?'

He pushes back the flop of hair. 'Isn't that a good enough reason?' The skin of his brow is like olive silk, a gleam to the grain of it. 'I've wanted to be a doctor since I was a kid,' he adds at last. Lord, he looks so young and lost.

'You told me.'

'Edgar said...'

'Edgar said what?'

'Doesn't matter.'

'It does, it does matter. What did Eddie say? Go on. Please.'

His hand clutches at the empty sleeve-end. If he had two hands, he'd be wringing them together, she guesses. Poor man. It's love she's feeling, a delicate kind of love. 'Please tell me what Edgar said,' she whispers.

He puffs a sigh, takes off his specs. Huge dark eyes, and silky lashes. 'He said that maybe one day, when I was trained, I could join the practice.'

'Daddy's practice?'

He nods. 'It was just something he said, when we were out there. He said I was a born medic, unlike him.'

'He *would* say that. *He* should have been an artist.'

'Yes, but he was a good doctor – *and* an artist.' He leans earnestly towards her. 'Honestly Aida, you should have seen him. The things he did. The way he improvised. And he was so *kind*.' A tear rolls down his cheek. 'So good with the men.'

'Don't,' she says, 'oh no, please don't. Darling, don't, please.' Though she tries to fight it, his grief has triggered her own, and together they sit and cry. She cries in a way she's never cried, not for Edgar, never in her life; she cries like an animal, as if something wild is getting hold of her and shaking her from the inside. Eventually, they quieten down and are left wet-faced and separate on the sofa, which suddenly strikes her as absurd, and she begins to laugh. He looks startled, but then he catches her hilarity, and they laugh and cry, wet and snotty, and she has to bolt to the loo not to wet her knickers.

In the bathroom – *Lord above! Henna everywhere!* – she splashes her cheeks with cold water, stares in the mirror at her awful blotchy face, swollen eyes and nose. Good God, what a sight. And poor Leonard. What a scene! As she holds a cold flannel to her eyes, something occurs to her, rises in her like yeast, the thought of what she could say. What she could offer.

How she could mend something. How she could try. It's rather a fragile sort of plan, a castle in the air and, as if balancing it in her head, she walks carefully back into the room. But he's got his coat on, ready to go.

'Take your coat off,' she says.

'My train.' His eyes are invisible now, the way the sunshine slants on his specs.

'Get a later one,' she says. 'I'll pay.'

He hesitates, sighs, exasperated.

'*Please*. Listen. This is important. Sit down.'

Shrugging, glancing at his watch, he removes his coat, slings it on the end of the sofa, sits down with a show of obedience.

'I have an idea.' She sits on his right side, takes his hand. It feels cold and thin in hers, insubstantial. 'What if... Don't say anything till I've finished. It's just an idea, a new idea; I'm going to think it out loud. All right?'

He makes a puzzled little noise, but doesn't pull his hand away.

'What if, don't interrupt, what if I went home tomorrow and asked Daddy if he'd sponsor your medical training?'

His fingers tighten, and his jaw. His naked eyes grow huge; there's a sort of jump right through him. A nervy jolt. *Lord help me,* she thinks. *I really do love him.*

'He would if we were to get married,' she says. 'And then you'd work for him.'

He takes back his hand, pushes it through his hair, brows pulled together. He opens his mouth to speak, but she holds up a finger.

'Shhh. I know. Neville. You're thinking of Neville aren't you? But honestly, my heart isn't in it. I could marry him, and if you say no, I will. I expect I'll carry on with it. But if *we* married, if you were Daddy's son-in-law, he'd sponsor your training. I'm sure he would. He expected Edgar to follow in his footsteps...' She swallows hard and takes a breath. 'Don't worry; I'm not about to blub again. We've both blubbed for England now.' A weird giggle finds its way out of her. The wildness of a new idea running through her is exhilarating. To shock everyone, to go charging off the rails like this, it feels blindingly right.

'You want to be a father to the baby.' She takes his hand again, presses it against her belly, which is rising and falling with excited breath. And he keeps it there, warm now, warm and light on the place where the baby is curled. 'And you want to be a doctor. You could have both the things you want.'

'Could I?'

'I'm saying you could.'

He turns to examine her face, his expression unreadable. Or it's as if a series of expressions are flickering there, a whole speeded-up movie of reactions. He reaches across and lifts her left hand, twists the ring on her finger. The diamond trembles reflected light onto the ceiling.

'What would *you* get out of it?' he asks.

'Well,' she says, after a pause. 'I suppose I would get you.'

'But...'

'Neville,' she says, and it comes rushing back to her how much she has to lose. How much she might be throwing away for this thin and shifty man, who doesn't even seem all that delighted with her beautiful idea. How terribly, terribly hurt Neville would be. And Mummy and Daddy and everyone, how shocked, and all the wedding plans – even for a hole-in-the-corner affair, there are many – and his folks who she's never even met, whatever will they think of her? And the Dublin honeymoon and the loch, and the forest. Is it all too much to give up? And all too stupid? It's the same wrecking impulse that's come over her, irresistibly, over and over in her life.

Shouldn't she resist this time, pull herself together, grow up and do what's best for herself and best for the baby?

'Can you feel?' The baby is kicking under her ribs. She puts his hand in the right place and hears him gasp as, for the first time, he feels the movement of his child.

# EPILOGUE
## CLEMENTINE

December 1946

She drains her champagne glass and surveys the little gathering in the sitting room. The christening, which she's been dreading, went without a hitch; it was every bit as quiet and low key as Aida demanded. Now, back from church, they await lunch. It's an intimate gathering: just Aida, baby, husband, and the two sets of grandparents. Grandparents who double as godparents; all very economical. She should make further conversation with these new in-laws, make an effort to get to know them. And she will, over lunch, which will be ready shortly. But for now, they all seem held in a pause. The champagne's finished; Dennis was only able to procure one bottle of *Deutz* – the first taste of really good stuff since before the war.

She surveys the room: a good fire crackling in the hearth, Christmas tree, holly and mistletoe and cards on the mantel and, most importantly, the collage, newly hung. It's in the perfect spot, on the wall where the light will catch it – where the light catches it now, in fact. It's meant as a surprise for Aida, though she hasn't yet noticed. The girl stands by the piano, smoking, and plinking a finger repeatedly on the same high note. She looks a perfect fright, hair still orange at the ends, pale at the roots and rather hat-squashed. But surprisingly, marriage and motherhood do seem to suit her. She's not quite so thin, or surly, or brittle. Still an awkward baggage, of course, and always will be.

Her husband, the baby on his shoulder – a bootee has fallen off – stands by the window, gazing out. What is he gazing at? What is he thinking? There's something about him she can't quite put her finger on. He seems perpetually wistful, as if part of him isn't truly present. Against his dark jacket, the christening gown is a pale smudge, above which the thick black hair of the infant shines – almost an indecent amount of hair for such a tot. She's an odd little creature: eyes startlingly blue in her olive complexion, a wary child who watches one with unnerving intensity, and doesn't waste her smiles.

Neville Guthrie would have been by far the more preferable match; she and Dennis agree on that much – a sounder and more wholesome prospect altogether. *Poor fellow.* He wrote a fine and tactful letter saying how much he'd enjoyed meeting them. He was quite open about how disappointed he was. To be jilted less than a week before his wedding! Humiliating for the poor chap. But he wished them well for the future. What grace. Aida herself says she didn't deserve him, and quite right she is, too.

Leonard (she cannot bring herself to call him Starling as Aida will insist on doing) is still looking out of the window. Clem picks up the fallen bootee, goes to join him, gazing out at the cars shining in the winter sun. She's about to make a cordial remark, but he moves away, and she sighs, remembering the night Aida came to tell them she was marrying not Neville

Guthrie after all, but someone else. Just like that. And not just someone else, but the very man who had taken them all for such fools at Christmas – well! There had followed the most undignified scene, and for once she'd been in full agreement with Dennis, as he stamped and ranted. It was as if someone had lifted the cloth from an elaborately set table, flung everything up in the air, let it land and then expected them to accept the mess – spilt tea, broken flowers, smashed teacups – and to live with it like that. No, it was bigger than that; it was as if someone had upended and shaken the whole world. And now the war comes to mind, of course. After all, accept is exactly what they did. In both cases. What choice had they?

When everything had landed and they were standing in the wreckage, it became clear that if they wished to keep Aida, if they wished to have their grandchild in their lives, they would have to accept the future on her terms. Dennis was so angry that she wondered if he'd cut them off; for a few days he seemed liable to – but in the end he came round. He never could refuse Aida anything. So here it is, the future on her terms. Dennis has bought the couple a flat in Maida Vale, and sponsored Leonard's training. When he qualifies they'll sell the flat, move to Seckbridge, and he'll repay his debt by working for Dennis. Effectively, he'll be filling Edgar's shoes. And that is painful. More of a cuckoo than a starling, he's turned out to be. Whether they can ever truly forgive him for his behaviour at Christmas is another matter altogether. Such outrageous deceit!

*No, do not dwell on that today.*

The wedding took place at a registry office in Sheffield, Leonard's parents the sole witnesses. She and Dennis were only told when it was a *fait accompli*. And that hurt terribly. But you can hardly blame them after all the fuss they'd made – she and Dennis, united for once in their outrage. And with the pregnancy advancing, there had been no time to waste. Of course, it was clear from the get-go that Leonard has darkie blood of some sort. Contrary as ever, Aida seems cock-a-hoop that her child is part Egyptian.

Amina is an acceptable name though, Arabic apparently, but not too outlandish. (Whether teasingly or not, Aida suggested Bathsheba, for God's sake!) When Clem gently suggested something more traditionally English, Aida hooted, 'Pot/kettle! You called me Aida! Isn't *that* Arabic?' Amina Clementine Rose Starling, the child's full name, is actually rather sweet and dignified. One must be satisfied with what one has.

And it is a good thing, after all, that Aida has married the child's natural father. With the dark colouring it would have been difficult to pass Amina off as Guthrie's. The question is: how does Leonard feel about the whole business? With such an inscrutable chap, it's hard to tell. There's something distant about him, something almost numb. But that will be to do with his POW experience, no doubt. Untold damage. And his missing hand, of course. How might Edgar have been, if he'd come home to them? She turns away from the thought, faces the room, forcing her mouth into the smile of a hostess.

Leonard lifts the baby from his shoulder, and seats himself on an armchair. Aida stops plinking, thank heavens, and perches beside him. 'Hello monkey,' she says, catching the tiny naked foot. 'Look at this edible thing!' She pretends to gobble it.

'Put her bootee on, she'll get cold.' Clem hands over the tiny white object, beautifully knitted by Rose.

But instead, Aida pulls the other bootee off. 'Look at those marvellous toes! I can't believe I made them!'

The elder Starlings, Rose and Bob, sit at either end of the sofa, clutching their drinks. They are clearly out of their depth, and she knows she must try to put them at their ease. Rose is tiny – more sparrow than starling. Her miniature feet are clad in shiny, bunion-distorted shoes, and her stick-like calves emerge from what is bound to be her best frock, an unfashionable maroon cretonne. She's the source of the Egyptian blood, the lovechild of some serviceman, apparently. Bob seems a thug on his best behaviour: stiff collar tight round his neck, a bulldoggish bulge to his eyes.

'Another drink anyone?' says Dennis and, eagerly she accepts a glass of sherry, lights a cigarette, sits between Rose and Bob to make conversation. After all, extraordinary as it is, they are all grandparents to the same child and will have to find a way of getting on.

'Lovely little thing, isn't she?' she says to Rose.

'She's a little duckie,' says Rose, 'the image of our Lennie as a babe.'

Dennis, pipe clenched between his teeth, distributes drinks, offers cigarettes.

'You wield a club at all?' he asks Bob, and it turns out that he does play golf, on a municipal course in Sheffield, so that's a godsend. As the men begin to compare handicaps, Rose smiles at Clem. Though her face is worn and lined, it transforms with the smile; her eyes and her cheekbones are rather beautiful.

'I couldn't be more pleased about our Lennie getting wed,' says Rose. 'Your Aida's such a dear.'

Clem blinks at this surprising notion.

'We've been worried sick about him since he got back; he were in a right shocking state, but just look at him now!' Leonard looks up, smiles at them and then back at Amina, who is kicking and blowing bubbles from between her serious little lips. He carries her across, and settles her on his mother's lap. 'Here you are, Mum, you hold her for a bit.'

'Who's Nanny's little duckie then?' Rose says.

Clem tries to exchange a glance with someone, but everyone's eyes are on the baby. '*This little piggy went to market,*' Rose begins, taking hold of a tiny toe, and there's a sudden sweet gurgle of baby laughter.

'Darling?' cries Aida. 'Did you hear?'

But Leonard's over by the hearth, examining the collage.

'Excuse me, Rose.' Clem gets to her feet, struggling a little – legs wobbly already, and she's barely drunk anything – and goes across to him.

'How on earth...?' demands Aida, coming to join them. 'How long have you had this? Why didn't you show me before?'

'Oh Diddy, I've been waiting for you to spot it.'

'Golly gosh!' Aida says, softening in her sudden way. 'Did you do it? It's simply marvellous, Mummy.'

'Sir Murray-Hill did it for us,' says Clem, with a warm bloom in her heart, thinking *Corin, Corin, Corin*. 'He's brought them together beautifully, hasn't he? Made out of all the scrappy bits, something *whole*.'

'Oh Lord, wouldn't Edgar *love* this?' Aida's voice is choked with emotion, and her face, gazing at Leonard's, shines with love. But Clem sees his minute flinch as he turns from his wife, blocking her view of the picture with his shoulder as he leans closer to it.

The door opens, and a heavenly smell of roast lamb drifts in. 'Lunch is served,' calls Elsie.

'Come on, darling.' Aida tugs Leonard's arm, but he resists. Shrugging, and pulling a wry face, she goes to lift the baby from Rose's lap. And Dennis and Bob, still talking golf, and Rose and Aida fussing over the baby who is herself beginning to fuss, all troop off to the dining room. At the door, Clem turns to wait for Leonard who hasn't moved away from the collage, and she sees him touch his fingers to his lips and press them to its glass.

## THE END

## ACKNOWLEDGEMENTS

Thanks go to Andrew Greig, Tracey Emerson and Joshua French for patient reading, and my agent, Bill Hamilton, for his help and sound advice.

# A NOTE FROM THE PUBLISHER

**Thank you for reading this book.** If you enjoyed it please do consider leaving a review on Amazon to help others find it too.

**We hate typos.** All of our books have been rigorously edited and proofread, but sometimes mistakes do slip through. If you have spotted a typo, please do let us know and we can get it amended within hours.

**info@bloodhoundbooks.com**

Printed in Great Britain
by Amazon